To Marie Walker

Enjoy Osbofahn

JW/Hah

25 Sept. 03

THE CLOUD DWELLER

The Cloud Dweller

Robert D. Hale

THE QUANTUCK LANE PRESS

Copyright 2003 by Robert D. Hale

Book design and composition by Gina Webster
Manufacturing by Maple-Vail Book Manufacturing Group

Library of Congress Cataloging-in-Publication Data

Hale, Robert D. (Robert David), 1928-
The cloud dweller / Robert D. Hale.– 1st ed.
p. cm.
ISBN 0-9714548-8-4
1. Eccentrics and eccentricities–Fiction. 2. Inheritance and succes-
sion–Fiction. 3. Conflict of generations–Fiction. 4.Children of the
rich–Fiction. 5. Rich people–Fiction.
6. Young men–Fiction.7. Mansions–Fiction. I. Title.
PS3558.A35715C545 2003
813'.54–dc22   2003019875

The Quantuck Lane Press, New York
Distributed by
W.W. Norton & Company, 500 Fifth Avenue, New York, NY 10110
www.wwnorton.com

W.W. Norton & Company Ltd., Castle House, 75/76 Wells Street,
London, WIT 3QT

1 2 3 4 5 6 7 8 9 0

For Lydia

THE CLOUD DWELLER

PROLOGUE: *Oshatakea*

THOUSANDS OF ACRES OF FERTILE LANDS ON BOTH sides of approximately forty miles of the Shatekye River were acquired in the eighteenth century by Thomas Fillmore, who came west from Cohasset, Massachusetts, seeking the proud people he had heard trappers talk about when they sold beaver and fox pelts to his merchant father. Whatever loose treaty Thomas and Seneca chiefs agreed to must have satisfied both parties because during all subsequent wars up to and beyond the American Revolution, whenever red men battled whites or were slaughtered by the French or British, Senecas and Fillmores retained strong alliances of friendship. By the time the Dutch arrived to parcel out that part of the country the Fillmores' hold on the Shatekye River valley was inviolate.

On a balmy evening in 1736 Thomas and his Seneca friend Gahah were seated on bales of beaver skins beside the river watching fog skim over the water's surface and creep in ghostly fingers into ravines and up forested hills. The next morning Thomas would begin the long journey east to marry Clara Southwick, a Cohasset girl. What kind of woman could this Clara Southwick be, Gahah wondered, to make Thomas ride many days and nights to fetch her? When she was among them, would she recognize the pain that dulled the eyes of Gahah's sister whose body had warmed and pleased Thomas through the circles of seasons he had lived here? If asked, Gahah's sister would gladly join Thomas in his new cabin, obscured now in the cloud of mist and fog that blanketed the top of the hill. Gahah had warned Thomas his Clara Southwick would be too much alone up there where the fiercest winds blew, the deadliest spears of lightning flashed and snow stayed days longer than in the valley, but Thomas was determined.

Always before Thomas listened to Gahah, who had taught him to hunt the Seneca way, how to trap the beaver and cure its pelt, how to live with nature. Thomas listened in silence when Gahah spoke of spirits and customs before relating his own tales. Smoking together in the evening had become a ritual for the two young men, one Gahah worried would not resume when Thomas returned with his white wife. Would there be no more discussions of truths, of dreams, Gahah's and this little man's, he who was without fear despite his modest size?

"You are frowning," Thomas said.

Gahah's countenance softened. He turned to look toward the long hill. "Up there Thomas, you will live in the clouds. You will be an Oshatakea, a cloud dweller."

"Oshatakea." Thomas said the word several times, as if he were tasting as well as hearing it. "Gahah, you have given me a name for the cabin. Oshatakea."

Six succeeding generations of Fillmores built increasingly grand houses on top of that hill without disturbing the original rough log cabin, leaving it intact on this original site as a reminder of their beginnings. The grandest was the rambling castle constructed by Farnsworth Phillips Fillmore II to contain hundreds of rooms he purchased in Europe, dismantled and shipped home. His collection included whole structures—a baroque theater from Austria, a convent from Spain, a monastery from Greece, a chapel from Dorset, an Italian villa. When he could not buy what he wanted, a Tudor banqueting hall, for instance, or a staircase from a stately home is Sussex, he had it duplicated down to the finest detail. FP, as he was called, filled his Oshatakea with as many treasures as it could hold, and he built warehouses to store more than enough to fill rooms he planned to add.

FP's grandson, Phil, is now Oshatakea's sole occupant.

PART ONE: *Phil*

Chapter 1

PEOPLE MADE RESERVATIONS WEEKS IN ADVANCE AND drove long distances to have lunch between noon and one o'clock at the Peasant Palate in the tiny village of Fillmore so they could report they had actually seen Farnsworth Phillips Fillmore IV. Once there they stared openly at him, having never looked upon anyone as rich or as mysterious. Some might say the chef's reputation or the town's quaintness were the lures, when in truth it was curiosity about the eccentric, reclusive multimillionaire that drew them to the picturesque town whose streets in 1984 were still illuminated by glass-domed gaslights on black iron stanchions. The gawpers' reactions varied, though most agreed he didn't look at all as they had imagined him. His photograph never appeared in any newspaper or magazine, thus they had little to go on beyond myths. That he was extraordinarily handsome, with wide-set, large, long-lashed eyes no one would argue, but many thought his shoulder-length black hair gave him an air of decadence. None, nobody, not even the rare nonjudgmental individual, could resist wondering why one so rich would dress so shabbily.

Fillmore residents also regarded him as exotic, but he was a constant in their lives. They had known him since he was born just before his mother's fifty-second birthday and shortly after his father had reached sixty-one. Because of his parents' ages, Phil was regarded as a minor miracle. When the old man in the village who collected newspapers and junk in his two-wheeled cart heard a baby had arrived up at Oshatakea, he suggested the infant be named Jesus after another whose birth was believed to be miraculous, but the boy was given the same name as his father, his grandfather and his great-grandfather providing a continuity the community found reassuring. Two-plus centuries of Fillmore family beneficence would apparently continue for another generation, barring unforeseen catastrophe. If the Fillmores were to die out, it was impossible to conjure what changes, what dire disturbances might occur in the valley. Few believed their lives would not be adversely affected. That was then, when FP was still alive as well as Farney, Phil's father. Now Phil, the last of the line, was approaching forty and displayed no interest in seeking a wife. His diffidence gave those whose lives he affected pause. Could his indifference mean the line would die out with him?

Sitting on a stool at the short counter, hunched over, concentrating on a piece of venison wrapped in home-cured bacon and grilled, Phil was unaware of the eyes gazing at him. Nor did he seem to hear incessant whispering between smartly dressed city women seated at small square tables where booths used to be. Loren Gage, proprietor of the Peasant Palate, standing behind the counter he had insisted on keeping when his son Danny came home from France and turned the diner into a gourmet restaurant, made no pretense of not listening. Annoyed by the women's curiosity, Loren silently vowed, as he had a hundred times before, he would overrule Danny and carpet the floor, maybe put those ugly tiles with holes in them on the ceiling to deaden sound so there'd be less chance of Phil overhearing what strangers were saying about him. Until that was done he'd continue trying to cover up their stupid comments. "Save room for dessert," he said loudly.

"I always do." Dessert today was a confection of dark, light and white chocolate with red raspberry sauce. "Nice thing about

Danny's food," Phil said, "it tastes as good as it looks. This torte will give me terminal toothache but it's worth it."

"I'll tell him you said that." Loren's proud-father smirk faded when he noticed tourists signaling waitresses for tabs, putting their heads together, getting ready to follow Phil out the door when he finished his lunch. Goddamn, Loren hissed. He'd like to take a broom and sweep the whole bunch into the street. Loren considered himself Phil's protector, had from way back when they were tots rolling across the lawns of Oshatakea. It was Loren who had pulled Phil from the thorny canes of rosebushes, Loren who scared bees away and swatted mosquitoes. His self-appointed role became more necessary as they grew up, when valley boys began making crude remarks to Phil because he was different. Of course he was different, he was rich and they weren't; Phil had tutors and they didn't. Bullies are seldom quick on the uptake, but in time they learned to keep their mouths shut about the Fillmore heir when Loren was present. Always big for his age and powerful, though peaceful until provoked, bullies didn't want to tangle with Loren, at least not one on one. Phil's parents were grateful for his protection, at least Phil's' father was. Farney appreciated Loren's staunch friendship as much as his guard-dog stance. He had reason. Loren was Phil's sole peer companion. Constant and loyal, almost a member of the family, the Gage boy had access to every part of Oshatakea, including the Portuguese Wing, which was strictly off-limits to outsiders. His sensitive intuition even as a small child made him aware that privileges he'd been granted above and beyond being tutored with the Fillmore scion had to be respected. Most important was the family's privacy. Before he knew what the word meant, he knew not to relate tales of what he saw or heard in the big house, and especially never to answer questions about the Portuguese Wing, the least-known segment of Oshatakea and so the part that aroused the most fervent curiosity. Those who lived in the valley had always been invited to Oshatakea celebrations, but to be given run of the place as Loren had was unheard of. Difficult though it was, Loren managed to keep his footing on the invisible line created by his unique involvement with the family that reigned over the valley while still remaining a vital part of the community, most of whose residents worked for the Filmore family.

That the last of the Fillmores could appear vulnerable enough to need a protector was an amazing turn of events, but Phil was the first of his family to be kept apart from valley people. Heretofore young Fillmores grew up with children who lived in the village or on farms along the river. Everybody was educated in the Fillmore Academy whether they came from mansions or ordinary houses, and they formed lasting and genuine friendships. Phil's mother, Catherine, was the only one of generations of strong women who chose when she married into the family to remain an outsider and determined her son should be insulated from valley people. This was as impossible as trying to keep a bear cub inside its birth den, and as unnatural. Catherine was forced to allow Loren Gage, born within days of Phil, to be brought to Oshatakea as a companion. That, she thought, was as far as she would have to go. She was wrong. Catherine could not change the course centuries had confirmed. The lives of everybody in the valley were intertwined with the lives of the Fillmores. The ongoing productivity of well-managed Fillmore lands and the success of their ever expanding vast business interests positively affected the life of each valley resident because of the generosity of Fillmore largesse. Fillmore money had established and continued to support the academy, the hospital and the library. Sociologists might describe this as a benevolent paternalistic society, but residents thought themselves fortunate indeed and prayed the good times would never end.

Loren's view was more particular. He regarded Fillmore as a remnant of paradise for the beauty of its fertile fields, the fast flowing river, hardwood forests, mostly good people and Phil, who was the sun in his small universe. Now, this crazy restaurant that Danny had come back from France and created was giving strangers from all over an excuse to invade the valley. They said they were coming to eat at the Peasant Palate when they were really coming to gape at Phil. Loren wished he'd never let Danny do it. When the place was just a diner, nobody but locals came in. "I'd like to kick their fat asses out of my restaurant and out of this valley, blow up the bridges at both ends so they couldn't come back."

Phil heard Loren's growl. "Asses?"

"What?"

"You muttered something about kicking asses."

"Did I?" Loren stroked his mustache.

Phil rose from the stool, preparing to leave.

"Phil, isn't it time you got a haircut? Those curls on your shoulders make you look like Cousin Levi." Loren cocked an eyebrow.

"Mother went ballistic when we called Levi 'Cousin.' She swore he'd changed his name from something nobody could pronounce to Fillmore just to annoy her."

"She also got pretty pissed when he'd arrive at one of those birthday bashes everybody was invited to and stink up the place."

"She hated it when he sat on an upholstered chair, and he knew it. To give her fits he kept moving, sitting in one chair after another while footmen served him champagne." Phil laughed. "Poor old Levi."

Loren harrumphed. "You probably haven't noticed, but we swab your stool with a Clorox-soaked rag every day after you get off it." When Phil didn't laugh, Loren raised his hands palms out in a sorry-bad-joke gesture.

But Phil hadn't been paying attention; he was fingering his black locks. "Probably time I had a trim. Miss Eleanor's not what she used to be and I don't want to hurt her feelings by taking the shears to myself. I tried that once and made a terrible mess."

"We do have barbers in town, you know. Always have. Now there's a unisex salon where Louis used to be. If you're addicted to a woman cutting your hair you can try that one."

"Nobody but Miss Eleanor has ever cut my hair—except when I hacked at it myself. I hate haircuts"

"It's up to you, but maybe people wouldn't think you were quite so, so"—Loren paused and glanced toward the starers at the tables—"oddball if you'd get your hair cut and, while you're at it, for Christ's sake stop wearing your father's old pants; they're too big for you around the middle and too short in the leg. Dig clothes out of your own closet for a change if you insist on wearing old stuff, and stop using a necktie for a belt."

Phil looked down at bare ankles where the pants didn't reach. "You don't like my father's—correction, these are my grandfather's pants. He bought them in London. The label says Jermyn Street."

"Save the label but burn the friggin' pants."

Phil shook his head. "I couldn't do that. I won't burn them, but I will have them cleaned."

"With any luck they'll dissolve."

"Hadn't better risk it. On the way home I'll see if Miss Eleanor is in a scissoring mood. Tell Danny I'm having terrible pains in my gut, must be something I ate. I'm leaving. Get out the Clorox. See you tomorrow."

At the door Phil stepped aside to let enter a stout woman in a flowered print dress with a flounce that emphasized her size. She took conspicuous care to stay clear of him. Then when he was outside she turned to her companion, put a hand to her mouth and cried, "Oh Alice, that was him! I know that was him. Wendy told me if we arrived promptly he'd be here. We're only half an hour late and he's gone. We drove all this way and we've missed him! Damn!"

THE PEASANT PALATE SITS ACROSS FROM THE VILLAGE square on the corner of River Road, which runs down to the docks, and Valley Road, the primary thoroughfare from the bridge at the east end of the valley to the pass some forty miles west. Valley Road became a state highway in the 1930s, but Fillmore influence in the legislature kept it from changing character; only periodic updating of the pavement and drainage is permitted. No stoplight brings traffic to a halt, or blinker signals caution at any cross road, but speeding is not a problem. Phil's grandfather FP insisted when the state took over that attractive but impossible-to-ignore signs be placed at both ends of the valley: "Anyone found guilty of driving over forty miles per hour on this highway will be fined ten thousand dollars." The same speed limit was enforced on trains that traversed the valley on tracks lying equidistant, approximately half a mile between Valley Road and the banks of the river.

The Fillmore Inn, a Fillmore Trust property, sits across River Road from the Peasant Palate on the corner next to the post office. Then comes the Fillmore Valley Bank, also owned by the Trust, and beyond that the Fillmore Free Library. The village square across Valley Road is not a New England village green, but the center of local commerce with a dozen, more or less, freestanding buildings of various vintages containing an IGA store, Fiske's Five and Dime, Wadsworth's Paint and Paper, Handyside's Hardware, Colgrove and Ryan Meats, the Home Dairy Bakery, which has salt-rising bread on Thursdays, and other establishments including the Unisex Hair Salon. Most are one-story edifices; the few that aren't house professional offices on the second floor. Morrison's Feed & Grain and Goodrich Lumber & Coal are situated on the right side of River Street headed for the river, as is Fawcett's Fuel Oil & Gas. On the left side are two automobile showrooms. Tom Herrick sells Ford products and Toby Best sells General Motors. Those who want Chryslers or Dodges or some other make of car have to leave the valley to buy them. Between the two showrooms is a farm-implement business. Back up in the square is a landscaped fountain ringed by benches, where old men meet their friends when the weather is good. At one time a horse trough at the base of the fountain was used regularly, but it isn't now, and where horses and wagons were tied up around the perimeter of the square cars now park. There are no meters. During cold months the congregation of retired farmers shuffles down River Street to gather around a woodstove and a coffee machine at Morrison's Feed & Grain.

Phil's daily departure from the Peasant Palate takes him diagonally across the square east of the fountain toward small white houses clustered where Ontyakah Road begins its winding ascent to Oshatakea. The road follows a path used by the Senecas when they hiked north to hunt game on the high plateau. Facing the square at the foot of the hill is the Presbyterian church, a classic planked-style white building, erected by settlers who followed Thomas Fillmore to the valley. Its tall narrow windows, stark interior with numbered box pews and the delicate steeple topped by a gilded gull-feather weathervane have been maintained unchanged since the day it was dedicated. After more than 150 years Presbyterian bells still mark time in the valley, striking on the hour and the half hour. Behind the church, an L-shaped construction of connected bays and stalls was used for sheltering horses and carriages during daylong services. The brown-shingled Methodist church on River Street, next to Fawcett's Fuel, is more modest, hunkering down beneath a squat flat-roofed belfry. Our Blessed Lady of the Valley, the last to be established in Fillmore's trinity of houses of worship, has late-nineteenth century stained-glass windows, a mansard-roofed brick rectory and a walled convent that nonbelievers find menacing. The old men sitting in the square speculate about what goes on in that convent. Few of them being Catholic, their speculation is often salacious.

About two hundred feet up Ontyakah Road, overlooking the Presbyterian carriage sheds, is the redbrick firehouse Theodore Roosevelt came to Fillmore to dedicate when he was president of the United States. Designed by Bryant Fleming to complement the architecture of the Fillmore Academy's original building, the oldest brick structure in the village, the most striking feature of the firehouse is its lookout tower. After Teddy cut the ribbon stretched across the front of the firehouse, he ran up two flights of stairs to the top of the tower, where he pronounced his blessing on the building and the good people of Fillmore, then proclaimed the wisdom of whoever had decreed the firehouse roof should not exceed the height of the church steeple's weathervane. "It wouldn't be right to look down on the house of God," he thundered, an anecdote repeated to those who came to peer at Phil and were enchanted by the village.

Henry Handyside was unrolling the awning in front of his hardware store as Phil came by on his way home from lunch in his Jerymn Street pants and crude thong sandals that made slapping sounds on the macadam. "Afternoon Phil," Hank called out, not expecting a response; Phil sometimes wasn't in a mood to communicate. Henry saw him on the way to and from lunch every day except Sunday, and it was a rare day the question of Pearl didn't pop into Henry's head. People don't just vanish, but Oshatakea's housekeeper Pearl did, disappeared the day Farney was killed. They say her room hasn't been touched, is exactly the way it was that morning she came up missing. Same thing for Catherine's rooms, locked tight; nobody's been in there since, except Phil of course, and the undertaker when he removed the body. That's what they say.

"Afternoon Hank," Phil replied.

Arne Swenson, one of six paid firemen in the mostly volunteer Fillmore Fire Brigade, was leaning against the wall of the firehouse, catching some sun on his face. "Think we'll get frost tonight?" he asked as Phil came alongside.

"Could." Phil didn't pause.

"Wife and I strolled through a few of your gardens yesterday; the China asters have never been prettier."

"Günter's crew does a good job.

Phil might be famous for his house, which locals said was the biggest in the US of A, and for his fortune these same experts said was so vast nobody could calculate the total amount, and he sure as hell was eccentric but he was reliable. Henry Handyside and Arne Swenson and anybody else who wanted to could set their watches by him instead of the Presbyterian bells. They all knew Phil opened the door to walk into the Peasant Palate as the bells started tolling noon, and emerged as they rang the half hour at one-thirty. Had done for years and years without missing a beat. The owner of the hardware store and the fireman were fairly consistent themselves, taking turns making comments about how peculiar it was that, though he must have more'n a dozen cars in his steam-heated garage, "Phil always walks." As far as they knew he'd never been behind the wheel of an automobile, and they couldn't recall seeing him being driven around by a chauffeur since Dick Fallon had brought him down to the academy for a few classes when he was a kid. Phil's answer when asked why he didn't drive—"I can walk where I want to go"—brought forth derisive laughter whenever it was repeated. Neither Hank nor Arne could remember which one asked him that question, but Phil's reply became part of local lore.

Arne stuck a toothpick between his cracked lips, wondering for the thousandth time if Phil really had murdered his mother. Not that Arne, nor most who knew Catherine Fillmore, would blame him if he had. She was a mean, difficult woman, haughty, thought she was better'n anybody else. Ruined her son's life, never acted as if she cared much more for him than she did people she despised, yet wouldn't let him out of her sight. Something more'n was generally known happened that day she and Phil and Farney were to board their private railroad car and head east toward Boston. Farney died, Pearl disappeared and Catherine might's well have. Nobody but a few nurses, Dr. Montrose and the four old women up Ontyakah Road ever laid eyes on her again. And Phil, of course.

Some say, when his mother got so nasty he couldn't stand it any longer, Phil put a pillow over her head and held it there. If he did, he must have paid off Doc Montrose because Doc left town shortly thereafter. Good riddance. Most people couldn't stand the sawbones who had replaced old Dr. Spoffard. Montrose had a little rat face, pointy nose, toothbrush mustache, and an attitude that made you want to hit him even when he was giving you something to make you feel better.

Walking past Henry and Arne and other valley people, men especially, Phil's stomach muscles cramped and his chest tightened. He forced himself to keep moving, hoping they wouldn't notice but sure they all knew everything there was to know about him. Well, not quite, there was one thing he'd managed to keep secret. Not even Loren knew about that. But, from the way Arne grinned that crooked grin at him, Phil surmised the fat fireman was thinking about the night in the carriage shed. Arne had been there, and had helped spread the word. By the next morning the only ones who weren't talking about it were buried in the cemetery. Phil believed the firehouse rocked with hoots of laughter every time he walked past as guys sitting around with nothing better to do reviewed one more time the ugly details of that night. Walking through the square, going to and from lunch each day, was for Phil like running a psychological gauntlet. He kept thinking it wouldn't bother him, but it did.

Up the hill beyond the firehouse, behind a rustic sapling fence from which the bark had long since peeled, Miss Eleanor's white clapboard cottage stood amidst a tangled garden that blossomed from early spring to hard frost. Visible from her kitchen window, in a sheltered corner of the ell, three hardy roses sometimes continued flowering into December. These English roses were her proudest achievement. Days after they faded, hellebores opened in the same bed, then came snowdrops. Miss Eleanor's sapling fence met with opposition when it was built; white pickets were considered more appropriate for her cottage, but she had insisted, saying the fence was in memory of her mother's garden fence in Cornwall. Miss Eleanor was too diplomatic to tell the truth. Her solid fence offered better protection from wintry blasts than the spaced pickets that fronted most yards in the picture-perfect village. Her fence and her careful planting of shrubbery to create a mini climate resulted in Miss Eleanor's being the longest-blooming garden in the entire valley. Its unkempt appearance also had a specific purpose. Miss Eleanor thought a cottage dooryard should be more welcoming than awe inspiring, as were the manicured gardens at Oshatakea. All the years she lived in the great house as Phil's nursemaid, she yearned for a garden of her own. Now, strangers as well as friends knocked at her door to tell her how pretty her flowers were, which gave her an excuse to make a pot of tea and pass a plate of cookies or biscuits. Since she did all the work involved in creating what those who don't garden call a gift from God, refusing assistance from Günter's army of men who cared for Isabelle Chapman's grounds as well as those surrounding Oshatakea, Miss Eleanor had exactly the garden she wanted. She sputtered about what was done for Isabelle, "It would do Isabelle a world of good to get down on her knees and plunge those soft pampered hands of hers into the earth." Isabelle, a much overweight, retired diva, would have none of it. She preferred looking down from her terraces onto the shoulders and backs of Günter's husky young gardeners. Phil tried as Miss Eleanor grew increasingly frail to persuade her to let his people help with heavy work, but she was adamant. "What gets so heavy I can't do won't get done."

She was clucking to a patch of fall-blooming crocus when Phil came through the gate. He was well along the path when she straightened up. "Phil! You startled me." She made a pass at wind-blown dandelion-down hair.

"What isn't behaving now?" he asked.

"Everything is behaving. I was just telling these lovely pink crochi how grateful I am to welcome them each fall. They delude me into thinking it's April instead of September." Her laugh was an almost girlish giggle. "Forgive an old woman her silliness. Come inside, or would you prefer to sit on the terrace in the sun? It's quite warm out of the breeze."

"I've come for a haircut."

Miss Eleanor clasped both hands to her left breast, a dramatic gesture she began using many years ago to indicate facetiously how taken aback she was by some announcement. It was after Katherine Cornell had come to Oshatakea to perform in a play by Christopher Fry and had clutched her bosom with such regularity Miss Eleanor said she reduced it to cliché. "You are requesting a haircut? I cannot believe it." Miss Eleanor's dramatic performance continued as she pretended her knees were buckling. Phil played along, allowing her to touch his forehead to see if he might be feverish. "Usually I chide you for months before you'll let me have at you."

Phil's disarming grin brought flashes to Miss Eleanor's mind of screen actors she thought especially handsome. Miss Eleanor was an ardent film buff. But no, Phil's look was his own; he didn't resemble a movie star, or anyone in his family. Maybe he was a miracle, as Levi had said. With his hair so black its highlights were indigo, and white skin covering features more refined than either his mother's or his father's, Miss Eleanor might think his background was black Irish if she didn't know better. Realizing how offensive such a thought would be to Phil's mother brought Miss Eleanor up short. She returned from her reverie. "If it's a haircut you want that settles where we'll sit. I'll shear you on the terrace which will be easier to clean up afterward. Bring out that blue stool from the kitchen while I get my barber kit." Moving toward the kitchen door, she said, "There will be no complaints when I'm finished, mind you."

"Do I ever complain?"

"Always!"

As he sat down on the stool he asked, "Would you mind if I face the other direction?"

"Your first complaint?"

"The sun is in my eyes."

She stepped back. He turned around on the stool, a barber's sheet tucked snuggly around his neck. "Better?"

"Fine."

"Good." She began to clip, and to hum. Miss Eleanor talked to her plants, murmured endearments or imprecations to food she was preparing, muttered while dusting or running the vacuum. The rest of the time, she hummed.

"Who'd have thought I'd become as peculiar as Levi? His hair was long and curly."

"Levi's curls were gray and greasy. He was also more than peculiar. There is peculiar and then there is particular, extraordinary. That description doesn't fit Levi."

"It was pretty extraordinary he had stashed away all that money he left to Beth Israel hospital in the city. I'm sure they think of him as particular. They'd never heard of Levi Fillmore, or whatever his real name was."

"Warshawsky," Miss Eleanor muttered.

"What?"

"Warshawsky. His real name was Leviticus Warshawsky."

"Hell, anybody can pronounce Warshawsky. Mother said it was something unpronounceable." The only sound for several minutes was Miss Eleanor's humming and the scissors snipping. "I am like Levi in one way. He had no heirs and I don't either."

"Not yet you haven't, but you will by the time it's necessary to have heirs."

"What's that supposed to mean?"

Miss Eleanor coughed. "You'll marry one day; Fillmore men marry late in life. Of course your grandfather married early and late, but he was unlike anybody else. You will marry when you marry and then you'll have children, heirs."

Phil turned to look at her. "Do you have a wife in mind for me?"

Her grin reflected his. "I'll not choose a wife for you. I changed your diapers and cleaned up after you, but some things you have to do for yourself, and finding a wife is one of them."

Phil laughed. "George Hunnewell says I have hard decisions to make. He keeps harping on it. Making decisions isn't my strong suit. I put off deciding anything as long as I can." Phil's curls were piling up in a glistening black circle around the stool. "Don't cut it all off, just get it off my shoulders."

"You want to look like Prince Valiant?"

"Very funny. No matter what you do, Isabelle won't be satisfied. She's forever making cracks about my hair."

Miss Eleanor sighed. "That's our Isabelle."

Together they cleaned up the mess. When all was neat and tidy and everything had been put back where it belonged, Phil thanked Miss Eleanor and bent to give her a quick kiss on the cheek. They were standing in her low-ceilinged kitchen; Phil had to duck to keep his head from banging against the beams. He inhaled the aroma coming from a pot of soup Miss Eleanor always kept simmering on the back of her stove, adding scraps and drippings each day. "That soup is making me hungry and I've just stuffed myself down at Danny's."

"Let me give you some to take home."

"No, no thanks, Adrian will have put more than enough food for me in the fridge." He moved toward the door looking fondly around the room. "Remember the night I gave you the key to this house?"

"I will never forget. It was your seventeenth birthday. You have given me the two happiest days of my life—exactly seventeen years apart—the first when you were born, the second when you made me the present of my own house."

Phil drew her to him for a long hug. "I don't remember the first, thank God, but I do the second. It was my happiest day too."

Miss Eleanor watched him sandal-slapping along her path and through the gate, pondering what he had said. If true, it was sad for a seventeenth birthday to be the high point in the life of a man not yet thirty-nine.

Across and up a few hundred feet from Miss Eleanor's cottage was a pink stucco villa built on several levels cut into the hillside. On each level French doors opened onto wide terraces. Wrought-iron balconies decorated the facade. Strangers to Fillmore, such as those who came to see Phil at the Peasant Palate, were thrilled by the sight of Isabelle's villa, the first mansion on Ontyakah Road, and the only one they could see from the road. Though magnificent, it was far from being FP Fillmore's most extravagant architectural transplant. He purchased it in Commachio, Italy, where it had stood for centuries on a bluff above the Adriatic, as a gift for a young soprano with whom FP hoped to have a significant dalliance. She had told him about the villa, calling it the most romantic house in the world, whereupon he persuaded the family that had occupied it for ten or twelve generations to sell the house with most of its furnishings for more money than they knew existed. Busy counting lire, not one of them shed a tear as their house was taken apart and put in numbered crates for shipment to Fillmore where it was reassembled, not overlooking a sparkling azure sea but a deep, swiftly flowing river coursing through a lush valley. Overwhelmed when presented with this splendid gift, Isabelle Chapman, the young soprano, at first refused to accept it because an ardent romance with her generous suitor was not possible, despite her deep and abiding affection for him. FP took his disappointment like the gentleman he was, told her it would give him almost as much pleasure to have her as a friend and neighbor, insisting she accept his gift with but one stipulation—from time to time she would sing for him, for his family and his guests. Few sopranos ever struck a better bargain.

Isabelle lived on long after FP's death in her pink palazzo crowded with its original furnishings plus treasures FP had allowed her to select from his crammed warehouses and quantities of decorative objects she acquired during a long career of worldwide concertizing. She no longer traveled nor performed in public, but would sing simple songs for FP's family, accompanied by Phil's cousin Adelaide Kropotkin, who in her late nineties had more control over her hands than Isabelle in her late eighties had over her vibrato. Ever flamboyant, Isabelle favored silk taffeta or satin gowns in brilliant colors and elaborate design, continuing to don many she had worn on stage. Whether in fancy dress or everyday Capri pants, she was bejeweled, her absolute favorite piece being a large ancient Inca breastplate of beaten gold encrusted with multicolored gems. Her friends referred to the breastplate as Isabelle's fender.

While Miss Eleanor had been cutting Phil's hair, Isabelle, her face covered with a cream to protect her skin, was taking the air on one of her high terraces. When she heard Phil's sandals flopping on the road, she arose from her divan, went to the rail and called down to him. "Who is the gorgeous man I see walking past my gate? How do you keep your Adonis physique young man while the rest of us fall apart? It's not fair."

"I've just had a haircut." Phil waved but didn't pause.

"Hurrah! Now get rid of those Mickey Mouse pants."

"Loren has already told me to do that, but it's against my nature to throw anything away."

"Committing a crime against nature now and then is good for you—gets the blood moving."

Phil stopped and looked up. "Isabelle, what are you suggesting?"

"Just that you change your pants Handsome. Pretend you are a tree; shed those trousers as maples shed their leaves. I would not, however, recommend you wait till spring to put on another pair." Her shriek of laughter was followed by a spasm of choking coughs.

"Easy Isabelle, one of these days your dirty mind is going to do you in." He waved again and continued his trek.

"Have you thought any more about letting us plan a birthday party for you?" Isabelle called after him.

"I'm too old for birthday parties."

"Thirty-nine, too old? God, what I wouldn't give to be thirty-nine again, or forty-nine or fifty-nine. When I was thirty-nine—"

"Stop before you have another spasm," Phil shouted. "I'm too young to hear what you were doing at my age." His laughter came back to join hers.

Would I want to be thirty-nine again, Isabelle mused. I think not, unless those who were around then could be with me now—and we'd all have to be the ages we were then. She shrugged off the foolish, depressing thought to watch Phil disappear around a curve in the steep road. Aloud she said, "More money than the Gettys, yet he looks like a bindle stiff in his grandfather's pants and wanders around alone in that granite pile, a ghost with no one to spook."

"You're talking to yourself." Lucile, Isabelle's maid, spoke from the music room door.

"I was talking to Phil."

"He's gone and you're still talking—to yourself. You'll be humming next, like Miss Eleanor."

"It's one of the privileges of senility."

"You were talking to yourself when I met you in Lyons before the Great War. You weren't old then, neither of us was old. You were older than I, still are, always will be. I find that comforting."

"Stop," Isabelle bellowed. "Who was on the telephone."

"Adelaide Kropotkin to remind you of dinner at the dacha this evening at six-thirty."

"She doesn't need to remind me for God's sake."

"Why so cranky? Behave yourself. Adelaide is an old lady."

Isabelle regarded her maid through faded green eyes, her lazy lids opened as far as she could stretch them. "So am I—not as old as Adelaide, nobody is as old as Adelaide."

"I wasn't telling you to be good because she is old, but because Adelaide is a lady. You missed my point."

The two women faced off, *en garde*, a stance broken when Isabelle's signature shrieking laughter shattered the quiet, scattering a flock of cedar waxwings that had been feasting on the berries of a nearby dogwood tree. When she stopped coughing, Isabelle pointed a gnarled vermilion-tipped finger at Lucile. "You, Mademoiselle Bigmouth, are fired."

"May I leave now, or must I wait for the next boat?"

"There hasn't been a boat in years. There is Air France, however, so dust off your wings."

Lucile rolled her eyes and disappeared back into the music room. The telephone was ringing again. Isabelle's gaze returned to the curve in the road. Phil had been dear to her since the chubby-cheeked curly haired infant about to be put into an embroidered ridiculously long christening dress was handed to her by Miss Eleanor. At the time of Phil's birth, Isabelle was in Europe entertaining American forces still waiting to be demobilized. The morning of his christening was their first meeting. More than a hundred houseguests had arrived at Oshatakea for the event. Ebullient FP was everywhere, ecstatic that he had a grandson. Farney was less enthusiastic than his father, but seemed pleased to have sired a son. Catherine refused to have anything to do with either the infant or the proceedings. Winston Churchill had agreed to serve as godfather, but could not be present; Randolph was standing in for him. Phil's godmother designate, Eleanor Roosevelt, interrupted her frenetic schedule to be on the scene. What, Isabelle had wondered, might be the future for a cherub with such powerful sponsors, adored by a King Midas grandfather who would spoil him, yet despised by a mother who would not look at him and had tried to exile her maid Eleanor Gaines when Gaines stepped forward in an emergency to care for the newborn? Surely there would be no second miracle to produce a sibling. As an only child torn between being pampered and being hated, how could he grow up to be anything but a monster? But he had not. How different his life would be had he been more concerned with his own needs and less with the demands of others. If that had been the case, Phil would be long gone from these parts. Or perhaps he would not. Since his father's death he hadn't shown the slightest desire to leave the valley. "He beguiles with those curls which I'm glad have been trimmed, though I do wish Miss Eleanor would not cut them that short," Isabelle muttered. "And those lashes, God would that I had had those lashes. While I'm asking Sweet Jesus, you could throw in those deep blue eyes as well!" She turned away, picked up a glass of iced tea and took a sip. "With his looks and sweet nature he could conquer the world, not that he needs to, he owns half of it."

Lucile again stepped out of the music room but she did not interrupt Isabelle's monologue. "What good does it do him? He's the last Fillmore, except for his two ancient cousins Adelaide and Louisa. As for friends, unlike his grandfather and father he never made real friends, except for Loren. Loren understands him better than anybody." She inhaled deeply and let the air out in a slow sigh. "Nobody is invited to Oshatakea—except the Kropotkins, Miss Eleanor, me and sometimes Loren for an occasional dinner, for Christmas Eve, but not like the old days. There hasn't been a houseguest since before Phil was supposed to leave for Harvard. God, what a day that was; I won't dwell on it. Difficult bitch that she was, you have to give Catherine credit, she put Oshatakea on the map. Sol Hurok could have retired on commissions from his contracts with her. Menuhin, Rubinstein, the Philadelphia, Ballet Russe, Martha Graham, everybody who was anybody, all the greats, came here to perform. Pons stayed a week, so did Flagstad. Paderewski considered it home. Artists of their caliber aren't around to invite these days. She didn't bring me here. I came long before Catherine, thrilled to be invited to sing for guests of the fabulous FP Fillmore. Nobody could have dreamed I'd keep coming, that he'd buy this dear house for me." She patted the balustrade. "And, here I'll be until the end, amen."

"Amen." Lucile cleared her throat.

Isabelle paid no heed if she heard. She was again gazing up the hill. "A full staff keeping everything immaculate up there, inside and out—who for, for what? Oshatakea used to feel like the center of the universe with footmen on duty twenty-four hours a day, better than the best hotel. There'd be no breakfast in bed now. Nobody lives in, except thousand-year-old Stefan tucked away in a stable apartment, so deaf a sound hasn't penetrated his thatch since bugles blew at Balaklava. Dozens of staff rooms under the eaves. I'd feel better if somebody lived in them, or slept up there at least so Phil wouldn't be alone at night. I'm surprised George Hunnewell doesn't insist if for no other reason than insurance."

"Mrs. Morrell is on the telephone." Lucile had moved close to Isabelle to deliver her message.

Isabelle jerked around. "How many times have I told you, do not sneak up on me, perfidious woman? I'm not here, what does she want?"

"She didn't say, not that she'd tell me. Mrs. Morrell doesn't converse with the help." Lucile dabbed her hay fever–tortured nose with one of the paper towels she kept in an apron pocket, Kleenex not being sufficiently sturdy for her powerful snorts.

"Elizabeth Morrell is a pain."

"You said it."

"And you think it." Isabelle adjusted pale green folds of the silk blouse that had twisted over her bosom. "Don't stand there dripping like a pelican, tell her I can't talk now, I'm in the middle of an orgy." Lucile started back toward the door, eager to deliver Isabelle's outrageous message to pushy Marguerite Morrell. "Wait just a minute, Troublemaker, you'd love to spread some such rumor wouldn't you?" Lucile's watering eyes smiled. "That Morrell woman keeps coming up with stupid reasons for me to take her to Oshatakea. The gates are never closed, she can go through the gardens anytime or visit the west-wing libraries if she has legitimate business there during the hours Fisher Ames and his staff have posted."

"You sound like a tour guide."

"It isn't a tour she wants, Klotzbach, she wants to be invited to dinner, has wanted nothing less since she bought the Simpson property thinking somehow that made her a branch of the Fillmore family. Nobody is invited anymore."

"He lets the Choral Society and the Playmakers use the Baroque Theatre. Mrs. Morrell should join one of those groups, or she can go as part of the audience," Lucile interjected.

"Those people never get beyond the loggia," Isabelle corrected her. " She's tried that route. I can't stand the nosy creature."

"Is that why you call her Margie Darling?"

"Eavesdropping again? Tell her I died, the funeral is Tuesday."

"You wand flowers?" Lucile spoke through a paper towel.

"Orchids would be mudge appreciated," Isabelle mocked her.

Phil slapped on up the road toward the towering gates of Oshatakea. He relished repartee with Isabelle. She always threw down a gauntlet, challenged him, stimulating him to rise to an occasion. When he was a child lulled into blind bliss by a worshipful grandfather and doting Miss Eleanor, Isabelle returning from her concert tours would greet him with horrified shrieks. "Phil, what happened to you? Your head turned into a pumpkin while I was away." Or, "I did not realize until this very moment you have one green and one red eye, the green is larger than the red and neither is in focus." He welcomed her teasing, found it refreshing, but Gramps did not, and Miss Eleanor repeatedly told her to stop: "You are not funny Isabelle." But she was. The strangest aspect of those joshings was the reaction of Phil's mother, who was beginning to just barely tolerate him when he'd reached the age where Isabelle knew she could kid with him. Catherine's frigid response to Isabelle's mock jabs was a silence of such intensity it frightened Phil. He had learned never to cry if he didn't want to be sent from the room, so, forcing himself to swallow sobs, with great trepidation, praying to not incite further fury, he would accept Isabelle's bone-crushing hug without making a sound.

In his early teens, Phil was more insecure than most pubescents, convinced he was a runt despite being tall for his age with the feet of a giant. It was Isabelle who had the imagination to tease him out of his depression. Phil's face was amazingly free of acne, yet a tiny pimple made him despondent. His voice was not to be totally trusted but did not crack constantly as often happened to boys during that period of development. The only thing about himself of which he was totally confident was his abundant black curly hair, which is why he collapsed into fits of laughter when Isabelle remarked, "If I were you, I'd bleach that mop platinum blond— after I'd had it straightened. Naturally wavy hair, yuck!" She treated him as an equal as soon as he was old enough to comprehend. This combined with her deprecating humor made him feel he and she belonged to a secret club.

As he approached Oshatakea's elaborate main entrance gates, which Isabelle once described as "overwrought to the point of hysteria," Phil met a vintage Daimler purring through, driven by a craggy-faced chauffeur whose uniform matched the dove gray of the stately black-trimmed automobile. Beside the chauffeur sat his wife, whose navy coat covered the uniform she wore as housekeeper for the Kropotkin sisters, who were ensconced in the rear. Adelaide, ninety-seven, and Louisa, ninety-six, went motoring after lunch every day, weather permitting, returning midafternoon to retire to their rooms for short naps before tea. The chauffeur answered to Boris, his housekeeper wife to Magda, though in fact his name was George Tillottson and hers Mary. Many, many years before, Adelaide and Louisa's mother, grief stricken by the loss of her princely Russian husband at the hands of Bolshevik forces, could not face the retirement of her coachman and housekeeper. Adelaide and Louisa hit upon the idea of easing their mother's staff transition by conferring the names of those who had just retired on the new coachman and housekeeper. The ploy became a tradition. There had been several generations of men and women in those positions willing to accept as part of the terms of their employment assuming, while on duty, the names Boris and Magda. After forty-three years, the present incumbents no longer thought of themselves as George and Mary.

"Phillips, how nice to see you." Adelaide wound down her window. "We are taking Lottie Christner a poppy seed cake. Poor thing can't get over Richard's death."

"They were married sixty years," Louisa piped up.

"Remember you are coming to us for dinner this evening?" Adelaide's tone of reminding someone thought to be absent-minded was softened by a radiant smile. She had been the plain sister when they were young, but as age refined her features she became quite beautiful, while Louisa's girlish prettiness had given way to a plumpness Louisa said made her look like a pudding.

"What time?"

"Cocktails at six-thirty."

"You have had a haircut Phil," Louisa exclaimed.

Before Phil could respond, Adelaide said, "You look splendid my dear."

"Why don't you wear kilts tonight, instead of those funny pants, to celebrate your haircut?" Louisa suggested.

"Can you control Isabelle if I do?"

Both women laughed gaily, and a smile brightened the face of normally dour Boris. "I'm going to tell her what you said," Louisa tittered.

"That's why I said it," Phil winked.

"Louisa you'll do no such thing." Adelaide remonstrated. "Please be on time Phillips."

"As the clock strikes," Phil promised.

"Drive on Boris."

Phil watched the limousine move sedately down the hill, then turned left inside the gate, taking the stable road for a short way before slipping through a break in the tall hemlock hedge lining the drive to enter a forest path that was his shortcut to the house.

Chapter 2

⸺

THEY LEFT THE CITY AT 10:48 A.M., DRIVING ONTO THE thruway twelve minutes later than George Hunnewell had planned because Jerrold Clewes was not waiting to be picked up at the Delaware Avenue entrance where he should have been, nor was he at the hotel's front door when Hunnewell's blue Mercedes 560SEC paused there, the steady sound of its powerful idling engine compounding growing impatience. George liked to start a journey when he said he was going to start. He wanted people to be where they were supposed to be when he had made a previous arrangement with them. He had signed a contract with Clewes for the most important, most lucrative appraisal the New Yorker's firm had ever undertaken. George hoped he had not made an error in judgment.

Jerrold Clewes was, thank God, at the Delaware door when Hunnewell pulled up the second time. "Sorry, I was on the telephone." He could tell; excuses were unacceptable to this unsmiling caretaker of the Fillmore fortune. "Talking to my London office." He could see Hunnewell was not impressed.

They rode in silence, the Mercedes cruising at a steady seventy-five miles an hour in the passing lane. After forty minutes, Jerrold was thinking he'd ask to have the heater turned up in an attempt to thaw the atmosphere. Instead, he took a small step toward a truce. "Living in Manhattan, I forget there's all this open land out here in the country. Makes me wonder what they mean when they talk about overcrowding, people falling off the planet if we don't slow population growth, that sort of thing." Hunnewell did not respond.

At 11:57, they left the thruway at exit ten, the Mercedes swinging into the parking lot of a facsimile 1940s diner at the end of the ramp. "The food here is adequate," George said.

"Smells good." Jerrold was being agreeable; actually, the odor of grease that had fried too many things over too long a period assailed his nostrils as they sat down in the single empty booth. He wanted to bite his tongue. Sarcasm wasn't likely to improve Hunnewell's humor. Glancing around, he surmised the two of them were the only non–truck drivers in the place. He doubted this would prove the old fable that truck drivers know where to find good food. How many cleanings would be required, he wondered, to rid his suit of the stink it was absorbing like a blotter. Probably have to throw it away. He'd put its replacement cost in the Oshatakea expenses column.

"There are two excellent places to eat in Fillmore, the Inn and the Peasant Palate, but Phil will be at the Peasant which eliminates that because I won't discuss private business in public, and the Inn is right across the street; he'd notice my car if we ate there, so this will have to do."

"Looks fine," Jerrold lied. He was becoming nauseated watching waitresses deliver heavy crockery platters heaped with slabs of pork and mountains of mashed potatoes swimming in pools of brown gravy. "Must be the special of the day."

"I advise you to stick with a BLT."

An hour later they drove onto a bridge across the Shatekye River. Jerrold Clewes purposely did not look down at the swirling water. His stomach was now in active rebellion though he'd eaten only half a ham sandwich. It was the glass of milk, "to wash it down," that did him in. Clewes was not a milk drinker, but he had friends in New York who consumed a thin bluish-gray liquid that was some percent milk, not at all like what the sweaty waitress slammed down in front of him. When he said he had asked for milk, she retorted, "That's what ya got honey—homogenized, straight from the cow." And, he blamed himself, he drank it!

"When we drive off this bridge we will be in the Fillmore valley," George explained. "Forty-three miles long and approximately eighteen miles wide. Once upon a time, the Fillmores owned every inch of it. Phil still owns a big chunk."

"Good Lord!" Clewes stared out at a landscape of vast fields that Hunnewell said were freshly planted with winter wheat, and that others had been harvested and were resting until spring when they'd be plowed for new crops. More cows than Clewes had ever seen at one time were lined up at long blue feed troughs in pastures that seemed to go on forever. On the wooded hillsides clusters of red barns dotted clearings alongside rambling houses, mostly white, though some were light brown. These, he would later learn, were constructed of cobblestone. "It's bigger than Central Park."

George laughed. "Bigger than a couple of European countries."

In the village of Fillmore the houses were smaller than those on the farms but again primarily white clapboard with a few brick, and some cobblestone, all set behind neatly trimmed lawns on quiet streets bowered by maple trees. They passed a white church with a multibayed carriage shed behind, obviously a relic of the past. Around three sides of a square was an assortment of stores including an apothecary, which caught Jerrold's eye. The Peasant Palate Hunnewell had mentioned was across from the square and, just as he'd said, across a side street from the Fillmore Inn. Along the main road, just beyond the Inn, an American flag fluttered in front of a handsome square granite building. "That's the post office FP Fillmore built and gave to the government because he told his friend FDR he didn't trust federal architects to put up a structure that would enhance his village. We'll drive through, then turn around. We get to Oshatakea up that road beside the church."

George identified a large stone and timber Tudor-style building as the library Hester Schuyler Fillmore had given to the people of the valley, and so richly endowed librarians found it difficult to spend the percentage of annual income allocated for books, though they frequently petitioned the estate for maintenance and staff salary assistance. Opposite the library, up from the road behind low retaining walls, was a Greek-revival brick building with six white pillars supporting a classic pediment, the original Fillmore Academy, established by Christina Farnsworth Fillmore. "That building is now used only for ceremonial events. The present academy is the group of later brick buildings you can see if you hunker down and look up to the left We didn't want to crowd the campus when new athletic facilities were needed, so eight years ago we created a second campus for them at the western edge of the village. That's where we'll turn around." As they made a U-turn in the parking lot of a gymnasium, rink, pool and playing fields complex, George continued. "From here to the far end of the valley is all farmed land, some of the most fertile acreage in the country, kept that way for more than two hundred years by careful scientific management."

On the drive back as they were approaching the Fillmore Inn and the Peasant Palate, Jerrold wished they had lunched in one of them rather than at the truck stop. His reverie was broken when Hunnewell said, "The warehouses FP built to store rooms and other architectural artifacts he hadn't yet incorporated into Oshatakea, plus stacks of leftover furniture and decorative objects, are down there, at the end of River Road."

"The legendary warehouses; I can't wait to get inside them," Jerrold said.

"They haven't been opened since FP's death."

"I know," Jerrold squealed.

Coming around the square Hunnewell nodded toward the foot of Ontyakah Road, "That is the firehouse built as were all public

buildings in the valley, and bridges, by the Fillmore family."
Before Clewes had an opportunity to comment they had started up
the hill. George continued, "The little cottage behind that strange
fence is where Eleanor Gaines lives. There she is, can you see her
in the garden bending over something? Miss Eleanor, as she is
called, came to Oshatakea as Catherine Fillmore's personal maid,
but she was always a great deal more than a servant. She reared
Phil, and still has a strong influence on him. Be good to Miss
Eleanor, she can be an important ally. Now, quickly, look to our
left. The pink stucco villa that is totally out of place in this valley
is home to Isabelle Chapman, a retired diva. She will drive you
bats. Avoid her if you can."

After the villa, Isabelle's well-kept terraces gave way to sloping
fields bright with fall flowers, blue chickory, goldenrod, joe-pye
weed, white and lavender asters. On the right Jerrold noticed a
high cut-stone wall continuing alongside Ontyakah Road as far as
the eye could see. When they came to a break and drove through
the tall gates, George smiled at his passenger's incredulity. "The
gates were commissioned in 1845 by Hester Fillmore. They had
terrible problems installing them because of their size. Wheels on
the bottom meant to carry the weight of the iron collapsed the first
time the gates were opened. They've not been closed since."

Hunnewell's Mercedes proceeded straight ahead along a broad
avenue bordered by terraces of specimen plantings designed to
give a protracted blooming season—azaleas, rhododendron, lilacs.
On the uppermost strata the waxy leaves and red berries of English
holly glistened in the sun. "The side road to the right just inside
the gate goes into a birch grove and the Kropotkin dacha. The
dacha had been in Prince Nicholas Alexandrovich Kropotkin's
family for generations. FP had it brought here from Russia before
the turn of the century. The prince's maiden-lady daughters,
Adelaide and Louisa, live there. They are Phil's first cousins,
which seems odd because of the great difference in ages, but FP

had two wives. I'll explain it to you some other time. The road to the left back there goes around to the stable block."

After half a mile the broad avenue narrowed and took on a very different character, curving around ponds in lightly wooded areas with specimen trees of numerous varieties and unusual shrubs, most of which were unfamiliar to Clewes. Nor did George know what they were. "The approach to the house was redesigned by Olmsted working with FP, who didn't like his mother's—Hester of the gates—plan. All of these trees, bushes, et cetera were planted to look as if each had sprung up by chance. Not so. In the spring the flowering trees are breathtaking. You'll be here to enjoy them." Hunnewell's demeanor was softening. He enjoyed pointing out sights to his passenger. "The house isn't as far from the gate as this drive makes it seem because we're crossing back and forth over and under the stone bridges. FP wanted visitors to have a series of impressions before making the final ascent, and Olmsted gave him what he wanted."

The woods gave way to a clearing. "We're coming into the circle that leads us around to an allée. Here we are. Now, look straight up through those rows of plaiched poplar trees, and you will get your first glimpse of Oshatakea." George laughed as Jerrold's jaw dropped. "Yours is exactly the reaction FP wanted people to have. From this spot the house appears to be floating in the clouds."

"My God." Clewes's eyes strained to take in the multistoried facade of a building that shimmered in the sun and seemed to stretch toward infinity in both directions. "It's unbelievable."As the car glided up through the poplars, gradually the totality of Oshatakea's south front came into view. "My God," Clewes repeated.

At the top of the rise they entered another graveled circle. George indicated a secondary drive branching to the right. "That goes around to the Portuguese Wing, a separate mansion FP built as a wedding present for Phil's parents. It connects to the main house through a picture gallery lined, I am told, with American Impressionist paintings that were part of the wedding gift, which you will probably not see; I never have. Phil's mother kept the Portuguese Wing closed to everybody but the very tight family circle, comprised of the Kropotkins, Isabelle, Miss Eleanor and Loren Gage, who was, still is, Phil's only friend—and servants, of course. Nothing in that wing is listed in the inventory because it is not part of the trust, so don't worry about it."

The Mercedes crunched to a stop under a large porte cochere, about the size of an ordinary house. Before mounting steps to massive double doors, which Clewes estimated must be fifteen feet tall, George pointed to the far side of the circle. "The road branching off over there is the one you will regularly use. It goes to the west and north entrances."

Hunnewell ignored the heavy knocker in the form of a fist holding a thick rod poised to strike a plate, instead pressing an ivory button to the right. After a few seconds, he pressed the button again, waited another few seconds, made an unpleasant sound of increasing impatience, pressed it a third time and then reached up to raise the fist holding the thick rod. As the rod struck the plate the door opened to reveal a tall, angular woman wearing a dark blue suit.

"I was downstairs," she said. "Is he expecting you?" She made no gesture that could possibly be interpreted as an invitation to enter.

"He is," Hunnewell replied pushing past her, the deepening red on the back of his neck contrasting with his perfectly groomed white hair. "I told him I would be here at two o'clock, and it is now," he consulted his watch, "two-twenty." As he strode on, he said, "Mrs. Gillons, Mr. Clewes."

"He didn't tell me he was expecting you," she raised her voice, directing it toward his retreating back.

"Come along Clewes, we'll be meeting in the Galleried Library."

"In a minute. Excuse me, ma'am," Clewes addressed Mrs. Gillons. "Is there a place nearby where I might—wash my hands?"

"Through that room, turn right." She pointed to the open door of a walnut-paneled reception room on the left side of the entrance foyer.

Hurrying over a deep red Persian rug—very fine, he thought— past burgundy leather sofas and chairs and paintings of horses and fox hunting scenes, Clewes did as he had been told and turned right into a men's room where six urinals of monumental proportion stood against one wall. As many sinks of similar size and vintage were opposite. At the far end of the room he saw six doors on toilet stalls that were larger than his New York apartment's closets. All hardware was the soft gold of scrupulously polished old brass. His first thought after he relieved himself was, I'm not in a private home; this is more like a resort hotel. As he washed his hands, he amused himself with the notion that the antique fixtures in this men's room from an earlier era were probably worth a great deal of money. Certainly somebody somewhere would consider them collectable.

"My name is Jerrold Clewes," he said, offering his hand to the taciturn woman waiting for him in the foyer.

"I gathered. My name is Mary Gillons, Mrs. Gillons. I'm the housekeeper." She shook his hand, then without worrying about offending him wiped hers on a handkerchief she pulled from her jacket pocket. "I'll take you to the Galleried Library."

He dutifully followed to the end of the foyer, and stopped dead when they walked into the Great Hall that rose five tall stories above a marble parquet floor. Tiered alabaster columns supported a ceiling painted with partially draped figures relaxing on cottony clouds around the base of a Tiffany glass dome. Jerrold knew the dome was forty feet in diameter because he'd read descriptions of it, but he was not prepared for the rays of bright September sunlight transformed into brilliant beams washing down onto a pair of white marble staircases that rose to a landing large enough to seat an orchestra. When Mrs. Gillons turned to make sure he was following, Clewes gasped his stock exclamation, "My God," then blurted, "It's a Portman fantasy."

"Portman?"

"Portman designs hotels with atriums that reach up to heaven."

"FP Fillmore designed this Great Hall, with engineering assistance from his own architects."

"I know. I've read about it, but I can't believe its impact, its splendor. You come through the long entrance corridor which is impressive in itself, yet it seems like a tunnel when you walk into this space, this magnificent soaring space." Clewes's neck was beginning to hurt or he would have peered upward longer. Twisting, he glanced left toward the Long Gallery, knowing FP's famous period rooms were off that gallery. He wanted to hurry over for a better look, but knew Hunnewell must be about to pop an artery, as he was when Clewes followed Mrs. Gillons under the marble landing into the Galleried Library. Once again, Clewes reared back. "My God."

"Do stop," Hunnewell reprimanded. "Mrs. Gillons, get on the telephone and locate Phil. The village operator will know where he is. When you find him, tell him we are waiting and I do not have all day." He was pacing in front of a cavernous fireplace between huge crewel-covered wing chairs arranged on either side of the hearth.

"Mmm," a retreating Mrs. Gillons muttered.

On a lower level, in the kitchen Adrian and his assistant Ethel Hovis were finishing their work for the day. They had prepared breakfast for Phil and breakfast and midday dinner for everybody who worked on the place, indoors and out, forty-eight people total. And Adrian had left food in a refrigerator ready for Phil to pick at whenever he was hungry. "There's cold chicken, beet salad, split pea soup and other things, not that he'll eat much here tonight, he's going to the Kropotkins' for dinner."

"He is," Mrs. Gillons agreed when she walked in.

"Who was ringing the bell?" Ethel asked, pinning a flat felt hat on top of her sparse bun.

"George Hunnewell. He's looking for Phil, but Phil isn't here. I don't know where he is." Mrs. Gillons picked up the cup of cold tea she'd been sipping when the doorbell rang.

"If George Hunnewell is looking for him, must be something important." Adrian pursed his lips.

"He told me to call Central and find him."

"Are you going to?"

"You don't see me doing it do you?" Mrs. Gillons took a long slow sip of tea.

Adrian winked at Ethel.

Upstairs, to keep his blood pressure from rising to a dangerous level while they waited, George Hunnewell took Jerrold Clewes on a fast tour of the first floor, merely pointing to an enfilade of three formal French drawing rooms, "all that's left of Hester's house," then down a long flagstone-paved passage toward the chapel. "Those tall doors on the right open into the gallery of American Impressionists I told you about that connects to the Portuguese Wing." After a quick peek into the chapel, he led Clewes back along the Stone Corridor and across the Great Hall into the Long Gallery. Nine of FP's period rooms on the left faced south, the facade that had so impressed Clewes when they drove up the allée. On the right were three dining rooms, the largest with a table that, George said, could seat one hundred, a smaller dining room that was a double cube, and a third called the Gibbons Room because of its lime-wood carvings by that great English artist, which Hunnewell explained was the one used by the family. Through north-facing windows in the Gibbons Room Clewes could see a large courtyard with a box-bordered flower bed. Between the dining rooms were pantries, service areas and stairs descending to kitchens on the half-belowground level and ascending to guest rooms above. To Clewes's great disappointment, George said, "I'll show you the period rooms later. There are many, many more on other floors and in other parts of the house, but these are the finest—these and the Spanish rooms above the Galleried Library that comprised FP's apartment and is now Phil's"

"Isn't the whole house Phil's," Jerrold asked.

"Of course, but, like his grandfather, he needs a place where he can be alone."

"I thought he was the only one who lives here."

"He is. Don't be obtuse."

Exiting at the far end of the Long Gallery, they came into the west entrance. Turning right, they went through doors that had been cut in a wall of sixteenth-century choir stalls and entered a different world. Citrus trees—oranges, lemons, limes—as well as mimosas and passion vines grew out of gigantic terra-cotta tubs spaced along a wall of antique glass doors, through which Clewes had a better view of the courtyard he'd glimpsed back in the Gibbons Room. "The West or Tiled Loggia is the public part of the house," Hunnewell said. "All the libraries are here, except the Galleried, which has since FP's time been used as the family living room." George opened a door. "This one from Italy is called the Red Library because of the red tooled leather on walls above the bookcases. The rarest books in the collection are housed here, and the validated old master paintings. Don't say it." He stopped Clewes from voicing another "My God." "Next door is the French Library because the room came from France, and then we come to the working library, a handsome room I think, but not original and ancient as are the others. FP could not buy the library he wanted in Brussels, so he had it copied. Access to two levels of stacks beneath all the libraries is from this room. Finally, we have in what was Catherine's office suite, when she had a staff to assist organizing events, offices of the librarian and his staff." When George opened the door an elderly gentleman examining an open book on a tilted table looked up. An equally elderly woman at a desk paid no attention, apparently deaf to the intruder. "It's only me, Mr. Ames, I'm just showing someone around. I'll bring him back to meet you in a few days," George called out, bobbing his head as he backed out forcing Clewes also to retreat into the loggia.

"What does a librarian do? I don't understand. Are the books— and I must say there are more than I thought there would be—are they available to the public?" Jerrold asked.

"Yes and no. They do not circulate, but they are available here for research purposes. I'm sure there are several scholars busy somewhere right now. Phil's, let's see"—George mentally counted generations—"Phil's great-great-great-grandfather was the first serious book collector in the family. He bought a number of private libraries as they came up for sale during the War of 1812. But the real bibliophile was his son who added thousands of books during his lifetime, and built the Galleried Library as a three-story freestanding building, which FP, Phil's grandfather, remodeled, enlarged and eventually incorporated into the present house. FP was a reader, interested in books for their content and not their rarity or monetary value. His contribution to the collection was as practical as it was bibliophilic. Every book is catalogued, and all are kept in repair by a knowledgeable staff, but, I am ashamed to say, the collection has never been appraised. I hope the man you signed on to do the job is up to it."

"He's the best there is," but, Clewes added to himself, I'm not sure he is ready for the months and months this job will take.

The red velvet and gilded cherub Baroque Theatre at the end of the loggia, just inside the north lobby, was almost more than Clewes could handle. Of Austrian descent, Vienna was Clewes's spiritual home. He sank down on a lushly upholstered bench against the back wall. "I am in Vienna, I hear Strauss, I smell chocolate," he sighed.

"Close," said George. "This theaer came from a castle quite near

Vienna. When Catherine needed more room for dance performances, she had the backstage area, wings, loft, dressing rooms, and
so on, enlarged, but I wouldn't let her change a thing in the front
of the house. It looks now exactly as it did when FP reconstructed
and refurbished it."

Clewes was stunned by the hammer beams, though his response
to the replica of Henry VIII's banquet hall was subdued. He was
beginning to suffer sensory fatigue. How much more could he
absorb? A casual visitor might simply be overwhelmed by the
house, its scale and magnificence, but Jerrold Clewes's entire life
had been spent studying decorative arts and architecture. He knew
what he was looking at, appreciated it on a level above and apart
from the pleasure an ordinary individual might feel. Nothing he'd
read about Oshatakea, and he had read every word he could find,
had sufficiently informed him of its visual and intellectually stimulating power. He had heard FP Fillmore II was a genius but
thought that appellation was an exaggeration expressed by synco-
phants. Now he believed the man was unique in his accomplishment. Signing contracts to inventory and appraise Oshatakea's
contents was the greatest coup of Clewes's career. Not only would
this single assignment when completed raise him to the pinnacle
of his profession, it would, with fees based on a complex formula,
bring him more money than he'd ever hoped to possess. He'd
never need to work again. Best of all, he would live like a pasha
while undertaking the task. But at the moment he wanted to just
sit down somewhere, close his eyes, lie flat if possible, perhaps take
a short nap. When Hunnewell suggested they return to the
Galleried Library to await Phil's arrival, Clewes nodded silent
agreement.

As he approached the house Phil didn't notice George Hunnewell's
Mercedes parked under the porte cochere until he almost bumped
into it. Mrs. Gillons was waiting for him, sitting in the ladies'
reception room opposite the gentlemen's into which she'd sent the

strange little man when he'd wanted to wash his hands. "Mr. Hunnewell and an odd duck in a shiny suit are here to see you. He said you are expecting them."

"I am? Where are they?"

"In the Galleried Library." Mrs. Gillons's moue expressed disdain. Accustomed to his housekeeper's unsolicited opinions, Phil acknowledged her silent comment with a shrug and headed for the Galleried Library.

Proceeding across the marble parquetry, his slapping sandals set up small echoes. George bored Phil. He was not impressed by the managing and senior partner in the law firm of Hunnewell, Hunnewell & Hunnewell, which had handled Fillmore family legal matters since 1885 when FP hired his former Harvard classmate A. Brayton Hunnewell. FP was Brayton Hunnewell's first client. Brayton never needed another, nor had the generations of Hunnewells that followed. As long as FP lived, members of the firm followed his directives, did not question, rarely offered advice except on fine legal points and learned in so doing how to grow money, protect investments and avoid liabilities. When FP died and his son, Farney, Phil's father, became head of the family a seismic shift in attorney-client relationship resulted, partially because FP's estate was tied up in trusts devised by himself and the Hunnewells that left little room for Farney's involvement, but also because Farney had no interest in finances. He cared only that money be available to support his passion for horses and his wife's obsession with music and the performing arts. Bringing the world's artists to Oshatakea was even more expensive than buying and breeding blooded horses. Fortunately, there was more than enough income to do both. Moving into the vacuum of Farney's disinterest, the Hunnewells made decisions, merely reporting trends and positive positions on a regular basis. When Farney was killed and Phil, at seventeen, became the sole male Fillmore, the Hunnewells consolidated their control. Phil was no more interested than his father had been. He knew nothing about managing his estate and had no desire to learn. If the Fillmores were among the world's wealthiest families, Hunnewell, Hunnewell & Hunnewell had by representing them become one of the world's most profitable law firms, and in financial circles exceedingly potent because of the capital at their disposal and the interests they managed in major industries and institutions for the Fillmore Trust. That they earned their keep was never questioned by knowledgeable analysts who admired the ability and agility of the Hunnewells to always be ahead of rising markets whether they be in minerals, services, technology or any other commodity, and similarly and perhaps more important sensing when markets would fall. FP had taught them well. That they could lose control of this empire on the day Phil reached forty, November 25 the following year, was a source of deep concern to economists and considerable anguish to members of the Hunnewell firm. Though only fifteen months away, Phil still hadn't thought much about it, one way or another. The extent of his personal expenditure was lunches at the Peasant Palate and recordings from Sam Goody. Each week, because Phil insisted, Loren sent a bill to George. It was paid promptly, with a handsome tip added, as were Sam Goody's bills, without a tip. Phil didn't know what pocket money was; he never carried any. The law firm also paid invoices for sound equipment Phil seemed to be forever installing. It was a less costly hobby than horses. All disbursements from the largest to the smallest for running Oshatakea, the farms, and every other aspect of the estate were made from the Hunnewell office. Until the approach of Phil's maturity as spelled out in the trusts, this arrangement satisfied everyone. If it all changed, as it might, depending upon Phil's decision arrived at either thoughtfully or on whim, George Hunnewell would not go hungry, but he would miss making moves that impacted the world of finance. He loved pulling strings and making men of substance dance as if they were marionettes. While his unsureness of what the future might be filled Hunnewell with foreboding, Phil had nothing on his mind when he walked into the Galleried Library, beyond hoping George would say whatever he had come to say and leave quickly.

The distinguished attorney stood when Phil entered the room. "I should have called to confirm our appointment today, but I assumed if it was not convenient for you to see us, you would have responded to my letter." Decades of authority and affluence had given Hunnewell a carefully cultivated bearing in his London-tailored suits. Yet though the power had long been his and would continue to be for at least another fourteen months, he recognized he was working for Phil and so dutifully, but without obsequiousness, he showed the younger man respect.

"Letter?" Phil shook George's hand, but was looking at the odd duck, as Mrs. Gillons had called Clewes, who was standing in front of one of the crewel-covered wing chairs. Clewes stared back, amazed that this apparition could be Phillips Fillmore. His features were striking and he was obviously a fine physical specimen, but why was he dressed like a tramp?

"I wrote you ten days ago to say I'd be bringing Jerrold Clewes this afternoon for a quick tour of the house, to meet you and to set the date when he and his assistants can move in."

"Move in?"

Rapid blinking replaced the forced smile in George's eyes. Phil's carelessness with mail was an old story; that he had no recollection of receiving a letter was not a surprise, but for him to repeat everything as if he were simpleminded was annoying. Hunnewell had assured Clewes that stories of Phil's eccentricities were exaggerated. It was maddening to have Phil carry on in a manner that made him appear foolish. Reining in the tad bit of temper he felt was justified because Phil had after all kept them waiting for more than an hour, Hunnewell tried again. "Perhaps you did not receive my letter. I should have telephoned." He took a deep breath. "At any rate, we are here now. Let me introduce Jerrold Clewes, formerly of Sotheby's, now head of his own firm, Jerrold Clewes Ltd. I enclosed his superb credentials with my letter, but I will repeat them for you now if you like."

"Not necessary," Phil replied. "Welcome to Oshatakea Mr. Clewes. I'm sorry I kept you waiting. Please sit down." When Phil didn't notice the hand Clewes offered to be shaken, nor heard Clewes say, "Call me Jerry," Clewes retreated to his chair. George and Phil parried over which would occupy the chair opposite, the one closest to the hearth that George knew had been FP's chair. Phil won by insisting, "I prefer to stand."

Hunnewell strived to bring back his cool smile. "Well then, shall we proceed? Suffice it to say, Jerrold Clewes is the most knowledgeable man in his field. We are indeed fortunate he is available at this time to do the required appraisal for us."

Clewes spoke up. "I am the fortunate one. To live for a year in this incredible, incredible"—he made a gesture to signal words were failing him—"house, which I believed I had visualized in fantasy, but I had not, to live here while examining its horde of treasures, and to sort through the contents of Fillmore warehouses that have been likened to Aladdin's caves, well it's, it's a privilege, more than a privilege, it's, it's, let's just say I am embarrassed to be paid to do it."

"Not too embarrassed to accept our checks, I presume." Hunnewell's laugh was hollow.

Clewes rattled on. "I must tell you, Mr. Fillmore, the revelation of what is in those warehouses is as eagerly anticipated by the fine and decorative arts worlds as was word from Egypt when Carter was opening Tutankhamen's tomb. I shall retire when I complete this assignment. Nothing, nothing I might be offered afterward could come close in prestige. Any later assignment irregardless would be anticlimactic." He looked as if he were about to clap his hands, but he didn't. His face flushed; he filled the ensuing quiet with a quick pass at his thinning hair to make sure the spray was holding.

George was thinking he would explain to Phil when they were alone that Clewes might seem a twit but he did know what he was about, much as he had earlier tried to explain to Clewes that Phil was not really crazy.

Phil interrupted Clewes thoughts. "Living here? For a year?"

"While they appraise the inventory." Phil's questions had been directed at Clewes but George answered.

"Inventory?"

"Phil, please stop parroting what I say." George's voice was firm. "When your grandfather created the '45 document, an inventory was taken of every item in the house, except for your parents' personal belongings in the Portuguese Wing and those of the staff of course. All furniture, silver, rugs, paintings, vases, everything," —his arm swept an arc to embrace the room—"was listed, as were contents of the warehouses, stables and all other buildings on the estate. Scale drawings were done to record architectural details and thousands of photographs were taken, all of which have been kept in a vault in my office. Every item was not only listed but appraised at its current, meaning 1945, value, except for the books. It took more than three years to do what we now have only fourteen months to accomplish. This time we do not need to photograph or make drawings—we have those from before; our major task is to verify the records, make sure everything is where it should be and update assigned values which have increased substantially in the intervening years."

"I'll say they have," Clewes could not resist affirming. "You won't believe by how much." Phil wished this birdlike creature would not perch so precariously on the edge of his chair.

George glared at Clewes. He did not want to lose momentum. "We have bound catalogs for every room wherein each piece is accurately and particularly documented for condition as well as location. If things have been moved, we will be able to note that. The warehouses will be the easiest inasmuch as they have not been opened since your grandfather's death. We will simply check against the lists to ascertain changes in condition if any and update estimated values."

"Yes they have," Phil said.

At the same time Clewes inquired, "I don't suppose there's climate control in the warehouses? If there isn't there's bound to be deterioration. It can't be helped, it happens."

"There is a kind of climate control," George said, then returned his attention to Phil. "You said, 'Yes they have.' What have?"

"The warehouses have been opened since Gramps died—lots of times. I've had them opened when people needed furniture, told them to take what they wanted. You know, young couples getting married who don't have much, and after the Hess family was burned out, times like that."

Shock at what he was hearing drained George's face. "Phil you had no right to do that without asking me, I would have stopped you."

"Why? It's mine, you confirmed the day of Gramps' funeral everything belonged to me. Why shouldn't I give away what I don't need, or want?"

George took a moment to catch his breath and to come up with a simple explanation for a complex issue. "Everything does belong to you, and it doesn't, quite. All is held in trust until your fortieth birthday when the trusts terminate. Though I would hope you might continue to rely on my judgment and counsel, on the day you become forty, or any day thereafter you can give away whatever you want, but not until then." George was using his father to son, now listen carefully to what I am saying voice. "I am responsible for the assets of the trust, and you are required, I repeat Phil, required to seek my permission before disposing of any asset."

Phil grinned. "George, I was four when my grandfather told me about the trusts and how they worked, and I guess you explained details to me again when Dad died, but that was years ago. There's no reason to get upset, I haven't disposed, as you put it, of assets; it was furniture mostly, some pictures—old stuff to tide people over until they could buy the new things they really wanted. Believe me, George, young brides don't think much of what they find in those warehouses."

Clewes looked as if he might faint, in which case he'd fall off the chair. George's respiration rate was rising. "I can't believe you actually allowed people, just anybody, to freely remove from your grandfather's estate antiques of considerable value. We'll do what we can to rectify your egregious error. Provide me with their names and I will attempt to retrieve what they took." George's cheek was aquiver, diminishing his aura of quiet authority.

"I couldn't do that. Nobody ever asked me for anything. I offered them the opportunity to go in and look around," Phil argued. "What difference does it make?"

"Try to understand me Phil. I am responsible, I and the other trustees. Everything must be is as it was when we assumed charge. We and our predecessors have carried a heavy burden all these years, for which we have been well paid, I am not complaining, but we could, if assets are gone, be accused of taking things for ourselves."

"No problem," Phil's good nature held. "Take whatever you want from the warehouses George, I'm sure Gramps would want you to."

"I'll do no such thing, and you are not to let anyone else in there, either. Is that clear?" A terrible thought struck George. "You haven't been letting people take things out of the house have you?"

"Nobody comes into the house, except, you know, Miss Eleanor, Isabelle, Adelaide, Louisa, Loren, sometimes Danny. There isn't much chance of anything being taken." As an afterthought: "Lots of people come in when there are performances in the Baroque Theatre, but they stay in the West Loggia area."

"I was thinking of members of the staff."

It was Phil's turn to anger, and he was angry, but he only shook his head. No, members of the staff had not been removing things from the house.

"Thank God we have the catalogs," George looked to Clewes whose perspiration was dampening his suit between his shoulder blades. As appalled as the appraiser was by what Phil might have given away with no awareness of its value, Clewes envied those who had an opportunity to pick and choose. He was also fascinated by this exchange between client and counsel. He had pictured a dim-witted Fillmore heir who if not subservient would be amenable to whatever his trustees decreed, whereas Phil seemed bright and feisty.

"Phil, please sit down," George requested. "We do have serious matters to discuss and I would be more comfortable if you were seated."

"Sorry George, there's no need for discussion. Take your inventory if that has to be done. However," Phil paused, pondering how to phrase what he would say next so as not to hurt the shiny-suited stranger who already looked extremely ill at ease, "Mr. Clewes said something about living here for a year. I do not want him, or anyone else, moving into the house. No offense."

George exhaled, exasperation reaching a danger point. "What has come over you Phil? Don't make every step of this essential process difficult. Jerrold and his assistants cannot drive out here from the city every morning, then drive back again every night and complete their work in the short time left to us. It doesn't make sense when there are accommodations in this house for many more than twenty or thirty appraisers. They will pose no problem, I assure you. If you are worried about the extra load for Adrian's kitchen staff, we'll hire Loren and his son to cater meals. It will all work out fine, you'll see."

"I will not see, George. No one is to sleep here. Adrian can do whatever needs doing to provide breakfast and lunch; he already does that for people who work here, but no one, I repeat George, no one is to stay in the house overnight." The break in Phil's voice surprised and confused George, who wasn't sure whether Phil was struggling to cover anger or fear. Phil continued, "No member of the household staff sleeps in. Everybody is gone by six or seven at the latest." He directed his attention to Clewes. "I understand why you and your people might not want to drive out from the city and back each day; I am sympathetic to that, but you will not stay here. Subject closed. I'd suggest you try the Fillmore Inn in the village. I don't know what their limits are, but if they can accommodate you, I'm sure they'd be happy to have your business for such a long period of time." Not giving George opportunity to argue, Phil added, "It has been an experience meeting you Mr. Clewes. I guess I'll soon be seeing you around the house." George's jaw dropped. "Thanks for all your trouble George. Let Adrian know how many to expect for breakfast and lunch and when. Stay in touch." He walked toward a bookcase that when pressed swung open to reveal a tiny elevator.

"Phil, it isn't as easy as that," George called after him, incensed that he had been dismissed like a footman and in front of someone he had hired.

Phil wheeled around. "Yes it is, George. Whatever authority my grandfather's trust documents give you, I'm damn sure they do not include allowing you to tell me who will live in my house with me."

Before Phil could pull the bookcase shut, George grabbed hold of it. "Wait, we must talk. I respect your desire for privacy and I know you hate to have people in the house, but I have legal as well as fiduciary responsibility. Phil, I insist you listen."

Phil yanked the bookcase out of Hunnewell's grasp. George could hear the quiet hum of the elevator rising to the apartment above the Galleried Library. There was a staircase in an oriel at the far end of the library, but George did not dare follow Phil. He had been in the apartment only once in response to a summons just before FP died. This time there would be no summons. He had lost the skirmish. Phil and George had frequently disagreed, but seldom with words spoken in anger. Not since Catherine's funeral had Phil openly defied him. He was embarrassed. "I can't imagine what has come over him, he's generally not like this at all, combative."

"Did I offend him?" Clewes looked worried.

"No, you did nothing, though it was what you said about living in the house that set him off, wasn't it?"

Neither of them heard Mrs. Gillons until she coughed. "I will show you out."

As they followed her across the Great Hall, George was tempted to inquire if Phil had been acting in a peculiar fashion lately, but then, face it, Phil frequently acted in an odd manner. George Hunnewell wasn't about to seek confidences from a servant. Striving to calm himself and sound positive as they drove out through the gates, he said, "I'm sure you and your people will be quite comfortable at the Inn. It's a lovely old eighteenth century building completely restored by Phil's grandfather and recently refurbished."

Jerrold Clewes was so bitterly disappointed he dare not respond, knowing his voice would betray his struggle to keep from sobbing.

Chapter 3

—

EMMETT DOBYNS HAD EXPECTED PHIL TO BRING HIS Haflinger stallion in from the paddock, as he always did after lunch, but was surprised when Phil put Taurus in cross ties and began grooming him. "You did that this morning."

"What? I didn't hear you Em."

"You groomed Taurus this morning. He doesn't get dirty out there on green grass."

"I thought I'd wipe him down before we go for a walk."

"Suit yourself." The old stable manager shook his head and went back to puttering.

Phil had not forgotten he'd groomed Taurus before breakfast, but he wanted physical contact with his horse. Brushing the taut, muscled body and wiping a soft cloth down the animal's neck and shoulders, across his back and flanks was a way for Phil to transmit some of the golden chestnut stallion's vitality to himself. He put his arms around the arched neck. Taurus nickered with a hint of impatience; he enjoyed being groomed, and was ever affectionate, but this was running-free time, what were they doing inside? When Phil stepped away, the horse turned his head to peer back at him, expressive brown eyes questioning. Phil apologized. "Sorry Tee. My day has been fouled up but that's no reason to cheat you. Let's go." He undid the cross ties and shouted, "We're headed out Em. Be back soon."

"I'm not going anywhere," came a voice from down the stable block.

Phil loved horses but hated riding them because, from the time he was a small child until he was sixteen when his father gave up and granted him a reprieve, he had been forced to ride every day. Riding with just his father and Pearl was misery enough, but racing across fields with the Fillmore Valley Hunt, jumping fences and ditches and dodging branches in the midst of a thundering herd of Thoroughbreds, Irish Hunters and Cleveland Bays, all following a pack of yelping hounds chasing a frightened fox, was pure hell. Thinking Phil would enjoy it more if he developed relationships with his mounts, Farney made his son take total care of each horse he was given, and relationships did develop to such an extent they became complications as Phil grew and developed skills that required a more experienced horse. Refusing to stop caring for Tigger, his first pony, and then Halcyon, his second, when the Irish Hunter Farney had imported especially for him arrived, thirteen-year-old Phil found himself spending two hours each morning mucking out stalls and feeding and grooming three horses. He could not have been happier with this part of the equine world, at one point going so far as to suggest he might work full time in the stables when he came home from Harvard, which was not what either parent had in mind for him. Stable boys were assigned to cleaning out his three box stalls and Phil's duties were reduced to feeding and grooming. Now, a lone adult no one could force to ride, Phil took great pleasure in caring for Taurus and walking with him.

In the aftermath of Farney's death, the only horse sold from the forty-seven that were housed at that time in Oshatakea's stables was a big, evil-tempered Thoroughbred, the last horse his father had given Phil. After being bitten, kicked and thrown repeatedly by the beast, Phil insisted he be sent to auction. This caused a furor because "Fillmores do not sell their horses, they retire them to one of the valley farms." Phil would not be dissuaded. "I want him out of the valley, out of the state, out of the country if you can find a country that will take him." Now, fewer than half a dozen of Farney's horses remained in the stable blocks, all at advanced ages but most in good health. As they died—Hackneys and Holsteiners that had been used for driving, Connemaras and Arabians for polo, Cleveland Bays, Thoroughbreds and Irish Hunters for hunting, and Morgans, as Farney said, "just because"—they were buried in a landscaped meadow, each grave marked with a headstone detailing dates of birth and death, sire and dam, awards won and a descriptive word or two on personality. "Beloved" Tigger and "Loyal" Halcyon had long since taken their places there.

Taurus ElBedavi, a Haflinger with supreme bloodlines and vast potential as show horse and stud, had been a thirtieth birthday gift for Phil from "the old women in your life, Adelaide, Louisa, Miss Eleanor and Isabelle." Isabelle had seen Taurus as a yearling when she'd visitedthe Duke and Duchess of Devonshire at Chatsworth. She persuaded the duchess to sell him, and by the time he lunged down the trailer ramp at Oshatakea his coltish palomino coat had deepened to a rich golden chestnut set off by an almost white mane and tail that floated in the air, not only when he cantered or trotted but as he moved swiftly over the ground in his long-stride walk. Walking had turned out to be the stallion's major occupation; he was never shown nor was he used for breeding. It was love at first sight between Taurus, desperate to run free after being kept in close quarters for the transoceanic flight, and Phil, emerging at last after years of living in a cocoon with his mother. It was the Haflinger's eyes that captured the young man, great liquid orbs that missed nothing as they scanned the world from beneath blond lashes, looking steadily into Phil's, inquisitive and calm, asking nothing, offering everything.

The bond between man and horse grew from immediate attachment and acceptance to total trust, resulting in actions that appeared to derive from a single impulse. Except for when he was being groomed, no halter, bridle or other controlling device was put on the stallion. Taurus came when Phil called and followed as if he were a dog trained to heel, including occasionally into the house when Phil absentmindedly forgot that the horse was with him and didn't close a gate. While most people thought this remarkable, Mrs. Gillons was not amused. She was especially upset if they clopped across the Great Hall. Keeping its marble mosaic floor pristine was Mrs. Gillons's major mission in life. Phil's inevitable excuse was, "He's not doing anything." Indeed Taurus never did do anything in the house, other than upset floral arrangements when he grabbed at them playfully in passing.

Their afternoon jaunts became essential elements in the psychological well-being of both man and beast. They were together and at the same time completely free of restraint as they moved side by side across fields and along wide wooded trails or wandered apart, each to explore his own space, but always keeping the other in sight. Phil talked to Taurus, sharing his thoughts and feelings, relating problems. He had found stating a problem aloud brought perspective if not always solution. When an answer was forthcoming, Phil thanked Taurus for his help, though of course Taurus had done nothing. If Taurus discovered something he wanted Phil to see, he whinnied for him to come and look. Never far apart, neither held the other back. The decision to head home was usually arrived at with only minor disagreement, Taurus sometimes needing a bit of persuasion if he wasn't quite ready.

On this particular afternoon, Phil needed to air George Hunnewell's threat to have a crew of appraisers live in the house. He had to hear himself say why it could not happen, why having them there would change his life, would disrupt his well-ordered existence. If his reasons sounded weak, he'd possibly reconsider, but he doubted he'd do that. For the first time in the span of years they had been together, Phil found himself too tightly wound to speak aloud to Taurus, to reveal even to him how important it had become to be in the house alone at night. When the horse ambled toward an open glade, browsing rather than grazing, Phil followed him to lie down on a sun-warmed outcropping of ledge. He closed his eyes. Enervated, he accepted his depression was the result of more than the unpleasant exchange with George. He was experiencing the same desperation that had panicked him at seventeen when he feared he might never be able to do what he knew he had to do. At seventeen he compromised. He would not compromise again. His life was not at all what he'd wanted it to be, but after a long lost period he'd settled into a routine that sustained him. Since his mother's death, he had settled for less, given up on fulfillment. He was also jittery about approaching the day when he would acquire control of the estate, which he cared not a damn about controlling. He hated that this whole business could mean losing the freedom and independence he felt he'd given up so much to earn. His life suited him; he wasn't bothered if others thought it strange, no one knew all its components. Why should he be forced to forfeit what was most important to him? He wouldn't! He would call George; tell him he could continue in control, doing exactly what he'd always done. A fortieth birthday meant nothing; let George make all decisions, guard the estate forever, regardless of what the damn trusts decreed. "Just leave me alone," he shouted. Taurus looked up from his browsing. Telling George that would solve nothing. George would still move a mob into the house. For twenty-five years Phil had lived according to the rigid rules and demands of others. His mother's death had given him his first real chance to be on his own, to make his own rules. All he had ever wanted was to follow his own path, hurting no one, but pleasing himself regardless of how queer some others might consider it. If he could not express his deep desire or his dread, couldn't give vent to his fear and confusion in words both he and his creature companion could hear and comprehend, how could he expect any kind of answer, any possible solution to arise from his own subconscious? All he said quietly was, "How can I hold back the inevitable?"

Taurus trotted over to nuzzle him.

THREE HOURS LATER PHIL, DAMP FROM A SHOWER, WAS slamming doors and drawers. He couldn't find what he was looking for after searching through every closet in his father's dressing room, pushing suits and jackets, trousers, coats and capes back and forth on their padded hangers. No one else had been in these closets; he'd worn the kilts Christmas Eve, and was sure he'd put them back where they belonged. "Goddamn George Hunnewell, he's discombobulated me." He found the green jacket he wanted, and argyle socks, a white silk shirt and silver thistle cuff links and studs; the links and studs were in a drawer with that Cartier box containing astounding rubies and diamonds, but where in hell were the kilts? He should have asked Mrs. Gillons before she went home, or Dale Morris, one of them might know, though he couldn't think why they should. "The cursed things are here somewhere," he shouted, kicking a closet door shut.

In his father's bedroom he picked up the outside telephone, shivering as he waited an eternity for Mrs. Taylor to answer at her switchboard in the village. "Yes?"

"I need Miss Eleanor."

"She's going to the Kropotkins' for dinner, but I haven't seen her leave her cottage yet." There was a pause. He knew the village operator was squinting through her living room window across from the firehouse. "I guess she's still home, unless she went out while I was dishing up my stew. I'll ring." When Miss Eleanor picked up, Mrs. Taylor said, "Ah, you're still there. Phil is on the line."

He didn't wait for Miss Eleanor to say hello. "Where are my father's kilts?"

"How would I know, for pity's sake? Let me think." Miss Eleanor started humming. "He kept them, I believe, in a drawer in the bottom of the short cedar closet in his dressing room. If you put them back after you last wore them they should be there; I doubt anybody has moved them."

"That's the only place I didn't look. Thanks." Phil hung up.

"Miss Eleanor, you be careful walking up that hill," Mrs. Taylor warned.

"Isabelle is coming for me," Miss Eleanor replied, no more surprised that Mrs. Taylor had listened in than she was that Phil expected her to know how his father's clothes were arranged.

Smartly clad in the dress kilts, sporran, sash, hunter's jacket, argyles, silver buckled brogans and kepi with a pheasant brush on the side, Phil whistled in an attempt to dispel his lingering black mood as he marched purposefully through the birch grove, stopping to bow low before a jack-in-the-pulpit with an obscene cluster of fruit, each fat red berry about to burst. "You are looking especially erotic this evening, Jack," he said. Whistling was helping. In the rosy dusk, black-streaked curls of bark peeling from white birch trunks whose slender branches were delicate silhouettes against the sky gave a surreal touch to scenery usually serene. "I think we're more Daliesque than Corot this evening," Phil said, nodding right and left to the trees. Adelaide and Louisa loved the birch grove as dearly as they doted on their dacha, which sat in its midst, striving to maintain both residence and grounds in the rustic opulence so successfully contrived by their parents. Marianne Fillmore, their mother, was FP's daughter by his first marriage, their father, Nicholas Alexandrovich, a Russian prince. The Kropotkin family lived as if under a bell jar in their simulated czarist province until 1917 when Nicholas returned to Russia to fight against revolutionary forces and was killed in the courtyard of his family's St. Petersburg palace.

"Would you look at those gorgeous hairy legs!" Isabelle shrieked.

She was first to notice Phil when he walked into the dacha's octagonal conservatory where the Kropotkin sisters served cocktails. Phil spun around to flare the kilt's pleats. "What is your answer to the age-old question young man?" Isabelle batted her false eyelashes.

"Isabelle, I haven't worn underwear since Miss Eleanor decided I was old enough to dress myself. Was I five Miss E? Or six?"

"Stop you two." Miss Eleanor was in her gray crepe de chine going-out-to-dinner dress, the one her mary janes climbed up inside the front of because the material had stretched and the dress was too long for her. She'd gussied up for the occasion—Isabelle's term for extras such as an angora stole in shades of lavender and the sapphire brooch Phil had forced her to take from his mother's safe. Miss Eleanor smiled. "You look quite resplendent this evening."

"Thanks to your skill with the scissors." He bent to give her a quick kiss on top of her head. "Ummm, smell good too." He sniffed the downy nest of white hair.

Miss Eleanor rapped him gently. "Behave."

"Those kilts belonged to his grandfather. I was with FP when he bought them in Edinburgh. I'm not going to tell you when that was." Isabelle's rumbling chuckle gave way to coughs.

"Grandfather has been gone thirty-three years this December," Adelaide said, "and he hadn't traveled abroad for years and years before he died, so Isabelle, it must have been . . . "

"Stop, stop," Isabelle cried. "I knew somebody would start counting. How can I be forty-seven now and have been in Scotland with a gentleman friend fifty years ago?"

"Good try." Miss Eleanor countered, "It was probably closer to seventy years ago."

"Anyone care to try for eighty?" Phil asked.

Adelaide laughed at the silliness of it all and patted the cushion of the white wicker sofa. "Phillips darling, sit by me. Did you tell Boris what you want to drink?"

"I did."

Adelaide was lighted from within tonight, playing hostess at a formal dinner. Kropotkin diamonds were sprinkled in her hair and scattered down the front of her black lace gown.

"You can't sit before you give me a kiss,' Louisa chirped, her face beaming above a cloud of amber organza. She was wearing every topaz in her collection, including a tiara suitable for a royal wedding.

"You are a vision Louisa, may I kiss your hand?"

"Oh young man, yoo hoo," Isabelle raised and lowered her penciled eyebrows in burlesque fashion, "do bend over to kiss Louisa again, a bit lower this time. From where I am the view is delicious."

"I didn't see anything," Louisa said.

"You're not sitting where I'm sitting."

"I'm ready for another." Miss Eleanor held up her glass.

"Be careful, too many of those one-two-threes and you'll pass out at the table," Isabelle remarked to Miss Eleanor whose cocktail of choice was one part sweet, two parts sour, three parts strong; in her case, maple syrup, lemon juice and bourbon.

"Have I ever passed out at the table?"

Dinner was splendid as Adelaide's dinners always were, starting with the caviar, which was a given, as well as gravlax; both, Louisa explained, because she and Adelaide could never decide which delicacy they preferred. Toasts with chilled vodka greeted every course as it was served, followed by more toasts as they were completed. When the party retired to the drawing room, Phil's black mood had dissipated. He and the ladies were aglow with good cheer.

Adelaide went directly to the piano, removed her rings and played a short Chopin étude. "And now, Isabelle, what will you sing for us?"

"I would like to do *Signore, Ascolta,* but it's too late in the evening for that."

"The evening?" Phil asked.

"Quiet, Kid! Let's see what you can sing when you get to be forty-seven." They all laughed. Isabelle and Adelaide conferred, and then offered a soft lullaby.

"Beautiful, beautiful." Phil clapped vigorously. "I'd whistle through my teeth if I'd ever learned how."

Isabelle pulled up both shoulder straps of her gown to bring her fender back where it belonged, resting on the shelf of her ample bosom. Fixing Phil with an unblinking stare, she raised a penciled eyebrow and said, "Flattery will get you everywhere. Didn't think I could do it, did you? Neither did I."

"Memories flood back." Adelaide rose from the piano bench and went to sit next to Miss Eleanor after giving a signal to Boris that he should serve coffee, chocolates and after-dinner drinks. "The music we have heard in this room! Grandfather and your mother, Phillips, were so generous with the musicians they brought to Oshatakea, or it may have been the artists who were generous, coming down here to play for us after they'd given concerts at the big house."

"They came to play duets with you Adelaide," Louisa said.

"Some did, but not all. Do you remember, Phillips? Of course you do, when the Boston, the Philadelphia, the Cleveland and other great orchestras came for concerts?"

"And individual artists," Louisa interrupted. "Mr. Kreisler's playing was heavenly."

"But he was difficult," Miss Eleanor murmered.

"Difficult?" Adelaide asked.

"Shy is perhaps a better description, but that made him appear difficult. He would not mingle, took meals alone in his suite."

"Mr. Paderewski wasn't shy," Louisa tried again. "He came here often and played on that very piano, didn't he Adelaide?"

"Indeed he did."

"I miss concerts at Oshatakea." Louisa's sigh was theatrical. "I wish we could have music at Oshatakea again." She pronounced each syllable of *music* and *Oshatakea* slowly. "Beyond the concerts and little operettas local groups put together I mean. They are nice, and you are kind Phil to let them use the Baroque Theatre, but they do not perform as real musicians do."

"We were having a delightful discussion before you arrived this evening Phillips," Adelaide said.

"Having to do with your fortieth birthday," Louisa leapt in.

"Louisa, let Adelaide tell Phil," Isabelle chided.

"What are you plotting?" Phil's eyes widened in mock alarm.

"There is no plot, though it would be fun to surprise you, if only we could."

"It would be impossible," Isabelle said.

"You mean I'm not easily surprised?" Phil asked and took a truffle from the tray of Belgian chocolates Boris was passing.

"I love surprises," Louisa cried. "Don't say another word. Let's do it as a surprise."

"How can it be a surprise if we discuss it while he is in the room?" Miss Eleanor inquired.

"What exactly are we discussing? I'll have another brandy please." Phil held up his empty snifter for Boris.

"Your birthday party," Adelaide beamed.

"I didn't know I was having one."

"You see, it can be a surprise. Let's talk about something else." Louisa's excitement was impervious to disgruntled glances from the other women. "Has anyone had news of the Tsarevich?"

Adelaide held up her hand to quiet her sister, then continued as if uninterrupted. "Phillips, we think your fortieth birthday should be recognized with a grand celebration, the way family birthdays used to be marked at Oshatakea. There could be a ball, a banquet and entertainments—concerts. Mr. Hurok is gone, but Isabelle believes she can, through connections with other agents, hire artists."

"I can, I'm sure," Isabelle confirmed. "Pavarotti, for instance."

"Pavarotti?" Louisa rolled the consonants around on her tongue like a candy drop. "Do I know him?"

"At the moment, he's the biggest draw in the world—a tenor," Isabelle barked.

"Oh. If we're going to have a singer, I prefer Chaliapin."

Adelaide reached out toward Louisa. "Mr. Chaliapin is dead."

"Dead? He can't be! I listened to him last week."

"That was a recording. He's been dead for many years."

"Why was I not told?"

"You knew, you have forgotten," Miss Eleanor entered the conversation.

"How could I forget such a thing?" Louisa's petty annoyance was evolving into a display of grief.

"Louisa please." Adelaide returned to addressing Phil. "Everyone in the valley would be invited, as they always were for birthday celebrations, and the four of us, well three actually, Miss Eleanor preferred not to participate, have been compiling lists of houseguests. It has not been a totally happy task because so many old friends are no longer with us."

"Has nobody news of the Tsarevich?"

"Not tonight Louisa! The guest rooms wouldn't be filled as they were in the old days, but we could gather quite a crowd. It would all be such fun. We haven't celebrated since your seventeenth birthday Phillips. Think what joy it will be for all of us to see Oshatakea alive once again. Please tell us you are as excited by the prospect as we are." Adelaide's voice was optimistically expectant though her manner was apprehensive.

"Has there been anything to celebrate?" Phil asked. "Where is Boris with my brandy?" What did Adelaide mean, see Oshatakea alive again? He thought he was doing a pretty good job of keeping Oshatakea alive, not filled with people but lived in the way Gramps wanted it to be.

Miss Eleanor concentrated on her gnarled hands clutching and unclutching folds of gray crepe in her lap. She was worried about where the conversation was heading. Isabelle and Adelaide exchanged fretful glances. Louisa slumped back to sulk, disappearing into a billow of amber organza.

To relieve heightening tension, Adelaide tried to mollify. "Phillips, the time has come to put sad things behind us. We all mourned your father's tragic death, and suffered with you through your mother's long illness."

Phil rose from the sofa and strode to the fire where he threw the brandy Boris had just handed him into the fire. Blue flames blazed up from the spitting logs.

Adelaide continued, tentatively, "We understood how difficult it was for you, but everything we tried to do seemed to make things worse because Catherine objected to our presence. After her death we left you alone because solitude appeared to be your preference. Now here we are, too many years later, and still you are reluctant to return to a full life. We who love you cannot allow it to continue." What began as mollification was becoming reprimand. "Your rightful place is head of this family. You inherited a position you have yet to assume."

"Head of the family, Adelaide?" Phil was incredulous. "You, Louisa and me? And, if we consider bonds beyond blood, as we do, Miss Eleanor and Isabelle? That's the family. Two women over ninety, two over eighty and a man approaching forty who everybody thinks is cracked."

"Whom," Miss Eleanor's correction was muttered.

"We are a family Phil, important to more people than you might imagine." Isabelle spoke quietly but with force. "Shortly you will take control of your fortune. There are few larger. Coming into your inheritance, and I speak not just of money and material possessions, is an occasion to celebrate. Think of it as your second coming of age. We could not celebrate your first for reasons you know too well, but we can your second. This time, you will reach the birthday your grandfather envisioned as your majority. You were FP's future, Phil, heir to all he was, not just what he owned—

and he was somebody, somebody very special. Don't disappoint him and those who looked up to him. Fulfill your grandfather's dream; isn't that reason enough to reopen Oshatakea?"

Phil stared into the fire. He worshiped his grandfather. Isabelle had hit a nerve when she said he would disappoint Gramps if he didn't reopen Oshatakea. Keeping Oshatakea alive was what he thought he was doing every hour of the day, trying to live in as many rooms of the house as possible, keeping all of them open and in order; nothing was covered with dust sheets, fresh flowers were kept where Gramps had fresh flowers, the grounds were maintained as Gramps had maintained them. He shook his head in bewilderment. "You are all using my fortieth birthday as an excuse for getting something you want. George thinks it gives him the right to move a raft of strangers into the house to live and snoop while they check off old lists and report back to him. You"—only Miss Eleanor was not staring up at him—"think it gives you a good reason to throw a party for people from God knows where, who— whom—I haven't seen since I was a kid and haven't missed, plus everybody in the valley, some I care about and a helluva lot I don't, and I'm supposed to jump up and down with joy? If seeing all the windows of Oshatakea lit up would thrill you, I'll light them every night of the week, but no house parties, not on your life—not on my birthday, nor any other day." He slammed his empty snifter down onto the malachite mantle, sending splinters of crystal showering into the room.

Adelaide and Isabelle exhaled in disappointment. Louisa's eyes teared. Miss Eleanor rose abruptly. "Phillips, apologize for your bad manners. You know better than to shout at your elders, and see what you've done—broken Adelaide's glass."

He would have apologized, but before he had a chance Boris spoke from the doorway. "Excuse me, ma'am, Constable Lindsay is here."

"Mike Lindsay? Whatever for?" Isabelle asked.

Adelaide sent a please-be-quiet glance in Isabelle's direction and stood. "Ask Constable Lindsay to come in Boris." Phil rested his elbow on the mantle, his head on his hand.

"Forgive me for barging in, Miss Kropotkin," Mike Lindsay said as he entered the room. " I've come to alert, and also reassure, you about a possibly dangerous situation."

Adelaide stepped toward him. "Dangerous?"

"Yes, ma'am, a patient has escaped from the state hospital for the criminally insane, a man who murdered his mother and father. I was notified he had been seen driving a stolen car into the valley. State troopers set up barricades on Valley Road thinking they'd cut him off at the square, but he smashed through and went up onto the church lawn, made a terrible mess of those big yew bushes by the walk before he crashed into the church steps."

"All while we were having a quiet dinner," Isabelle said.

"I thought I heard strange noises," Louisa began.

"Shhh," Adelaide stopped them. "Listen to what the constable has to say."

"Well, he ran up the hill past your house Miss Eleanor, and yours Miss Chapman, then disappeared. He couldn't have gone over the wall and we don't think he went into the field because there's no sign we can find with our lights that the grass has been trampled, so," he hesitated, "we assume he ran through the gates and must be somewhere here on the grounds of Oshatakea."

"You mean, he might be outside this house?" Louisa asked.

A shriek of terror startled them. Boris, who had been listening from the doorway, ran toward the kitchen followed by Constable Lindsay. The constable returned almost at once. "Your cook, Miss Kropotkin, was frightened when she saw lights through the window; it was only my men searching the immediate premises. More state police will be here soon with their tracking dogs. I'm sure we'll find him. I don't want to worry you, but I need your cooperation."

"How can we not be worried?" Miss Eleanor asked no one in particular.

"What would you have us do?" Adelaide was remaining calm.

"Stay in the house; lock your doors and stay away from windows."

"I don't know if we can lock the doors," she said.

"I don't own a key to my house, except a symbolic gold key you gave me. Do you remember?" Miss Eleanor looked up at Phil.

"There are no locks on any of our doors or windows," Adelaide said, "but I'll have Boris close the draperies on the first floor."

"We don't know if we'll find him before morning," Constable Lindsay said. "I think it would be best for all of you to stay here tonight, if that's possible."

"Of course it is possible," Adelaide replied.

"I'd be more comfortable at home, and you said he ran past my house earlier," Miss Eleanor objected.

"I don't want Lucile alone," Isabelle put in. "Come along Eleanor, I'll drop you off."

"You won't be able to do that Miss Chapman," the constable countered. "By now they have probably closed the main gates."

"I doubt that," Phil spoke up. "Those gates have never been closed as far as I know. It would take more than a few troopers to budge them."

"Even so, I bring orders from the state police officer in command. Nobody is to leave this house."

"Gives me the chills," Louisa said. "Do you suppose it was like this the night the Bolsheviks slaughtered the tsar?"

"Louisa please!" Adelaide's cool demeanor was cracking. "We will follow your instructions, Constable. Thank you for being concerned about our safety. Would you like a cup of coffee and perhaps a cordial before you return to work?"

"No, thank you, ma'am. I apologize again for breaking in on you this way. If you need anything, just holler."

"Exactly how are we to do that, for God's sake, open a window and scream?" He left before he could hear Isabelle's sarcasm.

In the confusion of all the women talking at once, they were unaware that Phil was no longer standing by the fireplace. Slipping from the room he found Boris in the kitchen explaining the situation to Magda and the weeping cook. "I'm going back up to my house," Phil said. Boris made a gesture to stop him, but he was gone.

In the drawing room, when she noticed his absence and thinking Phil had simply left them for a moment, Miss Eleanor, hoping to discourage further discussion of a birthday celebration, hissed, "I knew he would fly off the handle. Phil is adamant about keeping the house closed to all but us and a few others."

"I thought getting him to reopen Oshatakea for a birthday party would be a step toward acceptance of what is expected of him," Adelaide whispered in response, keeping her eye on the door through which she thought he might return. "If he doesn't come to his senses soon, Miss Eleanor, what will happen to him—and to our beautiful world here? I so much want to see Oshatakea filled with life again before I die, the way it used to be." Her face was a mask of despair.

"We have a murderer lurking in the bushes, ready to rush in here and bash our brains out, and you're concerned about some lost world Adelaide? Jesus H. Christ!" Isabelle fumbled in her tiny bag for a cigarette, to hell with the Kropotkins rule against smoking in the dacha.

"I hope you aren't keeping news of the Tsarevich from me." Louisa settled back into her amber cloud.

Adelaide went to the piano. "I think we should have more music before we retire. What will it be Isabelle?"

"How about 'Funeral March of the Marionette'?"

Chapter 4

MIKE LINDSAY'S MEAGER FILLMORE FORCE HAD MOVED on with their flashlights, and state policemen with powerful searchlights and tracking dogs had not yet arrived when Phil went out the dacha's kitchen door. Unseen, he loped back through the birch grove, crossing the strand several hundred feet in from the entrance. He could see a Fillmore police car parked across the drive between the gates, a partial but poor substitute for a barricade. Slipping through the tiered hedges he found his regular path in the woods and quickened his pace. He was jogging through the Italian gardens when he heard dogs barking in the distance, probably coming up Ontyakah Road. He didn't know if that meant they had found the escapee or were merely following his scent up the hill.

Inside the house he went through to the Portuguese Wing and up to his dad's dressing room, shed his Scottish regalia and put on a silk kimono he'd found during a recent foray into one of the attics. In spite of having eaten a big dinner only a few hours ago, he felt hungry, probably stress from all that had transpired during the day and evening, or maybe it was the run home. He went back into the main house and down to the kitchen to see what Adrian had left. Standing at the long butcher-block table he ate a drumstick and thigh in the light of the open refrigerator door. After returning the carcass to its cold shelf, he climbed stairs to the serving pantry between the Gibbons Room and the Double Cube Room. From the pantry, Phil entered the Long Gallery, dimly aglow because of a full moon shining through the arched glass roof two stories above. Moving silently, he reached his destination, the Italian Drawing Room, whose painted coved ceiling depicted scenes from Roman mythology. As a child he had memorized the names of the gods cavorting up there, preferring their exploits to the children's stories that were read to him. He could easily walk about the house in the dark because its configuration was fixed in his mind when he was a child and paid strict attention when Gramps repeatedly pointed out architectural details of each room, told him where the room came from and why it was furnished and decorated as it was. He knew where lamps were, but tonight he did not turn them on because they would destroy the effect of moonlight coming through tall windows. For Phil, artificial light was never as satisfying as moonlight. He put a match to the kindling Stefan had laid beneath logs in the fireplace, sat down in a chair that resembled a pope's throne and lifted his feet onto a tapestry-covered stool. But he was too restless to sit still. He gazed into the flames for only a matter of minutes, then got up and padded into the next room, a smaller Gothic fantasy that had once been part of a castle in Wales. Again, Phil set logs ablaze. This time he pulled cushions from a deep window seat and tossed them down on the floor beside the hearth. Finding the pillows more uncomfortable than the papal throne, he got up once more, wandered out into the Long Gallery and down to the Chinese Room at the far end where embroidered silk-covered sofas flanking a chinoiserie fireplace were of sufficient length for him to stretch out, which he did after, with only a slight pang of conscience, lighting the third fire in less than twenty minutes.

Stefan's grumbling came to mind. "It's not getting any easier for me, layin' fires, with this rheumatism that's bent me over. I'm not complainin' and I thank you for having young Reuben lug the logs, not's if he could lay a fire that'd burn, but I was wonderin' if you might content yourself with lightin' fires in only one or maybe two rooms of an evening instead of five or six as you seem to like to do. Have a fire in the room you choose to set in, and maybe one up in your bedroom, but more'n that hardly seems necessary." Stefan's complaint was followed by the fleeting thought that he might have gone too far. "'Course you're free to do what you've a mind to do, it's your house after all. My job is to lay the fires, I've been doin' it since long before you was born. That's what I'm paid to do. Just seems to me two fires a night or three at most oughta be enough for one man, 'stead of six or seven."

Phil didn't mean to be extravagant, and he was not unaware of Stefan's rheumatism, but he never knew where he might settle down for the evening. He was doing what his grandfather had told him to do: "Live in every room. Pearls lose their luster if they aren't worn; rooms die if they aren't used." It was a challenge for one person to live in dozens of rooms; he didn't bother with guest suites or any bedroom other than his own, the one where his grandfather had slept, but he had accepted the challenge and did not regret it. Trying to do what Gramps wanted was a joy, not a chore. The way George and Clewes had talked this morning, the house might as well be a museum, not his home. He rose from the sofa and began pacing, touching chairs, running his hands across their backs, consciously aware as Gramps had taught him to be of materials and lines. His fingers skimmed surfaces of tables and the fronts of cabinets, so attuned was he to each piece he could picture in his mind inlaid and carved designs he could not actually see. In a ritual he frequently performed to conjure his grandfather's presence, he picked up a porcelain bowl, cold to the touch but luxurious too in its smoothness and shape, turning it in his hands, holding it as if it were an offering or a relic. To George, the bowl, and everything else in the house, was a tangible asset listed in an inventory. To Clewes, all were valuable artifacts. But to Phil they were associations, the things he lived with, treasures collected by his grandfather and placed by him where they remained ever after. Each piece had a life of its own, a history of where it had been and a place where it belonged. These rooms, Oshatakea's rooms, constituted Phil's universe, their furnishings were his landmarks, essential parts of his environment. His thoughts returned to Stefan's request that he not light five or six fires each night, but lighting fires was a habit born and developed during years of living alone. When he couldn't sit still, as he could not tonight, when he needed to regain a sense of closeness to his grandfather, and with it the security Gramps had given him, the only way he knew to achieve that was by heeding Gramps' instructions. Nothing made a room more alive than a fire burning in the hearth.

He could live in just the Portuguese Wing, never venturing into the rest of Oshatakea, but his parents' house interested him the least of Oshatakea's many parts. Though designed and furnished by his grandfather, his mother's aura poisoned the air there, overwhelming any sense of the presence of either his grandfather or his father. Except for his dad's dressing room and green marble shower and the Portuguese Courtyard where he ate breakfast, Phil paid little attention to the mansion Gramps had built for his parents, Farney and Catherine. It was the rooms where his grandfather lived that sustained and nourished him. He roamed Oshatakea's corridors incessantly. What he did went beyond a duty to keep the rooms alive; he cherished this world Gramps had created.

His fondest childhood memories were of listening to the old man's tales of how the house had grown. "I first saw this room in Sussex, in a county house badly in need of repair. I could have bought the whole house or what was left of it, but I wanted only this room. I acquired it for next to nothing, yet look at the paneling Phil, feel it, there's none finer anywhere." Or, "This suite came from a château gone shabby in the Loire Valley owned by down-at-the-heel descendants of prerevolutionary aristocracy. Many ancient families were running out of steam in those days. In need of cash, they were happy to sell, though they were terribly condescending, as the French can be. They thought what they had was worth more just because it was in France. Typical." Or, "Everything in this room, including the Della Robbia babe in the overmantle, is exactly as it was in the Florentine villa where I found it. I thought I had discovered perfection, and bought it on the spot, but I couldn't remove a stick until the last member of the family died. She was about a thousand years old then but, to spite me, lived nearly twenty years longer. We made charts of the room to be sure every piece would be in its proper place once we installed it here. It was well worth waiting for. The rest of the villa is in one of the warehouses."

Gramps' stories were Phil's best education in history and geography and how people, albeit of a certain class, lived in other parts of the world. FP relished telling Phil details of negotiations, how sometimes he failed; owners would not part with what he wanted, but for a price would allow the stupendously rich American to construct a duplicate from detailed drawings. Gramps knew they sneered behind his back, said he was attempting to buy a heritage, while he saw their greed and more often than not their ignorance of what they had. Sometimes he purchased an entire structure to acquire one or two rooms, as in the case of the Della Robbia room, or perhaps just a wall or the moldings of a room, or the ceiling or the mantle. He stored the rest, if it was worth saving, or gave rooms to museums. This knowledge of origins and Phil's appreciation for what was special about each room, combined with his deep attachment for the entirety as well as the concept of Oshatakea, was his real inheritance from his grandfather. The Fillmore fortune made maintenance possible, but it was his love for the estate and his satisfaction in keeping the place as Gramps had known it that was his reason for being. His secret activity brought him bliss, but he liked to think watching over Oshatakea was what fed his soul. Left to his own devices, his life was full. His intensity of feeling and his need for absolute privacy to do as he wished within his grandfather's house was what angered, and at the same time chilled, him during the difficult encounter with George—and brought on the flash of resentment that resulted in a broken brandy snifter at the Kropotkins'.

"Inventory!" he shouted, putting the porcelain bowl back on the table. "Those bastards want to invade my house to take inventory!"

He stormed out of the Chinese Room and stomped the length of the Long Gallery, across the Great Hall and into the Galleried Library, where he turned on a floor lamp next to one of four spiral brass staircases leading to the upper level, the gallery that gave the room its name. On a stand in an alcove he opened an unabridged dictionary. Riffling through tissue India paper pages he came to: "Inventory/ 1: an itemized list of current assets, a: a written list or catalog usu. made by a fiduciary under oath of the tangible or intangible property of an individual, organization or estate describing the items or classes of property so as to be identifiable and usu. placing a valuation thereon." There was more, but Phil riffled the pages again looking for tangible property. "Tangible property/ property having physical substance apparent to the senses."

Apparent to the senses. He rubbed the burnished-walnut dictionary stand and turned, his eyes sweeping the room, most of it hidden in shadow, but he knew what was there, all of it apparent to his senses. He listened to the heavy *tick, tick, tick, tick* of a tall case clock that generations of Fillmores had listened to going back before the first Thomas, who had brought it from Cohasset, Massachusetts. Aware of the rooms' mingled odors, he thought, I wonder if tangible property includes the sense of smell. He inhaled deeply.

THE SEPTEMBER AFTERNOON'S MODERATE TEMPERATURE had dropped when the sun set. Cold clear skies allowed the full harvest moon to cast elongated shadows in the topiary garden, shadows more curious than the towering creatures that were clipped out of yews and box bushes. From the outside, Oshatakea's banks of windows were blue mirrors. In the Great Hall, lunar brilliance, softened by Tiffany's stained-glass dome, glimmered down upon white staircases.

Directly below the center of the dome, Phil sat naked and motionless on the marble floor, crouched in a fetal position, arms wrapped around legs, knees pulled tight against his chest, forehead resting on knees. During seconds of silence he held this position, not moving even as the opening bars of Ravel's *Bolero* began. The quiet, insistent throb increased in tempo and volume as imperceptibly as smoke rising to curl up into the dome itself, ever more urgent, never pausing, intensity deepening. Phil's body sinuously unfolded, slow, smooth, deliberate, opening like a night-blooming exotic. Arms uncoiled from around legs in undulations coursing to the tips of his fingers; then rapidly recoiled, and slowly opened again, quickly closed, reopened, each time wider, faster, with expanding extension. Opening, extending, closing, withdrawing, opening, extending. His torso rose, sank back and rose again, then back and up, higher each time, the music pulling him as the moon pulls tides. Receding and rising until, standing erect, he lifted his chin from his chest and in an agonizingly tight, calculated motion twisted his head from left to right, backward and forward rotations, as his arms drew in languid clasping embraces around his torso, then opened, embraced, released; twist, embrace, release, slowly, then quickly. There were no seams in his rigorously controlled movements. He started turning in place, turning, turning, opening, closing, opening, closing, rotating, everything quickening, quickening, quickening, gyrating, until with a screeching crescendo the music stopped and the dancer collapsed.

For a time all was still, and then in the echoing silence Phil began to recoil, withdrawing each leg until knees were again tight against chest and each arm was wrapped around his torso as in the initial embrace. Tightly rewound, his head slowly lowered to rest upon his knees, resuming the fetal position. Beads of sweat on his pale body glistened in the moonlight.

A sound like a warning cry made him raise his head to look up where, from over the balustrade of the top balcony, he assumed Pearl, or the ghost of Pearl, watched as he believed she had before. But instead of sensing approval raining down from above, there was only a feeling of cold terror. Movement in a shadow by the doors into the Long Gallery made him jerk his head in that direction. A large man stood there in the moonlight, grinning at him.

"Who are you?" Phil knew who he was; not his name but that he was the man who had escaped from the prison hospital, the guy who had murdered his mother. "What do you want?" Phil didn't expect answers to stupid questions. The man's grin scared him. The power grid was under the stairs. If he could ease himself back and flick a switch, the Great Hall would light up and the man might go away. "I'm cold," Phil said. "I have a robe in the closet. I'll put it on and be right back."

"Stay." The man's voice was light but raspy.

"I'm cold; I worked up a sweat dancing."

"Dancing?"

"Yes."

The man's grin relaxed. "I thought you was having a fit. My brother had fits. He choked to death having a fit. My mother didn't do anything, just watched him die."

"Please, may I get my robe? I'm freezing. There's nothing in the closet but an old kimono."

The man took a step toward him.

"Okay," Phil said. "I won't move if you don't want me to but, please, don't you move either. We'll talk where we are. All right?" Phil didn't know how to let Mike Lindsay know the guy they were looking for was here in the house. When he was little, Phil was afraid of bears, not that he'd ever seen one except in picture books, but he was sure a bear hid under his bed who would chew off an arm if he let it dangle over the edge, or grab a leg if he tried to jump out of bed and run into Miss Eleanor's room. This guy didn't look like a bear, but he was big and at least as frightening.

The man heard dogs howling before Phil did. He spun around and bent over to peer into the blackness of the Long Gallery as if he could hear better and see more by crouching down. The clamor was coming closer. Phil thought the man must have entered the house through the north lobby and the bloodhounds had tracked him to that door. A keening cry that at first Phil didn't realize was emanating from the crouching figure became a whimper and then blubbering. What would he do, Phil asked himself, if the guy ran over and grabbed him as a shield? He should have gotten out of there while the guy was distracted by the baying hounds.

The rock crystal clock that had belonged to Peter the Great began striking the hour, its baritone *bong, bong, bong* reverberating around the Great Hall. The sounds Phil found reassuring when he heard them as he lay in his Chinese bed in Gramps' suite were too much for the blubbering man who rose up and rushed to Phil, collapsing at his feet and throwing his arms around Phil's legs, a crumpled bundle of misery, pleading, "Don't let them get me, don't let them dogs bite me."

Phil was bewildered when he reached down. The man was really little more than a boy; big, but a kid, a sniveling kid filthy from hiding under bushes and scrabbling about God knows where. His impulse from years of caring for his mother was to take him somewhere and clean him up. Hysterically barking dogs neared their prey as policemen charged into the Great Hall. "They'll bite me, they'll bite me," the boy screamed, climbing Phil's legs.

"I won't let them bite you," Phil said, shielding him with his arms.

The fugitive apprehended, the dogs were taken away. "You were crazy to let him get close to you," Mike Lindsay said putting shackles on the handcuffed escapee.

"He's not crazy, he's a dancer," the prisoner said.

"And I walk the high wire," a rough-looking trooper countered, looking askance at Phil's nakedness.

"You were in real danger, Phil. I told you to stay at the dacha," Mike scolded. "I hope the dogs didn't break anything tearing through the house. They were impossible to hold back once they had the scent."

Phil followed as they led the shaking prisoner away, watching from the steps when they pushed his head down and shoved him into the backseat of a trooper's car. Before the door closed, the boy who murdered his mother looked up at Phil and smiled.

PART TWO: *Catherine*

Chapter 5

—

CATHERINE DID NOT KNOW WHY SHE SAID YES WHEN Farnsworth Phillips Fillmore III asked her to marry him, but then Catherine did not care about the why of anything—never had, not even when she was six and her mother told her, "You are a disagreeable child; I will oversee your upbringing until you are twelve, after that you are your father's responsibility." Her father died when she was eleven, leaving her with only a mother to annoy. Catherine fought being sent to boarding school, knowing her mother's sole reason for shipping her off was to get her out of the house. She wanted to be a concert pianist, thanks to the student from the conservatory who came twice a week to give her music lessons. He was the one adult who spoke to her as if she had a brain, never asking, "Have we been practicing?" the way she was asked by others, "Are we not going to eat our carrots?" or, "Shouldn't we wear our rubbers when we walk in the rain?" For him, Catherine played the piano better than she thought she could, not for praise but in anticipation of the next and more difficult piece he would assign. Ignoring her daughter's apparent ability, Catherine's mother decreed, "Girls of your station do not pursue careers, musical or otherwise; they go to a proper school to prepare for coming out."

"Prepare for catching a husband you mean," Catherine screamed, adding, "Anything to keep the breed going." She was threatened with having her tongue scrubbed with brown laundry soap, but her mother's threats were empty.

Nor did Catherine pause for even a second to wonder why she hated her sibling, Teddy. Three years her junior, the first time she peered down at Teddy's newborn wizened face she found Edward Winslow Dudley revolting, and, as was her wont, stated her opinion. "He makes me want to throw up." If she had the vocabulary she would have proclaimed the infant "an insufferable bore," which is what she called him as soon as she knew the meaning of those words and for the rest of his life. Neither as child nor adult did she give thought to consequences that might result from anything she said or did, doing and saying whatever she felt like saying or doing. If her words or actions created a fuss, she was pleased by the achievement. Consideration for the feelings of others would always remain an alien concept to her. When Teddy turned twenty-one Catherine did not hail him upon becoming a man, but rather informed him he had grown into the complete boob she knew from his birth he was destined to be. Accustomed to her sarcasm, Teddy retorted that he was looking forward to the time when he, as head of the family, would no longer have to assume the duty of looking out for his old-maid sister. This caused Catherine to hoot, "The only duty you have assumed Tosspot is to empty Father's wine cellar." At twenty-four, Teddy fell overboard and drowned during a Marblehead to Bermuda race. "I'm surprised his ineptitude didn't take the boat and crew down with him," Catherine observed when informed of the disaster, maintaining her predilection for passing ever negative judgments. Gleefully rubbing salt into the open wounds of her mother's bleeding heart, she roared with laughter as Teddy's will was read revealing he had left the modest sum of money over which he had personal control to set up a slush fund at the Harvard Club to provide "drinks on me" for specified members of his class.

There were those who thought Catherine said yes to Farney's

proposal because no other man had asked for her hand in marriage, nor was likely to, and she was, after all, in imminent danger of becoming a life-long unmarried maiden. But Catherine didn't give a damn about being married, or what others thought of her single state. While she amused and occupied herself commenting on the multitudinous faults she observed in others, she could not care less—a phrase she used incessantly because it drove her mother to distraction—about what anybody saw as her faults. "I could not care less about Fanny Cabot's opinion of my response to Mad Soule's reprimand at the Myopia ball." In truth, Catherine would have been disappointed had she not caused a considerable stir when, after Mrs. Soule suggested that if she could not be pleasant she should remain silent, Catherine flipped a finger at the dowager and shouted for the benefit of those who hadn't seen the gesture, "Up yours." Madeleine Soule was the ancient and revered guardian of North Shore propriety; debutantes might laugh behind their white-gloved hands at her strict enforcement of rules of conduct, but they would never cross the old harridan, nor be disrespectful to her in public. The incident became a major topic of every conversation that summer in social enclaves from North Haven to Newport, but nothing Catherine did or said brought expulsion from Society. Dudleys were as top drawer as it was possible to be, closely connected to Boston's first families with trees full of Forbeses, Searses, Thorndykes, Saltonstalls, Cabots and Lowells. Whenever and wherever Brahmins gathered Catherine Cabot Dudley was discussed. It was suggested by those who did not approve of Boston's most independent hostess, Isabella Stewart Gardner, "Having Mrs. Jack for a godmother hasn't helped. Catherine thinks it gives her the right to do as she pleases." When members of her most intimate circle advised Mrs. Soule to banish this unpleasant young person, Mad responded, "Indeed she is a monster, but she is one of our own." The old arbiter shook her head in puzzlement. "As for Farney, poor darling, a sweet, charm-

ing man—Harvard '09—I don't think he knows what he's getting."
Farney's charm eluded Catherine.

Gossips had much to say about Farney's excessive, to the point of
being embarrassing, fortune, but certainly Catherine could not
have said yes to increase her income; she didn't give a fig for
money. Dudley family wealth, amassed over two centuries of profitable trade in whatever commodity was most in demand at the
time, some of which "the less said the better," had been handled
carefully, "hoarded" wasn't too strong a term, and funneled down
to her in irrevocable trusts that perhaps could not in their combined totality compare with the Fillmore riches, "but whose can?"

"She certainly is not marrying for social advancement," Mrs.
Soule emphasized. "If she were, she would not marry a Fillmore."
If Catherine had thought about such levels within the world of
Boston Society, it would have tickled her to tweak the noses of those
who thought they made the rules by "marrying down." While the
Fillmores had been among the group of early colonists to became
proper and prosperous in New England, and had, after Thomas
Fillmore went west to what was then the frontier, for generations
epitomized the upper extreme of landed gentry with acres measured in square miles, over which they reigned like royalty from a
hilltop castle, none of the Fillmores had bothered with any social
order beyond the boundary of their own valley. Listed since the first
editions in both the Boston and the New York Social Registers, they
ignored whatever éclat that was supposed to bestow. Nouveau riche
New Yorkers who had pushed themselves to the pinnacle of that
city's high society retaliated by pretending Fillmores didn't exist.
Bostonians, unable to pretend, made a point of ignoring them with
an aggressiveness intended to scorch residents of Oshatakea. One
Beacon Hill matron saw fit when commenting on Catherine's
engagement to sneer at the "savage origin" of the Fillmores' name
for their estate, forgetting, for surely she must know, mustn't she,
why her commonwealth is called Massachusetts. Names were more

important than money to these women. It was assumed one had money if one possessed a good name. New Yorkers tended to be rather crudely splashy with their wealth; Bostonians kept relatively low profiles, almost but not quite adopting the adage that the more one mended one's stocking, the more stockings one could actually afford. One New York hostess was heard to joke that Bostonians who had diamonds wore them on the backs of their brooches. In the circles where Catherine grew up some were genuinely offended by the world's awareness of the Fillmores' wealth. Add to that the Fillmores' disregard for Society's opinion, and they became "renegades with eccentricities beyond toleration," as Mrs. Sears Pingree wrote to her sister who resided in a cottage at McClean's. "Perhaps it is this renegade aspect of life at Oshatakea that appeals to Catherine," Mrs. Pingree's sister replied, which made Mrs. Pingree wonder if her dear sister would ever be well enough to come home. Insular as only social groups can be when they close themselves behind walls and doors, friends of Catherine's mother inquired if she was not worried about Catherine going "way out there," as if, in 1928, scalps were still being taken west of Albany.

There was no open speculation about passion, which was just as well because passion had nothing to do with Catherine's acceptance. Farney's passion was horses, and Catherine had experienced the dampness of carnal love only once, for an instant, when her piano teacher embraced her on the occasion of her final lesson as he told her she had talent and urged her to not give up music. Then he was gone. She would never see him again, but he remained the object of unshaped fantasies throughout her adolescence and beyond. She and Farney first met when he accompanied his father to Catherine's father's funeral. At the time, because he was twenty-two and she eleven, neither paid much attention to the other. They met again during her coming-out year when the chasm between eighteen and twenty-nine had narrowed. Still, neither made any impression on the other. Farney was her dinner partner at Fenway Court about a decade later, but made a poor showing when he fell asleep while everyone else was listening if not raptly at least attentively to a long discourse by Henry James. Then they danced at a ball having to do with one of his Harvard reunions and from then on he called when he was in Boston and served as Catherine's occasional escort to the symphony, to the theater or the ballet, that sort of thing. Beyond offering her his arm for the short walk from the automobile to the entrance, or perhaps his hand supporting her elbow as they ascended staircases, there was no physical contact except when they danced quite properly at waltz evenings. They were both graceful dancers. Though of medium height, Farney carried himself with the easy gait of an athlete. A receding hairline did not detract from a generally attractive appearance enhanced by genuine geniality. Catherine would have preferred him less genial and more intellectual. She wanted late supper conversations about the music they had heard at a concert or the play they had attended but, despite giving the performances his complete attention, he had little to say about them afterward. Made aware of her disappointment, he tried agreeing with everything she said, only to realize she was angered by what she called his "going along like a simpleton." He returned to silence, a stance she then adopted because she was too bored by him to try thinking of anything to say. It was while in this mood that the prominent jaw she had inherited from her paternal grandmother became most evident, thrusting forward, letting the world know, if it had not already suspected, that this was one exceedingly strong-minded woman. She had as a teenager accepted, because she had no choice, that the jaw would result in her being regarded as handsome, never pretty, not that she cared one way or the other. Even so, she worked to keep her full-figured body firm and allowed herself the luxury of paying considerable attention to an abundance of titian hair, of which she took great care. Neither she nor Farney were ever moved to remark on the other's comeliness.

"YOU DO KNOW HER MOTHER HAS A PROBLEM?" FP ASKED when Farney told his father he was engaged to marry Catherine Dudley, a question FP regretted even as the sound of his words hung in the air. He didn't want to say or do anything that might discourage his son if he was at long last thinking about a wife. On the contrary, he'd do all he could to promote a development he'd given up expecting would happen. Pleased that Farney was considered by everyone to be a perfect gentleman, FP sometimes wondered if he wasn't too gentlemanly where women were concerned, had even wished Farney's baser instincts would overtake his perfect manners and perhaps lead him thence from lust to love. He wanted to believe there had been experiences of a sexual nature while Farney was at Harvard, experiences no young man was expected to share with his parent. As far as he knew Farney had never taken advantage of housemaids, which was admirable, but for a number of years FP placed his bets on Pearl, the housekeeper's niece, who made no attempt to hide her adoration, her eyes filling with longing every time Farney glanced in her direction. FP could not decide whether Farney was stupidly unaware of Pearl's feeling or not responding because he was avoiding that kind of relationship with a person he regarded only as a close friend and perfect riding companion. Farney's father thought Pearl was a fine, sensible young woman who would make his son an excellent wife. She'd have strong children, perhaps a son to carry on the Fillmore name. As when Louisa had wanted to marry that young farmer, FP would have supported a union between Farney and Pearl.

"A drinking problem?" Farney's response to his father's question was a question.

Hesitating, FP said, "That's right."

"Mrs. Dudley doesn't drink too much; she has a low tolerance for alcohol."

"Whatever it is, she can make those around her uneasy at times. I've never paid attention to old wives' tales, but there's one you might think about. Look to the mother to learn what the bride will become."

"Dad, would you rather I not marry Catherine? I thought you wanted me to get hitched, you've dropped enough hints."

"Hints?" FP laughed and clapped his hand on Farney's shoulder. "When I remind you at least once a day you are not getting any younger and that I want a grandson more than anything—those are more than hints my son."

Chapter 6

—

ON HER OFFICIAL PRENUPTIAL VISIT TO FARNEY'S FAMILY, Catherine found Oshatakea not to her liking. The house was too vast with way too many rooms, and though the period rooms were sublime in their perfection, the opulence of others offended her. Overpowering masses of marble and alabaster in the Great Hall assaulted her senses, "and that Tiffany dome!" To Catherine, the space that FP considered his masterwork was a cross between the Ziegfeld Follies and the Paris Opera House, neither of which she thought appropriate for a private home. What bothered her more than the house itself, however, was its busyness; there were too many people doing too many things at all times. The Fillmores were gregarious, and being geographically distant from metropolitan centers of politics, finance and the arts, all of which intrigued them, they kept Oshatakea filled with people prominent in those worlds, and kept their guests occupied with every kind of activity one would find at a resort. They were constantly coming and going in tennis togs, golfing or riding outfits, croquet costumes, dressed for cards, billiards, bowling, reading, walking or merely talking. The traffic and the changing of clothes gave Catherine a headache. Most houseguests stayed several days, but some were there for weeks. Europeans tended to settle in for indefinite periods. Rarely did FP suggest to a lingering visitor it was perhaps time for their visit to conclude. Add to this the Fillmore tradition, going back to Thomas from Cohasset, of inviting everyone living in the valley to Oshatakea for celebrations of major holidays and all family birthdays. The mass confusion could stagger one who had grown up in a household where occasional dinner parties for six were the rule. When the custom of everybody in the area celebrating at Oshatakea began, it meant a few dozen people coming up the hill, but as the population expanded hundreds ascended for food, drink, dancing and entertainment several times each year. This crush of humanity invited to meet Farney's fiancée the evening of the day she arrived made Catherine claustrophobic, and she was appalled by the mingling of farmers, shopkeepers, mechanics, housewives, teachers, craftsmen, anybody and everybody including the dirty little man who collected junk, along with diplomats, international bankers and performing artists. She cringed watching Pierpont Morgan in deep conversation with a man she supposed was a hired man. The hired man shouldn't be here, but was Morgan condescending? She loathed condescension, not that this particular financier had reason to condescend to anybody in her estimation. She well remembered her mother's horror when a member of the Morgan family proposed to a member of her family. "Thorndykes do not marry parvenus!" Mrs. Dudley had said.

Catherine could not care less, she thought, about social classes, and she believed herself to be free of prejudice; yet she found it impossible to countenance the free-for-all style of Oshatakea. One might rebel as she had; being rude to people she didn't like (she couldn't think of many she did like) and doing things that would disturb the placid waters of polite society was amusing, as was breaking rules to give stuffy women something to talk about and replacing edicts with her own code based solely on doing what she wanted to do, feel and think and, a lovely phrase she'd picked up, "the devil take the hindmost," but Catherine would never compromise her place in the top echelon of America's caste system.

The way Fillmores lived did not meet her standards. Her actions conflicting with what she thought were her philosophies might have been seen as ambiguity, used by Mad Soule as reason enough not to blacklist the difficult Miss Dudley, except that ambiguity would not be in either Mrs. Soule's or Catherine's lexicon.

On this visit as fiancée of the heir apparent, Catherine was examining everything through a microscope. Her conclusion: Oshatakea might as many said be the grandest house in the western hemisphere, though she would have to admit she'd never heard any member of the Fillmore family make such a crass statement, but she found fault with the way it was run, certainly not up to the criteria for Dudley houses on Beacon Hill, in Dover and Prides Crossing. That she professed to hate each of those family homes was beside the point. Even in Dover and during North Shore summers, she was accustomed to unbendable distinctions and insurmountable barriers, not just between family and servants but between those who worked upstairs and those who worked below. At Oshatakea, all staff members regardless of where they toiled, inside or out, were treated as friends, colleagues, everybody working together to keep the enormous estate functioning, all enjoying what they were doing and all on intimate terms with the family. Nobody called either father or son "Mr. Fillmore." It was FP and Farney even to the servants. Only the Kropotkin sisters were properly addressed. Incredible. There were footmen galore, footmen tripping over one another, with nobody but a housekeeper who wore tailored suits instead of a real uniform to oversee them. At least maids and footmen wore identifiable uniforms. FP told Catherine when she made a negative comment about this, "If you wonder why I don't have a butler, Mrs. Blackburn is capable of running the house without interference from some pompous ass in a stiff shirt looking down his nose at the rest of humanity including those who pay him his wages." Catherine did not argue, which was unusual for her, but she swore a silent oath that no servant would address her as anything other than Mrs. Fillmore when she became mistress of the manor.

The visit began badly with her first breakfast. Farney had warned her that it was his habit to take breakfast mid-morning after a long cross-country ride. When Catherine complained about this, saying he should make an exception and breakfast with her while she was at Oshatakea, he explained he could not because it was essential for him to exercise his numerous mounts if they were to stay in top condition for hunting.

"Isn't that something stable boys, or grooms, can do?"

"Oh they can," Farney said, "but the horses are mine. I must make sure they do not develop bad habits."

Catherine frowned. "It is you who have developed bad habits." Farney gave in, assuring her he would come to table in the breakfast room, at least on her first morning, before she and his father finished their meal, apologizing that he would not, however, be on hand to greet her when she came down from her suite.

The one thing she approved wholeheartedly in this crazy house was the family practice to not engage with guests before 12:30 lunch, therefore Catherine descended that first morning not by the marble staircases in the Great Hall but by hidden stairs under the landing and thence down a short passage to the private breakfast room, where there was no one to greet her except a footman who addressed her as Miss Dudley. He introduced himself as Raymond. As she approached the table, Raymond inquired if she would like to inspect the contents of covered silver dishes being kept hot on a long sideboard. "That will not be necessary," she said. "For breakfast, I have a small glass of freshly squeezed orange juice, a single egg softly scrambled, two thin slices of crisp bacon, a piece of dry toast with a small serving of dark marmalade and a single cup of black coffee, no sugar." He pulled a chair away from the table for her, then gently pushed it back before moving briskly to the sideboard to pour a glass of freshly squeezed orange juice from a silver pitcher dewy with drops of condensation. As he placed the juice before her, she said it was "too large a glass, twice as much as I want," but told him he not need replace it. "However, please remember the next time." He said he would. She waited impatiently for Raymond to return from the pantry with her scrambled eggs. When he did, they were not as soft as she had requested, and the crisp bacon was too thick. "I asked for an egg softly scrambled and two 'thin' slices of bacon." Raymond acknowledged that was what she had ordered, saying "I will ask cook to do another egg for you and tell her to slice the bacon thinner. It's our own bacon, cured here; FP likes it sliced thick." He removed the plate and returned to the pantry. Awaiting replacement, she drummed her fingers on the table. The second attempt to please her fared only marginally better. She pushed gelatinous egg around with her fork, didn't touch the bacon, took one bite of toast, found the marmalade not as bitter as she was used to, sipped coffee that was too hot on her first try and tepid on her second.

Wishing Farney would appear so she could complain to him, she was about to leave the table when she looked up and saw Farney's father coming in. His appearance stunned her. FP, fresh from the swim that was part of his morning ritual, was clad only in a gaping-open robe that revealed the entirety of the elderly man's pale body. Noticing her pallor he asked if she had seen a mouse? "It's either an occasional mouse in here or nasty traps, isn't that so Raymond?" The footman mumbled something that sounded like 'Tis true. "I hate cats and traps, but I don't mind mice," FP said, his bare feet leaving watery prints on the tiled floor as he paced back and forth uncovering and then recovering the array of silver dishes. "'Wee, sleekit, cow'rin, tim'rous beasties,' as Bobbie Burns sang. Don't be afraid, my dear, mice don't really run up a pretty woman's leg."

Manners didn't keep Catherine from saying it wasn't a mouse that had startled her, not that a mouse would have, had there been a mouse; it was finding words to explain to this old fool that it was his disgusting nudity. She gestured for Raymond to remove her plate.

"Finished?" FP inquired. "Did you try Tilda's kippered herring? Tilda's our breakfast cook. There's untouched cheese grits here, sausages made on the place, blini, a glorious deep-dish apple pie in the square warmer. Raymond will bring you some ice cream for it if you like, or that pitcher at the end is heavy Jersey cream."

"I do not eat pie for breakfast." Catherine's tone was contemptuous.

"Pity." Sitting down in the chair opposite her, FP remarked, "I noticed when I visited your father in Boston his family was stuck in a bacon-and-egg rut. Branch out Catherine." A fork full of kippered herring washed down with a swallow of half cream–half coffee from a huge cup brought forth a low moan of pleasure. "You don't know what you are missing. Trouble is, if you'll forgive me for saying so, the reason you don't have more of an appetite at breakfast is because you crawl out of bed and come directly to the table. That's a very pretty wrapper you are wearing by the way. Farney goes for a long ride first thing, and I swim at least half an hour." He was cutting up a sausage whose pungent aroma Catherine reacted to as if it were a personal insult. "Why don't you come swimming with me before breakfast tomorrow? You'd find it invigorating. Not in the big pool down by the grotto; I have my own pool surrounded by a high wall and lots of greenery. Most people don't even know it's there." He mistook her grimace for horror. "You think it's too cold to swim this late in the season? You expect water to be chilly in October. Believe me it gets a sight colder before my pool is drained for the winter and I swim right up to the last minute. If you start going in now, you'll not notice temperature later."

"It isn't the temperature of the water that concerns me." Catherine's tone chilled the air in the breakfast room. "The Atlantic Ocean at Prides Crossing is at least as cold in July and

August as pool water is here in October." Her eyes, as icy gray as the North Atlantic, stared directly into his.

FP stopped cutting his sausage. Turning away from Catherine's unblinking gaze he searched Raymond's face for a clue. Raymond directed his eyes toward FP's lap. "Oh." FP placed his knife and fork on his plate and, twisting away as he stood up, turned his back toward Catherine, pulled the robe tight around his body, secured it with a firm yank on the ties, then facing her again sat down, retrieved his utensils and returned to his sausage, offering as an apology, "Oft repeated acts make one an automaton. I don't wear a bathing suit when I swim alone, and it's rare for me to sit down to breakfast with anybody." He relaxed with a resounding laugh. "I forgot you'd be here Catherine. I promise I'll not come to breakfast bare assed again." He winked at Raymond. Catherine's maelstrom of emotions congealed into embarrassed agitation. FP's light acknowledgment of his nudity had made the situation worse. She considered herself tough, not prone to feminine blushes, but a flush rose in her cheeks when she observed FP winking at the footman who was standing only a few feet distant, a slight smile playing across his face. "Don't worry about Raymond, he's seen all of me there is to see, haven't you old friend?" Raymond, alert now to Catherine's discomfort, was no longer smiling. He nodded an abrupt but positive response.

Would this impossible conversation never end? "I am going to my room to write letters." Catherine's voice was tight. Raymond moved to pull her chair away from the table.

"Let me know if you want to swim tomorrow morning, Catherine; I promise I'll wear a bathing suit." FP's grin, meant to be reassuring, was received as mocking. Obviously, he wasn't taking Catherine's discomfort seriously. "Meanwhile, I'll speak to Farney, tell him he should give up morning rides with Pearl while you are here. If he joins us for breakfast, maybe he can jolly you into being more adventurous."

"Pearl?"

"Pearl Reid, the assistant housekeeper, Mrs. Blackburn's niece. Came here to live when she was orphaned at thirteen. Farney was about sixteen at the time. They hit if off, started this everyday early-morning ride together way back then. His going away to Harvard didn't stop them—they'd go out together every day when he was home." FP's insensitivity to the impact of what he was saying to Farney's fiancée was brought up short by the expression on Catherine's face. "I'm really putting both feet in it this morning. Don't fret my dear; Farney and Pearl are just friends. She's as crazy as he is about horses, that's all there is between them. There was a time when I thought something more might develop, but it never did. I supposed you knew about Pearl; don't let my blather upset you."

"Why should I be upset?"

"You shouldn't be. Go write your letters." FP stood when she left the table and was still standing when she left the room. Resuming his seat, he and Raymond exchanged meaningful looks. "Damn, hope I haven't botched things." His contrition quickly gave way to musing. "On the other hand, I'm not sure somebody who leaves a plate full of scrambled eggs and home-cured bacon will be happy with us here at Oshatakea in the long haul."

THE FIRST THING CATHERINE SAID WHEN FARNEY CAME to her suite an hour later was neither a simple good morning nor a blast for not showing up in the breakfast room when he'd promised he would; it was, "Tell me about Pearl."

Farney appeared surprised. "She's a good friend, you met her when Dad introduced you to people in the house. You may not remember; she's quiet." Instead of leaving it at that, he added with genuine enthusiasm, "She's the best woman rider I've ever seen. Why modify the statement? Pearl is the best rider I know. When she jumps a hedge you can't tell whether the horse is taking her over or she is taking the horse. I mean it. She and her mount are so synchronized, so smooth, they are equal partners. They take your breath away. Beautiful, beautiful!" He shook his head in amazed appreciation. "Everybody says so."

Catherine didn't know what was happening to her. She was at that moment more emotionally stirred by Farney than she had thought possible. She wanted physical contact with him. She wanted to attack him, that's what she really wanted, to wipe that stupid smile off his face, knock him down, kick him in the ribs. She felt as if her blood were racing through her veins, threatening to reach the boiling point. This is not jealousy, she assured herself. I am not jealous! This is hatred, pure and undiluted. I loathe this disgusting excuse for a man, standing there like a grinning ape as he pictures the perfection of Pearl's horsemanship. He was involved with another woman when he asked me to marry him, an assistant housekeeper, a housekeeper's niece for God's sake! Fleetingly, she considered returning to Boston on the first train east, but immediately she dismissed the notion. Their engagement has been announced, the wedding date set, stupid unwanted gifts were arriving at Mount Vernon Street. She would be a laughing-stock if she walked away now. She didn't care if they all hated her, she enjoyed being hated, but she could not take being laughed at. Besides, walking away wasn't what she wanted; what she wanted was to strangle Farney. The urge to kill was stronger than any desire to depart, to get away from this damned place, to never hear Oshatakea or the Fillmores mentioned again. "Dense," she wanted to scream at him, you are beyond being an idiot, you are dense, standing there unaware anything might be wrong as I am on the verge of exploding. She said none of those things. What she did say was, "I'm tired, I am going to lie down. Call me when it's time to dress for dinner."

"Dinner?" he asked, incredulous. "Dinner is hours away. Aren't you going to join the other guests for lunch? They will expect you. Don't you want to do something this afternoon? There are a lot of things we can do."

"No thank you."

Catherine saw little of other guests or family members during the next two days. She took all meals in her suite, including dinner, received no visitors nor responded to notes sent by Farney or his father. Adelaide Kropotkin knocked on her door and pleaded to be let in. "I so want to get to know you," Adelaide called out. Catherine did not reply. She refused to accept a telephone call from her mother, who had been alerted that Catherine was behaving in a peculiar manner. Members of the house party had commented on the strangeness, the impropriety of a fiancée coming for a prenuptial visit unaccompanied by her mother, not knowing Catherine had said she wouldn't go if Mrs. Dudley insisted on going with her. Oshatakea's guests were now provided with the deliciously open-ended topic of Catherine's presence in the house and her absence from their presence. It confirmed rumors that the about to be Mrs. Farnsworth Phillips Fillmore III was peculiar, a law unto herself. "What does she do all day?" they asked.

What she did was think. She thought seriously about taking up riding, becoming expert at jumping and hunting. She already knew how to ride, any fool could ride a horse, there was nothing to that, but this business of jumping over hedges and ditches would take practice. She'd love to show Farney the Fart it was no great trick to take a horse over a fence as smoothly as his bitch in heat did. But would that be playing his game? Did she want to play his game? She did not. If she could simply go out there, get up on a horse, preferably a stallion with a reputation of being impossible to ride, take off like the wind and leave them all gasping for breath as she sailed over every obstacle, then return to the paddock, get off the damn beast and never go near a horse again, that is what she would do, just to show the SOB. Showing him, not joining him, is what she wanted. She might trample Pearl while she was astride the killer stallion. That would be a plus. Then, and only then, she'd board the train, go back to Boston and to hell with what anybody said.

But she hadn't brought a riding habit, hadn't worn one since she came home from boarding school, probably couldn't get into it if she could find it, would never buy another. Forget that.

She also thought about what she was getting herself into if she actually married the dog. Nobody, absolutely no one thought she should marry him. Did she really want to bury herself in this treasure-stuffed mausoleum? What would she do with herself all day every day here? In Boston she could go to the movies. Movies weren't highly regarded in her circle, which was one of the main reasons Catherine loved them. She went to the movies when she said she was going to the Athenaeum or the Museum of Fine Arts or the Junior League, and was never asked when she returned home what she had seen or read, or what good works she had done for those less fortunate than herself, so she didn't lie. It made no difference whether the movies were good, bad or terrible; she went directly from one to another, frequently seeing three or four in a single day. Did her mother never wonder why her clothes reeked of buttered popcorn? She adored popcorn. She supposed she could watch movies somewhere in this castle, but it wouldn't be the same, Oshatakea's couldn't match movie theater popcorn. Giving that up when she married Fart Face would be a sacrifice.

Worse would be putting up with Farney, as big a boob as her brother Teddy. Too bad they weren't together on that Marblehead to Bermuda race, Farney might have made a lunge to save Teddy when he went overboard and gone over himself. Two dull blades eliminated in a single accident. "God, I'm bored," she muttered. I must be, I'm not even married yet and already I'm thinking about how marvelous it would be if he drowned at sea. Maybe he'll fall off a horse and Pearl, the world's wonder horsewoman, will in a synchronized jump clear a hedge and land right on top of him. Better chance of that happening than dispatching him in a sailboat, he's probably afraid of water. She lay down on the bed. Thinking evil thoughts could be exhilarating or exhausting.

Another reason for her fatigue may have been because Catherine had forced herself awake hours before dawn so she could watch from the windows of her suite when Farney and Pearl rode by on that side of the house. Beyond the lawns were fields with hedges and stone walls, where neither of them paused before flying over. If she had appreciated such things, she would have granted they were both skilled riders. After they disappeared, she contemplated what would happen if she asked Pearl to come to her suite for an encounter. Wouldn't it be part of an assistant housekeeper's duties to respond to a request from a houseguest, a special houseguest, fiancée of the heir? What would she do if Pearl did appear at her door? Scratching her eyes out wouldn't satisfy; that is what jealous females do in double features. No, she would look her over, appraise her coldly, make sure she felt the full force of the fiancée's antipathy. Antipathy? Repugnance, scorn! Catherine decided she would coat each utterance to the housekeeper's niece with full-bore Dudley disdain. She did remember Pearl, a well-proportioned, neither attractive nor ugly woman who seemed to know her place and kept it. Perhaps, she thought, I should give up my self-imposed exile, join the house party, of which I am supposed to be guest of honor, so I can take another, closer look at the odious hag who makes Dodo's face light up when he describes her astride a mount, light up so he appears years younger than he is. Astride a mount indeed!

FP was delighted when Catherine sent word she would be coming down for dinner. His note to express his pleasure went on to importune her to join him at the pool "before breakfast tomorrow morning." In a short response carried back by the footman who brought her FP's epistle, she politely declined. She feared that even if she had wanted to swim, in her present mood she might drown the father as substitute for his son.

At dinner, following a toast to the happy couple, FP announced he'd stopped all planning for an Iberian wing to incorporate rooms he had not used in his apartment above the Galleried Library, "including some beauties from Portugal," to concentrate on a fine house for his son and soon-to-be daughter-in-law. His architects were working on drawings and specifications, he said. "Construction can commence within a matter of weeks, and we're hoping to get footings in before the ground freezes. The house," he smiled down at Catherine seated to his right, "will be ready for you when you return from your year abroad." His assembled guests applauded.

"When may I see the plans?" Catherine asked when FP resumed his seat.

"You may not," FP replied. "The house is my wedding gift to you. It must be a surprise."

"What if I don't like it?" Catherine was being Catherine.

"You will."

Those two words, spoken with affectionate affirmation, set her on edge for the remainder of her visit.

Chapter 7

—

CATHERINE BECAME MRS. FARNSWORTH P. FILLMORE III
in the double drawing room of her mother's Mount Vernon Street
house, with a small company of family present: FP, Adelaide and
Louisa from Farney's side, Mrs. Dudley, two second cousins and one
third from Catherine's. After a dinner remarkable only for being so
ordinary, the couple was driven to the Ritz Carleton, where they
spent an awkward wedding night in a large suite. The marriage was
dutifully consummated. Catherine was neither disappointed nor surprised that she did not enjoy an exercise engaged in without enthusiasm or affection. Farney was as disinterested as was she, lumbering
through his conjugal commitment by remembering a night many
years ago in a Boston hotel with a young woman from Ohio.

The following afternoon they sailed for Europe, a crossing that
was interminable. They walked the promenade deck around and
around and around, attended every social function, including tea
dances and bridge tournaments. For hours, they endured uncomfortable deck chairs wrapped in blankets, pretending to read while
staring out at intimidating waves on a gray ocean, its bleakness
preferable to confinement in relatively commodious quarters. By
the time they docked at Southampton and were transported to
Cliveden where they were to be guests of Waldorf and Nancy Astor
for ten days, both understood their marriage was a mistake.

Catherine was furious with herself. She had stupidly walked into a trap, and stupidity could not be forgiven. Farney was saddened. He had been totally content with his life as it was at Oshatakea, had acted only because he knew his father wanted him to marry. Now he was in an unnerving, impossible predicament, for which he assumed all blame. He wanted to offer balm to his bride, tell her she could leave him if she wished, or if she thought that would be impossible, he'd do whatever she asked to improve their situation. At the very least he wanted to tell her he was sorry, but she would not listen, turning her back whenever he approached in a placating manner. When they were on the continent, in Italy perhaps where it would be warm and sunny, he hoped the frigidity between them would thaw and they could engage in quiet conversation.

Upon their arrival at Cliveden, Lady Astor announced, "I have given you separate but adjoining suites. Having lived through two honeymoons of my own, I know how you must hate the sight of each other." The newlyweds were surprised by her remark, but grateful for her arrangements.

Their old-fashioned grand tour honeymoon was supposed to last a year, but in Sienna one morning, after just under three weeks in Italy, whose sun had no discernible warming effect on the relationship—there had been no quiet conversations—Farney said he could not stand being away from his horses. "I have booked space on a ship sailing Saturday for New York. You," he spoke gently to Catherine sitting across the table from him, "may accompany me, or return later if you wish. I don't want to deny you the rest of the journey."

Catherine actually smiled when she answered, "Gaines and I will finish the trip."

The only thing that had kept this hideous charade of a honeymoon from being a complete catastrophe for her was quiet but ever cheerful Eleanor Gaines, a young woman assigned to assist Catherine with her clothes and hair when the bridal couple arrived at Cliveden. Nancy Astor could not believe Catherine was traveling without a maid. "Bostonians," she snorted, "are so close with money you deprive yourselves of basic necessities. My dear Catherine, one cannot traipse across Europe and around the world alone. Husbands count for nothing. You must have someone dependable with you, a personal maid." When they departed Cliveden, Lady Astor insisted on loaning her Gaines, "my treat."

Having been dragged through every cathedral, museum, park and palace by his father, some several times over, Farney had no interest in seeing them yet again. Happy to leave him behind, but not wanting to go alone, Catherine asked Gaines to be her sight-seeing companion. While Catherine feigned indifference so as not to be mistaken for a tourist, her reaction to what she saw being either simple affirmation of what she expected or disappointment because it did not live up to preconceptions, for Gaines each structure, each garden, statue and painting was an enthralling discovery. With no advance knowledge of architectural orders or classic rules of line and proportion, she responded viscerally, felt attraction to and appreciation of what she was seeing. She was rarely unmoved, never disinterested and always completely free of concern about whether or not her reactions matched opinions of historians or critics, none of whom she had read. Catherine watched and envied Gaines's unabashed enthusiasm, and in an attempt to share it worked to change her own strictly-by-the-book approach. Assuming an attitude of naïveté was not totally successful, but she did find herself experiencing an elation that was quite at variance with the condescending, ever so slightly bored posture that had been bred into her. Even more surprising was setting out on excursions with an open mind. For someone whose mind had always been made up and set, usually in a negative position, before consideration of any subject, this openness was phenomenal. There was danger in the new approach. Sharing felicitous experiences with Gaines could lead to a camaraderie she had heretofore resisted, not that it was difficult to avoid with girls at boarding school or with daughters of her mother's friends, where contempt was mutual. The present situation differed from any she had known before. Catherine had to constantly remind herself that Gaines, though exceedingly bright, quick to learn and infinitely agreeable, was still a maid. That the young Englishwoman was fun to be with could not be argued, and, for Catherine, fun was a whole new experience. If happiness was a concept she thought about, she might be tempted to record the weeks following Farney's departure as a happy time, but, aware that such ridiculous thoughts were creeping in, and to keep them from taking root, she came down firmly on the side of safety, choosing to regard their laughter-filled days as further potential traps. She was not about to stupidly walk into one again so soon after the one that bound her to Fapfaw. However, she was also unable to maintain the strict discipline of proper distance, and so, after a week of sleepless nights worrying about the problem, Catherine decided to allow herself the delight, admitting she found Gaines's company delightful, of continuing as companions when they were where no one knew them. Remaining unknown was essential to relaxation of her usual stance. Thus in Italy, Spain, Greece and every other country they visited on the European continent and in North Africa, she made no attempt to call on those to whom her mother, Farney's father, the Kropotkins or Lady Astor had given her letters of introduction. Efforts at anonymity went beyond not calling. Because these friends or acquaintances of the family were mostly in major cities where social sets gathered, to avoid happenstance meetings Catherine rearranged bookings, canceled hotel reservations in what she was sure were preferred places and made them instead in tiny hostelries with no reputation at all and few amenities beyond cleanliness. If such was unavailable, she and Gaines moved on to obscure villages in the hills or along the shore without must-see sites, only sublime views, sometimes interesting antiquities and almost always welcoming strangers. Here in these out-of-the-way places she felt free to be reckless, to experience with what she thought was wild abandon, whatever new adventure might arise. She was confident she would never lose her compass, but to keep Gaines from becoming confused, the easy relationship that existed during days of sight-seeing ended at their hotel entrance where Catherine made clear through attitude and tone of voice that it was time to revert to a more formal exchange. At dinner, if taken away from the hotel, they again became chatty companions, and at the evening's entertainment they discussed what they were hearing and seeing, disagreeing when their reactions differed. Regardless of where they were, or in which mode, Gaines was always addressed as Gaines; Catherine was either Ma'am or Mrs. Fillmore.

The possibility of Gaines returning to Oshatakea with Catherine was a frequent topic of conversation. She would need a maid, Catherine said. No one she knew at home had a personal maid, but she did not reveal that. "We've had such a good time traveling together, I hate to send you back to Cliveden." That she who had been appalled by the closeness between the Fillmores and their servants was actually inviting a maid to join her at Oshatakea, not because she was excellent at her job, as she was, nor really needed, as she wasn't, but because Catherine didn't want to be separated from this individual who had become her friend, was incredible, as Catherine realized. Naturally, she did not speak of friendship in attempting to persuade Gaines. Never open a Pandora's box that must be kept closed. But Gaines was not stupid. She exhibited hesitancy about going with Catherine to the United States and perhaps remaining there, even though she had dreamed of one day doing just that, because she heard Catherine's casual invitations as too urgent pleas. Both women had reservations about the developing relationship, yet seven months later, the decision made, they sailed together from Yokohama to San Francisco, where the Thomas Jefferson, the Fillmores' private railway car, waited to carry them across the country.

On their last night in Japan, probably because they were tired and a bit melancholy that this yearlong adventure was coming to an end, they tittered when they should have been awestricken by the art of the Kabuki. Neither could remember which one broke up first, not that it mattered, but once they started they could not stop, to the consternation of highly offended Japanese sitting in their vicinity, for whom these foreign devils were despoiling the profound performance of a near sacred ritual. Back at the inn Catherine ordered saki and invited Gaines to join her in a "final night of freedom" nightcap, though neither ordinarily drank more than a glass or two of wine with dinner. The sweet warmth that should have been savored by sipping dissolved Catherine's resolve as she drank too much too fast. When the little cruets were empty, she told Gaines to order more. When these were consumed, a third set was sent for. Catherine thought it must be almost midnight, but wasn't sure, when she said, "Let's reverse direction and return to the States the way we came, retrace our steps, go backwards, more or less, if you get my point—which means we will arrive at Oshatakea approximately one year from now, give or take a day or two, whereas if we proceed as planned, get on the ship that sails within hours, it will be a mere four or five or six weeks—too soon, too soon—when we knock on that big front door and are admitted into the most ostentatious of all Great Halls. Gaines it makes Cliveden look like a dog kennel. Do I hear a second?" Gaines smiled but said nothing. "Discussion? If there is no discussion, I declare the motion carried by acclamation. Hurrah! Aren't you proud of me, knowing how to run a meeting? I learned that at the Junior League." She applauded her own attempt at humor. Gaines was so still, Catherine wondered if she had passed out. Shaking an empty porcelain cruet over her tiny cup, Catherine took up the subject anew. "If we do it all backwards Gaines my girl"—she shouted these last words in Gaines's ear to revive her sagging companion—"we can see things we missed the first time around, starting with the point of that silly masquerade we sat through this evening, last night, when was it? Maybe the second time, if we pay strict attention and you don't start snickering—you did start it—I would never laugh at a living work of art. I only did to keep you from feeling embarrassed, which I hope you appreciate, but," she was tittering again, "will you ever forget that hideous man in the fright wig with great big eyes flashing from one side of his floured face to the other, tippy-toeing around trying to convince us he was a chaste young maiden dying for the love of . . . of a samurai warrior who was half her/his size?" Shaking with laughter, she could no longer speak, nor did she try, giving in by falling back onto cushions scattered around the tatami mats.

There was no laughter aboard ship. The first day they were suffering such acute morning-after agonies, that sounds of bells and whistles made them cringe. That night they became seasick, remaining unhappily indisposed as the ship rolled and throbbed on a Pacific Ocean made turbulent by severe seasonal storms. Neither began to feel they were again part of the human race until close to sunset of the fifth day, when Catherine remarked quietly, "They will throw us to the sharks if I refuse one more invitation to dine at the captain's table." Gaines helped her select a gown, a dark green velvet dinner dress purchased for her trousseau and never worn until that evening. She also helped Catherine with her hair, though Catherine insisted a simple knot would do. Conversation was cursory as these simple tasks were undertaken and completed. The captain's table did nothing to lift Catherine's spirits. Her mood grew darker as the ship sailed east, each turn of its screws driving them nearer San Francisco. The morning of their arrival, they watched from the rail of the first-class deck as tugs eased their liner up to the dock where they would disembark. Gaines appeared calm but was truly excited. Would the America she'd heard so much about, the land of the free and home of the brave, also be as wild as her mother had warned her? The thrill of it all, and perhaps the threat, caused her to tremble as she followed Catherine down the gangplank. At the exact moment the young woman set her first foot on California soil, Catherine turned to address her. "Gaines I do not want you to become familiar with the Oshatakea staff, nor will you want to I'm sure, but some of them will be in close proximity on the train. I have no idea how many came with the Jefferson, but I will insist you have a stateroom to yourself even if that means somebody else has to sleep standing up."

They did not go to the St. Francis Hotel, where a suite over-looking Union Square had been reserved for them, Catherine demanding instead to be driven directly to the Jefferson. If the loathsome "homecoming" at Oshatakea could not be avoided, and she knew it could not, she wanted it over and done with as quickly as possible. She stepped onto the elegantly appointed private rail-way car, removed her hat, handed it to Gaines and gave the order to pull out as soon as their luggage was stowed. Gaines witnessed her first full-blown Catherine rage when the steward said that it would be impossible inasmuch as they were not scheduled to depart for three days. "FP thought you would want to spend time in San Francisco, perhaps see the redwood trees." Threatened with the loss of his job if they weren't rolling east "before noon tomor-row," the steward, stunned by the vehemence of Catherine's reac-tion, hurried away to consult via telegraph with FP. New arrangements were made. The Union Pacific would attach the Jefferson and its attendant staff car to a Chicago-bound train shortly after dawn the next morning. Gaines was sorry not to see the city by the bay.

During the overland journey, Catherine would be asked period-ically if she wanted to have the two railroad cars disengaged and parked on sidings so she could enjoy a respite from travel and do some sightseeing but, much to the disappointment of others on board, she always answered, "Absolutely not." There was no con-versation between Catherine and Gaines beyond Ma'am's basic requests and her maid's responses during the emotionally and physically exhausting eight days it took to cross the continent. No pleasant memories of the recent past were shared, no anticipations of the future mentioned. Catherine sat with an unopened book in her lap, staring out at bleak prairies and dark forests, stubbled crop-lands and the depressing sections of cities that lay along railroad tracks. Gaines sat in her own stateroom down a narrow passageway from Catherine's bedroom looking out at the same scenery, recon-sidering her decision to stay in America, wishing she had not told her mother and notified Lady Astor. Changing her mind now would not do. She would bide her time, stick with Madame for a few months, and then resign. She had saved some money, enough she thought to pay the least-expensive passage home to England. Catherine's deepening misery on the train did not surprise her; the bride's bitter unhappiness had been apparent during those few weeks her new husband was with them in Europe. What dismayed Gaines was Catherine's rude treatment of the extraordinarily kind and thoughtful people who had been sent from Oshatakea to greet her and see to her every need. Each of them, a soft-spoken foot-man, a fine cook, the cook's able assistant and the attentive stew-ard, did his best to please her, went out of his way to anticipate her wishes, but Catherine was never anything but venemous to them, worse than Lady Astor had sometimes been to people who worked for her, and that American-born lady could slice through bone with a sideways glance. Gaines was grateful the question of where she would take her meals had not arisen after they had left Japan, it being understood she and Catherine would no longer eat together. What little food Catherine consumed was served in the Jefferson's paneled and chandeliered dining room with only the footman in attendance. Gaines, though ordered not to associate with the Oshatakea staff, enjoyed jolly banter and good food at their table in the other car, which was a buffer between the Jefferson and public cars in the train. Catherine never entered staff quarters; actually, she never stepped out of the Jefferson from the moment she entered its lavish interior in San Francisco until it reached its destination in the village of Fillmore. The people from Oshatakea welcomed Gaines and she became fond of them. She surmised she'd need all the friends she could gather once she and Madame were residents in their new home.

Catherine never knew of the friendships Gaines made on the Jefferson, but she came to realize it was Gaines's quiet presence that made it possible for her to survive the first months at Oshatakea as Farney's wife. She felt as if she were suffocating, wished she would. Everyone else kept busy. Catherine had nothing to do. She assumed she would occupy herself with the new house, arranging furniture, unpacking barrels and placing wedding gifts, those she didn't throw against a wall, but the house FP had begun constructing before she and Farney were married, promising it would be finished when they returned from their yearlong trip, was not. This she discovered upon her arrival. She and Gaines were met at the Fillmore Village depot by FP and Farney, the Kropotkins and Isabelle Chapman with flower-decorated carriages. Curious villagers drawn to the spot to observe the reunion of a groom and his bride who had gone on an extended honeymoon without him stared from a distance. When the family came forward to greet her with hugs and kisses, she tried to fend them off, stiffening and turning her head away. At Oshatakea, as she alit under the south front portico to cheers from a throng of servants, she thought she was being taken to her own house when FP holding on to her hand led a procession around the end of that part of Oshatakea he referred to as Hester's, but there, behind Hester's wing, to Catherine's horror, was what looked like a monstrous package, crudely boxed in a four-story wooden crate. "Your almost finished wedding present, Mrs. Fillmore," FP said, and made a sweeping gesture. "Almost ready to open."

Catherine could muster no response.

For the next eight months Farney and Catherine lived *en famille* in a two-bedroom guest suite above Hester's gilded drawing rooms. FP was gracious and generous, but not to the point of relinquishing so much as a smidgeon of responsibility for the running of Oshatakea. Nor did he anoint Catherine hostess, which she thought she would automatically became as his daughter-in-law. "Oshatakea hasn't had an official hostess since Farney's mother died," FP explained. "My granddaughters Adelaide and Louisa and my good friend Isabelle Chapman take turns serving as such when one is needed. You are welcome to join that rotation." Astute enough to see that this did not satisfy her, he reminded her she would eventually be chatelaine, "when I am gone, but you must be patient my dear; we Fillmores live forever. Meanwhile, your own house will soon be ready, you will be mistress there."

Her days empty and her nights black holes, Catherine chafed, complained and was impossible to please. She gave Farney no peace. "If I am miserable, he will be miserable too," she swore. "If it weren't for him I wouldn't be in this mess." Farney threw faggots on the flame when he exhorted, "Be patient." No two words infuriated her more. Patience was as impossible for Catherine as withholding judgments. Impatience and passing judgment were basic components of her character. She saw it as her absolute duty to speak out, to voice her opinion, let the world know what she thought, and to show impatience with stupidity. Deadly boredom wafted explosive vapors over ever present embers. Catherine's shrieks of frustration seared Farney's ears and soul. No one was sacrosanct. She listed the myriad things wrong with him, his father, this house, and the Kropotkins.

"What have Adelaide and Louisa done?"

"They play at being pleasant when they hate me."

"They have no reason to hate you." Farney explained that the Kropotkins were like sisters to him. They had urged him to marry Catherine. He tried to tell her yet again that their mother,

Marianne, was his half sister, born of his father's first marriage. "His second wife was my mother. She was much younger than he, and died giving me birth. Adelaide is six weeks older than I. I was an uncle when I was born."

"Enough," Catherine shouted. "I've heard more than enough about your family history. Why did your father never marry that ridiculous Chapman woman, the hussy in the pink palace? Don't answer, it's obvious, nobody in his right mind would marry her. He doesn't need to does he? The old goat can sleep with the painted trollop any time he wants."

Farney sighed. There were things he could say, but she wouldn't listen.

"I will not eat every meal with him. He and I are alone at breakfast, with him stark naked under a skimpy robe. Then we follow along, part of the flock of sheep, to whatever room his whim has dictated for lunch or dinner. Is it never possible for us to eat by ourselves?" As she spoke she wondered why in the world she was suggesting she and Farney should eat by themselves when being alone with him was tedium beyond endurance.

"Catherine, it would be rude for us to eat by ourselves, apart from our guests, and when there are no guests we shouldn't leave Dad to eat by himself."

"When are there no guests? Tell me, don't the two of you ever feel the need for some privacy?"

"Dad doesn't see houseguests until lunchtime, and I go riding before anybody is up, which gives me all the privacy I need. People come and go at Oshatakea; they always have. You get used to it."

"I will not 'get used to it.' I refuse to participate in communal living."

Farney did not admonish, merely stated fact. "I seriously doubt, Catherine, you will change the way we live at Oshatakea as long as Dad is around."

"Why do you think I'm in such a state? Are you totally oblivious? I'm nothing more than a stranger in this hotel of a house, just another guest with no departure date. I have nothing to do. I'm drowning and nobody cares."

In truth Farney was more attuned to her unhappiness than she knew, but he was powerless to help her. That he would not comment on her distemper, or on what she called the state she was in, was his conscious effort to avoid confrontation. Commiseration enraged her. Trying to reason caused her to scream that he was jumping down her throat. Being literal minded, there were times when that is what he would like to do. When he tried to calm her with the slightest display of affection, she reacted with a revulsion so virulent he was sickened by it. All of which added to his sense of failure and inadequacy. Thinking his presence made her worse, he spent as little time in her company as possible, which led to accusations he was spending all his time with Pearl. He had repeatedly denied any relationship beyond friendship with Pearl based on a shared interest in horses, but nothing lessened his wife's suspicions. In an attempt to alleviate Catherine's agitation at having no role to play at Oshatakea, he asked his father to please consult her about decorating and furnishing their new house.

FP demurred. "If she doesn't like something when it is finished, she can change it." For sixty years, FP had designed, built, adapted, decorated and furnished, and seen to the smallest details of every installation in Oshatakea; he wasn't going to now change his way of accomplishing results that experts in their fields had for years told him were the epitome of perfection. Farney understood that if his father asked Catherine what she wanted in the rooms she would inhabit, her meddling would subtract from the surprise and delight the old man wanted her to experience when they were unveiled. He prayed his wife could maintain some equilibrium until that moment arrived.

"If I hate this wedding-present house when I finally see it, I shall return to Boston and never come back," Catherine said to FP at breakfast.

"I am sure you will do whatever you feel you must do." He did not look up from his oatmeal.

Adelaide and Louisa tried diverting Catherine with invitations to join them on their rounds of visits to valley residents. On the first such visit Catherine observed in silence, neither conversing nor making a pretense of touching a cup of coffee poured for her. The Kropotkins were nonplussed by what they deemed offensive behavior, but gave Farney's wife the benefit of doubt, agreeing, after they had dropped her off at Oshatakea, she was shy. Two days later Catherine remarked to an elderly woman whom the Kropotkins were calling on because she was mourning the death of her husband of fifty-seven years, "Too bad there isn't a movie theater in the village. Watching a good movie would make you forget him." The bereft widow's jaw dropped in disbelief.

On the third attempt to distract Catherine from her self-absorption and continuing to believe they could inculcate the idea that it was her duty to develop caring relationships with valley people, as had all Fillmores, the three women were driven by Boris to visit a new mother, Molly Bean, and her firstborn, a round-faced, bright-eyed son. Adelaide presented a tiny sweater she had knitted from yarn Louisa had spun from the wool of their own flock of Romney sheep. While Molly unwrapped the gift, Louisa cooed at the infant in her arms. When it was Adelaide's turn to hold him, she commented on how much he looked like both his parents. "You will not remember, Molly, but I held you and Greg when you were this little one's age." The beaming mother told Adelaide she still had the baby sweater the Kropotkin sisters had made for her. Then Molly offered Greg Junior to Catherine. Catherine threw up her arms to ward off the tightly wrapped bundle. "I despise babies. They smell and they all look like frogs." Adelaide and Louisa did not ask her again to accompany them on their valley visits.

Upset as they were with Catherine for her cold arrogance when with valley people, they felt compelled to do something to ease increasing tensions at Oshatakea. The depth of Catherine's unhappiness was made clear when she told them she felt as if she'd been found guilty of a crime and was confined for life in a prison whose opulence offended her. Their solution was to suggest a clothes-buying trip to Paris. "Everything we have is outdated," Adelaide explained. "We hope you might care to join us."

"Three months is an excessively long time," Louisa interjected.

Adelaide hushed her. "It takes that long to inspect all the offerings, and then, after we've made our selections, fittings require weeks." She was overstating the case. When she had asked Grandfather what he thought of their idea of taking Catherine away for a while, he was elated, offering to pay for the excursion if they would extend their stay in Paris to three months. He thought he could complete the wedding-gift house in that length of time.

Louisa did not drop her objection. "But Adelaide, they have all our measurements."

"I'm sure some of mine, and yours too dear, have shifted." Adelaide returned to Catherine. "We will also want to take trips into the beautiful French countryside as we always do."

Catherine at first rejected their invitation; she had been in Europe only a few months ago, and she had closets full of clothing purchased for her trousseau but never worn. Shopping bored her. But then the notion of being away from Oshatakea and Farney became too appealing to turn down. Perhaps she and Gaines could get away from Adelaide and Louisa and, while on their own side trips, rekindle some of the spark of their round-the-world journey.

Approximately four weeks after accepting the offer, Adelaide, Louisa, Catherine and Gaines—"I won't go without her," Catherine had stated, though neither Kropotkin raised the slightest objection—departed from the depot on the Jefferson. Apprehension almost exceeded anticipation. Catherine hoped she would not be driven to distraction by the Kropotkin sisters and they prayed she would not be so disagreeable they would regret coming up with this venture. The staff car and the Jefferson rolled out of the valley to the main line of the New York Central where they were attached to the rear of an eastbound express. From her tiny stateroom — she did not have the one she'd slept in coming across the country; that one was occupied by Adelaide — Gaines looked out to marvel at the immenseness of FP's warehouses and the lushness of mile after mile of Fillmore farmland. In the Jefferson's drawing room, Catherine opened a book, turned her back to the windows and read. Adelaide and Louisa sat at a table playing a fierce game of bezique. Barring mishap, they would arrive at Grand Central Station at 6:40 the next morning, when the women would be taken to rooms at the Plaza to freshen up and have breakfast before boarding the *Mauretania* at pier 14. Oshatakea people who had traveled in the staff car would see the ladies' luggage safely aboard, make sure there were flowers and fruit in their staterooms and then, after the ship sailed, they would return to Fillmore.

At sea, Catherine began to relax. She hoped the inner turmoil that had become sanity threatening would disappear before the ship docked at Le Havre. She was amused to be looking forward to this silly junket with greater expectations than she had her wedding trip. An easy routine was quickly established. Brisk morning walks around the first-class deck she found so bracing she was able to ignore Adelaide and Louisa chattering at each other. After lunch they played a rubber or two of bridge with Gaines as fourth. Because Gaines was exceedingly competent and highly competitive, these games turned out to be challenging rather than a yawn for Catherine, who ordinarily wasted no time on cards. Naps followed, prior to dressing for dinner. Catherine was pleasantly surprised by Adelaide's breadth of knowledge. She was more than able to hold her own on a wide variety of subjects with fellow guests at the captain's table. The news that Adelaide held a share in the Boston Athenaeum amazed her. While she hadn't thought about it, she assumed no one beyond Beacon Hill and Back Bay owned part of that august institution. Catherine's smile verged on the impish when she revealed to a startled Adelaide the many afternoons her mother thought she was reading in one of the Athenaeums's lovely rooms when she was actually sitting in a movie theater on Washington Street. Catherine suspected Adelaide was incapable of deception. No matter. Adelaide's knowledge of and love for music deeply impressed Catherine, to whom music meant more than anything.

She was slower to accept Louisa, whose precise imbalance was difficult to define. There were moments when Catherine thought the younger Kropotkin was mad as a hatter, others when she was sure Louisa was faking. Louisa could be quite funny and was almost always eager to do whatever was suggested, which somewhat offset the nuisance of her flights of fantasy. Catherine noticed that she inquired about the health of the Tsarevich only when she was being emotional.

The Kropotkins also breathed easier once they were under way, concluding after several days without a scene that perhaps Farney had not made a totally stupid mistake when he married Catherine, even if she showed little promise of taking on the roles that were expected of Fillmore women. And thank God for dear little Gaines, so smart and the best bridge player of them all. They suspected it was Gaines's presence that made Catherine quite pleasant when she wasn't finding fault, which she continued to do rather more often than they thought necessary. It wasn't just her judgmental statements that bothered them, but her habit of purposely making remarks that were overheard by the person who was the object of her scorn. "That is the most obviously cheap wig I have ever seen," Catherine proclaimed in the dining salon the first night out, not flinching when the red-haired woman at the next table reacted as if she were looking for a knife to throw at her. On the plus side, Adelaide was thrilled that Catherine could and would play piano duets with her.

Within days of their arrival at the Hotel Meurice the growing conviviality between the sisters and Catherine was strained by a score or more Russian refugees who appeared each evening for almost a week. Claiming close blood ties to the Kropotkins, Adelaide and Louisa greeted the boisterous Russians effusively and entertained them royally with a seemingly inexhaustable supply of champagne, caviar and oysters. Naturally they insisted Catherine and dear little Gaines join them. At first Catherine found the grand dukes, duchesses and lesser nobles curiously intriguing, but she soon became disenchanted. They never stopped talking, carrying on heated conversations in a mélange of Russian, heavily accented French and English English. On rare occasions when someone realized Catherine might be feeling excluded because, unlike the Kropotkins, she did not speak Russian nor could she decipher their French or English, that individual would appoint himself or herself to translate while the rest of the company swore in loud voices that henceforth they would speak English exclusively and slowly so as to not be impolite. They did try for a moment or two but seldom longer because they could not contain their excitement at being reunited with the daughters of their beloved cousin, the still mourned Prince Nicholas Alexandrovich, who had married an American heiress, the beautiful Marianne of Fillmore. Reverting to shouting in assorted tongues, they wept copiously and laughed uproariously at shared memories.

As Catherine had insisted she would not make the trip without Gaines, Adelaide insisted Gaines must join them on their visits to the houses of fashion, and indeed be included in their party at lunch and dinner and whatever entertainment they undertook in the evening. Catherine balked at first, but she gave way after she and Gaines made a few quick and secret visits to dressmakers to acquire a wardrobe for Gaines's social appearances.

Returning one afternoon to the Meurice from lunch at a tiny café Adelaide had remembered from earlier visits, the women were hailed by the concierge who scuttled out from her nook to hand a message to the elder Kropotkin. Assuming it was a communication from one of the exiled Russians, Catherine continued upstairs. When Adelaide was alone in her bedroom, with shaking hands she opened the sealed envelope, removed a single sheet of paper and read handwriting she recognized at once. "My dear Adelaide, your cousin Igor informs me you are in Paris. I hesitate to scold you for not sending word to me in advance because when last I wrote to you at your home in Fillmore, my wife, my daughter and I were in Budapest where I was teaching at the conservatory. My family is still in Hungary, however, as of four months past, I am playing with the orchestra of the Paris Opera. Inasmuch as we are by good fortune in Paris at the same time, please, may I call upon you? I remember with great joy my summer at Oshatakea. A reply handed to the concierge will reach me promptly. With high hopes, your always and ever devoted, Franz Ausenbach."

Adelaide did not answer when Louisa tapped lightly on the door and asked if she was asleep. A short time later she slipped out and tipped the hall porter to take her written response down to the concierge. That evening at dinner, when Louisa asked about the message, Adelaide said, "It was from an old acquaintance." As fate would have it, she alone did not have a fitting the following morning. This time when the women returned to the hotel, it was Louisa to whom the concierge handed an envelope. She opened it at once while Catherine and Gaines waited. "Dear Louisa," Adelaide had written, "Franz Ausenbach, the gentleman cellist who was at Oshatakea one summer, and who is as you will recall a close friend of Cousin Igor, has invited me to join him on a drive through the Bois de Bologne. If I have not returned by lunchtime, please go on without me. I trust the fittings went well. You are both going to be belles of the ball in your new frocks."

"Who is Franz Ausenbach," Catherine asked.

"A lovely man, a cellist, Hungarian," Louisa replied, "with a drab wife and a frightful daughter, at least she was frightful as a little girl, I suppose she is quite grown up by now. Edgar hated her."

"Was he a close friend?"

"Edgar was Mother's King Charles spaniel."

"The Hungarian cellist, was he a close friend?"

"He's Austrian. What gave you the idea he's Hungarian?"

Another note was delivered late afternoon to Louisa's suite where she, Catherine and Gaines were having tea. "Dear Ones, Franz has asked me to dine with him at a little inn near St. Cloud. Please do not worry if I am late returning to the hotel. I embrace you all, Adelaide."

The corners of Catherine's mouth plunged earthward. "I cannot believe Adelaide is doing this. She is so particular about being properly dressed for every occasion; certainly she would not consider something she'd put on for a ride in the Bois de Bologne, or even for an alfresco lunch, suitable for a dinner party."

"She doesn't say dinner party," Louisa corrected her. "She says, 'Franz has invited me to dine with him at a little inn near St. Cloud.' 'Me' and 'him' means Adelaide and Franz, a deux."

Catherine rose from her chair. "We must contact your boorish cousin Igor to find out exactly who this Franz person is. Adelaide may be in danger."

"I know who he is, I've told you who he is," Louisa snapped. "He's quite handsome, with a little mustache, the sort they call a tickler."

"Louisa stop grinning; you look gaga."

"I am gaga. I believe my sister is having a tryst." Gaines made a movement to depart, but Louisa reached out and pressed her back into her chair, ignoring Catherine to address her remarks to the embarrassed maid. "I think Adelaide may have planned this months ago. It was she who suggested the trip, and made all the arrangements. Perhaps her reason wasn't to get Catherine away from Oshatakea at all or to buy clothes we don't need, but so she and Franz Ausenbach could see each other again." She clapped her hands to her face. "Oh, I do hope they are making love."

"Louisa," Catherine groaned. "You are a silly twittering old maid. I'm going to my room."

"Poor dear," Louisa chirped with genuine sympathy, watching Catherine depart.

She settled back in her chair and let her mind wander back to when she and Adelaide were young. She could hear Adelaide calling from the dacha, "Louisa, come back here." "I'll be back," Louisa waved gaily and ran on through the copse of birch trees whose silvery leaves quaked in a slight breeze. "I know where you are going," Adelaide cried. Louisa's tawny hair floated freely about her head; she had removed both the crown ribbon and the snood her mother insisted she wear. Her embroidered sheer linen dress blended with the gray-white bark of the trees.

Scott Shelburn was waiting at the entrance to the grotto where Seneca sachems had secreted tribal relics. "I thought you weren't coming." She ran into his arms. He held her tightly. His shirt was damp with perspiration, but she was aware only of the fragrance of new-mown hay. "Let me look at you." He stepped back so his eyes could caress her face and body. His hands followed his eyes, lightly touching the outline of her breasts, her waist, her hips. "You are so beautiful." His voice was husky.

"So are you."

"Men aren't beautiful."

"You are." She put her hands on either side of his head. "Your face is . . . I love your mouth." She touched it. His lips parted and he gently nipped her fingers. She brushed his lashes with the tips of her fingers.

"How much time do we have?"

"Enough."

"Can we take our clothes off? I want to see all of you." His voice was light but his hands on her hips were urgent. He led her into the grotto.

"I haven't a stitch on under this dress," Louisa said, pausing between him and the opening to the grotto where she knew he could see the contours of her body as light from the outside shone through the thin material.

"Louisa!" He sounded shocked, but responding to the revelation he reached out to bring her into his arms again.

"You first," she teased. "I want to see all of you first." She dodged past him, took his outstretched hand and pulled him along the narrow path around the small pool into which water dripped from an overhead ledge and then through a low tunnel into a smaller cave that opened high in the face of a sheer cliff overlooking the river. It was warm here with the sun shining in. "Now," she said. "Take everything off as I watch you. I lie awake at night trying to picture you undressed."

He did as she asked, unlacing and removing his boots, setting them to one side. Then he took off his faded bib overalls, blue denim work shirt and socks. Louisa covered her mouth to stifle a snicker when he stood before her in his summer-weight union suit, long-sleeved, legs covered to his ankles. "If you make fun of me, I'll go no further," he said sternly. She passed her hand over her face from bottom to top as children do to wipe away a grin and replace it with a serious mien. "That's better." As he undid the row of buttons that started just below his Adam's apple and ran down to his crotch, Louisa's expression turned to rapture. She moved closer to touch the curls of hair that covered his chest, but then backed away as he stepped out of his underclothes so she could view his nakedness.

His eagerness, plus the simple act of undressing in broad daylight in front of the one he loved, aroused him. He tried to hide his erection with cupped hands when he kicked the discarded union suit out from under his feet.

Louisa appeared not to notice. "Turn around please, slowly."

"Louisa, you are shameless."

"I am. Turn around, all the way around." He did as requested. "May I touch you?"

"You may."

"Anywhere?"

He hesitated. "Everywhere."

She put her hands on his shoulders, and let them fall once more onto the mat of chest hair. When she touched his nipples and they hardened, she smiled. "Just like mine when you touch me." He nodded. "Turn around again please." He did, no longer attempting to hide anything. "Your back is as beautiful as your face." She traced her palms across muscles developed by laboring in the fields. When he shivered, she moved her hands downward, cupping his buttocks as if she were holding the rarest of icons.

"Louisa, you are cruel. I can't stand here much longer."

"Turn around then." Before he was fully facing her she had pulled the linen dress over her head, standing as naked as he, her yearning nipples as hard and obvious as his erection. He put his calloused hands around her waist and lifted her into the air. She wrapped her legs around him and reaching down guided him into her. Their lovemaking was fervent, loud and long.

He was the first to stand up again after they had lain in each other's arms. Pulling Louisa to her feet, he said, "I have to tell you something. I've enlisted." Brushing bits of leaves and twigs off her back, he added, "I leave Saturday."

"Why? You don't have to go."

"I do, it's the only way for us. If I am just one of your grandfather's farmhands, I can never hope to marry you. Maybe, if I go to France and make something of myself, when I come back your mother and FP will consider me a fit suitor." He wrapped his arms around her, holding her close to his naked body.

"Marry me? You've not mentioned marriage."

"I told you often enough I love you."

"Ask me."

He drew her closer. "Louisa Kropotkin, will you marry me?"

Louisa thought she'd faint from not being able to breathe even though her heart was beating so fast it threatened to pound its way out of her chest. She wanted to shout her answer in a voice that would ring the news across the entire valley. "Yes Scott Shelburn, I will."

"That's settled." He kissed her, then releasing her he bent over to begin dressing. "They'll think I've already gone to France if I don't get back to work soon."

He left on Saturday, kissing Louisa just before he stepped onto the train, after he had said good-bye to his mother, father and younger brother. Scott was not killed, but he came back broken in body and spirit, his lungs so seared by mustard gas they would never heal. He would not let Louisa see him, not even when she cried outside his bedroom door and begged to be let in, nor would he talk to her on the telephone or reply to her letters. Unable to live as he was, the desolate young farmer laid down on the tracks in front of the 7:20 A.M. freight train, an act FP said was as heroic as anything he might have done in France.

Louisa's memory became selective after that. She chose to remember only good things, happy times; all else unhinged her.

Later, upstairs in her bed at the Meurice, she prayed for Adelaide to be as happy in a little inn near St. Cloud as she had once been in the grotto overlooking the river.

Chapter 8

SEVEN MONTHS AFTER THE WOMEN HAD RETURNED from Paris with trunks full of couturier finery, and twenty-two months after Farney and Catherine's wedding, FP escorted his son and daughter-in-law along the stone passage toward the chapel, stopping where swags of blue velvet covered a wide section of wall from ceiling to floor directly opposite a side entrance to the Galleried Library. There he made a ceremony of presenting a heavy iron key. "It does fit this door to your house, but we never lock doors at Oshatakea." Farney's expression reflected his father's amusement. Catherine, in the grip of muscle-cramping stress, knowing beyond doubt she would hate what she was about to be shown, could not force a smile. She had tried to lessen the torment by telling herself moving into this cursed wing that had taken forever to complete was preferable to living in guest rooms, regardless of how hideous FP's so-called wedding present might be, but even that did not help. She hadn't slept through the night for weeks, waking up hours before dawn to despair about what she would do, how she would handle the impossible situation.

FP grasped a gold-tasseled cord hanging to one side of the draperies and placed it in Catherine's hand. "Please," he said. Why all this idiotic folderol, she wanted to ask, but racked with fatigue and vexation she gave the cord a tug. The blue draperies separated to reveal a pair of massive cypress doors. FP explained, "They are approximately six hundred years old. I found them in the ruins of a Greek monastery. Because they are so heavy, you will not want to open and close them most of the time, nor did the monks, which is why they had a smaller door cut into the right panel." He pointed to the door within a door. "However, since this is a special occasion, let's pretend we have a trumpet fanfare and go all the way." Using both hands, he grasped the pair of iron rings, turned them and, pushing with a grand flourish, forced the pair of tall doors to swing open on huge fish-shaped hinges. Before them was a gallery with a series of long landings broken by sets of steps descending to a fourth and bottom level and a second set of doors. From the relative darkness of the Stone Corridor, Catherine's and Farney's eyes had to adjust to bright daylight flooding through a glass roof. "In the architects drawings, I refer to this as the Stepped Gallery, but you may want to call it something else," FP said. "I will leave you here to go on by yourselves, but before I do, a word about the paintings on the walls by American Impressionists, purchased from time to time because I could not resist their allure. I had no proper place to hang them until I built this gallery, so it is not just as a connector between your house and mine, but a home for these paintings. Mr. Vose advised us on light, both natural and artificial, and came out from Boston while you were in Paris, Catherine, to hang the pictures as he thought they should be arranged. They are part of your too long delayed wedding gift; rearrange them if you wish."

Awed by the length of the gallery and by what she could see of the collection of paintings, Catherine made no sound nor changed her expression of barely repressed concern. FP took her hands in his. "I understand these past months have been difficult for you. I regret everything took so long, but I wanted your new home to be as fine as I could make it. Now it is finished, but I meant what I said, if there is anything you do not like, change it to suit yourself." He leaned forward to give her a paternal kiss on the brow. Her reflex was automatic, an abrupt turn away, allowing his lips to touch only the side of her head. FP did not acknowledge the rebuff, beyond making a statement he might not have otherwise made. "I will never enter this wing, Catherine, unless I am invited. Whether or not you choose to use the key, your privacy in your house will be respected."

Farney's gut was churning. He wanted to slap Catherine for her attitude and gracelessness in the face of his father's generosity. This response to a simple gesture of affection was an insult. He felt he should hug his father, hold him to ease FP's obvious hurt, but conflicting emotions made him slow to either physically comfort FP or tell him there was no need for formality; he would be welcome in their house anytime he wanted to visit. Before he could speak, Catherine interjected, "Thank you." It was apparent to her, from his remark, that FP had known she was unhappy about not having privacy at Oshatakea. The sound of her voice released Farney from momentary paralysis. Embattled and embarrassed, he embraced his father.

Catherine walked away from them, stepping through the wide portal onto the first of four blue and rose Persian rugs FP had commissioned for the landings. The Stepped Gallery was of sufficient width to allow proper viewing of the paintings, and they were breathtaking. Years of listening to Aunt Belle Gardner talking about how to appreciate art made Catherine aware of that. This is much more than a passageway, she thought, as she moved toward intricately carved doors at the far end opening into a large hall with a richly detailed staircase going up to second and third floors. Opposite the stairs was a third pair of doors. When she opened these she gave voice to enthusiastic approval for the first time. "He's given us our own front door," she cried. Not having to cross Oshatakea's Great Hall to enter or leave her house pleased her more than anything else he could have done.

Off the hall to the right was a drawing room that gave her pause because it was a duplicate of the music room from Mount Vernon Street, the only room in the Beacon Hill house that she missed. In the corner between two windows was her own piano, the one on which she had practiced long hours to please the young man from the conservatory who was her teacher. She sat down on the bench where they had sat, touching the ivory and ebony keys, recalling her dreams of one day becoming a concert pianist. A tall case clock with a scrolled bonnet ticked majestically against the wall. It was the Thorndyke clock from Mount Vernon Street, she could tell by the slight dent in the left brass finial, a dent she had caused when she threw a jade box at Teddy. For this crime she'd been locked in her room, a small price to pay for attempted murder. How had FP persuaded her mother to part with the family heirloom? She could not tell if the pair of Adams mantles on the long outer wall were the originals from Boston or clever copies. Nor did she know about the Queen Anne highboy, the Georgian secretary and other furnishings — round Pembroke tables, high-backed chairs, sofas and slipper seats from later periods. Surely her mother had not permitted FP to strip the music room. Everything here looked as if it had always been where it presently sat, accumulated by generations, as had the furniture in her family, but whereas on Mount Vernon Street the room was comfortable but drab, FP's touch made it resplendent, warmer than it had ever felt when it was her refuge. If it was her family furniture, and she was sure it was, FP had had everything refurbished. "Your father is a genius," Catherine said, responding to Farney's "This is nice," as he walked into the room.

The morning room across the hall was cheerful and bright as a morning room should be, with chintz-covered sofas and chairs. By an east window was a lady's tambour desk meant for writing thank-you notes and invitations, which made Catherine wonder if she was to have a staff of her own or would she use the Oshatakea staff under Mrs. Blackburn. If she had her own, this is where she would meet with the servant in charge who would pass on her instructions. "Very English," she said about the room itself. And so was the library behind, across a narrow passageway. Paneled in aged pickled oak, FP had hung George Stubbs horse paintings in there and upholstered the furniture in soft leathers to please Farney.

Not English at all was what lay beyond the library and the morning room, at the end of that narrow passageway — a four-story atrium with three walls of apricot-tinted stucco in which clusters of tiles were embedded, their rich colors muted by centuries in the sun. Lacy wrought-iron balconies underlined each window on the upper levels, and stairs curled around a small pool up to a landing. All this was from a village square FP had come upon north of Odemira, Portugal. Water dripped from a lavabo into the pool. Passionflower vines trailed from the balconies, their deep purple blossoms a contrast to the apricot walls. Lemon and orange trees bloomed in terra-cotta tubs that ringed the perimeter of the red tiled floor, scenting the air with fragrance. The fourth wall and the sloping roof were glass, bringing the sky and views of lawns and gardens, meadows and forest into the courtyard. Two places had been set on a round glass-topped table in the center of the room. "He is an amazing man," Catherine said quietly. Had he read her mind, or had she been more transparent than she realized? "This," she proclaimed, "is where we will breakfast."

At the top of the curved iron staircases the Portuguese courtyard was extended into a conservatory–cum–sitting room with white bamboo and rattan furniture and grass cloth carpeting. Separate suites for Catherine and Farney on the second floor were connected by a private passage in the guise of a balcony over the front of the main hall. Each contained an enormous bedroom, a sitting room almost as large, a wardrobe dressing room and a bathroom, hers with a step-down marble tub of a dimension Catherine's Boston breeding made her view as indecent. In Farney's bathroom there was no tub but a green marble shower stall the size of a small room with myriad nozzles to spray water from above and three sides. Shades of mauve and silver gray predominated in Catherine's suite, another result of FP's research. These were the colors Catherine had selected for her bedroom at home the one time she was given a choice.

On the top floor FP had created a cozy apartment for Gaines, an elaborate nursery suite and two attractive guest rooms. Catherine and Farney scowled when they saw the nursery suite. He said, "Dad doesn't forget a thing."

She said, "Your father works wonders, but there are some things even he cannot bring about."

Instead of hating the house FP had built for them, and using that as an excuse to walk away from a hopeless marriage and return to Boston, which she had planned to do, Catherine was so pleased with what she found she did not want to change a thing. Her attitude toward her father-in-law changed. She recognized the trouble he had taken to provide what he thought would make her happy, the breakfast table in the courtyard for instance, her favorite colors, her piano. She also realized his genius as a designer and decorator. Soft ashen greens used with the lovely Aubusson rug turned the morning room into a garden when the sun's rays were refracted through the chandelier's Waterford prisms. She was not a morning room person, but she found herself lingering there on her way to breakfast in the courtyard, and afterward. In the stair hall vibrant wallpaper with a powerful almost military pattern inspired one to walk with shoulders back, head held high to matching the dignity and importance of the space.

Though she rarely exchanged letters with her mother, she was moved to send a note to Mount Vernon Street. "What he has done is too splendid to describe. Each room as you enter it is more sublime than the one you are leaving. The ultimate is the Portuguese Courtyard, which rivals Aunt Belle's. Ours may not have an ancient Roman floor, but it is no less distinctive. When FP asked if we would care to call our new house the Portuguese Wing, we agreed at once, though it is indeed a quite separate house and not a wing at all. I have been studying the paintings in the connecting gallery, and reading about the artists represented—Cassatt, Chase, Hassam, Twachtman, Weir. We have two by Prendergast, which are magnificent. I don't respond as favorably to Glackens, but have grown quite fond of Sloan." Her uncharacteristic effusiveness did not extend to inviting her mother to visit, nor did she put in her letter that for the first time in her entire life she felt comfortable and at ease in her own home.

In the spirit of her friendlier attitude toward FP, she made the effort to join him several mornings a week for a pre-breakfast swim, and was amused to observe his frown of frustration when she did because it meant he must go into the bathhouse and put on a bathing suit. She swam only a few laps, then left him to his own devices. Reduced animosity did not weaken her vow to breakfast in the Portuguese courtyard. Attempting to placate Catherine and prolong her improved disposition, Farney rearranged his own morning routine to rise at first light and go to the stable so he could get in at least an hour on horseback prior to appearing in the courtyard to eat with his wife at 7:30 A.M. He was not agreeable, however, to her skimpy menu of orange juice, toast, bitter marmalade, bacon, eggs and coffee. After a testy discussion, she relented and allowed to be laid on in the courtyard a reduced version of the extensive buffet FP had spread out in his breakfast room. Trying not to make a misstep that would shatter Catherine's gentler mood, he did not tell her Pearl preferred earlier rides because it meant she was back in the office she shared with her aunt, Mrs. Blackburn, to review staff instructions before maids and footmen finished their meal in the servants' hall and started the day's work.

As Farney and Catherine sat at the table reading yesterday's Boston and New York newspapers that had arrived in Fillmore on the midnight train, they presented a picture of reasonably contented domesticity. If both tried, they could converse without rancor, though they did not always do so. Remaining silent was easier for him than for her. She found it impossible to be unaware of what she saw as his faults. Attempting not to comment required monumental effort and built up bile. To vent her spleen she substituted negative comments about him with complaints about Isabelle Chapman. "I want to be sick when I think of her and your father as, as whatever they are to each other."

"They are friends."

"She's his concubine."

"Catherine, my father is eighty-five."

"He is now, but they've been playing house for years. What other reason would he have for giving her that tourist's postcard love nest? She brags he opened the warehouses and turned her loose to take anything she wanted. He's never let me inside and I'm his daughter-in-law."

"That's what makes you itch about Isabelle, isn't it? Not the possibility she and Dad may have slept together." He snapped his newspaper. "I'll remind him you want a guided tour. Let's see if that will make you forget this other nonsense."

Farney did speak to his father who, now that he wasn't worried about Catherine despoiling his work of art before it was finished, immediately invited her to accompany him to the storehouses, where she was overwhelmed by what she saw. Their contents exceeded expectations, but when FP asked if there was anything she wanted taken up to the Portuguese Wing, after long consideration she declined, telling him, and meaning it, she did not want to add a single piece, nor take one away. She also didn't want to close the door to future possibility. "May I take a rain check."

"Don't be coy Catherine. When you decide you want something here, ask. The items are catalogued in the architects' offices, you may look at them any time."

Her tour of the warehouses provided material for weeks of breakfast-table monologues. Giving detailed descriptions of what she had seen, she asked Farney's opinion whether or not she should request objects she found especially intriguing then didn't wait for his response. There was a six-panel lacquered screen she could not get out of her mind. She brought it up several times before Farney interrupted to suggest she decide where she would put it before making the request because his father would want to know. When there was nothing more to discuss about the warehouses, they fell back to silently reading the newspapers.

Catherine read only Boston papers, confining her perusal to reviews of music, dance, theater and films. Details of performances at the Opera House, Symphony Hall, the Colonial, Majestic, Wilbur, Schubert and other theaters made her regret she hadn't been present. "We should have a house in Boston so we could be there part of the time and not miss everything that's going on." She scanned the Society pages. "For laughs," she said. She had never understood why people take themselves so seriously. Who cares what the Cummings girls wore to the opening of the flower show, or who was with whom and in what at the Tosca gala? She had hated having her appearances commented upon because she was sure columnists yawned as they wrote, "Miss Catherine Dudley accompanied her mother." She never wore anything worthy of note, and made loud snide remarks about those who had killed themselves to outdress everybody else. Public events were bad enough, but formal private affairs were worse. "The only parties I ever truly enjoyed were Aunt Belle's," she said one morning apropos of nothing.

"I beg your pardon."

"What?"

"You said something about a party?"

"Did I? I have taken leave of my senses if I gave you the idea I was talking about giving a party."

"Are you?"

"No!" She shook her head as the footman offered her more coffee. "Well, maybe. No. Yes, I am going to have a party. Why not? A dinner party."

He folded his newspaper. "I love parties."

"Relax Farney, it won't be an Oshatakea party with hordes of people. I will invite a few guests and have one or two top-drawer artists to entertain us, perhaps an orchestra for dancing."

"Artists doing what?"

"Who doing what?" She was trying to think. This party idea had just come to her; she was talking off the top of her head and he kept interrupting her.

"You said, 'one or two top-drawer artists to entertain us.' I'm asking, doing what?"

"Singing, playing instruments, juggling, whatever—I haven't decided yet."

"Singing, juggling, dancing during dinner?"

"Why not? That's preferable to the oompah bands and fiddlers your father brings in so the locals can do cute country dances, the Virginia reel for God's sake, before they line up like sweating pigs at troughs for mountains of food."

"Pigs don't sweat, and they don't line up. Pigs push."

"Precisely."

"What you call cute country dances are quite complex. We're rather proud here of our ability to do old English patterns properly and with considerable grace. The Virginia reel is strictly for fun, but we work at the others. You might enjoy dancing them if you tried. As for the musicians Dad brings in for valley parties, they are amateurs, but that doesn't mean they are without talent or skill. Dad hired period professionals years ago to teach the musicians what to play and the rest of us how to do the dances. Stop looking down your nose."

Catherine was not listening. "We will have a superb dinner, no tubs of lentils or Belgian stew, something exquisite. I don't know what, I never think about food." Brought up in a family that eschewed anything smacking of fancy and whose guests usually left the Dudleys' spartan table unsated, she had no gustatory experience until Adelaide and Louisa introduced her to choice restaurants in Paris. "I will need help planning a menu." Remembering only the big all-inclusive valley parties FP gave while forgetting his elaborate house parties, she continued developing a plan for oneupsmanship. "Our guests will engage in intelligent conversation about what is going on in the real world. There will be no groaning about lack of rain. I haven't a Henry James or Henry Adams to bring in as Aunt Belle did, but we'll manage nicely on our own." She paused to look directly at her husband with a cold eye. "Farney, I'll kill you if you so much as breathe the word *horse* at my dinner table." Returning to her daydream, she said, "A string quartet will be on the landing." She glanced up where the iron staircases met. "They will be playing when we come into the courtyard after drinks in the music room, and between the first and second, no, the second and third courses, yes, that's a better time, between second and third courses they will play a waltz or a foxtrot that we will find irresistible. We will all get up from the table and dance."

"Isn't it a comedown from an orchestra for dancing to a string quartet? I didn't think bringing in an orchestra sounded like you. Most Boston parties I've been to are lucky to have somebody's dried-up daughter strumming a harp." Losing interest, he went back to his newspaper.

Dismissing his derision about Boston parties, Catherine continued, "There were no strumming harps at Aunt Belle's suppers. When she felt things needed pepping up, she didn't dance, she dunked herself in the Roman bath." She raised an eyebrow as she looked toward the pool beneath the dripping lavabo. "Which I may do if I become overheated."

Farney put down the paper. He had never seen Catherine in a playful mood.

All he could think to say was, "In your dinner dress?"

"Why not? Better to ruin a dinner dress than come naked to the table as your father does."

"Only at breakfast. He wears a robe—he just forgets to close it."

Catherine wasn't listening. She got up. "This magnificent, glorious space"—she raised her arms—"is made for a party. It's a stage set awaiting an overture to, to, to *Carmen. Carmen!* That's it! The musicians will play *Carmen's* entrance, as we are relaxing at table after dinner, and I, quite spur of the moment mind you, will invite the old tart to sing." Her voice became velvety soft and seductive. "Isabelle, surely you must have sung *Carmen*. Won't you please sing an aria for us now? You can enter at the top of the stairs and slowly descend to vamp us." Catherine laughed, a deep dark-edged bark of a laugh. "We'll see if Isabelle Chapman is everything she claims to be. If she wears that fender on her fat front she'll be so top heavy she may roll down the stairs and land in a heap at our feet." Catherine's voice changed again, this time to the sugary syrup of solicitude. "Oh Isabelle, did you hurt yourself?" Another bark of laughter followed.

Fascinated and repelled by Catherine's performance, Farney spoke up. "I'm surprised you plan to invite Isabelle, knowing how much you hate her, but I would insist she be here if you have the family. Regardless of the relationship she has or does not have with my dad, Isabelle is part of our family. I understand you have an ulterior and rather nasty motive for including her, but be prepared, Catherine, she may surprise you."

"I do hope so." Catherine looked at her husband as if she felt sorry for him. "No I don't. I'll not be surprised. Isabelle will sound as overblown as she looks, and that won't spoil a thing. I'll be generous, if hypocritical, with my applause. She will know exactly what I'm thinking. The success of this dinner party could accomplish a multitude of things. It may prove to your father that I am more than ready to be chatelaine of Oshatakea. And," she added with a broad smile that was quite unlike her, "I may show up balloon-breasted Isabelle at the same time."

"Can't we be vulgar when we want to be? I'm confused, I thought you were going to hire singers, top-drawer artists, to entertain us."

She didn't answer; she was plotting a course as she walked around the room. "My first party in my own house will be the best party Oshatakea has ever seen. Your family thinks me a cold roast prig, but when I'm through they will think differently. The great FP Fillmore II isn't the only person on this hill with imagination. Prepare yourself husband. My debut as hostess in the Portuguese Courtyard will change forever the way things are done in the cavernous castle to which we are attached."

Farney wondered if she was losing control. He had been optimistic about her recent high spirits, but now he saw that her mood was swiftly shifting from delightful to demonic.

Chapter 9

PLANNING CONSUMED CATHERINE. SHE GAVE UP ANY semblance of socializing with Adelaide and Louisa, dropping as if it never existed the casual and cordial relationship developed during their Parisian shopping spree, a relationship that had been threatened by Catherine's pique over Adelaide's late-night escapade, whatever it was, dinner or more than dinner with some Hungarian. Adelaide never offered an explanation. Congeniality was revived when the Kropotkin sisters shared Catherine's enthusiasm for the Portuguese Wing. They came regularly for tea, a ritual Catherine had said was a waste of time, and bridge on Thursday afternoons, a game she still found dull but was willing to endure because Adelaide and Louisa so enjoyed being in her beautiful new house. She had even acquiesced to their suggestion that Gaines be asked to make a fourth, a breaching of barriers Catherine thought permissible only when abroad. The alternative was to invite Isabelle, which forced Catherine to give the nod to Gaines. Now with a party on her mind, she was too busy for teas and afternoons of bridge.

She set up a command post in her upstairs sitting room, moving a drop-leaf table from behind a sofa that faced the fireplace to a window overlooking the courtyard and opening both leaves to provide a large flat surface on which to stack folders containing scribbled notes on slips of paper from a pad she kept by her bed and pages of more detailed descriptions she developed later. There were folders for hors d'oeuvres, entrées, desserts, flowers, decorations, and entertainment, and two marked "music," the first with "dance" in parenthesis, the second with "background." Most mornings she spent at her table desk writing on lined yellow pads, scratching out but never discarding in case she might want to reconsider ideas that at the moment she was putting aside. Catherine did not hold meetings in the morning room with a head of staff as she had envisioned, because other than Gaines she had no separate household in the Portuguese Wing. Oshatakea maids and footmen performed all necessary services for her. Nor were there menus to approve after she had agreed Farney's breakfast buffet in the courtyard could duplicate his father's in the distant breakfast room, and the kitchen knew her own rigid requirements for breakfast. Lunches and dinners continued to be taken with FP and his guests.

Never having paid much attention to how the components of a meal came together, she would need help from Mrs. Fuller, Oshatakea's head cook, in planning food for her dinner party. Without giving thought to the politics of going through channels, such as asking Mrs. Blackburn to speak to the cook, Catherine simply had Gaines ring the main kitchen and tell Mrs. Fuller she wished to see her upstairs at once.

"I can't come now," Mrs. Fuller shouted into the telephone. "I'm in the middle of doing lunch."

"When would be convenient for you?" Gaines asked.

"*Convenient* for her?" Catherine snapped.

"I go to my room for a nap as soon as lunch is served, and I don't come down again till it's time to start dinner. What does she want?" Mrs. Fuller sounded querulous. She had the telephone so close to her mouth her voice was blasting into Gaines ear at the other end. Gaines held the instrument away from the side of her head, thus

Catherine heard the cook's every word as well as her labored breathing.

"Hand me that telephone. Mrs. Fuller, this is Mrs. Fillmore speaking. I will see you in my suite at two o'clock sharp." She handed the phone back to Gaines who replaced it in its cradle.

Mrs. Fuller had satisfied FP for many years with bountiful meals of food prepared from top-quality fresh ingredients, succeeding her mother and her mother's mother, who had in their turns presided over Oshatakea kitchens. She knew what FP liked and he did not interfere with what she cooked. Mrs. Fuller had seen Farney's wife only once, on the day Catherine came home from her husbandless honeymoon, and she wasn't overly impressed. She thought the new Mrs. Fillmore was pale and plain, not near as pretty as Pearl who everybody wanted Farney to marry. As for going to what Mrs. Fillmore called her "suite," Mrs. Fuller normally ventured into the front of the house only to see the decorations at Christmas and then to attend the staff party a week or so later. FP came down to her kitchen now and then to say hello, but it was Mrs. Blackburn who relayed messages about how many to expect for meals. She wasn't sure she liked being told to be in some suite at two o'clock sharp. Not that Mrs. Fuller was surprised by Catherine's call; she'd heard about her highfalutin' ways. Anybody who'd had anything to do with her said Farney's wife thought she was better'n everybody else because she came from Boston. Gaines never said that about the lady, of course, Gaines never spoke ill 'bout anybody, Gaines came from England but she fit into Oshatakea easy as an old shoe. Farney's missus would never fit. Too bad she didn't learn some manners from her maid.

Led by a footman up back stairs and through long service passages, Mrs. Fuller knocked on Catherine's door a few minutes before two o'clock. It was opened by Gaines who greeted her with a friendly smile. Before she walked in, the portly cook, puffing from the unaccustomed trek, turned to the trim young footman.

"Dale, don't you budge. Set yourself on that chair over there and wait for me. If you was to leave I'd never find my way back." She spied Catherine sitting at a table by the window, a second chair drawn up opposite her. Other than removing her apron and quickly passing one of the combs she used to secure a bun on the back of her head through her hair, Mrs. Fuller had made no preparation for this interview. "Pretty room," she said, attempting to calm herself; she had high blood pressure and she was sure this encounter was sending it higher. "But all rooms are pretty at Oshatakea. I can't stay long. I get down to the kitchen at four-thirty in the morning, so I'm tuckered out this time of day. If I don't get a decent lie down nobody'll get dinner."

Catherine's eyes surveyed the elderly woman, who carefully lowered herself into the indicated chair, her knuckles bulging from arthritis, a red scar from a recent nasty burn on one wrist, an overabundance of wrinkled flesh draped on a large frame. She was an icon of exhaustion, not just from being on her feet since 4:30 that morning but from too many years of too long days standing over a hot stove. It was readily apparent to Catherine that Mrs. Fuller was not up to providing what she needed to plan her dinner party. She was looking beyond the experience of a competent cook, seeking serious creative support in designing a memorable meal based on nebulous fantasies. "I won't keep you," Catherine said. "Go lie down."

Mrs. Fuller's jaw dropped. She swiped the back of a clawed hand across her lower lip. "Now that I'm here I can spare a minute or two."

Catherine closed her eyes and dismissed her with a wave. Acute disappointment was bringing on a throbbing headache.

"Well, I never." Mrs. Fuller heaved herself to her swollen feet. At the door she hissed, "What was that all about?" Gaines pretended she had not heard.

"Impossible!" Catherine cried before the door closed behind the cook's broad posterior. "I can't do it if I have to work with people like that."

"What is it you want to do?" Gaines asked.

Catherine glowered. "How can I tell you when I don't know myself?" She got up from her chair. "I've gone to dinner parties all my life and hated most of them, except for a few at Fenway Court, but I've never given one. I have in mind making the Portuguese Courtyard more beautiful than it already is, with flowers and candles, hundreds of candles. In this flickering setting I want sumptuous food impeccably served, food to make everybody exclaim, 'This tastes as fabulous as it looks,' while music to match the perfection of what we are eating wraps itself around us." Catherine paused. Gaines detected glistening moisture gathering in her eyes. "I can't do it by myself Gaines, I just plain damn it to hell do not know how. I need help. The only thing I can do is select music— but how do I find musicians to play what I want?" Her resigned sigh of self-pity was long and deep. She threw up her hands. "I'll forget the whole thing. It was spur of the moment idiocy."

Catherine had been so involved, so positive in her outlook during the early stages of planning her party, that Gaines dreaded having her fall back into the constant fault finding, impossible to please, mean-dispositioned person that preceded this feverish activity. "It is not idiocy, but it is a challenge." She grappled for a solution to keep Catherine occupied and on track. "Can you contact the people who planned the Fenway Court dinner parties?"

"No. I want my party to be better than parties were at Fenway Court—not more highbrow, the intellectual level of Aunt Belle's dinners would be impossible to achieve way out here, but aside from that I want to astound my guests, top anything they have experienced, not to impress, I couldn't care less about impressing them, but I want to prove a point—and in the process, purely for my own amusement, create a bit of mischief. The whole thing from start to finish has to appear easy for me, as if it were something I do every day, nothing special, as natural as it is for a female rider I will not name to take a horse over a hedge."

Gaines had listened for hours to Catherine ranting about Farney's admiration for Pearl's horsemanship; it was not necessary to explain how they had made the transition from planning a party to jumping a hedge. Her next thought was suggesting Catherine contact Lady Astor, whose parties had set Britain agog, but she didn't voice that idea knowing Lady Astor was still "ripped," as the lady put it, with Catherine for not returning a Cliveden maid, herself, who had been loaned, not given. To fill an awkward silence Gaines offered a sop. "If you want everything to be the tops, go to the top for help."

Instead of Gaines's unsolicited advice turning Catherine's sulk into a snarl, she smiled. Lights were turned on to dispel darkness. "Brilliant! The Ritz Carleton dining room is fast becoming the best in Boston. I'll consult the Ritz chef about a menu. And while we are there, I'll talk to the concertmaster of the BSO about music and musicians. Somewhere in Boston we will find an extraordinary floral designer. On Charles Street there are a pair of women who do unusual things. Pack your bag Gaines, we're headed for the hub."

The journey was delayed long enough to have enlarged and tinted photographs of the Portuguese Courtyard made, essential if the Boston advisers were to have a sense of where this unique party would be held. She filled time overseeing the preparation of hand-lettered invitations to Mr. Farnsworth Phillips Fillmore II, Miss Adelaide Helena Kropotkin, Miss Louisa Marianne Kropotkin and Miss Isabelle Anna Chapman, informing them, that the honor of their presence was requested by Mr. and Mrs. Farnsworth Phillips Fillmore III at a formal dinner dance in the Portuguese Wing at seven o'clock on the evening of Tuesday, July 3l, 1931. "Respondez s'il vous plais." Dale Morris, Mrs. Fuller's footman guide, was bewildered by Catherine's insistence he wear white gloves when he delivered the invitations. It could have been worse; she had a momentary fancy to make him wear a powdered wig over his dark brown hair.

FP complimented Dale on the gravitas of his demeanor when the youth handed him the envelope with a deep bow as Catherine had instructed. Playing along with his daughter-in-law's grandiloquence, FP told Dale his reply would be forthcoming, and then had his affirmative response illuminated as well as hand lettered by a member of the academy art department. The Kropotkins sent separate notes on stationery embossed with their father's princely coat of arms, saying they were delighted to accept the gracious invitation.

Isabelle Chapman, as bewildered as a dragon awakened from winter slumber, opened the outside door on the bottom level of her villa. "Why are you knocking down here?"

"Mrs. Fillmore told me to deliver this to your front door."

"Nobody for Christ's sake uses my front door. What's the matter with your hands, are they covered with poison ivy or something?"

"No ma'am. Mrs. Fillmore made me wear white gloves to deliver these envelopes."

Isabelle harrumphed. "You're lucky she didn't force you into pink satin knickers." She eyed the embarrassed young man. "You'd probably look pretty good in satin knee pants." Dale made no reply. "Well come in, come in, don't stand there gazing at me like a lovesick gazelle. Have I ever told you your opalescent green eyes make my knees go weak?"

"Yes ma'am."

"I have? And still you make me trudge down two flights of stairs to open a door? Hand me the envelope before I attack and then be off." Dale didn't budge. "Doesn't my threat frighten you, make you the least bit nervous?"

"No ma'am. You are always teasing me."

"Teasing? You think I'm teasing? If I were to charge I'd flatten you like a Clydesdale thundering through a pea patch." Dale tried to not laugh, but a wide grin showed his teeth. "My God, boy, your teeth are better than your eyes."

"Mrs. Fillmore asked me to return with replies. So far, nobody has given me a reply. I hope you will be the first. I'll wait."

"How can I reply if I haven't read the damn thing yet? And I can't read it here because my glasses are upstairs somewhere."

"I could read it for you."

"No you couldn't, and you are not to come upstairs. I'll not have people whispering about callow youths following me around." She winked at Dale. "How am I to retain my aura of intrigue if you see me wearing bottle bottoms on my nose? Sit on that chair Gorgeous Green Eyes, I'll yell down when I have something to say." Isabelle went up the stairs, found her glasses, opened the envelope, read the invitation, blew her nose and picked up the telephone. "Find FP for me," she ordered when the operator asked who she wanted. When FP answered, she demanded, "What's this with white gloves on Dale Morris? The poor kid was beet red from embarrassment. And the too, too laadeedaa invitation! Who is Catherine pretending to be?" After FP told her to join in the spirit of the game, Isabelle pulled out a sheet of watermarked stationery imported from London and wrote, "Miss Isabelle Anna Chapman thanks Mr. and Mrs. Farnsworth Phillips Fillmore III for their invitation to dine on July 31, 1931, and accepts with pleasure." Isabelle was tempted to sign it Lucille LaFleur, Lady in Waiting to Miss Chapman, but she didn't. Nor did she spit on the flap of the envelope, as she was also tempted to do, instead dampening the sealing edge with her stamp sponge.

Invitations delivered and replies received but photographs still not ready, Catherine turned her attention to what she would wear for the party. In Paris, she had purchased dinner dresses to make the trip worthwhile; now she was having a difficult time deciding which one might do. "None are strong enough," she complained to a fatigued Gaines who had taken them out, one by one, and held them up. Ordinarily Catherine gave little thought to what she wore, to any event anywhere, including her wedding. If her mother had not insisted Catherine be in white, she'd have never submitted to the bother of acquiring a dress for the farce of a ceremony that took all of five minutes. Dudley women, and most collateral relatives, were content to clad themselves in quality materials tailored along simple lines. It had been the practice for generations to find a cut and style that suited and have "frocks" duplicated in several fabrics. That was it. Period. The same was true of hats—black or navy blue, straw or felt, all purchased from R. H. Stearns. No time wasted; no worry about what was "in fashion." Fashionable clothing rarely provided sufficient warmth for women who inhabited large houses heated only to the point of "taking the chill off" and fashion was not a requirement if one had proper background and breeding. Following fashion was frowned upon. Innate, uncompromised dignity demanded understated steadiness in demeanor and dress. For those who subscribed to this dictum, and that included Catherine Dudley Fillmore, brown wren was preferable to Baltimore oriole. But not for this event. Catherine knew what she chose to wear at her dinner dance would be integral to the effect she hoped to achieve.

"What about this?" Gaines asked bringing out an evening dress unlike all others hanging on padded satin hangers in the large wardrobe closets. Lustrous burgundy silk gauze with a deep neckline softened by rolls of delicate fabric draped from the shoulders, the dress would reveal more cleavage than Catherine was comfortable showing. Louisa had teased Catherine into trying it on during a long morning in Paris when they were restlessly waiting for Adelaide who was in another room undergoing a complex fitting. Two narrow panels in front with oriental designs embroidered in gold thread floated from the waist to the floor. A similar but longer and wider panel attached at the neckline in back trailed down into a short train. In the couturier's showroom, Catherine had strutted and slowly rotated in the highly exaggerated manner of French models, striking poses that made Louisa laugh until she cried, much to the chagrin of the saleswoman, who disapproved of these rich Americans making fun of her master's creation. It was the saleswoman's superior manner, and her unspoken implication the dress was too good for this client, that made Catherine say, "I'll take it."

"You will never wear it," Louisa protested, wiping her eyes.

"This minion needs to be put in her place, and I like the color. It reminds me of raspberry sorbet."

"There must be a less frivolous way to erase a French smirk."

That was then. Now, this gauzy confection might be just what she needed for her premier party. With Gaines's help she donned the dress and stepped into her mirrored alcove. "Ludicrous," she muttered. Her shoulders slumped. "I feel naked. No sleeves and next to nothing to cover my front." She tried pulling up the neckline to hide her bra but there was nothing to pull. She placed her right hand over the deep cleavage, but she could hardly maintain that pose throughout an entire evening. The answer would be to draw the rolls of silk close together and secure them with a brooch. She hoped the material would hold if it were pulled taut. That wasn't the only problem. Her not ordinarily evident body contours were outlined when tightly encased. Full rounded hips below a svelte waist topped by breasts that combined to form an even more ample curve than the one below brought forth the exclamation: "This dress turns me into Mae West."

"Reubens," Gaines countered.

"Whichever, without strong support from an undergarment I do not now possess, flimsy silk is not going to contain me. My breasts will plop into the soup."

"I will bind you," Gaines said quietly.

"Bind me? Wrap me up like a mummy?"

PHOTOGRAPHS OF THE PORTUGUESE COURTYARD READY at last, Catherine and Gaines traveled to Boston in the Jefferson.

On the way Catherine told Gaines she was to sit in on all meetings. "And please feel free to make suggestions. You are the only one who understands what I'm trying to do. I value your ideas." Unsure what Catherine had in mind other than showing off to Farney's family and causing Isabelle Chapman embarrassment, Gaines agreed to add whatever she could to the discussions.

Catherine's mother was not invited to sit in, or to make suggestions, but she did both when Catherine received the executive chef of the Ritz Carleton and his sous-chef in the library of the Mount Vernon Street house. Mrs. Dudley had not forgiven her daughter for never once inviting her to visit Oshatakea after she had been persuaded by FP to part with furniture that had always been in her Mount Vernon Street music room. FP paying her more than the pieces were worth did not lessen her ire. The matriarch strode purposefully into the library minutes after everyone was seated. The men from the Ritz jumped to their feet. Overlooking the second in command, Catherine's mother skewered the executive chef with a disdainful eye." I am Mrs. Edward Ropes Dudley."

The chef bowed his head in acknowledgment and gave a small click of his heels. He would have kissed her hand had it been extended to him. "I am Etienne d'Auguste."

"I did not invite you to this meeting," Catherine interrupted the ceremony.

"I don't need an invitation to my own library." Mrs. Dudley sat down. Noticing Gaines about to resume her seat across the room, she asked, "Is her presence necessary?"

Catherine did not give her the satisfaction of a reply. "Chef d'Auguste, I want an extravagant dinner, comprised of extraordinary dishes. I expect compatibility but I also want surprise."

"But of course Madame," d'Auguste replied.

"Proceed Monsieur."

He began with lengthy descriptions of hors d'oeuvres: Roties de Homard Amandine, Fois Gras en Brioche, Canapes Micheline,

Turkish Beurrechs and three or four others. "All of them, I want all of them," Catherine said. Mrs. Dudley raised her eyebrows. Catherine closed the folder that contained her own thoughts on what might be served with cocktails without making a single suggestion.

D'Auguste next offered explicit details of two "superb" soups: a Puree of Pheasant à la Royale and Consommé Cyrano with Quenelles de Brochet. Catherine chose the duck consommé. There was disagreement over the fish course. The chef preferred oyster-stuffed smelt, a dish he had invented and named after himself. It would be served hot. Catherine said she wanted something cold, a mousse perhaps. He said the smelt dish was most unusual and "absolutely delicious." He kissed the tips of his fingers. "Stuffed or not, a smelt is a smelt," she said. His mustache twitched. "I can give you a Salmon Mousse en Bellevue, which is beautiful, but I thought you wanted surprise."

"There will be surprises, we are far from finished."

Alerted by Madame's tone that he may have offended her, and not wanting to do anything that would deter acceptance and delay payment of the substantial fee he planned to charge for this personal service, he hastily complimented her highly unusual awareness of the importance of varying textures and temperatures to sharpen the palate. "It is also obvious Madame knows about the use of colors on a plate." She accepted his praise but would not let him talk her into either Soufflé aux Pommes de Terre or Brandied Sweet Potato Soufflé, pouncing instead on Asparagus à la Polonaise and Truffles au Vin Blanc. She offended him when she rejected two veal offerings: Veau à la Alsacienne and Noix de Veau à la Conte. He bridled and sniffed, but she held firm.

"I want game."

"Stuff and nonsense," Mrs. Dudley cried. "A small roast beef and a pan of Yorkshire pudding are quite enough for family."

D'Auguste looked from Mrs. Fillmore's grimace to Mrs.

Dudley's glower. He was working for Mrs. Fillmore. "Ah, Madame should have said so. Game it will be. I recommend a haunch of venison seasoned with sprigs of lavender discreetly placed in numerous spots throughout the muscle and then slowly roasted on a spit while it is frequently drenched with an aromatic combination of wines. This could be the hot entrée. To make the plate look pretty we would place beside the sauced venison a slice of cold terrine of partridge."

"Now we are getting somewhere," Catherine smiled.

"Or . . . " d'Auguste closed his eyes, tilted his head back and touched his fingertips to his brow. Was he going into a trance or was he picturing a feast in the halls of Araby?

"For excitement, we might do Canard Sauvage à la Presse. This dish requires great skill. Final preparation is at the table, in a chafing dish from which Canard Sauvage à la Presse is served flaming directly onto the plate."

"Perfect, perfect," Catherine clapped her hands.

"Which Madame?"

"All three, we will have all three, the venison and partridge together followed by the flaming canard."

The chef's eyebrows arched to match Mrs. Dudley's expression of stupefaction. He thought Catherine was being excessive, and could not resist reminding her of his superior grasp of menu planning. "There is a problem Madame. We should not have duck consommé for the soup course and pressed duck flambé as an entrée. Your guests will think we lack imagination."

"I am not giving up the chafing dish, we will rethink the soup." They settled on the Puree of Pheasant à la Royale only after he had explained every step of its preparation. Then it was Catherine's turn to upstage the chef. "Harking back to keeping the palate keen, we need something savory between the rich hors d'oeuvres and the velvety soup."

"Touché," d'Auguste smiled. "I have just the thing—a centuries-old recipe from my family for escargots that is particularly pungent, with much lemon and garlic."

"These guests have eaten escargots hundreds of times."

"Not like mine Madame, I assure you."

"I'll take a chance." Catherine then accepted with no argument his plea for the simplest of salads to follow the three entrées, crisp Boston lettuce with superb olive oil and balsamic vinegar. He was too tired to challenge her when she insisted on two desserts: Soufflé aux Marrons and Les Religieuses."

As his assistant was closing the notebook in which he had never stopped writing during the morning-long planning session, Catherine said, "Now we must decide on wines to be served with each course." Chef d'Auguste asked if she might allow him two days to come up with such a list. He told her it would take a bit of time to confer with the sommelier. Could she come to the hotel, "let us say, Thursday morning?" to taste the wines? She said she could. She thanked him for all his help, asked if he would write out complete and detailed instructions for the preparations and serving of each dish, as well as a list of ingredients, thanked him again, assured him she would be at the hotel on Thursday, and bade him good-bye.

As the door onto Mount Vernon Street closed behind the men, Catherine said she was going to her room. "But you haven't had lunch," her mother said.

"I don't want lunch."

Mrs. Dudley went to the dining room alone where a piece of cold haddock and five spears of cold asparagus awaited her on a plate under a silver dome. Gaines went down the backstairs to the servants' hall where she asked for and was given a bowl of cornflakes.

Chapter 10

"MAGNIFICENT! SPLENDID! SUBLIME," THE TALL, BONY one exclaimed, she who had done all the talking. Imperious, with short gray hair, she didn't string words together, but pronounced each one in a deep alto bordering on baritone with seconds of silence in between, which her short, stocky partner filled with grunts of endorsement. They were inspecting large photographs of the Portuguese Courtyard. Catherine and Gaines exchanged glances. After a few minutes of variations on a theme, Catherine interrupted to point out where she planned to place the dinner table, where the musicians would sit, where the guests would dance. The florists offered no comment.

Then the tall Miss Coughlin inquired, "What dishes will you be using?"

Catherine said she was not yet sure; she was leaning toward a Wedgwood service that was formal, or a Spode, both sets left to her by great-aunt Amelia Saltonstall.

"With crystal I suppose?"

"Waterford."

"Naturally." Miss Coughlin rolled her eyes and looked down at Miss McCaffery, whose eyes were also rolling. "Wrong, all wrong! This heavenly space calls for pottery—Portuguese of course, but we will settle for Italian. And Mexican glassware."

"With bubbles in it." Miss McCaffery could talk!

"Do you have Italian pottery? And Mexican glassware?"

"No."

"Come." Miss Coughlin dashed out the door onto Charles Street in the direction of the river. Catherine and Gaines hurried to catch up. Miss McCaffery turned the key in the lock, then skittered along behind. They paused in Carbone's front showroom only long enough for clipped introductions, then followed Miss Coughlin's flat heels into the warehouse where dark-skinned, heavily muscled young men with bandannas tied around their heads were unpacking barrels of brightly colored dishes while their blood brothers checked orders on clipboards and picked pieces from the shelves. "Don't loiter," Miss Coughlin commanded. "What we are looking for is on the next floor."

Sweeping past bubbled glassware at the top of the stairs, Gaines spied an array of blown goblets similar in color to Catherine's silk dress. "Look." She touched Catherine's shoulder. Catherine let out a small cry of wonderment.

"What's the problem," Miss Coughlin asked.

"These glasses are close to the color of the dress I will be wearing."

"Aha!" Miss Coughlin grabbed a goblet from the shelf, clutched it to where her bosom would be if she had been blessed with a bosom and scuttled off.

Three hours later, having been convinced it mattered not at all that her dress was of lighter-than-air silk delicately embroidered with fine gold thread while the Italian pottery that complemented it in color was heavy and decorated with peasant patterns and the Mexican glassware was crude, Catherine purchased a complete service for twelve, plus pottery in another pattern to serve six and a full set of the Mexican glassware in blue, which she couldn't resist. For the same reason she bought an assortment of ceramic baskets filled with sculpted arrangements of fruit and flowers. "We haven't talked about flowers, which is why I came to you," she addressed Miss Coughlin, "and I am late for a meeting with musicians. Gaines, call the maitre d' at the Ritz and tell him we will be a larger group at lunch than expected. We can talk music while we taste wine."

"Don't worry Mrs. Fillmore"—Miss Coughlin's tone was assured and the smile on her weather-wrinkled face irrefutable—"we will fulfill your floral expectations. I presume you want us to come to Oshatakea. Give me the name of your greenhouse man so I can find out what he will have available. The rest we will bring with us. You have not mentioned where you will be having drinks before dinner—in the drawing room I expect, that's where you use crystal and silver. Do you want us to do flowers for the drawing room as well?"

"Why not?" Catherine had bridled at being instructed on when and where to use crystal and silver, but was feeling more than a trifle overwhelmed. She gave bossy Miss Coughlin a telephone number for the Oshatakea greenhouse and told her to speak to Mr. Colantonio.

Having grown up trodding Beacon Hill's uneven brick sidewalks, Catherine set a pace climbing Mount Vernon from Charles Street just short of a jog. Gaines found the rapid ascent tricky. Afraid of tripping or turning an ankle, she kept her eyes cast downward. "Hurry," Catherine called over her shoulder, relieved to be free of Miss Coughlin. "We have much to do. I'd think this all good fun if I were sure I hadn't made terrible mistakes. That scrawny woman took over this morning, didn't give me a chance to say a word. No wonder her short friend grunts. Neither told me what they plan to do about decorating the courtyard, which is all I wanted of them. I don't need dishes. I have barrels filled with dishes we've never unpacked. I could have done without this morning, thank you very much, especially following yesterday when that Frenchy chef ran over me as if I were standing in the middle of the street, but at least he described the food he was suggesting so we could come up with a menu. Do you realize neither Coughlin nor McCaffery mentioned a single flower? I think I'll fire them and look for somebody else, or do it myself with Ron Colantonio's help. He's a bright young man with taste. Together we will come up with new ideas. It won't happen selecting music I can tell you. I hold my own when it comes to music. God, do I have a headache." She banged the knocker on her mother's door.

Five musicians from the Boston Symphony Orchestra, counting the concertmaster, were polite but chilly when a glistening Catherine and an out-of-breath Gaines entered Mrs. Dudley's library. The men stood. Mrs. Dudley did not. "You are late," she admonished from the depths of her chair.

"Count on you to state the obvious," Catherine snapped at her mother but was conciliatory when she spoke to the musicians. "I am sorry I've held you up, but do come along now. Did I forget to tell you we are having lunch at the Ritz when I made our appointment? Forgive me." Without taking time to go splash water on her face or have Gaines run a brush through her hair, Catherine reached out to take the concert-master's arm and, unheedful of muttered objections or attempts at introductions, swept out of the room and house. Mrs. Dudley watched in disapproval from the window as her daughter, her daughter's maid and five grumpy musicians stumped down the hill, Catherine talking and gesticulating, not bothering to look in either direction when she marched her troops off the curb into the street. "She has lost her mind. I'm not surprised." Catherine had always been unmanageable, and there was a strain of madness on the Dudley side of the family; a cousin was still kept hidden away in a house behind a tall hedge in Brookline. "Thank God she lives where nobody knows us. I hope the Ritz dining room is empty. I'll hear about it if she makes a spectacle of herself, lunching with paid musicians—and a maid!"

Catherine was not making a spectacle of herself; she was an avid student alert to what she was being taught, an unusual experience for her. From earliest nursery days she had rebelled against "being told" anything, but as the sommelier explained the subtleties of each wine presented, she absorbed his every word and tried valiantly if in vain to taste hints of autumn, raspberry aroma and lingering essence of oak and cloves. Chef d'Auguste had prepared samples of the menu he and Catherine devised for her dinner and the sommelier had chosen at least two wines to be tried with each course. Catherine was supposed to choose those she would ultimately serve after listening to the wine steward's advice. It required total concentration to taste what he told her to look for in the wine and at the same time be aware of how that wine complemented the food she was eating. The chef, expecting only three participants for the taste testing, was forced when three turned into seven to divide food into minuscule portions, which meant they were eating very little while sipping substantial quantities of wine. The mellowness that resulted compromised Catherine's decision-making process. She solved wine selection by telling the sommelier to have a case of each vintage sent to Oshatakea where she would taste-test them again in the order of his recommendations, which Gaines had written down in a little notebook.

The same mellowness loosened the musicians' tongues. Relaxation softened their professional stance and obliterated offense taken at being kept waiting, also blurring the edges of mannerly hesitancy. Catherine began the conversation about music for her dinner party with a rambling discourse on her admiration of and appreciation for obvious composers—Bach, Beethoven, Corelli, Handel, "Grieg when he's not being lugubrious," "romantic Puccini"—then explained, that she didn't want the obvious, she wanted "unusual" music as background that would complement the food being served as beautifully as the wine she would so carefully choose. When she added, "And support conversation at table I hope will arise from each particular course," the musicians exchanged dark glances. Their brows furrowed, their lips pursed, their heads shook.

"Mrs. Fillmore," the concertmaster said after taking another sip of a sweet dessert wine, "we are not lounge musicians. People do not eat while we play, they listen, and they never talk."

"They don't even cough." The violinist swiped a napkin across his mustache.

"What you want," the concertmaster continued, "is a trio or a quartet whose purpose it is to provide innocuous music that does not capture the imagination and draw one's attention away from dining, such as they have playing here in this dining room. I'm sure the Ritz management could give you a list of such people to contact."

"A pianist would do," the violist said.

"Or a harpist," the cellist suggested. "A harpist is what you want."

"A harpist is exactly what I do not want." Catherine was losing control; she had had enough of people telling her what she wanted.

"I'm sure whatever you want is easily found, Mrs. Fillmore," the concertmaster said trying to appease not backtrack, "but you are looking in the wrong place. I for one would not play for you under the conditions you describe—for any amount of money."

"Why are you wasting my time then?"

"Let's not get into an argument about who is wasting whose time," the violinist said, throwing his napkin down into the sticky residue on his dessert plate.

"Don't raise your voice at me," Catherine hissed.

The dining room was empty of the ladies and few gentlemen who had been in for lunch, but busboys and waiters going about their tasks hovered as close as they dared to witness more drama than was the usual Ritz fare. Gaines, alert to their presence, asked, "May I make a suggestion?"

"About what?" Catherine barked.

"Lady Astor occasionally had music when guests were entering the dining room, but never while they were eating; she wanted nothing to disrupt the conversations. And then, of course, after dinner for dancing." Gaines did not reveal that dancing at Cliveden was more often to the music of a record player than live musicians.

"That's what I want," Catherine exploded, "but these idiots think they are too good to provide it."

"That isn't what you said you wanted," the cellist erupted.

"Don't tell me what I said I wanted."

Incredible as it seems, after long acrimonious minutes of back and forth as to who said what, and what exactly did that mean, ideas for music to enter the courtyard by began to trickle into the noisy debate, then gave way to a spate of thoughts on pieces to play between courses, with the musicians falling all over themselves to come up with complementary music. Should they concentrate on something that said salmon mousse after the mousse had been eaten or before? If before, they'd need a venison piece next. These exchanges led to absurd suggestions everybody thought were hilarious. Even Catherine laughed. They almost came to blows over what to play that was guaranteed to pull diners out of their chairs to dance, but agreed at once on which aria from *Carmen* would entice Isabelle to rise and sing. All animosity evaporated as the men from the orchestra at last understood Catherine's desire to make her guests not merely listen but to hear what the music was saying, to let it become a part of permanent memory of that moment in time. They responded with enthusiasm, bursts of laughter and questions. Realizing she wanted them to come to Oshatakea to play this unique program, they began stating the obvious, "If we do that piece, we'll need woodwinds, and tympani, brass . . . " The list of required instruments grew as Gaines jotted composers' names and titles of pieces into her little book.

"Whatever." Catherine threw up her arms in happy acceptance. Everybody was talking at once when the conversation came to an abrupt halt shortly before four o'clock because the concertmaster remembered a dentist appointment. He assured Catherine he would send her the complete program he understood they had arrived at by consensus along with a list of musicians, anticipated costs, etc. Without demur Catherine accepted, telling him they should plan on coming to Oshatakea prior to the dinner for rehearsals in the courtyard, "and plan to stay on for several days after for a holiday." The concertmaster embraced her warmly, as did the other musicians before they reeled out of the dining room.

"I did it again, didn't I?" Catherine sighed.

"You did fine," Gaines assured her.

When the maitre' d asked if he should put the charges for lunch on Mrs. Dudley's account, Catherine laughed. "An excellent idea."

In Mrs. Dudley's library, before going upstairs for a nap, Catherine thanked her mother for her "generous" hospitality without being specific. She said she and Gaines would be returning to Oshatakea the next day.

"I do not approve of what you are doing, Catherine." Mrs. Dudley tone was crisp, her reprimand delivered as to a naughty child.

"You never have." Catherine's high spirits engendered by the fun she had had with the musicians were dashed. A headache that seemed to plague her whenever she was with her mother made it imperative she lie down at once.

"Don't walk away from me, Catherine. Catherine, I will not have you turn your back on me. Have you forgotten who you are?"

Catherine closed the library door behind her and went up to her girlhood bedroom.

Chapter 11

—

CATHERINE WISHED SHE'D THOUGHT TO HAVE A hairdresser come from Boston with the florists and the musicians. Gaines said her figure wrapped in burgundy silk was stunning, a description that made her nervous, but her hair, unless something special was done, would be ordinary. When she complained of this, Gaines said she had learned a few tricks from Lady Astor's maid if Catherine was willing to trust her. She would have trusted Gaines with her life. Not only had the sensible little Englishwoman saved her sanity numerous times since they'd met at Cliveden, she joined in the planning of Catherine's party with enthusiasm, which was more than could be said of the Oshatakea staff. Mrs. Fuller, after proving herself incapable of accomplishing what Catherine wanted, actually threw pots and pans when presented with written step-by-step instructions "from some foreigner at a fancy hotel." The how-to-cook part was bad enough, but this so-called *chef de cuisine* had the effrontery to send photographs of how each dish should be "presented."

"I guess I know how to put food on a plate. Frenchy names don't mean a thing. It's no different from what I've been cooking in this kitchen for years. I'll do what I've always done. It'll be as good as you'd get at the Ritz whatever and with a lot less fuss."

Catherine was persuaded to go down to the kitchens when Mrs.

Blackburn told her Mrs. Fuller was upset and had no intention of following orders. Keeping her own temper, which amazed those who witnessed the encounter, Catherine insisted in a calm cold voice, "The instructions you received are to be followed precisely as written. There are differences in your cooking and Chef d'Auguste's, which would not ordinarily matter, Mrs. Fuller, but this time they do." She breathed deeply. Pleading was not easy for her. "Please do what he says with no shortcuts and no substitutions."

Mrs. Fuller would have none of it. She whipped off her apron, threw it down on the floor, wiped her feet on it and stormed out of the kitchen. Her second cook, an Englishman named Ernest Bones, stepped forward. "Don't worry Mrs. Fillmore, we will give you what you want."

"With no deviations?"

"With no deviations. I look forward to the challenge." His yellow-toothed grin reassured Catherine.

Nor were men who worked in the greenhouses and had always done flowers for Oshatakea thrilled when told two women were coming from Boston to decorate and do floral arrangements for Mrs. Fillmore's party. However, when the Misses Coughlin and McCaffery arrived at the Fillmore depot dressed in dark slickers and flat felt hats, and with no nonsense set about checking long lists as crates of plants, exotic flowers and equipment were offloaded from the freight car, Ron Colantonio and his men found their pique turning to amusement. As the actual work progressed in the Portuguese Courtyard the women, whom Ron's men called "tough birds," and the men, to whom the women referred as "well-meaning lumps," formed a mutually rewarding relationship. Ron's crew showed their admiration of what the women were doing by acceding to their every demand, and were pleased as punch when their own suggestions were accepted, usually with Miss Coughlin remarking, "Splendid idea, quite splendid."

FP hadn't blinked an eye when Catherine told him she had

invited what turned out to be twenty-three people, counting several musicians' wives, to be houseguests for two days prior to her party and two or three days after. No other guests being scheduled for that week, Mrs. Blackburn gave them rooms on the south front so they could enjoy views of the valley. Ever hospitable Farney tried to coax them onto horses. He was successful once, but not a second time because the three who had tried riding were barely able to walk after the experience. Everybody, including the Misses Coughlin and McCaffery, accompanied FP on walks through the parklike grounds. They took pictures of the Italian garden designed by Christina Farnsworth Fillmore, FP's grandmother, and of the herb garden planted by Thomas Fillmore's second wife, Emma Freeman, FP's great-great-grandmother. Nine Bostonians succeeded in getting through the boxwood maze without assistance. The musicians rehearsed in the courtyard as decorators worked around them, and they were delighted by the acoustics. Curious Louisa wanted to invite the entire group to the dacha, but Adelaide warned they should not interfere. "We will after Catherine's dinner." Isabelle observed the activity, and chuckled.

Preparing Catherine's hair, Gaines tried a variation of her usual French knot, placing it higher on the back of her head and releasing a single curl onto the nape of her neck. Catherine liked the effect, but said, "I feel a chill." On Mount Vernon Street the possibility of a chill would have made her forgo the high French knot, but she decided she'd risk it. "Are you sure the curl isn't too Gibson girlish?" Gaines assured her it was quite sophisticated. Wrapped in a dressing gown Catherine went downstairs to make a quick tour of inspection, first of the drawing room where drinks would be served before dinner. The florists had fashioned arrangements echoing those in paintings on the walls; pink roses for a Renoir, anemones substituting for poppies in the Redon. Catherine remembered Miss Coughlin's remark about silver and crystal in the drawing room and appreciated the sumptuous displays. She hoped FP would not think them too much. As she went along the corridor between the library and the morning room toward the courtyard she became aware of the sweet odor of stephanotis hanging from iron arches that supported the glass ceiling and suffered a moment of panic; would they be overpowering? Too late to change now. What had only hours ago been a shamble of ladders, netting, tools, water jugs, clippings and other paraphernalia was now a paradise. Moss-stuffed nets covered with ginger leaves and studded with assorted shades of asters and centura, cynara, Lady Diana sweet peas, cornflowers, scabiosa, sprays of white cymbidium and tiny Rothschildiana orchids draped walls on both sides of the iron stairs, brilliant living tapestries. Miniature box and myrtle topiaries lined the stairs. Balconies held pots of lavender. FP's tubbed citrus trees around the perimeter of the courtyard were integrated into a terra-cotta landscape of eggplants, kale and several varieties and colors of tomatoes and peppers. There were no flowers on the table to pull the eye away from vivid patterns of Italian pottery, mixed colors and shapes of Mexican glass and jumbles of candles in differing heights on a coarsely woven apricot cloth.

Catherine wished Aunt Belle Gardner could see this. "Make sure all candles are lighted when we come in for dinner," she said to a footman. He assured her they would be.

Gaines helped her into the burgundy silk gown and talked her out of using a gold bar pin to gather together rolls of filmy material falling across her breasts and thus reduce the exposed cleavage. "You will ruin the lovely bodice lines. Don't worry, you are quite secure in the undergarment we ordered from Crawford-Hollidge." Sitting before her dressing-table mirror, Catherine watched with increasing unease as Gaines incorporated a string of pearls into her coiled hair, then placed a diamond and amethyst broach in the back just where that single curl began its drop. The broach and a matching necklace that Gaines put around Catherine's neck were wedding presents from Farney.

Rising carefully from the bench, lest a wrong move cause everything to fall apart, she turned slowly in both directions within the mirrored alcove. "I look like a lampshade."

"You do not," Gaines said. "Stand still and let me apply a bit of rouge to your lips and add a blush to your cheeks."

Catherine stood still, but fretted. "Gaines you are transforming me into a circus performer—pearls in my hair, a neckline that scares me to death and now paint on my lips and cheeks."

Gaines rubbed on the rouge, dusting it lightly with a rabbit's foot. "While we're at it, close your eyes and keep them closed until I tell you to open them." Again Catherine obeyed and felt Gaines brush something on each lid. When told she could look, she was astonished by the reflection staring back at her. She'd always thought her face was a blanc mange, but as she stood gazing in the mirror she saw discernible and not unattractive features. "Gaines you are a magician. Where did you get all this makeup?"

"Paris. I thought after you bought the dress you might need matching rouge one day."

"No more now or I'll be as grotesque as Isabelle." The expression on Farney's face when he came in and saw his wife was of such bewilderment Catherine asked, "Do I look that weird?"

He bowed as he had been taught to do as a boy in dance class. "Take my arm Mrs. Fillmore and we will go greet our guests."

Their guests were assembled in the drawing room when Farney and Catherine entered, as Catherine had planned. The practice at Oshatakea was for guests to be greeted upon arrival. Catherine knew the protocol, but she wanted to make an entrance. She was the leading lady of this drama; leading ladies are never on stage when the curtain rises. Prepared for their disapproval at what they would think a faux pas, and expecting FP to make a curt remark, she was not disappointed when they faced her with a phalanx of frowns, nor surprised by her father-in-law's "We thought we had come the wrong night." What she was not prepared for were frowns giving way to wonderment. The weighted silence was broken when Louisa chirped, "Catherine you are the Tsarina in that dress. It's her favorite color."

"Is that why you persuaded me to buy it?"

FP, the next in line, was beaming. "You are well worth waiting for my dear." He leaned forward to kiss her. She did not turn her head. As his lips brushed hers she was swept by an unwelcome emotion. No one ever said she was worth waiting for. There was more approval in his words than she'd ever had from her family. Not expecting what she hadn't known, deep sadness mingled with elation. She had no proper response. Dudleys do not show emotion. Catherine wanted to acknowledge FP's kindness, but all she could manage was a tight smile. It was the burgundy dress, she believed, and her makeup and coiffeur that brought forth FP's lovely comment and made the others regard her with such open admiration. How could she know it was the light in her eyes and the spark of eagerness barely subdued and not previously apparent that amazed them? They had not thought it possible she could be as gracious as she was being. For Catherine's presence and poise to illuminate a room was astounding. Her defined gestures, controlled movement and perfect carriage, viewed before as condescending hauteur, this evening were coming across as innate elegance.

Adelaide, stepping back from Catherine, said the flowers in the drawing room were exquisite. Isabelle threw her arms around Catherine before either woman realized what was happening, and neither could pull back without being obvious. In fact, they could not pull back at all until Adelaide disentangled Isabelle's bejeweled fender from the rolls of silk barely covering Catherine's nipples. "I would have returned from Europe for this party—had I been in Europe." Isabelle laughed and hitched the fender back where it belonged.

Recovering from a momentary sentimental lapse and the shock of Isabelle's embrace, quickly glancing down to make sure nothing more had been exposed during their encounter, Catherine replied honestly, "There would have been no party if you weren't here Isabelle." As she spoke she realized what had been devised as an assault on her husband's family, and an attempt to unmask the diva, was in its first few minutes becoming an extraordinarily convivial event. Did she or did she not, with no ulterior motive, want to entertain these people? She had no choice but to let the evening play out as meticulously planned.

When a phalanx of footmen came in with canapés more intricate and diverse than was ordinarily served at Oshatakea, Catherine's guests were as impressed as she had hoped they would be. "Each one is better than the one before, and then we begin again," Louisa cried. "Surely this must be dinner, who could eat anything more?" Adelaide said accepting another Fois Gras en Brioche. "I can," FP said. They were finishing a second round of drinks when music, the players having been cued by a footman who passed on Catherine's discreet signal, was heard in the distance. Catherine took FP's arm and, after thanking him for his generous hospitality to the musicians, said, "Shall we follow our ears?" She might also have thanked him for allowing her to monopolize the greenhouse staff and apologized for throwing his kitchen into an uproar, but that did not occur to her. Together they led the party from the drawing room across the hall and along the narrow corridor that was FP's signature architectural trick of a relatively long low passage opening onto a space of soaring height and dimension. The Portuguese Courtyard was aglow with hundreds of candles in sconces on walls, in citrus trees, on tables, stairs and floor. Catherine, who knew what to expect, was transfixed by the shimmering beauty and shadows of the room.

Adelaide and Louisa touched fingertips to their lips like awestruck little girls. "Good God in heaven!" Isabelle exclaimed. FP took in every aspect, savoring details so carefully worked out.

"Oshatakea has never seen anything to match this," he said quietly. If nothing happened after that, if the party stopped for some reason in that instant, Catherine would have felt vindicated by FP's reaction. She knew her father-in-law believed that the Oshatakea he had created was among the world's magnificent houses. For him to say what she had done surpassed earlier events in the history of his house was more than a compliment. This party's purpose was to make all Fillmores, and Isabelle Chapman, aware of who she was and what she could do. Once they understood—cried uncle, to put it in the vernacular—they could take a flying leap into the abyss, Farney included. That had been her attitude, but the need to show them, to make them admit something, was diminishing, and the evening was just beginning.

Behind each of six chairs surrounding the table stood a footman not letting on by gesture or blush how foolish he felt in the peasant costume Catherine had had made for him. Place cards indicated FP was to sit on Catherine's right, Louisa on her left. Farney sat across with Adelaide on his right and Isabelle on his left. Catherine realized this put Isabelle next to FP, which bothered her, but she had no choice. If she had switched Isabelle with Adelaide it would have implied Isabelle was the female guest of honor and that would not do. Beside the place cards were copies of the menu written in minute script. As always, Louisa was the first to notice and comment. "Escargot d'Auguste! I've never heard of them d'Auguste, but I love snails." Catherine, who could take snails or leave them alone, patted Louise's hand.

Isabelle raved over the Puree of Pheasant à la Royale, saying she had been served it only once before. Farney said if he could have as much as he wanted of the Salmon Mousse en Bellevue, he'd require nothing beyond that.

"You would be sorry I think," Catherine replied.

FP inhaled deeply as a plate of richly aromatic venison was set before him, with a beautiful to behold slice of partridge terrine.

Before he had time to taste either, a smaller plate containing Asparagus à la Polonaise and pungent Truffles au Vin Blanc was placed to one side. "It's too much," he said cutting into the venison. As the plates for this course were being removed, the orchestra began a Strauss waltz. "I cannot sit still when I hear 'Where the Lemon Trees Bloom,'" FP exclaimed. "Would you think this old man senile, Madame if I were to ask you to dance?"

Catherine smirked at Farney through the forest of flickering candles. To FP she feigned surprise. "In the middle of dinner?" Off they waltzed.

Adelaide laid her napkin on the table. "Farney, dance with me."

"Isabelle, I'll follow if you lead," Louisa cried. The mismatched pair of women spun across the tile floor. If they danced too close Louisa's nose banged up against Isabelle's fender; if too far apart, Louisa had trouble following, or perhaps it was Isabelle who was having trouble leading. Whatever, their laughing, lurching progress made the others laugh as well.

FP laughed so hard he stumbled. Please God, no falls in this dress, Catherine prayed. "Shall we return to the table?"

Glistening from exertion and the rising temperature in the courtyard because of masses of burning candles, the only diner prepared for the presentation of flaming Canard Sauvage à la Presse was Catherine. Adelaide's eyes reflected the conflagration. "Catherine your dinner surpasses those we attended at court in St. Petersburg." She looked across at FP. "Grandfather, have you ever been to a more glorious dinner party?"

"Never!" FP raised his glass of a newly poured wine. "To Catherine."

"Tell us your stories about Edward Seventh's coronation banquet," Isabelle urged.

Throughout that course and the crisp salad that followed, FP regaled them with humorous anecdotes about the English king's dinner, from the grotesque quantities of food consumed by the rotund monarch, to tales of Edward's exquisite Queen Alexandra who came in late. The deaf queen frequently misunderstood what was being said to her and came back with totally inappropriate replies. "None of which made the slightest difference," FP said. "Everybody loved her. She could be as late and irrelevant as she chose to be." He sipped some wine. "As one who knew her well, I am convinced she heard more than she let on. She made everyone shout because it amused her."

They danced a fox trot after the salad course, with different partners but the same gaiety. Following lighter than air Soufflé aux Marrons, Les Religieuses were served on plates decorated with candied violets and spun-sugar birds. Adelaide again raised her hands in admiration. "I don't want to eat this, I just want to look at it." But eat it she did. They were settling back, sated, when the stealthy opening bars of Bizet's entrance music were heard from above. Isabelle took the bait as eagerly as Catherine had hoped she would. "*Carmen!*" she cried. "Perfection, Catherine, absolute perfection, you have an ear as well as an eye for detail. Those stairs were made for Carmen. If I'd known I would have prepared."

"You can do it Isabelle," Louisa egged her on.

"Shall I? Should I try?"

"Only if you want to." Adelaide cast a wary eye on Catherine.

"I wasn't asked to sing for my supper," Isabelle said demurely, "but if you don't object . . . " she looked across the table at her hostess. Catherine's smile was noncommittal.

"Oh, what the hell—in for a dime, in for a dollar." Isabelle rose majestically from her chair.

"Please don't if you are too tired Isabelle," Catherine heard herself say.

"Au contraire, I am exhilarated from dancing and dining and drinking, which translates into don't expect too much, but with *Carmen*, it's mood that counts." She strode across the courtyard toward the iron staircases. "Gentlemen!" She clapped her hands to get their attention. They stopped playing. The concertmaster looked down. "Thank you. Are you prepared to play through this aria?" The concertmaster affirmed they were. "Well then, take it from the top. I will sing Carmencita, you fill in the chorus." She climbed the stairs and disappeared momentarily behind a pillar in the conservatory sitting room.

What followed was not worthy of an opera house, but it was an accomplished singer playing with words and music she knew well and understood. Isabelle was the cigarette girl as much for her own merriment as to entertain an intimate audience. Singing directly to them her tone was rich and her French flawless. "L'amour est un oiseau rebelle que nul ne peut apprivoiser, et c'est bien en vain qu'on l'appelle, s'il lui convient de refuser." She made them accept that love is a rebellious, untamable bird. Turning her head to flirt with the musicians—"Rien n'y fait, menace ou prière, l'un parle bien, l'autre se tait"—the gypsy winked down at FP. "Il n'a rien dit, mais IL me plait."

During "L'amour, l'amour," which rolled in luscious liquid tones across the courtyard, she spread her arms to those sitting around the table, then assumed an air of intrigue, "L'amour est enfant de bohème," and tossing her head in defiance started her descent, brazenly imitating a current diva's guttural interpretation: "il n'a jamais connu de loi." The musicians grinned. At the foot of the stairs, Isabelle gave her generous torso a final seductive twist, raised her arms and, hanging on to the stair rail, knelt in a half curtsy.

"Olé, olé, olé," Farney shouted, the first on his feet. The musicians joined in a standing ovation. Catherine's astonishment made her the last to rise.

"I need a drink, a real drink, bourbon will do," Isabelle laughed, pounding her fender and fanning her face when she returned to the table. Her eyes met Catherine's. "Didn't think I could do it, did you?"

"I didn't, but you were marvelous Isabelle."

Isabelle's delight at Catherine's capitulation was expressed in a rush of coughing laughter. She winked and raised the glass of bourbon brought to her by a peasant footman. "Never underestimate an old fire horse."

Shortly after midnight Catherine and Farney bid their guests good night. Adelaide, Louisa and Isabelle departed through the Portuguese Wing's front door where the Kropotkin Daimler was waiting. Catherine and Farney walked with FP up the Step Gallery to the monastery doors. "A splendid occasion, Catherine" he said. "How superbly you designed the evening around your guests." His smile was wise as well as benign. "You underestimated Isabelle — and I have underestimated you. We must put your special talents and abilities to use at Oshatakea."

Catherine silently cursed. What is this emotional thing? Emotions are a damned nuisance. "Thank you," she said in a small voice.

"Good night." FP patted Farney's shoulder and stepped through the door within a door.

"Well, you did what you wanted to do. You won them over, every single one. They were eating out of your hands." Farney led the way back down the Step Gallery.

He had broken the spell. "I don't want them to eat out of my hands. I want them to respect me, nothing more."

That night when he knocked on her bedroom door, as was his custom on those rare occasions he ventured across the hall balcony, he didn't wait for an invitation to come in. "You were beautiful tonight," he said, switching off the table lamp. Catherine wasn't sure if he had had too much to drink, or if he assumed he had played a role in her triumph. With no further conversation they proceeded to engage in sex that was, for him, somewhat more animated than usual, but for her no less disagreeable. The deed done, he rolled away and fell into a deep snoring sleep. It took vigorous prodding to wake him so he could be sent back across the balcony to his own room.

Alone in the dark, Catherine lay with her eyes open, going back over the long lovely evening before Farney's intrusion, dismissing from her mind that aspect of an otherwise sublime experience. FP had invited her to assume a role at Oshatakea. She mused on her almost friendly feeling toward Isabelle. The Kropotkin sisters had been more than affectionate. Most gratifying, as well as surprising, was her realization that, more than winning a skirmish with people she had thought of as enemies, she had actually had a good time at her own party. She felt fulfilled for the first time since coming to Oshatakea, perhaps the first time anywhere.

Chapter 12

MORE THAN THE DYNAMICS OF CATHERINE'S RELATIONSHIPS with members of Farney's family and Isabelle changed that night. Oshatakea's employees, everyone from FP's architects to stablemen and gardeners, saw her in a new light. Mrs. Blackburn, kitchen assistants and parlor maids, footmen and florists discussed details of Catherine's dinner dance as if he or she had been there. By noon the following day, a legend was launched that wouldn't stop growing. Dozens of candles became thousands. Trailing stephanotis became garlands of gardenias hanging from rafters to floor. A string of pearls entwined in her French knot became ropes encircling her body, and Catherine's display of cleavage was described as near naked breasts, nipples visible through diaphanous silk. Even those who knew the truth enlarged upon facts to enhance their own roles in the grand event.

No one was more overjoyed to tell and retell tales than Mrs. Fuller, avowing she had dreamed up the fabled menu.

Ernest Bones alone remained silent about his truly major role in the dinner's success. He didn't want to ruffle Mrs. Fuller's feathers, and he had something more important than bragging in mind. When Catherine asked to see him the next morning, he went to the Portuguese Courtyard prepared. Her praise and expressions of gratitude were genuine as she handed him an envelope containing a check in a generous amount written on her personal Bank of Boston account. He accepted the check after a halfhearted attempt to refuse it. Squaring his shoulders and, on the brink of nervous prostration, he asked in a tight voice if she thought there was any chance he might go to Boston to apprentice for a short time in the kitchen of Chef d'Auguste?

Catherine's response was agonizingly slow. She was startled that Bones's request for a leave of absence was made to her rather than to Mrs. Blackburn, who would need to ask FP. Flushing with pleasure at this crack in Oshatakea's lines of authority, she said, "I will contact the Ritz to see if such an arrangement might be made, and then I will speak to Mr. Fillmore about a leave. I don't think he will object." After Catherine assured the chef she would underwrite all expenses and pay Bones's wages, d'Auguste agreed to the apprenticeship. FP approved the scheme, and shortly thereafter Oshatakea's second cook went to Boston, the first such learning experience in a variety of venues Catherine would arrange for Bones in years to come. Mrs. Fuller was made aware she could never satisfy Catherine's demands, and accepted retirement as soon as Bones returned. Publicly she blamed her varicose veins for leaving Oshatakea's kitchen and moving into a small house FP provided for her in the village, making it possible for Ernest Bones to take charge without causing a wrinkle in the below-stairs fabric. Catherine silently celebrated her first victory in a battle for dominance.

The most significant external change was that valley residents shortly after the dinner party began referring to Catherine as Mrs. Fillmore, a step up in the popular lexicon from "Farney's missus" or "the bitch from Boston." She would not then or ever attain FP's and Farney's level of affectionate recognition, being called by her first name, but she would have hated that assumed familiarity. She was not yet chatelaine of Oshatakea, but FP did invite her to participate in planning Oshatakea events. This came after the family had bidden farewell to the musicians and the Misses Coughlin and

McCaffery, having stayed on for several days to enjoy FP's hearty hospitality—and to be enjoyed. Adelaide and Louisa gave a splendid tea that turned into an impromptu musicale when Isabelle and the concertmaster discovered a shared enthusiasm for "Knees Up Mother Brown," a bawdy English music hall ballad that they proceeded to bellow. This led to Farney and Louisa attempting a silly dance routine they had devised when they were in their teens. Then Adelaide played the piano while the jolly cellist led everyone in singing rounds. Hilarity filled the dacha. Catherine applauded, but could not be persuaded to join in.

"I've had more fun these last few days than I've had in years," FP said waving to the caravan of cars taking musicians and decorators down to the depot. He asked Catherine to join him in the Galleried Library. Seated in wing chairs on either side of the massive hearth, they regarded each other with unblinking speculation. "It has been a tradition at Oshatakea going back many years to have long weekend house parties from late spring through New Year's. Our weekend parties have not greatly differed from other country house gatherings. We play games, dance, ride, all pleasurable pursuits but not particularly memorable. I think it's time we added something new. If I give you guest lists for weekends starting next May, would you plan the menus and some special entertainment? All usual daytime, indoor and outdoor activities will be available of course—Farney would have a fit if he couldn't entice people into hunts and coaching. I want you to concentrate on the evenings— and food. For someone I thought had a limited view on eating, you served us an amazing dinner."

Without hesitation, Catherine replied, "I will." Thus casually the first step in Catherine's climb to fame as a hostess and major force in performing arts circles was taken. She set to work at once, not waiting for dates or guest lists before sending letters to the just departed concertmaster and cellist asking them to return to Oshatakea. She explained she needed to pick their brains for a

major undertaking, adding, "You will be well paid for your advice."
She wrote a similar letter to Chef d'Auguste. The two musicians
responded first, positively and eagerly. Mutually agreeable dates
were set and rooms on the south front reserved with Mrs.
Blackburn. Chef d'Auguste, curious to see the estate of which he
had heard stories, said he would be "happy to travel to Oshatakea
to help Mrs. Fillmore." He would arrive approximately one full
week following the musicians' departure. Catherine was glad it
worked out that way. Music was her passion; food, despite FP's
compliment, she still thought of as fuel except when it was
designed to serve a special purpose. She could immerse herself in
stimulating discussions with the musicians if she could devote full
time to them when they were at Oshatakea. A week later she'd
force herself to learn more from d'Auguste about the gustatory arts
than she cared to know.

"I will need a place to work, and a clerical assistant. There will
be many letters to send and files to keep."

"I heartily approve approaching the task as a professional," FP
replied. "Let me see what I can do." What he did was convert a
suite of three rooms at the far end of the west loggia into offices,
furnishing them with antique desks, sturdy Jacobean tables and
comfortable chairs placed on fine rugs. On the walls he hung
assorted textiles: two small Brussels tapestries in one room, a
Navajo rug in another, an embroidered silk kimono in the third.
All of this from his warehouses. Steel file cabinets were concealed
in especially built wooden credenzas. A house phone was installed,
as were two outside lines. When he showed Catherine her offices,
and introduced her to Annie Dingle, a fiftyish spinster sister of
Darcy Dingle, one of Farney's stablemen, Catherine was pleased
with the suite of rooms. She was not pleased with Annie Dingle.

"I can't work with that woman."

"Why?"

"She's a mess. Did you look at her? She slumps, her hair is

unkempt, her skirt hangs down in front and hikes up in back. There are cigarette burn holes in her cardigan, and her blouse is a blot of what she'd had for a week's worth of meals. Shall I go on? What could she have been thinking, coming to be interviewed for a job with old cotton stockings falling down around her ankles?"

"She wasn't coming to be interviewed," FP said. "She was reporting for work. I have already hired her."

"You find something for her to do, she's not working for me."

"She comes highly recommended. Try her, Catherine, for a few days, and then if you decide she is impossible, we'll find a replacement,"

When Annie appeared the next morning in the same disgusting outfit, Catherine greeted her with a bark. "No smoking."

Unbidden, Annie flopped down in the chair on the other side of Catherine's desk, a cigarette with an inch of ash dangling from her lower lip. "I'll do my best." She stubbed the butt in a paper cup withdrawn from her sweater pocket. "I don't take dictation."

God is good! The baggage had provided an excuse for immediate dismissal. Catherine concealed her exaltation. "You are of no use to me if you don't take dictation."

Annie's protuberant, blue-veined, milky eyes peered with the belligerence of a Jersey bull over greasy glasses resting on the red tip of her nose. A partially opened paper clip substituted for the lost screw meant to secure the left temple to her frames. "How much dictation do you give?" Annie didn't wait for an answer. "Don't fret. I'll keep up. What do you have there? Letters to be answered? Give them to me." As if cast under a spell by Annie's uncowed comeback, Catherine made no sound when the two pieces of paper she had been holding, notes from the concertmaster and d'Auguste, were snatched from her hand. Annie glanced at one. "He wants to know if his wife can come with him. Can she?"

"No. He's coming to work, not vacation. Oh, I don't know, what difference does it make?" Catherine fumbled for coherence.

Annie withdrew a dingy handkerchief from somewhere behind the tired bow on the front of her blouse and blew her nose. "Are you adamant about no smoking?"

"I am."

Annie groaned. "Now this one—she scanned Chef d'Auguste's letter—"he'll be here when you want him. Should he bring his knives and will you want him to cook?"

"Why would he bring his knives?"

"How do I know?"

"He will not need knives and he won't have to cook."

"I'll do these after I go to the toilet."

Annie's audacity was beyond comprehension. The woman was obviously going to the bathroom to smoke. Should Catherine follow her and make a scene? What a stupid way to begin the first day. Catherine forced herself to breathe deeply, exhale, breathe, exhale as she pondered the next step. She would delay decapitation until the wretch presented her with typed replies to the two letters. They would certainly mirror the typist's own disarray, providing the last straw, pounding a final nail into the coffin of dirty Annie Dingle. Her spirits lifted, Catherine picked up the guest lists FP's secretary had laid on the desk, smiling when she heard sounds of Annie's rapid typing in the outer office. The products of reckless speed and abandon could only be catastrophic.

A rancorous odor of scorched wool preceded Annie as she shuffled back toward Catherine's desk. Swiping ashes off her front, she slapped down two sheets of Oshatakea note-size stationery. Catherine retrieved them with the tips of her fingers, and peered down as if from Olympian heights. Joyful expectations plummeted when she saw two immaculate, perfectly centered and spaced documents awaiting milady's signature. "Of course you may bring your wife to Oshatakea," Catherine read in the letter to the concertmaster. "There are many things for her to do here while we are busy at work. I look forward to welcoming both of you on the sixteenth."

The response to Chef d'Auguste was equally succinct, more concise than Catherine might have been able to phrase it, yet the voice was hers. Her heart sank; she yearned for a sentence to change, for a mistake she could correct, a fault to find, but there was nothing. Without looking up she brusquely scrawled CDF above her typed signature and handed the letters back to Annie.

"You are most welcome, Madame." Annie bowed in case her sarcasm was missed. "When you want me, you know where I am." If that were all that was expected of her, this job would be a lead-pipe cinch, she mused—after she taught hoity-toity Mrs. Fillmore the facts of life. Dropping the letters on her desk in the outer office, she pulled a crumpled package of Camels from her cardigan pocket and headed down the hall in the direction of the ladies' room.

Catherine quickly came to depend on Annie Dingle, to such a degree that she wanted her available around the clock. When asked to move into a staff room on the top floor of Oshatakea, Annie demurred. "Snowy, my cat, wouldn't know what to do if I didn't come home. Call me anytime." Unsatisfied with the arrangement, but accepting she could not change it, Catherine wildly abused the privilege of calling her "anytime," whenever a thought occurred as she lay in her big bed in the Portuguese Wing, regardless of hour or urgency. "Ron Colantonio tells me we will have blue flag and bachelor buttons to use on the table for Friday night dinner, which means we'll want white cloths, blue linen napkins and the Canton china. Remember that when we discuss food with Bones." Annie never complained about middle-of-the-night calls—and never stopped complaining about the no-smoking rule. Though she appeared to be a walking disaster, she proved to have amazing skills and was able to translate Catherine's frequently snarled commands into masterpieces of precise but friendly prose that made her a partner in an enterprise that would expand from weekend house-party planning into a highly complex organization for producing indoor and outdoor performances of theater, dance and music involving hundreds of people. This did not happen overnight.

Nine days before the first house party, during family dinner in the Gibbons Room, FP asked Catherine for a progress report. The simple request raised her hackles. It took her back to boarding school when she had refused to provide answers she knew perfectly well because she suspected Miss Tucker's questions were a scheme to make her appear incompetent as well as intransigent. This enraged her. Intransigent yes, of that she was guilty. She strove to be intransigent, but incompetent? Never! "We will be ready," she told FP.

"I'm sure you will, but you haven't shown me work sheets."

"Work sheets?" Was her father-in-law's expression positive or disdainful? Did he think she was not up to the assigned task?

"Menus. Entertainment," FP prompted.

Catherine tensed. "You asked me to plan menus and evening entertainment. That I have done. Food orders have been placed, contracts signed."

"Contracts signed? Catherine you have no authority to sign contracts having to do with Oshatakea." His tone was that of a disappointed father addressing the daughter who has let him down, telling her rules should be obvious and followed.

She glared across the table. Who did he think he was, God passing tablets to Moses? He could, if he chose, destroy everything she had set in motion. "I did not realize." She could not control the anger in her voice. "I thought you trusted me."

"I do trust you, but I want to know what is planned. Send me work sheets in the morning."

She didn't go to bed until after three A.M. Lying down was impossible. She paced. She cursed. She threw Dresden figurines against the fireplace. "The old bastard, the goddamned bastard."

The next morning, Catherine had Annie type fresh copies of

menus for all meals, from Friday afternoon tea through Monday luncheon, for the first house party in May. These she put into a folder marked "Menus." In another folder she placed typed programs for Friday, Saturday and Sunday evenings, with information about each artist and what he or she would be doing. She had engaged a mime and a puppeteer for Friday night to amuse guests who would be tired from travel. They would perform in the Baroque Theatre. For Saturday, she scheduled a chamber music group to play in Hester's white drawing room. A soprano and baritone would sing French art songs following Sunday "supper" in the Long Gallery.

Within the hour after a footman had delivered the folders to FP, Catherine was summoned to the Galleried Library, where she found FP sitting at the refectory table examining her work sheets. St. George slaying the dragon hovered above in a stained-glass window. "These menus are too fancy. People don't come to Oshatakea expecting exotic food. However, since you ordered supplies, which you should not have done, I won't ask you to change menus this time. But these programs, Catherine, these programs are all wrong. They aren't at all what I had in mind. The mime and puppets are passable I suppose, but chamber music? On a Saturday night? What could you have been thinking? You might enjoy chamber music, and perhaps Isabelle and the Kropotkins like French art songs, but, and this is the most important but, my guests will not. Esoteric entertainment two nights in a row?" The way he said "esoteric entertainment" it sounded like exquisite torture. "I'll not let you do it. Friends aren't invited here for enlightenment, I want them to have a good time."

"Did you read the list of pieces on the two programs?" Catherine interjected. "They will be very different."

"I did. They mean nothing to me. We will bring in local musicians for Saturday night so people can dance. Now, we need to think up something for Sunday. How about charades?"

She ignored his suggestions. "Neither Saturday nor Sunday programs are esoteric. Fine music can be lighthearted you know—undemanding and entertaining, which is what you said you wanted. Most of the music the quartet will play was composed specifically to divert people after dinner. Your guests will be delighted." Inwardly, she was raging. Why do I toady? Why don't I tell him to accept what I've done or forget the whole thing? I'll have nothing to do with stupid oompah bands or charades.

FP watched her eyes, noticed the clenching of her jaw and decided it was time to give ground. "At this late day I have little choice but to take your word for it, however, be prepared to cancel Sunday if one person shows the least hint of boredom Saturday night. Heed my warning Catherine, don't ever again commit us to two arcane programs the same weekend. Chamber music is bad enough, but French art songs? I can see Jay Vanderbilt flying into the billiard room."

"Let him fly." Catherine made no effort to soften the edge on her voice. "We won't call them French art songs if they are likely to upset Jay Vanderbilt. God forbid. We'll simply say Genevieve Pieluska and Larance Smith are here to sing for us."

Isabelle Chapman unwittingly saved Catherine's life that first weekend when FP showed her the work sheets and she remarked on the quartet's selections, "It's what my friend Virginia Eskin calls 'high-class potted palm music.' As for what Gen and Larry will sing, Catherine once again has shown a special gift, ending the weekend with songs people will go out the door humming." Indeed, the French art songs were a hit. Jay Vanderbilt was first to stand as the duo finished, leading applause that brought on encores. A bemused Catherine wondered as Jay later followed the luscious Miss Pieluska from room to room if it was Debussy and Poulenc or décolleté plangent and pulchritude that kept him from flying off to the billiard room.

Chapter 13

CATHERINE WATCHED THE FRIDAY NIGHT ENTERTAINMENT
sitting alone in a tiny hidden box on the right wall of the Baroque
Theatre. From there she observed FP's guests as they laughed at
the mime's antics and applauded the incredibly lifelike puppets.
Reacting to FP's opposition to chamber music, she was nervous
about Saturday night. Though she sneered at his concern, she
could not ignore his threat to bring everything to an abrupt halt if
even one guest appeared bored while the string quartet was playing. That would mean he'd not permit her to present the French
art songs on Sunday. While listening to rehearsals she realized how
much she hungered to hear the music she had planned for both
evenings, and vowed she would not allow FP or his guests to spoil
the performances for her. She would listen to music and ignore
guests. If the stupid philistines were bored they should not diminish her pleasure.

Catherine selected Hester's white drawing room as the venue for
the quartet because of its intimacy. She had Louis XIV settees,
chairs and delicate tables moved into groupings with inlaid cabinets and other furnishings along the white silk walls. In the center
of the room small gold chairs were lined up facing a raised platform. To shield herself from any restive behavior, she had a wing
chair placed behind a screen of mirrored panels down front and to

the right of the audience. While the quartet was welcomed with polite applause, Catherine slipped, unnoticed, into her chair from the adjacent green drawing room, where, in greater comfort than that provided by spindly gold chairs, invisible to all but the musicians, she listened as if she were alone. It was sublime.

A pattern was established. Catherine always sat apart and alone during a performance. Nor did she mingle freely with guests before or after. FP spoke to her repeatedly about her absence from the Great Hall when people arrived at Oshatakea. "If you see yourself as hostess, you must be the hostess." She told him she was unnecessary because he was always there when each person was ushered in to be greeted before being sent off with a footman to an assigned suite. Most guests caught glimpses of Catherine only in passing, but basking in the warmth of FP's attention they were unaware they bored her. "She's incredibly shy," said one who did not know her. "She is not," countered another who knew her well. "The only remotely gracious Dudley was her brother, Teddy." Said a third, "Yet when he fell overboard, nobody made much of an attempt to save him."

And so it went through Catherine's first season as house-party planner at Oshatakea. She was not personally popular, but in spite of FP's nit-picking every aspect of each party was an unqualified success. Thank-you notes received from weekend guests included exclamations about the "exquisite food" and "delightful evenings of glorious music."

FP continued to question her entertainments. "Ballet? Who wants ballet three nights in a row?"

"They are doing three very different ballets—highly comical on Friday night when everybody wants to laugh, more serious but romantic on Saturday and short pieces, some light and some tours de force, on Sunday." She dared to be increasingly firm against his objections to chosen artists as time went on, aided and abetted by the guests themselves, who wrote about being "thrilled not only by their superb performances, but actually getting to know them!"

Ironically, it was FP and not Catherine who was responsible for performers consorting with houseguests. Remembering the wonderful time he had had at the Kropotkin tea, he decreed that paid performers were also guests at Oshatakea. Everyone ate together and joined in activities that intrigued them. More than a few romances sprang up between dancers and business tycoons, or the wives of tycoons. Romance has always been part of the fun of house parties.

If Catherine had had her way, artists would have been available only to her. Jealous of any time they spent with "those plebeians," she considered breaking her rule of keeping the Portuguese Wing off-limits to everyone by housing some there, but then abandoned the notion. She did invite favorites to breakfast in the courtyard, or to come to her drawing room for relaxed late-night conversations, when she could ask them about other performers she should invite to Oshatakea. It was during these breakfasts and late nights that friendships formed. Catherine, having no experience in nurturing such relationships, pulled back when she feared greater intimacy was being offered than she could handle, and nearly collapsed with embarrassment when two young dancers leaving after midnight spontaneously hugged her and one said, "Mrs. Fillmore, we all love you."

Isabelle Chapman, not one of her ardent supporters, told Catherine, "Stick to your guns and if you need backup, let me know. FP will listen to me."

To date she hadn't needed Isabelle's backup, but then at dinner, when it was just the family in the Gibbons Room, on a Tuesday evening following the final house party of the season, after which guest-room floors would be closed for the winter, FP told her how much he was going to miss the events. "But we don't need houseguests to have music and dance," FP said. He wanted Catherine to schedule a major entertainment to which valley residents would be invited each month until the house opened again. "Locals won't stay overnight, so we need to house only performers. What do you say?"

Catherine said she would need time to think about it because the audience would be quite different. She wasn't about to waste her time on hillbilly music.

"While you're thinking, let me give you something else to ponder. The prince of Wales is coming in June on the way to his ranch in Canada. I've invited him here for a few days. When they tell me how many will be with him we'll know the number of other houseguests we can invite. We'll have a formal ball, of course, but I want a lot of all-American things going on. I trust you to do it right Catherine."

Catherine accepted FP's charge as an athlete accepts a challenge to enter world-cup competition. She went into training, learning all she could from the experience of others. Adelaide and Louisa were wise to the ways of royalty; she had watched them preside with aplomb over exiled Russian nobility in Paris, and the sisters were on nodding acquaintance with members of extant ruling houses.

Actually, the Kropotkins were of little help with the prince of Wales, as neither was fond of him. "He's a dim bulb," Louisa commented, a remark Catherine found odd coming from her.

"Let Farney entertain the prince," Adelaide suggested. "They can ride horses and jump fences all day. Then in the evening line up a few empty-headed girls to dance with him and you're home free."

That settled they moved on to her other assignment. Catherine was startled by Adelaide's response when she said she was concerned about FP's desire to have big events for valley people. "What can I possibly plan for them?" she asked.

"Exactly the same kind of programs you had for Grandfather's house parties."

"I don't think farmers and tradesmen would appreciate Bach and Vivaldi," Catherine said.

"There has been an orchestra comprised of farmers and tradesmen in Fillmore for as long as I can remember that plays nothing but classical music."

When Catherine reported this conversation to FP, he remarked, "Your ignorance of working people is vast." What a peculiar statement, she thought, from the man who had not wanted chamber music for his houseguests. Was he implying the taste of valley people was more refined than the taste of financial and industrial giants?

"If that's the case, I'd like to bring in a full orchestra, the Boston or Philadelphia. I'm tired of petit point music."

"Fine," FP nodded assent. "Stop talking about it Catherine. Do it."

Unsure how to go about hiring a major symphony orchestra, Catherine decided it was time to take up Isabelle's offer of help. Isabelle had contacts. Catherine knew no one in Philadelphia, but had decided she wanted the Philadelphia orchestra with Leopold Stokowski conducting. If she was going to ask a favor of Isabelle, the diva might be more amenable if she were casually visited at home rather than being summoned to Oshatakea. Catherine was willing to bend her rule of conducting business only in the office.

Isabelle was suspicious. "She has never darkened my door without a specific invitation," Isabelle rasped to Lucile when Catherine telephoned to ask if she could drop down. The singer's warning signals were lit. The meeting began as a standoff. Isabelle offered Catherine tea. "Or do you want a drink? I'm having a double martini."

"I'm not here to drink." Coming right to the point, Catherine said she was seeking Isabelle's help. The singer's eyes widened with surprise. Catherine continued, "How can I persuade the Philadelphia orchestra to come to Oshatakea?"

"Is that all you want? Offer them money," Isabelle roared, "lots of money. Sit where you are Sweet Petooty, don't move a muscle and don't make a peep until I give you permission." With gestures as broad as if she were giving a bravura performance on stage, Isabelle put through a call to Sol Hurok. Their declarations of devotion done with, Isabelle cut to the chase, telling him what she wanted, as if bringing Stokowski and the Philadelphia orchestra to Oshatakea was her idea. The agent must have said something about cost because Isabelle yelled into the telephone, "Don't worry Sol, big bucks are available. We want a February date."

"February?" Catherine heard the impresario's incredulous cry. He explained orchestras schedule a year, two years, three years in advance. "You don't just call up and say, send me the Philadelphia."

Catherine's heart sank, but Isabelle was undeterred. "Sol, get this straight. We, Catherine Fillmore and I—you've dealt with Mrs. Fillmore before, you know she means business and you know how much she has done for a number of your clients, don't disappoint this woman Sol, and don't disappoint me—Catherine Fillmore and I want the Philadelphia to play at Oshatakea with Stokowski on the podium in February. Don't but me no buts, baby." Isabelle winked at Catherine and gave her a thumbs up. The telephone conversation proceeded for another few minutes though Catherine heard little of it. Isabelle grinned at its conclusion, dropped her French telephone into its cradle and took a slug of martini. "He'll be in touch in a couple of days. Be prepared darling, he'll charge you your head and shoulders—even FP may choke—but there's nobody in the world who comes close to Hurok in the booking business."

FP did blink when Catherine told him how much they were asking, but after only a moment's hesitation he told her to have a contract drawn up. In Philadelphia, it was said Stokowski threw an earth-shaking tantrum, calmed down and, admitting he was curious about this Oshatakea, set a price he thought would shatter all records for a single performance, then informed his musicians they were going on a trip to "never-never land."

For March, Catherine booked Katherine Cornell's new play,

which was going on the road after its Broadway run. Ballet Theatre would come in April. Determined to have the ballet in the Baroque Theatre, which seated only 320 people, she booked two performances and struck a deal with the company's management that the second could be canceled if they danced the first to a half-empty house.

Approximately forty-eight hours before the orchestra was to arrive, FP threw Catherine when he complained that he hadn't seen menus. She said she thought performers would eat with the family and those menus did not require his approval. FP reprimanded her for not regarding performers as houseguests, but what really upset her was his demand to know what she would serve at the post-concert supper to which everybody in the audience would be invited. "Everybody?"

"No one leaves Oshatakea unfed Catherine. When people come to your house in the country they expect to be offered something to eat. You've been here long enough to know that. Increase quantities of whatever you were going to give the performers for a late supper - after I have approved it."

Why did he, over and over again, when she was jubilant with expectations, bring her crashing down to bitterness? Worse than having to provide a meal for hundreds with only a few hours' notice was his dismissive tone. Did the old fool think you just snapped your fingers and the Philadelphia orchestra dropped in, or Katherine Cornell with sets and scenery and an entire Broadway cast and crew? She had been feeling triumphant, she who had been written off as a brat in school who could not be educated and now had three major professional companies coming to perform for her. Had anybody else ever done such a thing in a private home? She wished the old bastard would drop dead.

Bones came to her rescue and, as with FP's house-party weekends, her grand evenings for valley residents were spectacularly successful. Observing audience reaction from a hidden spot, she could not have been more amazed. Stokowski's flamboyance was for them whip cream on the delicious music they all seemed to know. In March they cheered Miss Cornell and her cast until tears came to the eyes of jaded actors. Most incredible was the near hysterical response to Ballet Theatre. The Baroque Theater was filled to capacity for each performance. Had it not been for the policy she had established, insisting on advance reservations for the free performances, there would have been a riot among those who wanted to see the ballet but could not get in. "I should have booked you for a week," she told the beaming company manger.

Disappointed neighbors gave FP the impetus for a spasm of new construction, an amphitheater first, on a south slope, in ancient Greek style, with a stage of sufficient size to accommodate anything Catherine wanted to bring in with enough seats for everybody. Farney sparked the idea for a big-band dance pavilion, an enlarged version of an eighteenth-century orangery surrounded by wide marble terraces. FP was most proud of the spring floor that became famous as word of it was spread by big-band musicians. The combination of top-dollar and unbeatable accommodations made bookings at Oshatakea exceedingly desirable. They were featured on résumés of artists who could brag, "Anybody can hire Carnegie Hall, but only Mrs. Fillmore can invite you to appear at Oshatakea." FP paid bills without complaint but never stopped nattering at Catherine about work sheets, though he made no changes in who would perform or what anybody would eat. Catherine left nothing to chance. Her goal was to have every aspect of every function contribute to a singularly satisfying experience. No matter how much hard work was required—of her and many others—she never failed to reach that goal.

Chapter 14

FARNEY BELIEVED WORKING TOWARD OSHATAKEA's bicentennial was what kept his father's energy level high. FP would celebrate his ninetieth birthday on the Saturday of the scheduled weeklong bicentenary. "The year marking Oshatakea's two hundredth and my ninetieth is the same, but I rearranged anniversary months so we can combine them in a single celebration," FP explained.

The president and Mrs. Roosevelt were coming for two days. The President's mother, Sara Delano Roosevelt, would be at Oshatakea the entire week. FDR would dedicate the classic Greek revival post office FP had built because he could not stand government buildings designed by federal architects. A brass plaque marking FDR's visit, similar to one on the firehouse unveiled by Theodore Roosevelt, was to be attached to the polished granite facade. FP smiled at the eagerness of his banking and commerce colleagues to be at Oshatakea when President Roosevelt was there. Most of them called FDR a traitor to his class and the worst calamity ever to befall the United States. FP was one of very few "fat cats" who wholeheartedly supported the New Deal, believing Roosevelt was the savior not the destroyer of capitalism. FP had courted Sally Delano before she married James Roosevelt, and known Eleanor since her birth. Both the Hyde Park and Oyster

Bay branches of the Roosevelt family had been friends of the Fillmores for generations.

Catherine booked the Boston Symphony Orchestra and the Metropolitan Opera Company for performances in the amphitheater at opposite ends of the week and was negotiating with Noel Coward and Gertrude Lawrence to play parts of Coward's *Tonight at 8:30* cycle on two consecutive nights. If she could not get them, Lord Dunsany and Eva Le Gallienne would bring their companies to Oshatakea. At the concluding event, a birthday banquet and ball, Duke Ellington's band would provide music for dancing. Bones and his staff planned enormous quantities of food. Farney organized polo matches, foxhunts, driving and dressage competitions. There would be a pageant in the village depicting the history of Fillmore and a parade organized by local residents. A cavalcade of carriages with polished fittings, pulled by teams of horses groomed until they shone, would transport guests from the depot or dock up to Oshatakea.

Everything went according to plan; villagers in period dress greeted guests as they were driven past lush dooryard gardens, bunting-draped public buildings and clematis-encircled iron-stanchioned gaslights. The president and his wife were the last to arrive, their special train pulling into Fillmore Station as the Fillmore Academy band played "Hail to the Chief." The president was carried smiling and tipping his hat from the rear of the train to the grandest state barouche in Farney's carriage collection. Once FDR and Eleanor, FP and Sara were comfortably seated and lap robes had been tucked over their knees, the Cleveland bays slowly moved out leading a procession of landaus, broughams, victorias, vis-à-vis, calèches, phaetons, and state, road and stage coaches north toward the square, where they turned west on Valley Road. Riders in carriages waved to cheering throngs lining the route. At the western terminus of the trip, they came to a large tent in a meadow by the river, where tea and lemonade, sandwiches and cakes were served to refresh the party before its return to the village and the ride up Ontyakah Road to Oshatakea. Here, in the meadow, two old Senecas, as wrinkled and drawn as venison jerky, awaited the president. Garbed in faded feathers and worn leather, the last of the beautiful people to inhabit this valley that had been their ancestral homeland when Thomas Fillmore arrived exchanged modest gifts with FDR in a ceremony that was moving for its simple dignity. The president was especially taken by the elder of the two, who used his Seneca name, Hetgah, rather than his cognomen Johnny Beal when representing what was left of his nation.

Throughout the week the weather cooperated, allowing tightly scheduled outdoor events to be enjoyed under clear, unthreatening skies. All seats were filled at performances in the amphitheater, and hundreds sat on blankets on the lawn. The hunt and trail rides attracted so many participants that Farney ran out of mounts. Pools and tennis courts were always full, as were woodland trails and garden paths.

When Friday arrived at last, with only the birthday banquet and ball before her, Catherine held a short conference with Bones, spoke briefly to Duke Ellington's manager and to technicians in charge of fireworks, then went to the Portuguese Wing to lie down. Gaines was massaging her feet when a footman delivered a note from FP. Would Catherine please join him and Sara Roosevelt in his apartment above the Galleried Library for a cup of tea and "to review details for this evening." Exasperated because she desperately needed an hour alone, she put on her shoes and returned to the main house.

The tiny elevator resembled an antique gilded birdcage more than a conveyance for human passengers, rising slowly and complaining all the way with creaks and groans that made the fainthearted nervous. As she folded the gate back and pushed the door open into FP's foyer, Catherine glanced into the sitting room where she could hear FP talking to Sara. From his extraordinary attention all week to the former Sally Delano, it was quite apparent the still handsome woman held a special place in his affections. Before Catherine stepped out onto the tiled floor, she heard FP say, "Catherine has been a bitter disappointment to me."

"Nonsense Farnsworth!" Sara's tone was incredulous. "She does everything perfectly. What more can you expect of her?"

"A grandson."

Blood drained from Catherine's head and torso, puddling in her lower limbs. Her feet were leaden. She wanted to rush into the sitting room and crush FP's skull with her fists. She felt faint and struggled to stifle a scream rising in her throat.

"Farney and Catherine were not young when they married," Sara said. "Childbearing could be dangerous for her."

"Perhaps, but I'm still disappointed."

Catherine managed to pull the elevator door shut and slam the gate back in place. She didn't want to hear more. "I hate him," she cried as the elevator lurched downward. She didn't care if her shrieks of rage carried up the shaft, hoped they would. She regretted she had not rushed into the sitting room to claw his face, spit on him. In fury and frustration, her anguish intensified by combined accumulation of exhaustion and stress so well controlled until now others were unaware of it, she broke. A sob escaped. She caught herself. "Dudleys don't cry!" She bit her lip and clenched her fists. Her father had told her that when she wept while they were burying her pet rabbit. "Dudleys don't cry! Dry-eyed we bury our dead," he said. The words became a mantra repeated again and again as she stumbled through the Galleried Library and across the Stone Corridor, then through the monk's door into the Stepped Gallery. Getting up to her bedroom took forever. She felt as if she were in that dream where you try to run to escape danger and each step requires superhuman effort.

Slamming the bedroom door, she startled Gaines, who was coming out of the dressing room. "Whatever is the matter?"

Catherine paused, not for effect but to catch her breath. "I want him dead. I want him dead now." She collapsed onto the chaise longue, stifling sobs with a gasping rattle. Gaines was frightened. She had never seen Catherine struggling to pull oxygen into her lungs as her chest heaved and she made terrible choking sounds. When she offered a glass of water, Catherine pushed it away. "I don't want water." Her voice was an icy whisper. "Bring me a glass of scotch."

Gaines was shocked. Except for a little wine at dinner, Catherine did not drink alcoholic beverages. "Are you sure scotch is what you want?"

"Positive."

Though Gaines instructed the kitchen to get a bottle of scotch and ice cubes up to Catherine's suite instantly, it took almost ten minutes, which may have been just as well because during that hiatus Catherine regained her composure. Lying on the chaise with her eyes closed, her breathing returned to a semblance of normalcy. Gaines thought she might have fallen asleep when at last she approached her with a bottle of single-malt scotch, a small bowl of ice cubes, a pitcher of water and a heavy Waterford crystal glass, but Catherine opened her eyes.

"No ice," she said. Gaines poured a small dollop. "More," Catherine prompted. After another dollop, Catherine snarled, "More for Christ's sake. I'll tell you when to stop." She didn't, but Gaines, unbidden, stopped pouring when scotch half filled the tumbler. Catherine raised the smoky amber liquid to her lips and drank as if it were barley water. Rising from the chaise, she said she was going to bed, not for a nap but to sleep. "I don't want to be disturbed. I may not get up for days." Gaines opened her mouth to object. Catherine pointed a finger at her. "Don't but me no buts, as ever clever Isabelle is wont to say. If my idiot husband or my bastardly father-in-law or anybody else wants to know where I am, including the president of the United States, tell him, tell all of them it's none of their business." The potency of the scotch was warming her, relaxing her tongue and her rigid self-discipline. "Better yet, dear Gaines, tell them to go screw themselves." She laughed. "I've always wanted to say that, 'oh go screw yourself,' but I never have. My sanctimonious mother would scold, it goes against my breeding. If dear old mother was standing here, I would, with a courtly bow and a broad grin, say, 'Mother, go screw yourself!'" She would have fallen had the chaise not been there as a support. "Dudleys don't cry. Dry-eyed we bury our dead." The mantra turned into a lullaby as Gaines undressed her. By the time she was lying flat the scotch was overpowering her senses, but through a lovely mist she knew she would take only a short nap. She had worked too hard for too long to make this bicentennial celebration a crowning achievement; it would be self-defeating to spoil it now just because she wanted to kill FP. She wouldn't give him any satisfaction by caving in at the last minute. If God was good, and she had no reason to think He was, FP might drop dead at the ball. She pursued that train of thought. A fireworks technician might cram one of those enormous rockets scheduled to go off at midnight up the old man's backside, and, by the rocket's red glare, send him shrieking off toward the moon. "Oh say can you see?"

Her eyes closed, she thanked Gaines for the cool damp cloth laid gently across her brow, but she did not sleep. Lying there she contrived a calm that took the edge off her emotional turmoil, masked it, as if it were put to one side, stored on a shelf until it could be used along with FP's other offenses to destroy Oshatakea. She was pondering the ways to bring this about when Gaines touched her and said quietly, "It is time." Catherine got up, soaked in the scented bath Gaines had prepared, welcomed the vigor with which Gaines scrubbed the cucumber sponge across her shoulders and back, stood silently, her head throbbing, as Gaines dried her. In the dressing room, she examined her reflection in the mirror and was relieved to see she looked remarkably unperplexed.

On the dressing table was a square blue velvet box with an envelope beside it. "What is this?" she asked.

"Mr. Farnsworth senior asked me to place it where you'd see it when you were dressing for this evening."

"Was that before he asked me to come to his apartment?"

"Oh yes," Gaines replied. "He gave me the box yesterday morning."

Catherine opened the envelope and removed a card on which FP had written, "This parerre belonged to my mother, Hester Schuyler Fillmore, who has always been regarded as Oshatakea's grandest chatelaine. She was, until you came along. I pass her jewelry on to you as a token of my gratitude and affection. FPF II." Catherine tossed the card onto her dressing table and picked up the blue velvet box with Cartier stamped in gold on the lid. Inside was an Edwardian-style collar of strands of diamonds interspersed with rubies, a wide diamond and ruby cuff and a pair of diamond earrings with cascades of ruby drops.

"Oh my," Gaines exclaimed from where she was peering over Catherine's shoulder.

"Mmm," was Catherine's only comment. She returned FP's fulsome card to the envelope, placed the envelope on the diamonds and rubies within the blue velvet box and snapping the lid shut tossed the box into the wastebasket. "We'd better move along, or I will be late getting downstairs."

The hardwood floor in the French pavilion ballroom tent that accommodated five hundred dancers was filled to capacity for every number the Ellington orchestra played. Ringing this were clusters of smaller tents, each one seating 120 for dinner. Pennants from a forest of tent poles fluttered above the canvas village. Inside, the tent poles were decorated with American beauty roses entwined with greenery and white satin ribbon. Fireworks lit up the sky above the valley after midnight, and then dancing resumed, to continue until dawn when hardy souls who were still on their feet lined up for a breakfast buffet in the Orangery that Lady Astor said outdid all breakfast buffets ever. It would take workmen the better part of two weeks following the ball to remove this carnival and a full year for the lawns to recover.

Saturday the welcoming processions from the prior weekend were reversed, as tired guests rode back down Ontyakah Road to the depot and the docks. The Fillmores, FP and Farney, Adelaide and Louisa, but not Catherine, said their farewells to all except the three Roosevelts, standing between the white marble staircases in the Great Hall. For the president, his wife and mother, whose train would pull out after a quiet family lunch in the Gibbons Room, all, including Catherine, trekked down to the station and saw them off amidst, again, cheering, flag-waving crowds.

Frequently during the long night of the ball, FP looked questioningly in Catherine's direction. He was puzzled as to why she was not wearing Hester's diamonds and rubies. They would set off the white ball gown she had ordered for the event. On Saturday, though he had numerous occasions to speak to her, he did not mention his gift, not even when he thanked her yet again for all she had done. He attempted an embrace, but she stiffened and stepped back. Upon their return from seeing FDR on his way, before FP went up to his apartment, he hesitated, again offering Catherine an opportunity to say something. She said nothing. As time passed, Gaines anticipated FP's question about the jewelry and wondered what explanation she would offer. There might also have been a question from Catherine about what had become of the Cartier box after she had thrown it into the wastebasket, but neither question ever came.

Chapter 15

THE FAMILY LUNCH, WITH ROOSEVELTS, FILLMORES, Kropotkins and Isabelle Chapman sitting around the table in the Gibbons Room, was Farney's time to talk, to express his concerns without fear of treading on the toes of either his father or his wife. Over lobster bisque and a chunky chicken salad, Farney questioned the president about the immediate outlook. "Will there be war, do you think?" FDR said he didn't see how it could be avoided if the Germans wouldn't back down from their ever increasing demands. He couldn't set a date, but predicted that when it came it would be devastating. He and Farney might have been alone. The conversation was theirs; others at table listened but did not participate. FP beamed when the president complimented Farney on his grasp of history and his appraisal of what was happening in Europe.

"Don't think me a foreign affairs expert. I keep in touch with stud farm friends in Britain and on the continent, who are concerned about the welfare of their horses. It may sound self-centered, but they don't want stallions and mares carrying bloodlines developed over generations to become cannon fodder, which is what happened during the Great War. England, France and Germany lost the best of their young men; the studs lost many of their best horses. I know one does not equate with the other, but horsemen do worry." He added as if it were an afterthought, "I'd like to help; maybe bring the most endangered animals here until things settle down. I'll make a quick trip over to see what is possible."

Catherine regarded him with amazement. She'd never heard him speak so fervently. He had made a small speech. If she had an emotional reaction to spare, she might have been embarrassed that he was centering the tragedy of a possible second world war on horses, but her emotions were spent. She tasted the watermelon sherbet a footman had placed before her. Delicious. She would praise Bones for his excellent lunch.

The president assured Farney he was not equating the loss of human life with the loss of blooded horses slaughtered in battle. As he was being wheeled from the room, FDR took Farney's arm and held it in his firm grip, forcing Farney to walk beside him. Roosevelt was speaking in a conspiratorial tone, rather than in his usual vibrant voice.

Everyone gone, entertaining ceased and an uneasy quiet enveloped Oshatakea, not the peaceful country house quiet but a profound silence disturbing to the staff. Instead of relief at lighter schedules following weeks of long hours, they fussed, knowing something was amiss. In whispered exchanges there was talk of a storm gathering strength as evidenced by brittle tensions as electric as lightning spears.

FP and Catherine had decided they would take the summer off following the June bicentennial, meaning no house parties were scheduled until mid-September, but a respite did not explain the rupture in the family's demeanor. FP, Farney and Catherine dined together each evening in the Gibbons Room, but according to Raymond who served them they ate in silence, which Farney tried to break from time to time, starting conversations that neither his father nor his wife continued. "Dad, I wish you'd come to the stables to see how well Radiant Blue's filly is doing. She's the finest Arabian we've produced." Farney thought FP would respond with a surprised, "Better than Buttons?" But the old man didn't let on he'd heard his son. Though FP seldom involved himself in the details of Farney's management of the farms, the patriarch had always been interested in his son's breeding program. In the months following his ninetieth birthday, he responded to very little that Farney said.

"I've been asked if we'll be having Marian Anderson back any time soon," Farney addressed his wife, and continuing when there was no reply, "Those who heard her want to hear her again. We should have her in the amphitheater next time." Catherine didn't even look at him.

In the housekeeper's office, Mrs. Blackburn interrupted working on her account books with Pearl to say, "What they need is company. The house doesn't function properly when it's empty. Isabelle Chapman and the Kropotkins haven't been here for dinner since the ball. Consider that! They have always had dinner here two or three times a week, until now. What's going on? Has there been a battle? Hardly. There's never been a family fight we don't know about down here." The housekeeper squinted through reading glasses across the account books toward her niece. "Maybe a lingering royal is tucked away in a bedroom upstairs. We'd better take a look, and if we find one, drag her out. That would take their minds off whatever is bothering them."

"Not possible," Pearl smiled. "We checked all rooms to make sure they had been properly cleaned."

"You and I didn't see anybody, but they could hide while we were inspecting and come out again after we'd gone."

"You read too many English novels," Pearl countered. "They'd starve to death."

"No they wouldn't," the housekeeper, whose idle conversation was turning serious, "they could sneak down to the kitchens when nobody was around and take whatever they wanted. Who'd know the difference?"

There may have been no conversation but there was plenty

going on in the heads of the silent diners in the Gibbons Room. FP
could not understand why he felt so burdened by fatigue since his
ninetieth birthday. How could ninety differ from eighty-nine? He'd
always been an early riser; now when he forced himself out of bed,
his first thought was how soon he could decently lie down again.
Feebleness could not come on that fast. He feared illness, not
death. The thought of lying helpless gave him nightmares. He
knew part of his melancholia derived from dismay that Catherine
had not mentioned the gift of his mother's diamonds. They were,
after all, not mere trinkets but family heirlooms he'd not offered
either of his wives. A thank you would be nice but wasn't necessary;
ignoring his gesture was what hurt.

FP wondered if Catherine and Farney were having trouble
again, or if the trouble that always existed between them had wors-
ened for some reason. He glanced at Farney to his left halfway
down the table and then at Catherine sitting at the other end.
Farney was eating; Catherine was pushing her food around. They
weren't a matched pair. Farney possessed a gentle wit. Catherine
had no sense of humor. Nor was she ever what could be described
as good-natured. Farney is too easygoing. Everybody loves him,
which is why the farms prosper. FP's gaze lingered on his son. If
Farney did go abroad on his horse-rescue mission, FP prayed he
wouldn't get caught between fighting armies.

Farney knew he and Catherine were in a new round of serious
difficulty. He didn't know what kind and he didn't know why.
Absolutely nothing he said or did was acceptable to her, which
wasn't unusual, but now everything, no matter how trivial, instead
of bringing on sighs of impatience, or disdainful glances, brought
forth spates of venom. If he barely spoke she accused him of starting an argument. He hated arguing, walked away from disagreement whenever possible, but she wouldn't let him walk away.
When she wanted to fight, she wanted to fight and would not be
denied. He couldn't converse with her. Conversation was an art

Catherine practiced only with musicians or dancers. Postprandial chat among members of the family became a thing of the past when Catherine came to Oshatakea. Impatient with the slow pace of others enjoying their food, the little she ate she consumed with dispatch, and then she made it apparent she wanted the table cleared. Her temper could be triggered if she had to wait to signal footmen it was time for removal. The instant the last course was finished, she stood and was on her way to wherever coffee was to be served. Farney missed the days when he and his father lingered at table and talked.

Catherine didn't care that her father-in-law was depressed. If his depression deepened, he might throw himself off the Tuscan tower. Not an especially long drop, but surely far enough to kill an old man. Fantasizing helped Catherine retain a semblance of sanity during interminable family dinners. Nor did she care if her husband was unable to figure out what her problem might be. He never could. As long as he had horses to play with and that woman to join him at play he was happy. She was bored with him, with FP, with this house and everybody in it. Screaming from time to time in the privacy of her suite was the only way she knew to keep her head from exploding. Gaines no longer made a fuss when Catherine threw her head back and shouted vulgarities, had given up attempting to calm her; instead the maid slipped out of sight during these tantrums. What a way to live! I'd like to shriek a few obscenities right this minute, she thought, and with a wide sweep of my arms, send plates, silver and crystal flying onto the floor. That might wake FP Fillmores second and third, give them something to think about—not that they do much thinking. She touched her wineglass. While the footman was refilling it, she thought, maybe she should go back to Boston. Why would I do that? Crawl home to Medea who would gladly list the hundreds of ways my return adversely affected her? Hardly. I'll never cross the Mount Vernon threshold again. I could move to New York City, acquire a nice house and live rather well there on my own income. I'd take no one with me except Gaines, Bones and possibly Annie if I decided I wanted to establish a salon similar to Aunt Belle's at Fenway Court. Not that I can stand New Yorkers any more than I can Bostonians. Still, it's something to contemplate. I could go to concerts, Broadway shows, museums—and movies! I could go to movies around the clock.

Following dinner FP, his son and his daughter-in-law moved to whichever chamber had been selected for that evening's coffee, their migration part of FP's determination to live in all the rooms in his extravagant collection. They crossed the Long Gallery from the Gibbons Room and entered the Italian drawing room, the Welsh, the Chinoise, or any of the others that opened off the gallery, or they might walk the length of the Long Gallery into the West Loggia if their destination was one of the libraries off that corridor. When they arrived in the chosen room, a fire would be burning regardless of the season because Oshatakea's thick granite walls made most evenings cool inside. A footman waited with coffee, chocolates and assorted savories.

FP and Farney occasionally played a game of chess or cribbage while Catherine flipped through magazines. In spite of FP's determination to rotate, the room used most frequently was the Galleried Library, of which FP always remarked, "This is my favorite room in the house." In the Galleried Library, FP had a footman put records on the big Capehart. When he and Catherine were communicating, he asked if she had a preference for music that evening. When they were not, he made the selection himself.

Regardless of where they were, between 9:15 and 9:30 P.M., depending upon how long the game of chess or backgammon took if one had been played, matter-of-fact good nights were said and the threesome dispersed. If he was not already there, FP went to the Galleried Library to read by the fire. Catherine retired to her mauve suite in the Portuguese Wing, undressed and sat at her dressing table while Gaines brushed her hair.

Farney always went, whether after a silent family dinner or following a birthday ball, to the stable block to check on his horses. Carrying a bucket of carrots he doled them out to muted nickers, rubbing a nose, patting a neck or tugging at an ear of each animal. If he felt like staying out of the house after he'd finished his rounds, he joined the night stablemen in their paneled lounge, happy to sit with them into the night playing cards and swapping stories. For Farney, there was no more soothing way to conclude a day.

Chapter 16

—

TIME MAY NOT HEAL ALL WOUNDS BUT IT DOES ALLOW emotions to cool. FP's animus toward Catherine dissipated, but his unbounded enthusiasm for life did not return, though he was able to dredge up sufficient energy to resume his old regimen, which included spending several hours each afternoon with his architects in their monastery offices. Aside from the pleasure of working on building projects, he especially enjoyed being in the monastery during spring and summer when windows were open and he could inhale the fragrance of roses blooming on the monks' terrace.

"We could construct a long gallery off the Stone Corridor, similar to the one we built for the Portuguese Wing, and put the Spanish rooms in an open square where the Italian Garden is now, east of the chapel." The chief architect presented sketches for FP to study.

"Next to the Portuguese Wing is geographically sound, and I like the open square idea, but it has taken so many years for the Italian Garden to reach maturity, I'd hate to sacrifice it unless we have no alternative. On these plans, the new gallery, and what a long gallery it is, would go off the Stone Corridor at an angle. I don't like angles."

The architect unrolled another set of sketches for another site. These had an arched arcade over the west front drive in order not to block traffic flowing around the house to the north entrance.

"What about the flow for people from that wing into the main house?" FP asked. "I wouldn't like them having to go outside and across the driveway, or worse climb up a set of stairs and then come over a covered bridge."

"They wouldn't need to go outside FP. We'd use the ground floor of the new wing for additional utilitarian space, which we are going to need — bedrooms for servants accompanying guests, workrooms, offices, wardrobes, that sort of thing. The Spanish rooms would be on the second level, which Europeans call the first floor, with a broad corridor the length of the wing continuing through the arcade over the driveway and connecting to the existing house slightly north of the West Portico. If we widen the staircase that is there now, people would come along the broad corridor and directly down a grand staircase into the lobby and to the Long Gallery. How's that for making an entrance? The Spanish Wing is where royals and toffs will want to be. Broad corridors and wide staircases make powerful statements."

"We could call this one the Spanish Steps," a draftsman quipped.

FP smiled. "That's exactly what we'll call it. Work up the plans. Do you think our Spanish steps might become as popular for flirtation and assignation as the Spanish Steps in Rome?"

"We can only hope," his architect said, relieved to have something positive upon which to begin the project they had been talking about for years. "How many Spanish rooms do we have to incorporate into this wing?"

"Check the warehouses. At least a dozen are complete, I seem to remember, and there are parts of many others — ceilings, paneling, mantles, overmantels, floors and so forth. I shouldn't have let Isabelle persuade me to be greedy when we were in Spain. If we use only the best, we can probably do six suites on either side of the corridor on the main floor and use parts and pieces for another twelve on the floor above. Specifications for the rooms and fragments are in the files with photographs. Pull them out and we'll begin planning placement."

Once FP and Catherine were again communicating in fits and starts at the dinner table, Farney returned to his habit of woolgathering, opening his mouth only to eat. If either his father or his wife were interested in any opinion he might hold, they did not ask for it. Not that he cared about what they discussed, now that it all had to do with scheduled weekend house parties once again. Family dinners with just the three of them resembled corporate board meetings at which only two officers participated in decision making. Wednesday and Sunday evenings, when Isabelle, Adelaide and Louisa were present, they and Farney did the talking. There was more than enough valley gossip to keep them occupied through five courses. FP joined in if he had something to add, surprising the others with tidbits of information they had missed. Wednesday and Sunday dinners were Catherine's evenings to wool-gather. Valley gossip did not interest her.

During the uneasy quiet following the bicentennial, Farney had, after much soul searching, decided to make a move toward Pearl, not to satisfy lust but the curiosity Catherine had aroused with her constant harping on a sexual relationship that did not exist. Making such a move was not easy. Pearl seemed oblivious to any change in him, beyond dismounting to walk in secluded spots, which he had never done before. "Is your back bothering you?" she asked.

"No."

"Well then, let's keep moving. I have more work today than I'll be able to finish."

As he donned his riding togs each morning he promised himself he'd touch her, put his arm around her, maybe both arms, and, if she didn't resist, try to kiss her. He'd be able to tell by her reaction at each step what his next move should be. But when the moment came, when such a simple opening gesture as touching her might be possible, he couldn't lift his arm. It took great effort to murmur, "No," when Pearl asked him if he was sure there was nothing wrong? After several days of this schoolboy nonsense Pearl was obviously becoming agitated. Rather than risk her displeasure, Farney gave up trying to screw his courage to the point of making a move, but though he stopped fidgeting during morning rides, it took a long time for him to stop wondering what it might be like to hold her in his arms in a flower-filled field or, wild thought, between the sheets on his big sleigh bed.

Catherine had during the lull contacted Manhattan real estate brokers recommended by Sol Hurok, using Eleanor Gaines's name as a cover, which caused Gaines more grief than Catherine's anonymity was worth because each time a realtor sent a packet of materials on available property, the Fillmore postmistress asked everyone who came to her window, "What do you suppose is in the oversized envelopes Mrs. Fillmore's maid receives from New York City?" Anything having to do with Oshatakea and its inhabitants was part of general conversation in the valley, and this was news. Life did not come to a standstill on farms and in the village, but its pace did slacken. FP noticed whispering among the feed-store wise men, and asked what they were buzzing about. After hemming and hawing, the postmistress's question was put to him, with the added information that the mysterious envelopes carried "a mint of postage because they are all overweight." FP shook his head, said he had no idea, but he'd ask her. He didn't. What Gaines's business might be with Manhattan correspondents was none of his affair.

Catherine pored over the descriptive materials, photographs and floor plans of town houses that were depression priced at "a percentage of what the house cost to build," but none was tempting. Oshatakea had spoiled her. FP was in his nineties, how much longer could he live? When he was gone, she'd have Oshatakea to herself, to do with as she pleased. Why should she give up that opportunity for some faux château on Fifth Avenue, especially when she felt as negatively as she did about New Yorkers? The wide availability of arts in the city was alluring, but she could import anyone she wanted to see and hear, and at Oshatakea she'd have them to herself. She had no access to museums in Fillmore, but if she wanted to view what was being exhibited in galleries, all she had to do was let them know she was interested and they'd come running with every etching, sketch, painting and piece of sculpture they had in stock. As for films, FP would probably build a movie theater if she said she wanted one, but that would mean admitting she was a fan and she didn't want that. No, she would bide her time, force herself to be patient. Soon, very soon she hoped, Oshatakea would be turned inside out and upside down, and when the dust settled she would be in complete control.

TIME PASSED, WEEKS THEN MONTHS THAT BECAME years, with few changes at Oshatakea. Actual construction of the Spanish Wing had not begun because of exceedingly complicated engineering challenges. It wasn't the rarefied world on the hill, but the real world that turned upside down and inside out. Hitler's blitzkriegs struck across Europe and Japanese armies marched through Asia. Austria, Czechoslovakia, Poland fell. Governments collapsed, monarchs fled, democracies died. The United States was not yet at war, and if the strident chorus of isolationist America Firsters had their way this country would never enter a fray beyond its own borders. As the world situation became increasingly critical, FP regretfully called a halt to planning for the Spanish Wing. A minute matter in the midst of what was happening, but a major setback for him.

The White House called in mid-May. Would Farney please come to Hyde Park the following Friday night to meet with the president?

"What can he want with you?" Catherine asked, denigrating "you." Farney shook his head in bewilderment.

FP said he would accompany Farney. "It will give me a chance to see Sally before she goes to Campobello for the summer." He was dissuaded by his son.

Farney drove off early the next morning. FP had asked him to call home when he got there, so they would know he arrived safely, but Farney didn't. When there was still no word Saturday, FP took it upon himself to telephone Hyde Park. Sara was delighted to hear from him, but in reply to his query she said, "Farney isn't here. He left before I came down this morning. He should be home shortly."

Farney did not arrive home shortly, or the next day, or the next. FP had the state police looking for him. Then a cablegram came from London, stating he had hurried off to check on stud farms and to look at a stallion that had unexpectedly come on the market. He'd not be gone long, he said.

"Not be gone long?" Catherine was incredulous. "How could he fly off to London, obviously he flew, without letting either of us know? He never said anything to me about a stallion, not that he would, but it isn't as if he's just run down to Virginia or Kentucky, chasing horses, he flew to England without a word to anybody!"

"And with a war on." FP couldn't believe it.

Catherine summoned Pearl and quizzed her about this stallion. Pearl said she knew nothing about Farney pining for a particular horse. "I can't believe he kept secrets from you, especially one having to do with breeding." Pearl did not respond then or when Catherine dismissed her.

FP tried to remain calm, but he was deeply distressed. "I wish he had not flown. Crossing the Atlantic in a ship is extremely dangerous these days, but flying is suicidal. If we knew where to cable him, I'd urge him not to fly home even if it means he'll be longer getting here."

Three weeks after he left to meet with the president at Hyde Park, an exhausted Farney reappeared at Oshatakea in the middle of the night. "I didn't like the stallion when I saw him, but I've made arrangements for a group of mares and several stallions to be shipped here for safekeeping." That was all he had to say when asked about his quick trip.

FP's sensitivity alerted him to a need for Farney to be unresponsive. He stopped asking questions, but Catherine would not give up. For the first time her husband intrigued her. He was obviously involved in something other than horses; they were a mere cover. She laid awake thinking about the sequence of events, figuring the mystery began when FDR spoke to Farney as he was being wheeled out of the Gibbons Room. Whatever Farney's secret might be, it involved the president of the United States, which made him vastly more interesting than his not-so-secret sordid affair with an assistant housekeeper—or anything else he'd ever done.

When the news came on September 7 that Sara Roosevelt had died, FP was shattered. This was more than the loss of a beloved friend; it was a door closing. She approaching eighty-seven and he now ninety-five shared so many experiences they conversed in code. All she had to say was "Mitzy," and FP would double over laughing while Sara shook with amusement as they remembered the funny things their beautiful friend Mitzy Christian did. Or they bickered affectionately over details of incidents from a shared past. When Farney tried to comfort his father, rubbing his hand in circles across FP's shoulders, the old man looked up and said, "Nobody will ever call me Farnsworth again."

Farney gave him a squeeze. "I thought you preferred FP."

FP's reply was muffled, "I do, that's not the point. Sally was the last."

Within hours the Jefferson was polished and stocked for a journey. Three staterooms were made up, but then Adelaide and Louisa received invitations to the funeral and two more were prepared. Though the services were for the mother of the president, it was very much a family and close friends affair. Dignitaries kept to the shadows at the church and at Springwood. When the time came to leave, FP insisted on stopping one more time at the churchyard, where he stood for several minutes staring down at flowers covering the new grave.

After they arrived home Farney said he had something to discuss with FP and Catherine. Closing the door to the Galleried Library he told them FDR had asked him to make another flying trip. "I will be back when I get back," he said. "I can't tell you where I'm going, and the president doesn't want you to mention to anybody that I am away. People will notice I'm not around, but don't make a big thing of it."

"Checking out another stallion?" Catherine asked.

"Precisely."

"Incredible, how you can traipse around playing with horses in the midst of a war. Do tell Pearl about it, she was rather upset you hadn't shared this horsy information with her the last time you left us."

"I will tell her exactly what I have told you."

There were paragraphs about stallions and bloodlines and breeding potential in his letters from Britain, but Farney also mentioned old friends he was seeing, the Spencers, the Churchills. He had lunched at Buckingham Palace, which surprised FP; the Fillmores were not on good terms with George VI and Elizabeth, who saw them as supporters of Edward VIII. Farney said he'd had a splendid dinner at Cliveden despite Nancy Astor's stinging rebuff upon his arrival. "She will never forget you stole Gaines."

Catherine was reading the Cliveden letter aloud at Sunday lunch to Adelaide, Louisa and Isabelle when Mrs. Blackburn came into the Gibbons Room to tell them that Pearl Harbor, the United States naval base in Hawaii, "is being bombed by the Japanese." Pushing away from the table they rushed to the radio in the Galleried Library.

"Sons of bitches," FP stormed. "They did it while we were negotiating terms. Our backs were turned. We've been concentrating on Europe and look what's happened! Sly bastards." His sources in the world of international finance had informed him there was a serious threat from the Japanese, but he was not prepared for this. He had believed the emperor's emissaries were talking in good faith with those at the U.S. State Department.

"At least the idiocy of should we or shouldn't we jump in is settled." Isabelle's look defied anyone to disagree with her. "I wonder what Lucky Lindy will say now? We're in this battle, and about time. If we'd waited much longer there wouldn't be anything left."

"Will you sing for the troops?" Louisa asked in a faraway voice, courteous and not curious. She was even more distracted than usual.

"I will if they'll have me," Isabelle said.

"Be quiet, so I can hear," FP thundered. His ear was almost touching the Atwater Kent. He was fearful for his son.

Adelaide's countenance was one of deep grief. The last war had changed Louisa forever, killed their father and subsequently her mother who could not live without him. What tragedy might this new conflict bring to her family? Farney, more brother than uncle, what if he could not get back from Europe? What is he really doing; surely his mission has nothing to do with Lady Astor or horses. He had seen Churchill, but Farney should not be over there.

Catherine stared at the radio as if she could see in the tapestry-covered speaker what the static-blurred bulletins reported. How could our Pacific fleet be so vulnerable? Would the west coast be bombed? FP was right, we'd been blindsided as a result of our concentration on the Nazis. Where was her husband? We weren't really at war when he left. Now that we were, would they press him into the armed forces? Didn't they want young men, not men his age? She heard herself saying to no one in particular, "I wish Farney were here." All heard her, but none was more surprised than she that she actually meant what she said.

Chapter 17

SOME WEEKS AFTER PEARL HARBOR A WHITE HOUSE aide telephoned to pass on a message from the president. Farney would be unable to contact them immediately, but he was fine.

FP ordered most of Oshatakea shut down to conserve fuel and electricity. After everything was covered with dust sheets in all but a few rooms, he bade sad farewells to members of the staff who had enlisted or were going to work in defense plants. Catherine was not as sanguine when Bones joined the air force. "You can't be drafted, you aren't a citizen." He said he'd had a guilty conscience ever since Britain declared war on Germany and he hadn't gone home to fight. Mrs. Fuller was coaxed out of retirement to replace him in the kitchen. Tubbed plants from throughout the house were lugged to the greenhouses in a futile gesture; they soon expired. The greatly reduced ground crew struggled to keep the estate from reverting to wilderness. Flocks of sheep were turned loose on lawns. They proved an unsatisfactory substitute for mowing, cropping irregular patches bare and leaving others to grow ragged, but there was no alternative, so Cotswolds and Romneys spent the war years dropping beans from which forests of thistles sprouted, which were beautiful when in bloom but a menace and nearly impossible to eradicate later.

FP holed up in his apartment above the Galleried Library, warming the study and bedroom with fireplaces kept fueled by Stefan, whose deafness made him unfit for military service. Catherine did the same in her mauve suite, inviting Gaines to join her. "We'll put a cot in the dressing room for you." Gaines declined, saying she never had a heated room in England and would be fine in her own quarters, but she did go along with the installation of a small wood-stove up there. Once she stopped fussing about the work she was causing men who brought her wood and carried ashes away, she found this wartime arrangement quite cozy.

FP made the decision that he and Catherine would take their meals in the servants' hall with remaining staff, but Mrs. Blackburn and Catherine joined forces to keep that from happening. "It wouldn't work," Mrs. Blackburn said, citing staff schedules as a problem. Catherine did not say it aloud, but she thought that speaking to servants and sitting down to eat with them were two very different matters. The solution was to set up simple buffets three times a day in the breakfast room, from which FP and Catherine served themselves. Though the smallest dining room in the house, the breakfast room was high-ceilinged. Two electric heaters set up at opposite ends of the table barely cut the chill, partly because of floor-to-ceiling windows that opened onto a courtyard. Mrs. Blackburn made heavy lined draperies, but draughts billowed them into the room during winter months. Catherine wore layers of clothing to meals, and at times a fur coat and fur-lined boots. Still she could not keep her teeth from chattering. The tradition of Adelaide, Louisa and Isabelle coming to dinner twice a week and lunch on Sunday was reversed. FP and Catherine went to the dacha where the dining room could not be described as toasty but was degrees warmer than Oshatakea's breakfast room.

Catherine's yearning for live music at Oshatakea had to be satisfied with recordings. This, she stated, was her greatest sacrifice. Unable to survive without complaining, each time she left her suite to join FP for a meal, she grumbled about "crossing the tundra to get something to eat," referring to the Great Hall, which was truly frigid. "I'd rather have a hard biscuit and stay by the fire in my sitting room." Gaines told her FP should not be left to eat alone, to which Catherine replied, "If he would just die, he'd put us both out of our misery."

After much nattering, Gaines persuaded Catherine to go with her down to the Village Hall Monday mornings where they and the Kropotkins joined valley women in tasks assigned by the coordinator of volunteers organized to support the war effort on the home front. Catherine had been asked by the Fillmore Board of Supervisors to be that coordinator, a post filled by mistresses of Oshatakea in national emergencies going back to the Civil War, but she declined and later commented sarcastically on the inability of the Presbyterian minister's wife who had taken on the job. Catherine and Gaines also took their turn twice weekly sitting in an aircraft observation tower that had been built high up behind Oshatakea, recording every plane they saw and ready to report sightings of "unusual aircraft." Gaines, terrified of heights, closed her eyes and clutched Catherine's skirt when she followed her up open outdoor stairs to a tiny plywood and tarpaper hut that was an oven in summer and an icebox in winter, and swayed in the wind. Neither woman was totally at ease on this rickety perch, but the duty gave them a sense of shared danger, not from enemy aircraft but from the possibility of being killed if the observation tower collapsed. Isolated in their aerie with sandwiches and a thermos of coffee, they recaptured some of the easy camaraderie they had enjoyed during their journey around the world. They took turns reading aloud while the other kept her eyes peeled for German or Japanese aircraft.

The bitter cold morning FP found crystals of ice in his orange juice he took a stand. "I am eating downstairs in the servants' hall next to the kitchen where it is a hell of a lot warmer than we will ever be in this breakfast room. Do what you want Catherine, join me or sit here and freeze your tail off." Catherine joined him.

It had been FP's thought simply to sit down with his staff, eating whatever Mrs. Fuller and her aged assistant put out on two long tables, but again Mrs. Blackburn and Catherine thought otherwise. The staff had breakfast at six, dinner at noon and supper at five. An adjunct schedule was devised. When the long tables were cleared after staff meals, a small table in the corner of the room was laid with a damask cloth, sterling and fine china, and lighted in the evening by candles. Here Catherine and FP had breakfast at eight, lunch at one-thirty and dinner at seven. Mrs. Blackburn and Pearl passed dishes. Catherine missed the buffets since they allowed her to eat as little as she wanted without making an issue of it, but life during the war consisted of compromise, so she went along with the new routine. She found herself looking forward to meals at the dacha, where Isabelle joined them when she was at home. Most of the time she was singing to troops in every theater of operation and sending cheerful letters to FP describing her adventures. "The guys groan when this old broad lopes across a platform. They expect Grable or Dietrich, but once I open up, tell a few off-color jokes and start singing, they settle down. I'm doing more music hall than concert hall, but what the hell, if it's good enough for Gracie Fields it's good enough for me!"

Farney, it became apparent from what little he could say in very short communications, was serving as a kind of liaison for the president. His official capacity was vague. He did not have a title or, as far as they knew, a rank. He did not wear a uniform but was allowed access wherever he went because it was understood he reported directly to "the old man." In three years he came home twice, each visit for only a few hours, and then, in March of '45, he was able to stay for a night and a day. He had hoped to return to the states from Yalta with FDR in January but was sent from that conference on a secret errand. Two months later, someone with authority who admired Farney secured a seat on an army plane and told him to take a quick trip home while everybody geared up for the final push. He landed in New Jersey, then made his way to Oshatakea.

Arriving unheralded, he went first to his father's bedroom. Mistakenly believing Farney was home to stay, FP said, "If you had let us know you were coming, we could have killed a fatted calf."

Catherine was reading when he walked into her bedroom. She found it difficult to accept this lean, tanned and vibrantly healthy individual as her husband. He sat on the edge of her bed, actually amusing her with anecdotes about Charles de Gaulle, Winston and Clemmie, and Stalin, or "Uncle Joe," as FDR called him. He went across the balcony that connected her bedroom to his and returned with a decanter of scotch and two glasses. She said she wanted only a drop but didn't object when he kept pouring. Sipping scotch warmed her. Farney couldn't stop talking. Everything about him was different from the Farney Catherine remembered. He seemed younger than he'd been when they were both young. He laughed when he told a funny story and so did she.

A clock striking four halted his monologue. "I'm sorry, I didn't mean to keep you up, but there is so much to say and I haven't been able to write any of the good stuff." He prepared to leave.

"Your rooms haven't been heated since you left," she said. "They are cold and damp. You will freeze if you try to sleep in there. For what little is left of the night, lie down here." She moved from the center of the bed to one side.

"Are you sure?"

"Would I ask if I weren't sure?" Inviting this stranger into her bed was giving her a slight frisson.

Farney was as startled by her invitation as she had been by his appearance. They never slept together. He wasn't sure how well he'd sleep lying next to her, and he was dead tired, but it occurred to him that going without sleep was not his major concern. He had promised himself, when they told him he could go home, he would say nothing and do nothing that would bring a frown to Catherine's face. By the way she was looking up at him, he thought perhaps she had made a similar promise to herself.

Chapter 18

FARNEY LEFT THE NEXT AFTERNOON, AFTER ASSURING his father the war in Europe would be won within a year. For him it was over within weeks. FDR died at Warm Springs, to be succeeded by Harry Truman, who had never heard of Farnsworth Phillips Fillmore III. The new president was simply told that Roosevelt had a coterie of rich cronies willing to volunteer time and risk their lives without credit or compensation, running errands and undertaking touchy tasks FDR considered useful in the conduct of world affairs. Farney was one of those. He felt no loyalty to Truman, but would have continued what he'd been doing if asked. He wasn't asked, nor was he debriefed by anybody in a new administration that was either unaware or uninterested in information and insight he might possess. FPF III simply ceased to exist as a participant in the Allies' march to victory. So abrupt was his nonstatus that, if it had not been for a friend who was a general on Eisenhower's staff, Farney would have found it impossible to get home from Europe. His cover of protecting equine breeding stock would deter rather than abet any chance of getting onto a ship or an airplane. But get home he did, to be greeted by FP with open arms and a glad heart. FP had said nothing about his conviction that Farney would be killed, meaning he himself would be the last of the Fillmores. This thought distressed the patriarch almost beyond enduring, hastening his declining stamina. Perhaps with Farney safe at home, he'd regain will and sense of purpose. After a short period of doing little, FP began thinking again about building the Spanish Wing, not that he'd be able to get construction materials for some time but at least he could dream. He couldn't dream too long because as soon as the war was really won, the Herculean task of returning Oshatakea to its proper state would commence.

Catherine did not greet her husband as FP had. "Did they decide they could win the war without you?" Whatever soldier of fortune aura he'd had for her during his March drop-in was gone. As far as she was concerned, he had returned to prewar dismal. His early morning rides with Pearl resumed as if they'd never been interrupted, and so did the ugly standoff between husband and wife. This time, on the evening of his unanticipated reappearance, she showed no regret that his room was cold and damp, nor suggest his bed should be aired before being made up, nor hint at an invitation to join her. When he ventured unasked into her suite later that night she ordered him out.

For several weeks her state of mind had been that of a cranky bear rousted from hibernation. Her body and brain were in turmoil. Something was drastically wrong. Dudleys frowned upon not feeling fit. To admit to an affliction was to surrender control. As everyone else grew more excited about imminent victory, Catherine remained in bed with the mauve brocade draperies drawn. The mention of food made her retch. She allowed no one but Gaines near her.

Adelaide explained, "Catherine is going through what women her age go through," attempting to reassure Farney when he made his wife's excuses for not attending a welcome-home dinner at the dacha. "It is difficult in ways men can't understand, and can continue for a rather long time."

Even Dudleys had to deal with menopause, and Catherine accepted that menopause was the cause of her misery. Her periods, always irregular, had stopped altogether, which was a blessing. "Thank God that's behind me," she said, but it didn't make her feel any better. Increasing discomfort angered her. Why couldn't she be one of the lucky women who breezed through the change of life? She lashed out at Gaines. "Why should I have such a hard time? I want to go to sleep and not wake up until the whole filthy process is finished. Is there a pill I can take?

Terror replaced anger when, one morning in the bath, she noticed her abdomen was swollen. It could only be a tumor and it might be malignant. More desolate than before, she told no one, not even Gaines, clutching her terrible secret as if revealing its presence might cause the cancer to metastasize. She could not sleep, lying in anguish as perspiration soaked her gown and bed linen. She must devise a plan. If the physical discomfort she felt now was making her crazy, how would she react when white-hot knives stabbed her, knives no medication could dull? She would kill herself. Analyzing how best to commit suicide became an obsession. A new doctor had recently come to the village, a ratty little man, she heard, was already prescribing sleeping pills and he'd never seen her. Sleeping pills would be better than a gun; she hated guns, and didn't have the courage to slit her wrists or put a noose around her neck. She thought of her brother Teddy drowning at sea. Could she drown herself? Probably not. An overdose of sleeping pills was the way out; she'd have Gaines call Dr. Montrose and start building a cache. Gaines would not be told what she was doing.

She had not yet launched her plan when, after Gaines finished brushing her hair one evening, Catherine got up from her dressing table and walked toward the bed with her body arched backward and both hands pressed against her lower back, where it ached constantly. Usually, she wore a loose silk wrapper over her nightgown, but tonight her thoughts were otherwise occupied. As she turned to sit on the edge of the bed, she heard Gaines speak but did not discern the words.

"Would you please stand again?" Gaines asked. Catherine pulled the sheet across her lap. "Stand up," Gaines repeated.

Catherine's eyes widened. "Are you telling me what to do?"

"I am, forgive me. Stand up." There was a moment of taut silence, then Catherine's shoulders slumped, her features collapsed and, with eyes closed as tightly as possible to stem a flow of tears and blot out the developing scene, she let the sheet fall away and stood. Gaines stepped forward to place gentle hands on Catherine's abdomen. Her touch turned into a caress. "Oh, what have we here?"

Hot tears fell onto Gaines's hands and wrists. "I'm dying," Catherine sobbed.

"I don't think so. Oh no," Gaines put her arms around Catherine and drew her close. "You are not dying my lady, you are pregnant!"

Catherine's recovery was instant. "Don't be a sap." She pushed Gaines away. "I am too old to be pregnant. How can I be pregnant when I'm menopausal, for God's sake, a damned ugly process by the way. Wait until it's your turn." She straightened her shoulders, which did not diminish the slight swelling. "I think Miss Know-it-all I have enough intelligence to recognize the difference between pregnancy and a malignant tumor."

Gaines tried not to smile knowing that would further upset Catherine. The symptoms of pregnancy were so obvious, how could she have been blind to them? "I suggest we call the doctor and get him up here to examine you."

"There will be plenty of time for doctors when the pain is too intense for me to handle." Catherine was weeping again. Crying made her furious with herself; Dudleys don't cry. "Listen well to me Gaines, I have never been more serious about anything, no one, absolutely no one is to be told about this. I mean what I say. If you wish to be useful, telephone Dr. Montrose's office tomorrow and tell him I need more sleeping pills."

Gaines did not reply until she was pulling the covers up and tucking Catherine in as if she were a frightened child. "I will keep your secret my lady, on one condition."

Catherine sat up so fast she bumped her head against Gaines's chin. "There are no conditions. You do what I tell you to do."

"The condition is, I will say nothing if you will allow Dr. Montrose to examine you."

Catherine lay back on her pillows. "That's some condition. You won't tell if I let a doctor in here to examine me to confirm what I already know, so he can announce it to the world."

"Doctors don't make such announcements. He'll not say a word if you insist, but much more important, he will prescribe proper care, medications rather than sleeping pills, whatever the truth may be. Your well-being is my major concern, you know that." Catherine let Gaines smooth the covers and tuck her in again.

"Stubbornness is your worst failing Gaines." Catherine closed her eyes. "He will insist on telling my husband and he's the last person I want to know."

"Perhaps," Gaines conceded, "but if what you believe to be a tumor is a baby, your husband should be told. Think of the satisfaction it will give you to tell your father-in-law. The poor man gave up hope of hearing such good news years ago."

Catherine's eyes searched Gaines's face. "What do you know about my father-in-law's hope?"

"I know only how happy he will be if you are indeed pregnant."

Catherine glared at her. She did not believe Gaines's too pat answer, but Gaines did not flinch, bidding her mistress good night and quickly leaving the room.

The next morning Gaines, risking wrath, informed Catherine that if she were not allowed to call Dr. Montrose at once, she would go straight to Farney and tell him what was happening. Strong words, epithets Catherine used only under duress, were hurled at her, but Gaines held her ground, and in the end, with exhausted resignation, Catherine capitulated.

Dr. Montrose came at once, as every person in the valley did when summoned to Oshatakea. Gaines waited for him inside the east portico and led him upstairs to Catherine's bedroom. Expecting to withdraw, she was surprised to hear Catherine, after she had sworn the doctor to secrecy, ask if Gaines could remain in the room while she was being examined. Dr. Montrose said he saw no reason why she should not. "I'll be right here if you need me," Gaines said, taking a chair in a corner where she could hear all that was said.

Twenty minutes after the doctor's arrival, he pulled the covers up, replaced several instruments in his black leather bag and said, "You do not have a tumor Mrs. Fillmore, you are carrying a baby, which, from what you have told me of your last menstruation I would judge to be into"—he took a small calendar from his coat pocket—"its sixteenth week."

Gaines clapped her hands to her mouth to stifle a joyous cry.

Catherine's face was devoid of relief but livid with rage. Worse than being told she was wrong, and she had always rebelled when corrected, she had made plans, devised a schedule, knew what steps she would take to reach the desired conclusion, and nothing exacerbated her temper more than having carefully laid plans altered. She drew on generations of Dudley self-discipline to calm hyperventilation and bring her breathing under control so she could speak. "May I see that calendar doctor?" She turned pages in his tiny morocco bound book, her eyes darting as she counted the weeks back to Farney's surprise visit shortly after the Yalta conference. An oath escaped her lips. She snapped the calendar shut and handed it back to him. "Your calculation is incorrect; this cursed thing has been growing inside me fourteen weeks and three days! If you tell me what time it is, I can add hours and minutes."

Within hours and minutes every person in the Fillmore Valley knew. Farney was told first when he was asked to come to Catherine's room. Shocked or, as his stablemen would report, flabbergasted, he tried to kiss his wife but she turned away. Not wanting icy aloofness to spoil his delight, he hurried off to find his father.

FP jumped straight up in the air, quite a feat for a man approaching one hundred, so thrilled was he by the prospect of an heir. Oshatakea's future was ensured. He sat down to recover his equilibrium before rushing up to see Catherine, entering her bedroom without knocking. His uninvited, unwanted intrusion heaped coals on the fire of her fury. She struck out, fighting off his attempted embrace with a blow that glanced off the side of his head. No damage done and respects paid to the prospective mother, FP hustled to the nearest telephone to call Adelaide and Louisa. He would call Isabelle if he knew where she could be reached in the south Pacific. The village operator listened in as the elated head of the Fillmore family informed Adelaide of the glad tidings. No further public announcement was necessary. Jubilation broke out from one end of the valley to the other. Another generation of Fillmores meant continuing good times. One would be hard-pressed to guess which was the most heartfelt phrase during those early hours of knowing: it's a miracle, or, it's God's blessing. It was upon hearing the news that Levi the junk man made his oft-repeated remark, "If it's a boy, they should name him Jesus."

Actually, arguments began at once between Farney and FP over the unborn child's name, a more acrimonious disagreement than was usual between this father and son. Farney was insisting the boy, and of course it would be a boy, should be Farnsworth Phillips Fillmore IV, "after you Dad."

"If you do that you are naming him after yourself or after my father, which is fine, but don't make out you're naming him after me," FP thundered. "We don't need another Farnsworth Phillips in the family, three is enough. It's time to get past my mother's pretentiousness. Show some originality Farney. Give him a heroic name, or go back to Thomas. It was Thomas who started this whole shebang."

The morning after public jubilation, it dawned on people that all might not go well and gloom descended like a hangover. Being pregnant at forty-seven was hazardous, and Catherine would be forty-eight when she gave birth. There could be complications, not only for the child but also for the mother. Much younger Fillmore wives had died giving birth or from the fever that followed. "Usually their babies survived," FP reminded Farney. For FP the infant's survival was of utmost importance. What worried him more than the birth was that Catherine might not carry the baby to term. "Dear God, don't let her lose it," FP prayed each of the dozens of times a day he thought of the miracle pregnancy. Dr. Montrose agreed there was a risk; precautions should be taken. FP hired around-the-clock nurses, which the doctor felt was unnecessary but allowed when he realized there was no way to stop the anxious old man. Catherine was told to stay off her feet as much as possible, a command she followed too readily. She would not have gotten out of bed at all in the weeks that followed if Gaines hadn't forced her. Catherine was suffering postpartum depression before the fact.

In her mind she had solved the problem of dealing with a malignant tumor; having a baby was a vastly different proposition. Damn it to hell, she did not want to be a mother, did not look upon what she now felt moving within her body as anything other than the Fillmore family's satanic vengeance. "I won't do it," she shouted. "I swear to God I won't do it."

Instead of lying awake considering ways to end her life when the pain of cancer was beyond endurance, now sleepless hours were spent thinking of what she could do to bring on a miscarriage. Falling down stairs was a cliché. If she were to go that route, which stairs would she fall down, and should she do it when she was alone or would it be more convincing if there were witnesses? The perfect place would be one of the marble staircases in the Great Hall, but what reason would she have for being at the top of those stairs and how would she get there when she couldn't walk across her bedroom without assistance? What if she broke her back when she fell and did not miscarry? "I could be an invalid and still give birth," she groaned.

"Gaines, what do women do in England when they find themselves pregnant and having a bastard means the end of life as they know it?"

Gaines was draping a bath sheet over Catherine's shoulders as she helped her out of the tub. "Girls in service you mean? Some run away before anyone notices, and some go to crones in dirty rooms. Lots of those girls bleed to death."

"Leave it to you to be cheerful."

Nothing that happened within the next months changed Catherine's perspective. Her disposition grew steadily worse. She refused to do the exercises Dr. Montrose recommended, or to participate in any aspect of preparing the nursery on the floor above. She would not open her eyes when FP brought paint and fabric samples for her approval, nor would she permit footmen to carry her up to inspect the suite of rooms after they had been redecorated. When Farney asked why the nursery needed to be redone since the rooms had never been used, FP said, "Colors faded, and dust accumulates. We can't be too careful about germs."

Gifts for baby Fillmore came from family and friends, local residents and former houseguests, musicians, dancers, actors who had played at Oshatakea. Miss Anderson sent a silver rattle, Eleanor Roosevelt a porringer. Clementine Churchill sent an antique silver drinking cup. Adelaide knitted a sweater and Louisa made a crib quilt. "We will never need to buy a thing," Gaines commented. Catherine paid no attention. To avoid temper tantrums, packages were not brought to her but taken up to the nursery suite where they were opened by Gaines and listed by Annie, who wrote thank-you notes in Catherine's name.

In the midst of all this excitement, word came from Joseph Wengren in Boston, the Dudley family attorney, that Catherine's mother had died quite unexpectedly from a massive stroke. Farney relayed the message to his wife, whose response was, "Do you expect me to do something about it?"

Icarus flying closer to the sun, Farney continued, "Inasmuch as you cannot, I think I should go to Boston to make arrangements."

"Why for God's sake? They know what to do. There will be a service at Emmanuel and they will bury her in Mount Auburn. You would only be in the way."

"But Catherine, some member of her immediate family should be there."

"I'm the only member of her immediate family. I'm not going, nor are you. Don't use this nonsense as an excuse to escape the mess you've created here, War Hero." She fixed him with a cold eye.

When Dr. Montrose talked to her about nursing the infant, she froze him with that same cold eye. "You must be perverted if you think I'd let any brat attach itself to my breast."

Word went out for wet nurses. Gaines interviewed applicants and FP checked their medical histories to make sure nothing threatening might be passed on to the infant. Three valley women were contracted and given deposits against future services. FP found a nanny with impressive credentials through a New York agency. She'd been trained in England, and written documents attested to her knowledge, experience and health. Miss Cooper moved into Oshatakea two months before Catherine's due date and promptly rearranged the nursery furniture. She said she pre-ferred Gaines's bedroom and sitting room across the hall to those that were part of the nursery suite. Gaines could have told her to disappear and would have been supported by FP, but she moved without objection to a small bedroom that opened onto the room where the baby would sleep. There she'd be able to keep an eye on how the wee one was faring in the care of this Cooper woman, whose personality was as starched as her stiff white cap and floor-length wraparound apron. A gaunt woman with a formidable black mustache, Miss Cooper even made FP wince. Following a short conference between himself and Gaines, Miss Cooper was dismissed and sent back to New York, a piece of rejected merchandise.

This brought on a flurry of urgent telegrams to the nanny agency, telling them what was unacceptable about their first candidate and specifying what they were looking for in a suitable replacement. FP's attention to the nanny detail was diverted when Catherine went into labor approximately three weeks before Dr. Montrose had said she was due. The doctor and two registered nurses were in attendance, with Gaines standing at the foot of the massive bed in the mauve bedroom. Farney and FP frantically paced the floor in Catherine's sitting room. After the initial signs everything seemed to stop. The doctor was asked if it had been false labor but did not reply. And then it began again, and stopped and started up again.

At about the twenty-seventh hour, Catherine remembered what Gaines had said about the agony of a crude abortion and thought it could not be worse than what she was suffering. Demanding relief, she screamed at the doctor and nurses that they were not doing a thing to help her through this shattering experience. "It is you who must do it Madame," one unwary nurse said.

"Get her out of here," Catherine bellowed. During the months since she learned she was pregnant, there had been times when she wondered if the birth process would ever begin; now she wondered if it would ever be over. She wished she had thrown herself down the stairs, any stairs, with or without witnesses. "God, won't someone pull this thing out of me," she cried.

Dr. Montrose had been standing at her side for seven hours without a break when Gaines persuaded him to go into Catherine's dressing room and lie down on a chaise. After a short rest, he put in another five-hour stint. Highly skilled nurses hovered, plumped pillows, took turns wiping Catherine's brow, tried to get her to sip water, but were otherwise "useless," as the patient screamed. Only

Gaines's presence calmed her though there was nothing Gaines could do. Farney was barred from the room. Catherine swore she'd never lay eyes on him again. The pain she was enduring, the emotional and mental turmoil flailing her she blamed on her idiot husband. She must have been crazy that night she saw him as a warrior. The boredom she had always felt in his presence and the general loathing for him as a person were magnified during those hours of labor into a soul-searing hatred that bored into the marrow of her bones.

"Out of here. I want everybody out of here. I don't want to look at your faces another minute." It was not quite dawn. Dr. Montrose nodded to exhausted nurses on either side of the bed. As they were leaving, Catherine screamed, "Gaines, where are you? Gaines don't leave me."

"I'm right here."

Through a door slightly ajar, a distraught Farney, a nearly comatose FP, a depleted doctor and two numb nurses listened to Catherine's cries and visceral grunts, believing they were the same as they'd been witness to for almost three days. Their postures were a tableau of defeat when, next door in Catherine's bedroom, Farnsworth Phillips Fillmore IV was at long last pushed upside down and backwards, bruised, blood-smeared and wizened out of his mother's womb and into Gaines's outstretched hands. It was Gaines who cut the cord, slapped the baby's bottom, rinsed the squalling infant in warm water and wrapped him in a flannel blanket. His father, grandfather and the professionals came running when they heard him cry, but Gaines refused to hand him over. "I'll tend to the boy," she said. "You take care of her, she needs attention."

Catherine was lying limp and lifeless, unaware of all that was being done for her or to her. Except for fractions of minutes she would remain in a semicomatose state, abetted by Dr. Montrose's sedation, for the better part of a week.

On the floor above, in the nursery, Farnsworth Phillips Fillmore IV slept peacefully, tiny but tight and strong, watched over by his adoring grandfather. The old man put his hand lightly on the newborn's swaddled form. "I didn't think you'd ever come along, little lad," he said. "There won't be much time for us to get to know each other, but we'll do the best we can, and we won't waste a minute."

Chapter 19

CATHERINE'S ENTIRE WORLD, SO CAREFULLY CONSTRUCTED and jealously guarded, had collapsed. She survived the war with a forbearance she didn't know she possessed, chewing her cheeks to keep from venting frustration with the severely curtailed life at Oshatakea, cut off from all that had become important to her. If she so much as murmured her desire to have a few guests with a string quartet to entertain them, or perhaps a small company of dancers, the quartet and dancers being what she really wanted, FP regarded her with a disdain that made his "Don't be silly, we are at war" redundant. Everybody had been so sanctimonious doing his or her duty. The whole thing made her sick.

Now, after giving birth, as far as she was concerned the worst experience hell had to offer, the very people she had entertained for years, as she also satisfied her own needs, turned against her. Instead of being the center of their attention, they cast her aside, the discarded packaging for an infant who was greeted as if he were the messiah. Her father-in-law had gone simple over the child and nobody stood up to him, no one told him he was fawning. She didn't care if the old fool spent all his time in the nursery; what she could not forgive him was his taking Gaines away from her. For that Catherine wanted to strangle him. Gaines, her only friend and companion in this hideous house, in the world! Adelaide was ever sweet, but Catherine wasn't fooled. She knew Adelaide and all the rest of the family wouldn't have paused for half a second if she'd died giving birth to their precious Fourth. Farnsworth Phillips Fillmore IV. That sequence of names passing through her head made her gag. Family names could be excused, but carrying this one as far as they did was sick. Maybe she was wrong, maybe Gaines wasn't her friend, never had cared about her, just used her as an excuse to get away from Nancy Astor. If Gaines did care, why would she be so quick to take on total responsibility for the brat when Catherine needed her now more than she ever had, more than any puling worm of an infant could?

As for her farce of a husband, that chapter in her life was closed. Why didn't Farney do her an enormous favor and run off with his horsy serving girl? Why in God's name hadn't FP taken the golden opportunity of Mrs. Blackburn's sudden resignation to send Pearl packing? What possessed him to make Pearl housekeeper? That happened while Catherine was in the agonies of labor. When Mrs. Blackburn's declining health forced her into retirement and Pearl was appointed her successor FP was so concentrated on the impending birth of an heir, that he paid no more attention to household matters than he had paid to his one hundredth birthday, which went unmarked except for greetings within the family.

Adelaide and Louisa came to visit on a morning so blindingly bright Catherine asked to have her bed curtains closed. The Kropotkins had the good sense to call on her before going up to the nursery to look in on the baby they had beheld many times while Catherine was still semiconscious and unable to see anybody. Twice a day they were driven up in their Daimler, then crept to the third-floor nursery. At Gaines's request the twice-daily visits fell back to once a day. When Catherine finally said she'd see them she complained about having to be polite to people she didn't feel like being polite to. Adelaide and Louisa entered her bedroom bearing fresh flowers from their greenhouse, huge yellow rosebuds and a spray of tiny spider orchids. Speaking up so she could hear them in her cocoon, Adelaide asked, "Is it all right if we visit with you for a few minutes?"

From behind the bed curtains, Catherine replied, "If you don't stay too long." When a maid pulled the hangings back she was revealed propped against pillows cased in mauve satin, her countenance devoid of expression.

Adelaide, her smile radiant as always, moved toward the bed in her particular imperial glide, placed the roses next to Catherine on the bed and leaned to brush her powdery cheek against the invalid's. "You must tell us when we begin to tire you." Catherine said she would.

Without comment, Louisa handed her gift of orchids to the maid who had shown them in, then exhaling a deep sigh sank into a lavender velvet slipper chair on the far side of the bed. Catherine interpreted Louisa's sigh as proof this was a duty call.

"When the sun came out today reflecting so brilliantly off the new snow after a long period of storms and overcast skies," Adelaide began, acknowledging with a nod a matching slipper chair pulled up to the bed for her by the maid, "I told Louisa, I believe our dark days are behind us." She unbuttoned her white kid gloves, removed them from her manicured pianist's hands and placed both on her lap. "The war is over, our people are coming home from working in defense plants, as are our men in uniform, though sadly some will never return." Her pause was significant. "And you dear Catherine are recovering from your ordeal and will soon return to your vibrant self." Another, more significant pause. "Most salubrious, in the nursery upstairs is a male heir to Oshatakea, a boy to carry on the Fillmore name. What further blessing could we ask?"

If Catherine had replied, she would have said she could think of a dozen or more without even trying. She did not appreciate her near death experience being included in Adelaide's litany of blessings.

Louisa was neither as doleful nor as cheerful, she was just Louisa. "That's fine and dandy Adelaide, but I won't believe dark days are behind us until Catherine is able to do her entertainments again. I didn't mind giving up butter and gas during the war, but I missed your parties Catherine."

"We gave up neither butter nor gas," Adelaide corrected her younger sister. "They were rationed, but we managed nicely."

"Rationing gas I could understand," Louisa retorted, "but why we had to ration butter when our dairies make tons of it each day is beyond me."

"And will continue to be, I fear." Adelaide's response was curt.

"Did you really miss the parties Louisa?" Catherine asked.

"More than I can say. I loved your parties Catherine, but it's the music I miss most. There were times during the war when I thought I'd never be able to breathe deeply again until I could listen to Flagstad."

Catherine would not have dreamed Louisa, whom she thought was next door to certifiable much of the time, could strike a spark in her scarred psyche to rekindle the fires that had driven her to become an impresario.

Louisa wasn't finished. "You carried on an old family tradition of forceful women marrying Fillmore men, but you brought something quite extraordinary to us. Our grandmothers established the Fillmore Academy and built the library, the hospital. You understood valley people needed to hear great music played by professional musicians and see ballets and opera and plays performed. We in the family can go to hear music, but most valley people can't. I think what you did, bringing performers to the valley, is as least as important as what our grandmothers did. I do, Catherine. Really, I do." Her excitement had mounted. When she finished her face was flushed.

Adelaide was amazed by her sister. Catherine's expression was unreadable. She had not for a single minute thought about fulfilling the needs of anyone other than herself, least of all people who lived in the valley. She did not make that point when she said, "Louisa, that was a lovely oration."

"I didn't mean to make an oration."

"Whatever you meant, I am grateful." She reached across the bed toward Louisa, who stretched her arm so Catherine could touch her hand. After the briefest contact, Catherine slumped back against her pillows. "Now, if you don't mind, I am beginning to tire."

They didn't mind at all. Adelaide and Louisa blew air kisses in Catherine's direction and departed, hurrying to the floor above where they joined FP and Gaines in a cooing circle around the cribbed cherub.

That evening, FP entered the Gibbons Room to find three places laid on the polished table. "Does Farney have a guest?" he asked, and was astonished by Raymond's reply. Mrs. Fillmore was coming down for dinner. FP sat down, then immediately rose again as Farney and Catherine walked into the room. She was leaning heavily on her husband's arm. "We've missed you. You are good to join us Catherine." FP's greeting was genuine.

There was little conversation until Catherine raised her knife and fork to cut into a veal chop, thanking God as she did so that Bones was back in the kitchen. "Now that my strength seems to be returning," she said, "it's time for us to think about reopening parts of the house. I would like to invite a few guests for a long weekend, not a large party, twenty at most. The staff is not yet back to its full complement, but they should be able to handle that number."

FP, content with only his infant grandson for company, didn't care if there was ever another houseguest at Oshatakea but was relieved that Catherine appeared to be recovering. "Splendid idea, splendid."

"I spoke with Sol Hurok this afternoon. He has several artists who interest me available for booking the weekend of May 16."

"May?" FP interrupted. "Phil will be six months old in May. We can have a proper christening and introduce him to the world. Farney, telephone Winston first thing in the morning. Tell him as godfather he has to be here."

Catherine slammed down her knife and fork with such force she chipped a rim of the Dresden dinner plate. "Celebrating an infant's six-month anniversary is not what I had in mind." Her eyes narrowed. "However, inasmuch as you have brought him into the conversation, I have made the simple request repeatedly, if this child is to be saddled with names and numbers given to him without either of you asking me what my preference might be, please humor me after the fact by not referring to him as Phil."

Farney's voice broke through. "Who is it that Sol has available?" Why couldn't Catherine behave like a normal human being? Why did she always have to throw a fit? He had told her the minute he knew she was pregnant he wanted to name the baby after his father if it was a boy. Her response then was that she didn't care if he named it after a horse. Probably they should have waited for the informal christening in the chapel until she was able to attend, but at the time he thought she'd never recover, not that he could say so now. She sits there like a conquering Caesar with that tyrannical look, as if she hates Dad as much as she hates me. I'd like to slap her hard enough to knock her down, not that I'd ever lay a hand on her but why does she make everybody's life miserable—or try to? Why did she come down tonight? Dad may have missed her, but I haven't. She should stay upstairs feeling sorry for herself.

Before Catherine could respond to Farney's question about Hurok's artists, FP picked up the reins, speaking quietly and in measured words, which forced them to pay close attention if they were to hear what he had to say. "Regardless of what you may or may not have in mind for reopening Oshatakea, Catherine, we will celebrate Phil's six-month birthday on May 25 with a grand party to which everyone in the valley is invited. Have as many houseguests as you can accommodate. I suspect only one level of rooms will be ready by then. I urge you to join me in planning the festivities because you have a talent for putting together memorable events. At that sort of thing you have no equal. However, if you do not wish to participate — or attend — we will manage without you."

Catherine's ashen features turned scarlet, giving her the appearance of one whose inner battle to contain emotion was causing sufficient stress to bring on a seizure. Always aware FP spoke again. "I believe you are not feeling as strong as you thought you were." Prepared to show concern, but not wanting her to think he was softening his stance, FP continued in the slow distinct voice. "If you wish to leave the table Catherine we will understand. Raymond, please take Mrs. Fillmore to her suite."

Farney's heart leapt into his throat. Considering Catherine's excessively evil disposition and a temper that was ever more volcanic since Phil's birth — witness her reaction when Dad called the baby Phil — what might she do after being dismissed from the table and sent to her room, for in truth, that is what his father had done. Raymond didn't move, standing steady, his attention concentrated on FP, awaiting further instructions. Farney could not remember his father ever dismissing him from the table. As a child, he had been reprimanded but never sent to his room. Catherine was not a child. She was a domineering woman who knew that the mere threat of a scene could result in getting what she wanted, but this time it had not worked. She will never forgive him, Farney thought. To be disciplined was bad enough, but to be embarrassed in front of Raymond was worse. Could Raymond's presence be what was keeping her from spewing a torrent of wrath at FP? Or was she building up a head of steam for a response that would blast her father-in-law out of his chair? The tall case clock ticked. Farney's muscles tightened; should he say something to lessen the deepening tension? What could ease the standoff between his wife and his father that would not appear to be taking either side?

"You are right." Catherine spoke as quietly and distinctly as if she were aping FP. "I am not as strong as I thought I was when I made the decision to come down for dinner. If Raymond can be spared to accompany me to the foot of our staircase . . . "

Farney pushed his chair away from the table. "I will take you back."

"Not you, I prefer Raymond." She leaned on the footman's arm, expending waning strength to keep her shoulders back and her head high. Nothing in her bearing as she left the room bespoke concession. If asked, Catherine could not explain why she accepted FP's dismissal without a fight, now especially when her antipathy toward him was increasing by the second. She had never been one to examine motives, least of all her own, but she was not withdrawing out of respect or common courtesy for one's elders. Retiring from the fray without a fight when FP laid down the law, some might think, remembering Catherine's enthusiasm for battle, was physical weakness resulting from a difficult labor and months during which she had done little but lie abed. Others might theorize that FP had given her explicit orders that could not be ignored, and Catherine, accepting ultimate authority, had allowed him to assume a strong patriarchal role while she obeyed, as a good daughter should, but that was laughable. Catherine had never been a good daughter. She would tuck away her rage toward her father-in-law, hoarding it with slights and slings from the past until they could be transformed into an act of vengeance equal to or exceeding their combined value. If he would not relent on his insistence that the postwar reopening of Oshatakea must be a cel-ebration of his grandson's six-month birthday, she would make it a party to remember. Introducing the old man's namesake and heir would make clear to everyone that FP's life was nearing its conclusion, an ending that couldn't come soon enough to suit her. Using Phillips to foreshadow his grandfather's demise would give the brat's existence a useful purpose.

"Thank you, Raymond," she said at the foot of her staircase. Without assistance, she climbed up to her suite.

Chapter 20

—

PHIL WOULD HAVE NO RECOLLECTION OF CELEBRATING his first six months of thriving on a plenitude of love from his grandfather and Gaines. Cuddled by one or the other since the moment of his birth, he was carried about, sung to, burped, bathed and changed by one or the other of his two devoted protectors, who with great reluctance handed him to a wet nurse to be suckled. Their doting attendance shielded him from a complete absence of attention from his mother and little from his father. Farney was afraid he'd hurt the baby if he tried to pick him up, so just beamed affection on his son. Catherine didn't go near the nursery and would not allow them to bring the infant to her. Defying orders and thinking Catherine would relent and fall under her baby's spell if she held him, Gaines carried Phil down a flight of stairs and pleaded with her to take him. Catherine closed her eyes and turned away.

Of the pictures taken at Phil's six-month celebration and formal christening, there are many of him with FP, with Gaines, with Farney, with both FP and Farney to record three generations, with Adelaide and Louisa and Isabelle and anybody else who wanted to be photographed with the newest Fillmore. One shows him on Winston Churchill's lap. The former prime minister's expression is grim; Phil is a tiny version of old Blood, Sweat and Tears himself. There is no picture of Phil with his mother.

He would not remember his first birthday party either, at which miles of home movies were shot to capture the momentous event for posterity. Dale Morris was assigned to keeping a camera focused on the celebrant, and did, photographing him lurching into the Great Hall from the Galleried Library, a dark-haired, round-faced, pear-shaped imp in a romper suit. FP walks on one side and Farney on the other, each bending to grip a tiny fist at the end of an upstretched arm. The waiting crowd must have frightened Phil, because after three faltering steps he screws up his face and starts to cry. There is no sound, but the pictures make clear Phil is bawling. Farney picks him up, even though Phil's arms reach out toward Gramps. Gaines hovers behind, her face creased with anxiety.

This tearful scene is followed by successions of people approaching to say hello, which Phil doesn't seem to mind, except for those who try to touch him. They are treated to a view of the back of his head when he buries his face in Farney's neck. There are reels of the toddler tearing open presents everybody was told not to bring, and more reels of him in a high chair, rearing back from a cake twice his size with a candle blazing on top. He reaches to touch the flame when Farney blows out the candle, and then thrusts both hands into the icing, which brings on more tears.

Raymond's assignment was to film guests and the general festivities. Panning through the crowd he caught Catherine staring at FP standing a few feet away talking to a young couple, unaware that if his daughter-in-law's eyes could shoot poisonous darts he would be dead. Catherine's concentrated contempt is chilling to contemplate. The flickering scene says much about the antagonists. FP, an old man, is happily chatting and enjoying life. Catherine has the appearance of a vengeance-driven fury. Celebrating birthdays was very big with FP. Celebrating anything. His entire life was a celebration—building his house, collecting rooms and finding ways to fit them together into an expanding mosaic. He collected not to amass treasure but to surround himself with glorious spaces in which beautiful objects could be placed and appreciated. To him, each piece was part of the celebration.

"Phil, I want you to notice," FP said when the little boy was three and standing beside him in the Chinoiserie Room, "the variety of elements the artisans used in this entryway. These doors have panels that resemble stacked pairs of vertical black-lacquered boxes with mythical rural scenes in gold. Surrounding the boxes, pay attention now, is a slanted lattice pattern repeated in the framework on either side." He tipped Phil's head back and lifted his chin with a gnarled index finger. "Above, way up on top, do you see delicately carved branches with realistic leaves and tiny buds? And there, in the middle is what? Is it a peacock tail or is it a scallop shell? It is both my boy! It is a stylized peacock tail and a scallop shell. Now then"—his hands on Phil's shoulders forced the little boy to bend—"what do you see framing the entrance, beyond the latticework? Pilasters of fish scales, carved golden fish scales and plumed capitals supporting a lintel with more carved natural designs capped by a classical scroll pediment. Quite magnificent, but also an elaborate joke. Fish scales and plumes, peacock tails and shells, indeed! These artisans played tricks on us, and they did it using only black and gold. A splendid piece of work, splendid. But now, lad, step away and see what we have on the wall in which this superb gold and black doorway is placed—hand-painted wallpaper busy with white trees and bushes on a luminescent blue background. Artistic license, trees and bushes aren't white, but here they are white to focus our attention on flights of exotic, brilliantly colored birds. We couldn't count the number of birds. This portal is majestic enough to be in King Tut's tomb. The wallpaper would be at home in a lady's bedroom. We put together an ancient doorway from China and chinoiserie paper from England, *et voilà*, we too play tricks. One masterpiece is enhanced by combining it with another. It works for me. What do you think?"

Phil had learned early to say something meaningful when responding to his grandfather. He couldn't reply, "Un-huh," or "It's pretty." If asked what he thought, he was expected to think and reflect his thoughts when he spoke. FP would accept differing opinions and welcomed questions, but empty pat phrases were not accepted. Gramps's descriptions always ended with words such as, "I could stand here gazing at it for hours." Or, "Each time I look at it I see something I've not seen before, and every time I thank those men of genius who created it." Coming back as if he'd been in another world during his musing, he would conclude, "I tell you Phil, this doorway is one of my favorite things in all of Oshatakea," a statement he made about nearly every object and architectural feature in the house. Phil believed his grandfather meant it each time he said it.

"I think the colored birds and the golden peacock are friends."

FP was delighted with Phil's answer.

He began showing Oshatakea to his grandson before the child could walk, pushing him in a stroller with Gaines trailing along. Between the first of these adventures and the last, a few months before the old man died, everything important about the house was explained, not to fill his heir's head with facts but to pass on passions. The trio covered the main floor numerous times, as well as important rooms on the guest floors, passing through dozens of others with Gramps merely pointing out special pieces, or perhaps how cleverly he and his architects had solved a problem. Of all parts of the enormous house, Phil thought it most rewarding to be taken up in a small elevator to FP's apartment above the Galleried Library, where he could dart through French doors shaped like Moorish arches onto a terrace built on the roof of the Stone Corridor that ran between the Great Hall and the chapel. At the far end of the terrace, stairs in a square Tuscan tower led down to Gramps's swimming pool, and another flight ascended to a room open on all four sides, from which he could look out over the roofs of Oshatakea, its gardens and stables, outbuildings and fields on the plateau to the north, and to the south the river and valley. Strutting around that room in the top of the tower Phil felt he was really king of the castle, a winter game he played on mounds of snow. Gaines had become Miss Eleanor, a change FP instituted when he said a little boy should not be calling his dear friend and loving caretaker by her last name.

The trio's perambulations started when Phil awoke from his morning nap and paused at noon for lunch, which arrived wherever they happened to be on a wheeled table with a warming oven. Sometimes they ate seated around this cloth-covered contraption, but more often a table in the room they were investigating was laid and chairs brought forward. "Rooms need to be lived in. If you don't live in them they turn into museums, a god-awful fate." After lunch, Phil was free to run around and touch anything he wanted with only an occasional "be careful" from Miss Eleanor. If he pointed to an ancient jade figure, a Della Robbia wreath, a Russian icon, he was lifted up to examine it. When Miss Eleanor worried he might break something, FP said, "It wouldn't be the end of the world if he did."

Exercise period over and afternoon nap looming, there would be another short lecture by FP on the fine points of their immediate surroundings. At two o'clock Phil was taken back to the nursery. Gramps rejoined him and Miss Eleanor for tea at 4:30. Miss Eleanor poured and passed food she had ordered from the kitchen, usually simple bread-and-butter sandwiches and seed cakes she remembered from her English childhood. Teatime was her chance to shine; it was she and not FP who told stories. If she was trying to teach Phil something, she and not his grandfather asked if he understood. FP made them laugh when he said, "Phil may get your meaning, but I don't, would you mind repeating what you just said?" At that he always reached over and touched her.

There was a lot of touching among the happy three. Phil climbed up into Miss Eleanor's and Gramps's laps, or leaned against their legs if he was playing on the floor. At the tea table, if he laid a buttery or jam-smeared paw on his grandfather's wrist it was not brushed off, even when he left traces of what he'd been eating. Miss Eleanor touched FP too, tapping his arm when she caught on that he was teasing her about her accent when he asked her to repeat what she'd said. To confirm something she'd taught Phil, he would lay a hand on her shoulder and say, "That's right, that's right." All three joined hands to sing songs. Only Miss Eleanor could carry a tune, but Gramps and Phil gave her loud support.

If the weather was good, part of each day's tour moved outside so Phil could exercise in the open air while he learned about Oshatakea's gardens, who planted them and how they came to be as they were at present. The oldest, and one he liked best to visit because it was the farthest away, down near the edge of the hill next to the tiny cabin Thomas Fillmore built, was a small square plot surrounded by boxwood bushes so old they nearly filled the space where herbs once grew. These boxwood were from cuttings carried west from Cohasset, and, Gramps told him, the boxwood in Cohasset grew from cuttings brought from England by an earlier ancestor. As they stepped inside the musty log cabin, Gramps said, "This is the real Oshatakea." Phil clung to his side. To Phil, the cabin was "creepy," but he loved drinking clear cold water from a spring in the corner of the room.

FP explained to him that each generation of Fillmores built bigger and bigger houses on the hill. Gramps was born and brought up in what he called a wonderful rabbit-warren house his mother tore down and replaced with a formal Georgian mansion, which he subsequently tore down except for a couple of wings so he could build his own house. "However, nobody uprooted their predecessors' gardens. You can trace the history of our family through Oshatakea's gardens. The boxed herbs came first, then the walled vegetable garden with espaliered fruit trees and next the planting of roses. Arches in the rose garden indicate our family fortunes were improving."

Better times brought parterres, water gardens, pavilions, pergolas, terraced stairs, the maze, the Moon garden the Italian gardens, a soaring glass palm house at the center of the conservatory. FP told Miss Eleanor and Phil about all of them. The child was acquiring a unique preschool education in horticulture and botany as well as architecture, furniture and the decorative arts.

As loathe as FP and Miss Eleanor were to share him, they accepted early on that others had to join their circle. If anything should happen to FP, whose age was a factor to be considered, the child's immediate world would shrink to two people, himself and Miss Eleanor. The first outsider to become part of Phil's life was Loren Gage, a farmer's son, nine days older than the Fillmore heir. Loren's parents were assured by FP that it would benefit both children if each had someone his own age to grow up with. A car was sent Monday, Wednesday and Friday to the Gage farm to pick up Loren, and for the first week his mother too, who accompanied her tot to the day nursery where he and Phil bonded on sight. Every other day was increased to every weekday as soon as morning naps were no longer required. The boys would have been together around the clock if FP had not wanted Phil to concentrate and be free from distraction when he was learning about his inheritance.

Phil's friendship with Loren firmly established, FP decided adult socializing was also necessary. He thought it imperative for the boy's parents to acknowledge the worth of the child they had produced. Thus, at age three years and four months, Phil joined the family for dinner in the Gibbons Room. Gramps and Miss Eleanor had drilled him on table manners; sit up straight, place the napkin in your lap, here is how you hold and use utensils. To practice for his downstairs debut, FP had Raymond serve lunch in the nursery exactly as dinner would be served in the dining room. There was no concern about his ability to participate in discussions at the table because they always included him in their conversations even when he didn't understand what they were talking about.

At six P.M. on the day he would have his first meal with his parents, Miss Eleanor gave him a small glass of milk and a graham cracker in the nursery to hold him over but not spoil his appetite. After the snack, he was scrubbed as thoroughly as if he'd been mucking about in mud. Dried, combed and polished, she dressed him in a dark blue suit that was a miniature version of those Gramps wore. The stiff woolen material scratched his legs. A bow tie was secured over the top button of a starched white shirt before he was helped into a jacket of the same scratchy goods. Black socks that wrinkled around his ankles and over the tops of hard-soled black shoes completed the outfit. Encased in this rig, Miss Eleanor made him walk back and forth across the day-nursery carpet to get used to the slippery soles she said she had scratched with sandpaper.

Then she sat him down at a low table with a book "to read" while she changed her clothes, returning a few minutes later in a long-sleeved black dress that hung almost to the floor. Phil could see she was also wearing new shoes. "Why do you have your nightgown on?" he asked.

"This is a dinner dress."

"It looks like a nightgown."

"Your grandfather ordered it for me from New York."

"Why are you shaking?"

"I'm nervous." It made him nervous because Miss Eleanor was never nervous. Something was happening.

"We mustn't dawdle," she said, giving his hair a quick brush though he hadn't done anything to mess it up since she plastered it to his head when he'd gotten out of the bathtub. "Your grandfather said we are to walk into the Gibbons Room at precisely six-forty-five." She checked her watch. "Which we will be able to do if we start now, and if you do not get distracted along the way." Phil was ready to go, but Miss Eleanor stopped once more and knelt down. Looking him in the eye at his level, she said, "Phil, promise me you will be on your very best behavior tonight. Please don't do or say a thing to disappoint your grandfather. Promise?" He promised.

They went as quickly down the stairs as they could in new shoes that were stiff as well as slippery. Phil's heels began to hurt when they were crossing the Great Hall where Miss Eleanor's shoes made scuttling and clacking noises on the marble floor as if they were too big for her feet. The sound distracted Phil. Miss Eleanor put extra pressure into holding his hand. As they approached the double doors of the Gibbons Room, Miss Eleanor again checked her watch. With half a minute to spare, she pressed Phil's hair down one more time and then she opened the doors. There before them was what, to Phil, looked like a pair of tall trees on which candles blazed, their flames reflecting on the polished surfaces of the table and the long silver plateau. He knew this room perfectly well, had been lifted up to touch the Gibbons carvings, but he had never seen it this way. Dazzled by the candle glow, he didn't notice Gramps standing to his left at the far end of the table, nor his father on the other side looking back at him, nor his mother to his right, opposite Gramps.

Catherine's voice startled him. "Are Adelaide and Louisa coming for dinner? It isn't Wednesday, why are five places set?"

"Because we are a family of five within the house," FP replied. "Miss Eleanor, please sit here on my right." Raymond pulled the indicated chair away from the table. Miss Eleanor stepped forward, hanging on to Phil's hand with a life-saving, bone-crushing grip. "And Phillips, you sit on Miss Eleanor's right, to your mother's left."

There was an unabridged dictionary on the chair Raymond pulled out for him. "If that isn't comfortable," Gramps said, "Raymond will fetch a pillow."

Raymond lifted him onto the dictionary.

Catherine sat with an annoyed thud when Raymond pushed her chair in.

"Good." FP smiled, as did Farney.

"Have we turned the Gibbons Room into a nursery?" Catherine tilted her head in a disapproving way, stretching her neck and her back into maximum perfect posture. From where Phil was looking up, her nose was a beak. Fearing she might bend over and give him a painful peck, he turned to make sure Miss Eleanor was close enough to protect him and saw her glancing first at his mother, then at his grandfather and back again.

"Not at all. It's time Phil, or, as you prefer, Phillips, joined us down here. He's very adept at conversation, an art that may return to this table with his company, and Miss Eleanor's. You may begin Raymond." The menu was designed to deflect any possibility Phil might make a fuss. He had been taught never to ask, "What is it?" And knew better than to say, "I don't like it" before tasting whatever was set before him, but had been allowed the privilege of "No more, thank you" after he'd tried something new. His first adult dinner consisted of several of his favorite foods, starting with cold strawberry soup, which he would have eaten more of had it been offered, and ending much later with chocolate soufflé.

His mother's silence during the long dinner did not disturb him, but he was aware something was wrong when Gramps spoke to Miss Eleanor and she barely answered. When they ate alone, she talked at least as much as Gramps. Phil could not understand. He knew Gramps was not directing remarks at him because he understood it was hard to concentrate on not making a mistake. His father was cheerful, but his mother remained mute until the main-course plates and silver were removed, when she said, "It is past your bedtime." Phil realized she was talking to him, but he was so proud of having cleaned up his plate and placed his knife and fork at twenty minutes past four, as well as still being mesmerized by the dancing candle light, he failed to reply. Besides, he was looking forward to dessert. "Phillips I am speaking to you." She reached over and tapped his wrist with her index finger, a tap so sharp he swallowed an "ouch."

"I didn't hear you."

"I said, Gaines is keeping you up much too late. We don't want to overplay this little drama. A joke that goes on too long becomes tiresome. You are excused. Gaines, take Phillips upstairs and put him to bed."

Miss Eleanor lifted her napkin from her lap and placed it on the table. FP gestured for her to stay where she was. "Phil and Miss Eleanor are here because I asked them to be here. If Phil is tired, we'll skip salad and go directly to dessert. What do you think Miss Eleanor?"

She turned to Phil. "You should eat a small salad." He said he was not tired.

FP laughed. "That settles it. Proceed Raymond. I think we might all move along a bit faster, however, to get to Phil's favorite. And then, my dear," he turned to speak directly to Miss Eleanor, "if you think cheese and savory is too much the first time, we'll excuse you both and send yours up to you." Which is what happened. Phil began to fade before finishing his soufflé, feeling only relief when Miss Eleanor whispered he should ask to be excused. He was sleepwalking by the time they reached the nursery, with blisters ready to burst on both heels.

From that evening on Miss Eleanor and Phil dined in the Gibbons Room with the rest of the family, or in any other room that was being used when there were guests.

In the beginning Catherine used the excuse of a series of sick headaches as reason to not join them, but these eventually abated and she resumed her place opposite FP, though she did not relax her stern demeanor toward Miss Eleanor and Phil. She tried several ploys to get them not to appear, such as, "I think you would both be happier if you didn't have to dress for dinner." Farney made a stand, saying he would miss them so much if they weren't there that he'd have to join them for dinner in the nursery. FP said this was a capital idea; perhaps they should all dine up there. Catherine said no more. She knew when she had been bested in a skirmish.

Chapter 21

—

AS HE NEARED HIS 106TH BIRTHDAY, FP SAID HE WANTED to make a complete tour of Oshatakea, look in every room of his house, starting at the top with attics, then staff rooms, third-floor guest rooms, mezzanine rooms for servants of guests, second-floor suites and the main floor. He took a deep breath. "Just talking about it I lose my puff, and I'm not finished. I want to see all the kitchens and pantries, the staff hall, wine cellars, the works, the entire house from one end to the other, top to bottom. And I want you with me Phil. Are you game?"

Phil's smile exposed a gap where he'd lost a baby tooth. "I'm game."

FP regarded Catherine across the table. "You will grant me permission to walk through the Portuguese Wing I hope. I promised when I gave it to you I'd not enter your house unless I was invited—but I'd really like to see all there is of Oshatakea one more time before I die. It will be my farewell tour."

"What nonsense," Farney joshed.

Phil thought farewell meant good-bye. How do you say good-bye to a room?

"You have kept your word," Catherine said. "Permission granted."

The tour was no simple undertaking. Because many guest rooms had been closed, a squadron of maids, footmen and cleaners was dispatched to remove dust sheets, vacuum hangings and rugs, polish floors and mirrors and return ornaments and pictures to their designated spots. As for their own rooms up under the eaves, members of the staff hustled to neaten up and put closets in order. Accompanied by Phil and Miss Eleanor, with Raymond along to give the old man physical assistance when needed—and he found it necessary to sit down frequently—FP began the tour riding the luggage elevator to the topmost level.

As they stepped off, he sniffed the air. "I love the smell of unfinished wood. That's why these attics have always been my favorite place in the house." If FP heard Phil's giggle, he didn't let on. They poked around in cedar-lined rooms containing clothing from generations of Fillmores. In box rooms FP pointed to trunks he had used when traveling in search of architectural treasures. "Those three over there that look like large wooden coffins I bought in Singapore to carry home bolts of silk I couldn't resist." While doing the staff floor, he voiced his admiration at attempts made by the occupants to transform quarters of modest dimensions into individualized personal abodes. "I forgot how small these rooms are. Why do you suppose I used so much golden oak?"

The next day, they started on the third floor where FP told Phil stories about furnishings he'd not explained to the boy before. They'd done only fourteen rooms when Gramps asked what time it was. Told it was a little before noon, he said he'd seen enough for now. "We'll skip the mezzanine and go to the second-floor suites after lunch." After lunch, FP repeated information he had already passed on to Phil about each room. He was getting tired. As the level of his voice dropped so did his pace. "The senior Rockefellers were the first to use this suite." A long pause and then, "I didn't invite them back. Old JD and I weren't fond of each other. He was a hypocrite." Another pause. Phil wondered when Gramps was going to speak again. "Abby and Junior come to Oshatakea often." Time out to breathe. "They prefer the west front."

FP had planned to walk through the entire interior of the house, including the Portuguese Wing, and then undertake an equally complete tour of the grounds, but when they finally got to the first floor, and had spent only a few minutes in the Tudor Banquet Hall, he said he needed a change of scenery. A cabriolet was called for. Hitched to a team of Farney's blood bay Morgans, the carriage drove up to the North Portico. The temperature was in the mid-forties, the sun was shining and there was no breeze. When FP, Phil, Miss Eleanor and Raymond were settled with lap robes tucked around their legs, FP told the coachman to take them to the foot of the plaiched lime allée where the statues of Thomas and Gahah stood. There, they sat for what seemed to Phil like hours while FP stared at his ancestor and the Seneca Indian who had found him floundering in the snow and saved his life. The child was itchy to move on, or better yet get out and run, but a glance from Miss Eleanor persuaded him to be still.

"Not brothers, but more than friends," FP read the short inscription below the names of the two men. The figure of Thomas Fillmore sat on a bale of beaver pelts; the Gahah figure stood slightly behind, his hand resting on Thomas's shoulder.

When FP returned from his reverie, he asked to be driven to the entrance of the Oshatakea estate. Trotting the horses along the boulevard and out onto Ontyakah Road, the coachman turned them to start back. "Stop," FP said. He gazed at the massive wrought-iron gates with the same intensity as he had at the statues, but for a shorter period of time. When he spoke he related yet again the tale of these gates being too heavy to swing on their hinges even with the support of rollers. "Fortunately the rollers collapsed when the gates were open, so we welcomed the world to Oshatakea." His laugh came as a faint echo. Delivered to the South Portico, Phil, Miss Eleanor and Raymond stepped out of the cabriolet, then helped FP. "I'm breaking down all at once," he joked, "like the one-horse shay." He asked Raymond to take him up to his room. He would not come down again.

Dr. Montrose said FP had no specific illness. "He is in remarkable physical condition for a man his age." When FP said he didn't feel remarkable, Montrose replied, "At one hundred and six your body slows down, Mr. Fillmore. You can stall nature's course but you can't stop it."

His birthday fell on Thanksgiving Day but was celebrated only by short visits from members of the family, including Isabelle, and a few favorite longtime members of the staff. Each, except for Catherine, came away depressed by his feeble state. The following Sunday morning, he sent Raymond to the stables to fetch Farney. Farney didn't take the slow birdcage elevator but dashed up the oriel stairs two steps at a time. He found his father in his nightshirt, unshaven, sitting at an awkward angle in an easy chair in his bedroom. FP's eyes filled with tears.

"Dad, what is it?"

It was difficult for FP to speak, but he managed to get it out. " I want to go. I love you all, but I want to go."

Farney bent to kiss him. "Let me help you get dressed. Raymond and I will take you down to the breakfast room. You'll feel better after you've eaten something."

FP shook his head and raised a hand to ward off Farney's. "I won't feel better. Please. Let me go."

Little more was said. FP stopped eating and drinking. He was offered water, which he swirled around in his mouth and then spat into a basin. He had convinced himself if he did not eat or drink he would soon die. It wasn't that easy. His body began shutting down, but the days of his dying dragged on, each more excruciating than the one that came before. Spasms of knotting cramps tortured him; the muscles in his legs contracted, drawing him into a fetal position. His kidneys stopped functioning. Yet his heart continued to beat. Farney spent nights in a bamboo carrying chair close to his father's bed. Adelaide, Louisa and Isabelle took turns sitting with FP during the day, after each had promised Farney she would not try to get him to eat or drink. "Not even ice cream," Farney said, "and don't ask him how he feels." Raymond stayed within whispering distance at all times. But it was Miss Eleanor FP wanted near him. He repeatedly asked for her. Miss Eleanor was torn between being with him and being with Phil.

"I have things to say to her," FP told Farney. Farney sent for her and she came. Reassured by Miss Eleanor's presence, FP reiterated what was uppermost in his mind. "I trust you to never leave Phil. Promise me." She promised.

Mid-morning and midafternoon most days, Miss Eleanor brought Phil to visit his grandfather. The little boy took the old man's skeletal hand in his, softly patting the purple-blotched skin so thin he could see blue veins through it. Gramps did not pull away, not even when Phil's gentle caress caused him pain. "How are you feeling today?" Phil asked, the only one allowed this privilege.

"Not good, but I'll soon be fine."

During afternoon visits, Phil reported everything he had done that day with the same attention to detail Gramps used in his stories, concluding with "I'll see you tomorrow Gramps." FP's response as long as he could manage it was a slight squeeze of Phil's hand.

Catherine stayed away. "I'd be a ghoul sitting there waiting for him to die. Why doesn't he just do it?" Her patience had never exceeded that of a spoiled two-year-old. She wanted what she wanted when she wanted it, and what she wanted was to reign over Oshatakea, answerable to no one at long last. The estate would be in Farney's name, but he'd not cross her. It wasn't that she was eager to possess property or money; she had money and property, as her mother's sole heir. Most of the old family money was tied up in trusts, but two terminated upon Mrs. Dudley's death, meaning the principal was now Catherine's, as were residences on Mount Vernon Street, in Pride's Crossing and Dover, with their contents. Catherine had done nothing about anything. She didn't ask to have family jewelry kept in a bank safe deposit box sent to her, nor did she go to Boston to lay claim to her property. No decisions were made about what was to be done with the real estate. Mrs. Dudley's small staff stayed on in the Mount Vernon Street house, as did caretakers at both Pride's Crossing and Dover. Catherine wasn't waiting for FP to die so she could inherit his possessions; it was his authority for which she hungered.

The years of his niggling control were coming to an end, but not fast enough to suit her. When she wasn't feeling frustrated at the slow pace of his demise, she rejoiced in the power she would soon wield. To channel the high spirits no one would understand, she took it into her head to make the tour FP had begun but not finished, setting out to systematically inspect every room but reversing FP's direction. Catherine started on the half-belowground level and worked up. She knew the kitchens but had never been in the housekeeper's quarters. There, on Pearl's bedroom bureau, she saw a framed photograph of a grinning young Farney astride a polo pony. Concealing her urge to smash the picture, Catherine relished the knowledge that within seconds of FP's final breath, Pearl would be sent from Oshatakea forever.

Her tour of inspection was not to look lovingly on what had been created, or to remember connections between people and things, but with cursory glances to consider changes. She'd never have the huge house-party weekends FP favored. There'd be no need for so many accommodations. It would be relatively easy to convert third-floor guest rooms into suites by taking down walls and opening doors. While she was at it she'd modernize bathrooms. Neither on the guest floors nor when she was walking through the main floor did she pay attention to the harmony FP had established through the artful placement of objects in his collection of rooms. What she felt as she looked—and she insisted on seeing every inch of every floor—was the exquisite pleasure she would experience when decisions concerning every aspect of Oshatakea would be hers to make. She would follow to the letter FP's requests for his funeral, and she was sure his wishes were written down, but after that, after he was sealed in the crypt beneath the chapel, she could do whatever she felt like doing with his house and his gardens. Not that she yearned to make change for the sake of change, beyond redoing the third floor and booting Pearl off the hill and burning every stick of furniture in the housekeeper's rooms. Farney would object to Pearl being fired, but Farney's objections meant nothing. He could go with his girlfriend if he wanted, or, if he chose to stay, he'd continue to be as insignificant as he'd always been. Free of all fetters, Catherine would not make major changes, but waiting until FP's treasure was hers to play with was trying her patience.

Shortly before dawn of the thirty-ninth day of his fast, FP asked Farney to bring Miss Eleanor to him. Miss Eleanor, in her wrapper, hurried to the bedroom above the Galleried Library. When she touched his shoulder to let him know she was there, FP asked, "Are we alone?"

"We are. Farney is in your study."

"Close the door."

"It is closed."

FP opened his eyes sunken deep in their sockets as wide as he could. The flesh on his face was so scant that the contours of his skull were sharp. "Help me."

"What would you have me do?" She leaned low to hear him.

"I didn't know dying would be . . . Please, help me."

Miss Eleanor took his hands in hers. "Dear friend, there is nothing I can do."

Raymond came with a small bowl of water in which ice cubes and slices of lemon floated to swab out his mouth.

On the afternoon of the forty-third day, at approximately four o'clock, FP went into a coma, not responding to sound or touch. Raymond took up his post at the head of the bed, and left only to freshen the basin of warm water from which he dabbed at FP's face with a washcloth. Miss Eleanor brought Phil to say good-bye, the third time the boy had been put through this. Phil kissed his grandfather's brow. Adelaide, Louisa and Isabelle joined Farney and Raymond for the deathwatch. All adults in the family were there except Catherine who compromised by coming to FP's apartment but refusing to enter the bedroom; she occupied herself rearranging small items in his cluttered living room. Though FP wanted to die, in a coma he lost the power to will it; his heart struggled to keep beating. Slightly past midnight, Farney said, "This may go on for hours, go get some sleep, I'll stay with him." All except Raymond followed Farney's suggestion.

At eight o'clock Saturday morning, Isabelle returned, followed an hour later by Adelaide and Louisa. They persuaded Farney to lie down in his father's study. This routine was duplicated Sunday and Monday. Catherine had returned to the Portuguese Wing Friday evening and did not come again to FP's apartment. Instead, she played solitaire in her sitting room and dined by herself in the Gibbons Room. Monday evening, a footman was left sitting in the day nursery to listen for Phil so Miss Eleanor could go to FP's bedroom. She told the family they would all collapse if they didn't get a full night's sleep. Adelaide, Louisa and Isabelle gratefully went to bed elsewhere in the house after Miss Eleanor said she would let them know if there was the slightest change. Before leaving to lie down again in his father's study, Farney said, "He has worked so hard to die, now he's at the threshold and he hangs on."

"Fighting to live is instinct," Miss Eleanor whispered. "If you tell him it is all right, he might let go."

"Will he hear me?"

"He might."

Farney leaned over, placed his hand lightly on the father's cold forehead, tried to not concentrate on the thrown-back sightless eyes and said, "Miss Eleanor and I are here, Dad. It's okay. What you are doing is okay. We understand. You can relax now. You've done it Pop, what you set out to do. We are all proud of you. I love you. Let go, please just let go."

The rattle in FP's throat halted, then briefly sounded again before stopping. After a few shallow breaths, the hand Farney held moved ever so slightly. A long slow exhale followed. Farney's tears dropped onto his father's chest. "Did I tell him I loved him?"

IN THE SILENCE OF THE NIGHT, HOUSE SOUNDS CAN BE heard, creaking floors, groans.

At Oshatakea these and other sounds were frequent as wall panels adjusted to changes in humidity, or when the wind whistled around the Tiffany dome and through the open portals of the Tuscan Tower. Those who lived in the house were accustomed to these noises, but when perturbed guests commented, FP had to explain that it was because he had fitted centuries-old rooms into new spaces against rooms from other centuries, other houses and other countries and encased them in a granite shell. "There's bound to be grumbling until they all settle down together."

FP's was the heartbeat of this house, the force that kept it vital. Oshatakea was his forever unfinished work of art. During the weeks of his dying, as his pulse slowed, Oshatakea's sounds diminished. During his final agony the house was without groans and creaks. The wind did not whistle around the dome or the tower. From foundations deep in the earth to tiled and leaded roofs that seemed to reach the clouds, Oshatakea's assembled parts held their breath. When the old man relaxed, let go, the stillness was broken. Oshatakea shuddered.

Chapter 22

SOME MAY BELIEVE SIX-YEAR-OLDS DO NOT UNDERSTAND death, are mystified by the sudden absence of a loved one and confused by displays of grief. Phil was not mystified or confused; he was terrified. He knew what had happened to Gramps, the one person who loved him without reservation. What he didn't know was what would happen to him now that Gramps was gone. Who would shield him from his mother, stop her shrieks, countermand her orders? Phil clung to Miss Eleanor with infantile desperation. He would not go to bed if she did not lie down beside him, something she had never done. He ate only because she plied him with special foods. Miss Eleanor told him everybody was worried about him, but he knew no one was as worried as he was about himself.

Gramps had explained to Phil what he knew of the process of starvation in as much detail as he earlier explained how a coffered ceiling was made, hung in a palace in Europe, taken down, dismantled and brought over to be rehung at Oshatakea. As long as he could, he had answered the boy's questions, and let him know at what stages he was. "I'm almost there," he whispered, "but it is taking too long." Phil felt like crying when Gramps said, "Thank you for coming along Little Man. We had a good time together, didn't we?" He wondered if Gramps would cry if his tears hadn't dried up. The last time Phil kissed him, his forehead was colder than it had been before, but it wasn't dry. The touch reminded Phil of the grotto's walls when he ran his fingers along them on a muggy day. He didn't say anything out loud that last time, but sent a message from his brain to Gramps's, something they'd done at the table when they didn't want anybody else to know what they were thinking. "I hope you like being dead Gramps."

After Raymond bathed FP's body, Phil went with Stefan and Ron Colantonio up into the Tuscan tower where they took turns pulling the rope of the big bell to publicly announce the patriarch's death. The sounds of the tolling—*da dong, da dong, da dong, da dong, da dong,* mournful but also grand—echoed in Phil's head for weeks after.

Famous people who came to the funeral did not overwhelm him. Mrs. Roosevelt and Sir Winston were his godparents. He'd met Mr. Baruch, the Rockefellers, Morgans, Morganthaus and Mountbattens, Achesons, Astors, Luces and most of the others who had come to pay tribute to a unique and greatly admired gentleman. When Mrs. Luce fixed her icy blue eyes on Phil, he thought she might be trying to hex him. To escape he slipped away and lost himself in the crowd. Hundreds of people from the valley as well as from afar patted his head and told him he had inherited a most distinguished name. They also said he had very big shoes to fill.

What happened in the Galleried Library following the service was somewhat confusing to him. While guests lined up at buffets in the banquet hall, the West Loggia, and the Long Gallery the family, including Miss Eleanor and Isabelle at the request of Charles Hunnewell, gathered in the room that was FP's favorite. Adelaide and Louisa lifted black crepe veils from their faces and draped them over their hats as they sat beside Isabelle on a long sofa opposite the fireplace where the two Hunnewells—father and son, Charles and George—stood with their backsides to the fire like generals about to address their officers. Miss Eleanor and Phil perched close together on a high-backed Queen Anne settee near the chair to the left of the fireplace, where Farney sat staring into space.

Catherine was busy rearranging the spiderweb-delicate Venetian blown glass decanter and goblets on a table next to FP's wing chair. Flecked with gold and lapis, the decanter and goblets had belonged to England's Virgin Queen Elizabeth. FP said he cherished them for their romantic history as much as for their delicate beauty. Fearful they might be broken, he had written "Do Not Touch!" on a white card placed on a small easel that stood in front of the glass objects. As casually as if she were removing a speck of dust from the lapel of her smart suit, Catherine picked up the white card, ripped it in two and, stepping behind George Hunnewell, tossed the pieces into the flames. This brought a squeak of dismay from Louisa. No one else made a peep, though all, including FP's attorneys, were startled by her action. Catherine then turned and sat down in FP's chair rather than the chair in which she always sat when the family gathered in this room. Nobody but FP sat in that chair, ever. Farney straightened as if to reprimand her, but he did not speak.

Charles Hunnewell cleared his throat. "I apologize for taking you away from your guests, but George and I leave shortly to catch a flight to London where we will reassure participants in Fillmore European and Asian ventures that all will continue as before. We don't want them to panic do we?" When no replied, he continued. "I will keep you only the minute or two it will take to explain a few things. FP did not leave a will. He had nothing left to bequeath."

This statement caused a stir. Catherine's eyebrows shot up as if she were questioning the attorney's sanity. Adelaide and Louisa exchanged shocked glances. Isabelle crossed her arms over her ample bosom. Farney looked quizzical. Miss Eleanor took Phil's hand and held on so tight he thought she'd break it.

"Four years ago," Charles said, "FP put his substantial affairs in order. At that time, he made a few final distributions, adding capital to the '32 Kropotkin Trust, for instance, though neither he nor anyone in our offices thought it necessary because income from that and earlier trusts seemed more than adequate for the needs of the beneficiaries, Misses Adelaide and Louisa Kropotkin. Most years ladies you do not spend all available income, which we reinvest for you." He bobbed his head toward Adelaide and Louisa. "However, your grandfather wanted to be sure you'd have enough." Adelaide nodded graciously; Louisa's brow furrowed.

"He also increased the Isabelle Chapman Trust."

"I never have any unused income," Isabelle chortled. "I'm pleased of course. FP was always generous."

"Indeed he was." Mr. Hunnewell's tone was dry, but then his attorney's smile returned. "I asked Eleanor Gaines to join us because she is unaware FP also set up a trust for her. You will begin receiving income from this trust January first." He was businesslike but beaming benevolently at Miss Eleanor. "You may ask for disbursements from capital if you require further funds. FP's instructions were to give you easier access than is usual. I'm sure you know, Miss Gaines, he was very fond of you, and exceedingly grateful."

Miss Eleanor's "Thank you" was an embarrassed and grief-stricken whisper. Phil pulled his hand free of her clutches and placed it on top of hers, trying to stop her from worrying to tatters the handkerchief she held in her lap.

"FP established almost three hundred sealed savings accounts in varying amounts in his Fillmore Valley Bank, none with less than ten thousand dollars as an initial deposit, some with fifty thousand, for current and former members of the Oshatakea staff and for a number of valley friends. They will receive letters of notification and their savings account books tomorrow. These accounts are separate from their retirement. The recipients should be pleased. As will householders, farmers and business owners in the valley whose mortgages were held by FP's bank. As per his instructions, those mortgages and all other outstanding loans were forgiven on the date of his death. Deeds of clear title and loan documents stamped paid in full will be forthcoming."

Catherine was losing patience. She raised her arm to consult her wristwatch. Phil tensed, expecting his mother to demand that Gramps's attorney get on with it, but she only punctuated her increasing displeasure by shifting in the chair and exhaling loudly to let them all know she was bored.

"Farney," Charles Hunnewell continued, "you are familiar with your established annuities, which, with access to income from estate trusts, will take very good care of you and Catherine. Catherine"—his head turned so his eyes could meet her's—"while your father-in-law did not know the totality of your own family inheritance, he assumed, correctly I am sure, you require no further monetary resources." Without giving Catherine time to react, he turned quickly toward Phil, who was afraid he'd been caught fidgeting. "Having seen to all that was required of him, on January 1, 1947, in this room actually, FP signed documents transferring everything he possessed, all assets real and personal, to his grandson, Farnsworth Phillips Fillmore IV." Charles Hunnewell's smile was benign as he looked and spoke directly to FP's heir. George Hunnewell also radiated warmth in the boy's direction. "Phil, you have owned Oshatakea and all Fillmore holdings since you were two years old. It amused your grandfather to be a guest in his grandson's home and, as he put it for a small private joke, to be living on his grandson's money."

Phil didn't know if he was supposed to say or do something. He stopped patting Miss Eleanor's hand when he realized, from the way she was looking at him, that she already knew what Mr. Hunnewell had just said. Out of the heavy silence, Farney asked in a gravelly voice, "I assume there are trustees, guardians?"

"Of course. You and Catherine are naturally Phil's guardians. FP could do nothing about that. If he could, he would have named

Eleanor Gaines guardian. You succeed your father as the family trustee on this '47 trust. I am the managing trust officer, to be succeeded by my son, George, who is presently my assistant. This is per FP's instructions. He wanted a younger trustee, one who will be around when these trusts dissolve and Phil acquires control of the estate, on his fortieth birthday. Judge Julian Washburn is a trustee, to keep us honest, your father quipped, and so is Lem White, the senior officer of Morgan Guaranty Trust. You and Catherine are to have life use of Oshatakea. Hunnewell, Hunnewell and Hunnewell will continue to manage the property and all finances as we have done since January of '47. And we, I actually, until George takes over, will serve in an advisory capacity on staffing and-or any other matter that has to do with the outlay of money, inasmuch as we are entrusted with protecting Phil's income as well as his assets. If you or Catherine need extra funds for something special, you may apply to me. All bills and invoices having to do with Oshatakea, the farms, all estate business expenses will be paid by my office out of estate income, which has been and will continue to be channeled through us. FP showed great faith entrusting us with full responsibility. Phil's investment portfolio I am happy to report has grown substantially since we assumed that responsibility."

"Phil's portfolio or yours?" Isabelle inquired.

"I beg your pardon?" The interruption surprised him.

"Are you referring to your firm's portfolio or Phil's when you say it has 'happily grown substantially'?" Isabelle did not soften her sarcasm.

Mr. Hunnewell did not have opportunity to reply because at that moment Catherine began making noises that sounded like growls coming up from deep inside. When she could no longer contain herself she rose from FP's chair emitting a high-pitched scream; Isabelle later described it as the wail of a dying Valkyrie. Catherine raised tightly clenched fists high above her head, unable for an instant to release this paroxysm of fury. Then, with a rushing roar, she lashed out and swept the virgin queen's Venetian glassware from the table onto the hearth, where it shattered into tiny shards of glittering gold-flecked, blue-gray opalescence. Adelaide moaned. "Damn him," Catherine cried. "Goddamn him."

Farney leapt from his chair. "Enough."

"Not nearly enough," she spat. "It will never be enough. Nothing I did was ever enough. I did everything he wanted, and more, more than he imagined I could do, but nothing satisfied him. I could have died giving him the stupid grandson he wanted." When it looked as if tears were ready to flow, she added in a completely controlled low-pitched voice, "I have not believed in the existence of hell, but if there is a hell, and I pray God there is, I want your bastard father to burn there."

How Farney came suddenly to be so close nobody knew, but there he was. Nor would anyone remember him raising his hand, but those present would never forget the sound his hand made when he slapped her face. They could not believe what they were seeing and hearing. Farney never raised his voice, never used a riding crop no matter how badly a horse behaved. Now he had struck Catherine with such force she struggled to maintain her balance. Phil froze, as did Louisa. Adelaide's posture stiffened. Isabelle's hands flew to her cheeks to hide the smile of satisfaction that Farney was at last taking charge. Miss Eleanor wept.

George Hunnewell looked as if he'd like to run. Charles Hunnewell cleared his throat again. "We've kept you too long. I have said all that needs to be said for now. If there are questions I'll answer them when I return from London on the twenty-second. He removed an envelope from his jacket pocket. "Your father wanted me to give this to you." He handed the envelope to Farney.

Farney, instantly reverting to his gentle, polite self, nodded, took the envelope and put it into his own pocket as he shook Charles Hunnewell's hand. "Thank you. We appreciate all you have done, and all you did for Dad." When the Hunnewells were gone, Farney said Phil must be tired after the long funeral service and sitting through the session in the Galleried Library, suggesting to Miss Eleanor, "He should probably be taken to his room for a rest."

"I haven't had lunch yet," Phil protested. "I told Loren I'd eat with him."

"If you are concerned about keeping family secrets, forget it. I'd be willing to bet there isn't a person on the place or in the valley who doesn't know all there is to know," Isabelle said.

"Are you talking about Gramps giving me Oshatakea when I was two?" Phil asked. "If you are, I've known that for a long time. I forgot, but I did know because he told me."

That snapped Catherine out of the shock she'd been in since Farney slapped her. "What did you say?"

Phil reached for Miss Eleanor's hand. "Gramps told me on my fourth birthday. He said I was to not tell a soul, not even Miss Eleanor or Loren, so I didn't." For a second Phil thought his mother was going to come at him the way she had lashed out at that decanter, slamming and smashing him as she had destroyed Venetian glass. Instead, she turned and left the library through the Stone Corridor door.

A keening Louisa rushed over to kneel on the hearth. "If I had a box I could collect the pieces. I'm sure Pearl knows somebody who can put them back together."

"Get up Louisa and come along, we must return to our guests. They will think something is terribly wrong if we neglect them a minute longer." Adelaide was assuming the role of hostess.

"Right," Farney muttered.

"May I please have lunch?" Phil was hungry and he didn't want to be sent back to the Portuguese Wing where his mother lurked in a killer mood.

Farney glanced toward Miss Eleanor who shrugged and dabbed at her eyes and nose with what was left of the shredded handkerchief. Farney gave in. "You may, but Phil, it might be best if we keep the secret you and Gramps shared for a few more days. Don't discuss it with anyone who was not here in the library, and please don't mention anything else that happened here, not even to Loren. Okay?"

"Okay, but Isabelle said everybody knows."

"I exaggerate," Isabelle snorted.

"I never thought we'd hear you admit it," Louisa crowed.

Chapter 23

NO ONE WAS IN THE STONE CORRIDOR WHEN CATHERINE crossed and entered the Stepped Gallery through the monk's door. She hurried upstairs to her suite, her face burning, chest ready to explode, bile-soured stomach churning. Safely inside, she slammed her sitting room door. If she could she'd slam it hard enough to splinter into fragments as minute as those pieces of glass on the library hearth. Too bad Dudleys don't cry; tears might cool the heat of Farney's blistering handprint on her cheek. Her lily-livered husband who had never dared stand up to his father had slapped her, struck her in front of those pompous-ass Hunnewells. The embarrassment, the shame of that slap would never be forgotten; for the rest of her life she would bear its invisible scar.

"Why?" she shouted. Why had the old man destroyed her? He challenged her in every conceivable way from the moment of her engagement and kept her on the defensive. He threw her tidbits with this Portuguese Wing, said it was hers alone, her refuge. Now even that was no longer hers. Along with all the rest of Oshatakea, her own house belonged to her sniveling little sneak of a son who knew and never let on. Unlike FP, she was not amused to be his guest. Worse, that smug toad Charles Hunnewell made it clear he was in charge. While FP was alive she'd felt free to act and do as she wished at least within the Portuguese Wing, but from now on she'd also have to answer here to Hunnewell. "Why for God's sake?"

FP was jealous, that must be it. The old fool had never shared credit for anything at Oshatakea until she did what he asked her to do. The bastard basked in her glory, told her no one entertained with as much style and imagination as she did. It wasn't just balls and country dances, nor concerts and ballet companies, nor professional theater, it was the way she integrated everything, he said. And he crowed about Oshatakea's food surpassing any that was served in other great houses. "I don't give a damn about food," she cried. What she cared for was perfection, making sure every detail coordinated with every other detail from decor to dinner to entertainment. She knew the old goat loved what she did. Over and over he proclaimed, that no previous chatelaine had come close to her, not even the legendary Hester, yet it must have nearly killed him to acknowledge that she had burnished Oshatakea's unique aura. After all, she was not a true Fillmore. "That's what boiled his pea brain," she muttered. It wasn't his son, and certainly not his beknighted grandson, who added to Oshatakea's luster; it was a daughter-in-law. My God, he couldn't just accept that, he had to punish her.

She wailed and paced, wept without knowing she was weeping. He might as well have plucked out her eyes as to take away what she yearned for, being in all ways her own person, answerable to no one. That's what she wanted. To hell with what she wanted. What she wanted was gone and she was worse off than she had been before. There were no words to convey her hatred for him. She fervently wished she'd killed him, crept in when he was alone and smothered him. Strangling would have given her greater satisfaction, watching his face as he struggled, aware of what she was doing. She would feel justice had been done if only she'd killed him instead of standing meekly to one side while the bastard starved to death.

"Enough!" she stormed. "Thank God I am not a Fillmore, I am a Dudley, the last of the Dudleys. In Dudley territory, I don't have to answer to anybody." Joe Wengren had his hands on some trusts, but neither he nor the trusts mattered. She would leave Oshatakea as fast as she could get off the hill, within the hour if possible. She yanked on the bell pull.

Giselle, the most unsatisfactory lady's maid in a series that followed when Gaines took on caring for the baby, was sitting with a group of village women in a corner of the Banquet Hall when a footman found her. "Mrs. Fillmore wants you, and you'll get up there PDQ if you know what's good for you." When Giselle said she hadn't finished lunch, the footman said, "It's your head, girl." Another footman was wheeling a steamer trunk through Catherine's sitting room into the dressing room as Giselle arrived.

"Where have you been?" Catherine was pulling dresses and suits off hangers and tossing them in the direction of the trunk. "Pack these and shoes to match—and underwear, nightclothes, everything for an indefinite stay. Pack a suitcase for yourself. Hurry, we haven't much time. The stationmaster gave me grief but he's stopping a train for us, and there isn't another eastbound passenger until tonight. We'll have to change in Albany but that can't be helped. Don't stand there, idiot, move."

After spending five and a half bone-jarring hours on outdated coach seats, nothing else being available, and close to three hours on a wooden bench waiting for a connection in Albany's cold empty cavern of a terminal, then another three-plus hours, again in coach, Catherine and Giselle stepped onto the platform of Boston's South Station at 6:40 A.M. A porter, who appeared to be sleeping standing up, was awakened and handed their baggage checks. With their luggage on a handcart, he led them outside in search of a taxicab. Catherine had called from Albany to alert the Mount Vernon Street staff that she was on the way, and had not been heartened by the restrained reaction of Ernestine, who answered the telephone. Ernestine, eighty-four, was in charge because she had been there longest, cooking more than fifty years for the family when Mrs. Dudley died. Mary-Frances, the maid of all work, with an almost as long tenure, was Ernestine's junior by fourteen months. Tommy, the youngest of the trio, was somewhere in his seventies; he didn't know exactly where. Tommy had recovered physically from removal of a brain tumor, but the little sense he had prior to the operation was removed with the fibrous growth. These three slept in rooms on the top floor of the big brick town house, creeping down five flights of steep back stairs each morning to spend their days in the basement kitchen and servants' hall, crawling heavenward again each night. Ernestine had not ventured into the family quarters since Mrs. Dudley's death, but Mary-Frances shuffled on a rotating schedule through a dozen rooms that overlooked the iron-fenced front yard or a rear courtyard, opening and closing draperies, flicking a feather duster, occasionally running a vacuum, though she preferred a carpet sweeper. Twice a year, before Easter and before Thanksgiving, she washed the insides of windows on the first, second and third floors. Seven mornings a week Tommy polished the brass kick plate, knocker and handle on the front door and went up again at noon, except on Sundays, to retrieve mail pushed through a slot by the postman. The three retainers were sitting around an oilcloth-covered table in the kitchen waiting when Tommy heard Catherine's unmistakable pounding of the knocker on the door upstairs.

Farney was not worried by Catherine's hasty departure from Oshatakea. After a short conversation with the Fillmore station-master he ascertained that she had gone to Boston. He understood some of her reaction to Charles Hunnewell's revelations; he too had been unnerved. "A few days away will be good for her," he told Pearl as they rode through the woods.

Pearl might, if she made comments on Farney's relationship with his wife, have said, "And good for you," but though she had many thoughts on that subject she didn't express them. However, she did not hesitate to question Farney about himself. "Are you going to be okay? Learning through a lawyer what your father did must have hurt."

"He explained in his letter it was for tax reasons. I wish he'd just told me that himself."

"Why didn't he?"

"He wanted to avoid a scene with my wife. He knew I would accept what he had done, but was sure Catherine would not." It was unusual for Farney to use Catherine's name in his conversations with Pearl. Regardless of how distant their marital relationship was, he had not in deed or word been disloyal to her.

Life at Oshatakea would never again be as it was when FP's powerful presence charged the atmosphere, but the tranquillity that followed his funeral and Catherine's flight came as a soothing balm to its occupants. Quietly reassuring routines were continued and those that were new were quickly established. Instead of going to the breakfast room to start the day with FP as they had done before his retreat to his apartment, Miss Eleanor and Phil joined Farney for breakfast in the Portuguese Courtyard after his morning ride. He enjoyed their company. He had always dreaded walking into Catherine's silence, never knowing when she would explode about something. Now he was greeted by giggles and laughter as comic strips from the newspapers were shared. The same cheerful liveliness prevailed during dinner in the Gibbons Room—after some confusion the first evening. Raymond had retired immediately following FP's funeral to be succeeded as dinner footman by Dale Morris. Dale, thinking he was doing the right thing, set Farney's place at the head of the table where FP had presided. "No, no," Farney objected, with a touch of emotion but no annoyance. "I will sit where I always sat, but thank you Dale for your thought," he added to ease the footman's embarrassment. "If I am to preserve decorum while dining with these two rowdies, I must be able to look at Miss Eleanor and Phil straight on." All, including Dale, laughed.

About a month into their blessed repose, while they were having dinner, Farney said to Phil, "I have business at the far end of the valley tomorrow. If you want I can take you with me, drop you off at the Gage farm in the morning to play with Loren, then pick you up on my way back midafternoon."

"Are you serious? Loren has asked and asked, but Mother would never let me go." He jumped up from the table. "I'll call him right now."

"Sit down and finish your dinner. Miss Eleanor made arrangements with Mrs. Gage this afternoon."

The Gage farm was as foreign to Phil as the jungles of South America would have been. Long pungent cow barns were nothing like the stable blocks at Oshatakea. "I like the smell of horse manure," he said, "but cow manure stinks." The Gage horses were draft animals, workhorses, plodding giants with monstrous furry feet and colossal heads larger than Phil's torso. Loren's father lifted the two six-year-olds onto the backs of a team of dappled gray Percherons then went off to finish his chores. Being up that high on a shifting beast was frightening. Phil's feet tingled. "How will I get down?"

"When you are ready, move back over her rump, lie flat on your belly and slide off feet first. I'll show you," Loren said, and did. "Hang on to her tail to keep from going down too fast."

"Won't she kick me?"

"Daisy doesn't kick."

There were early lambs whose still unbobbed tails jiggled when their mothers nursed them. Older Cotswold ewes didn't mind the boys trying to pick up their babies, but first-time mothers stomped their front feet as a warning to keep away. For lunch, Mrs. Gage gave Loren and Phil French toast made from thick slabs of her own bread with fresh maple syrup boiled down from sap gathered in the Gage's sugar bush, and sausage patties that had once been Gage hogs. Phil ate three helpings.

Starting when they were five, Phil and Loren attended kindergarten classes in a room next to the day nursery where Polly Nash, a teacher on leave from Fillmore Academy, was in charge. Catherine was as adamant that Phillips would not go to public school with valley children as she had been about not allowing him to play at Loren's house, but when she had still not returned to Oshatakea by the middle of May, nor given any indication when she might be coming back, Farney surprised Phil a second time. "Miss Eleanor and I have talked it over and agree you should be enrolled to start first grade at the academy in September."

"Loren too?"

"Loren too. I don't know what your mother has in mind for you, but I went to the academy through eighth grade, as did Adelaide and Louisa, and we seemed well enough prepared for what followed."

"Aren't there twelve grades?"

"There are. I was sent off after eighth grade to Phillips Exeter in New Hampshire. Adelaide and Louisa went to finishing schools in Switzerland. But that was before the new science building and other improvements. I see no reason why you shouldn't go straight through the academy. Recent graduates have gone to Harvard, Princeton, Yale. I don't think you'll have any trouble."

It was a perfectly normal decision, or as normal as it could be for a child who possessed one of the world's predominant fortunes, but the semblance of normality was short-lived. One day at the Gage farm, playing alongside a creek that was overflowing its banks from freshets of spring rains, Phil fell in, followed by Loren when he tried to pull Phil out. The boys were swept a short distance downstream but managed to stay afloat thanks to swimming lessons they'd had in Gramps's pool. They scrambled ashore unhurt except for scratches from low-hanging branches and a few bruises. However, the water was cold. By the time they trudged in sopping clothes through the pasture and onto Mrs. Gage's kitchen porch, their teeth were chattering and their lips were blue. Loren's mother stripped them, put them into a tub of hot water and gave them doses of Epsom salts.

Loren suffered nothing more than sniffles from the misadventure, but less robust Phil developed bronchitis that turned into double pneumonia. Farney called Catherine. If Phil had been aware of what his father was doing, the near-comatose child in an exercise of mind over matter would have willed his lungs to clear and his body temperature to drop, but Phil did not know. When, after several days of delirium and spiking fever, he awoke to see Catherine standing over him, Phil cried out. The next morning, his fever broken, spent but past the crisis, he told Miss Eleanor he'd had an awful nightmare. "I dreamt I opened my eyes and my mother was staring down at me."

"Ssh, ssh," Miss Eleanor cajoled. "Your bad time is over. Now you must think about getting better."He did get better, but he was given much more than his state of health to think about.

Catherine had needed the excuse provided by Farney's call to return to Oshatakea. Nothing suited her in Boston. She found it difficult to breathe in the stuffy rooms of the Mount Vernon Street house. Accustomed to the spaciousness and opulence of Oshatakea, derided by her prior to her marriage and still considered ostentatious by her Boston connections, she now found those grand open spaces difficult to do without. She also missed being waited on. The servants who survived her mother were beyond real service and Giselle was just plain useless. But Catherine most missed the splendid richness and beauty both inside and out that one's eyes feasted on at Oshatakea. Her hatred of FP had not diminished, but in hindsight her admiration for his creation had grown. The Beacon Hill house was smothering her in its cramped, musty embrace.

"Sell it," she told Joe Wengren, "as is, contents included."

"Surely you want to keep family pieces, portraits, silver?"

"There isn't a piece in the place that isn't 'family,' sell the lot—now!"

She had tried staying at the farm in Dover. That lasted for two weeks. "I hate it," Giselle whined, "there's nothing to do." Ernestine,

Mary-Frances and Tommy were along to do on the farm what they were supposed to be doing on Mount Vernon Street. They too hated it. Catherine didn't say so, but there really was nothing to do out there even if the terraces and screened porches made the farmhouse less claustrophobic than Mount Vernon Street. With Ernestine doing the cooking, the food in Dover was as bad as it had been in Boston. Why had she never noticed when she lived at home? It was beyond reason to expect she'd accept the thought, but Catherine had been spoiled by FP's table, laden with largesse that was always fresh and flavorful. She appreciated Bones most when she dined at the Ritz and was disappointed; obviously Ernest Bones had moved into realms beyond those of Chef d'Auguste. At Oshatakea she was sarcastic about beef Wellington, fresh peas in butter, potatoes Anna, all favorites of FP, but she had been seduced. Faced with Ernestine's overdone or raw roast accompanied by a tiny boiled potato and one small beet from a can, she recoiled. Such fare had sustained her until she married Farney. Back then she didn't know better. She toyed with the notion of moving to Pride's Crossing, but only for an instant. Seacliff, a large shingled cottage devoid of charm, would be catastrophic. Wooden panels nailed over windows and doors at the end of summer to protect the house from storms and vandals had not been removed since years before her mother had died. Generations of raccoons would have settled in the attic and chimneys along with millions of mice. No, Seacliff was not the answer. There was nothing to do with Seacliff but burn it.

Farney's call to come home rescued her, provided an excuse to go back to Oshatakea with no loss of face. She would not acknowledge, nor would she ever admit, that for a fleeting instant she'd had the thought that if Phillips were to die of pneumonia her dream of complete control might yet be realized.

Chapter 24

PHIL DID NOT ENTER FILLMORE ACADEMY THE FOLLOWING fall; such was Catherine's edict. His recovery from pneumonia was slow, not because of a few minor complications that set him back but because he resisted getting well. He was afraid his mother would snatch him away from Miss Eleanor's protective custody the minute he no longer needed her nursing care. His fears were justified.

"Phillips is too old to be encumbered by a hovering nanny," Catherine said.

"I try to not hover," Miss Eleanor replied. "And I do not consider myself a nanny."

"Whatever you may consider yourself, Gaines, you are my maid. I have been patient while you played nursey, but now I need you."

"I promised Mr. Fillmore I would never leave Phil—Phillips."

"My father-in-law is dead. The almighty lord and master is no more. You are superfluous to Phillips's life. From here on, I make decisions having to do with him, and it is my decision you and he should be separated. You are easier to move than he would be. I will have your things brought down to the north guest room. A chapter is closed. Gaines is back, Miss Eleanor is gone." Miss Eleanor turned to leave, her facial muscles twitching. "Don't cross me Gaines or you will regret it."

Catherine's reason for assuming control of Phillips had nothing to do with motherly concern; she wanted power over the one who had deprived her of what would have been hers had he not been born. Hunnewell said she was Phillips's guardian. The authority that came with guardianship could not be challenged. She would show those who cared so much about her son, the cynosure of their hopes and dreams, that the child king was to her a pawn she could move in any direction. As far as enrolling him in the Fillmore Academy was concerned, she made it clear she had no intention of following family tradition. If this child was a messiah she was the matriarch who would use him to achieve her own goals. Everything might belong to Phillips, but Phillips belonged to her.

The day Charles Hunnewell learned Catherine was taking Miss Eleanor away from Phil, he drove to Oshatakea and demanded a meeting with Catherine and Farney wherein he reminded them that, hewing to the spirit of FP's trust documents, all staff changes were to be sanctioned by him. It was not his desire, Hunnewell said, to restrain Catherine from having a personal maid, or indeed to have any say as to whom she might hire, not that he could in fact since the wages for that position became Catherine's responsibility the day she left Oshatakea and moved to Boston taking Giselle LaFleur with her. "Eleanor Gaines is on the Oshatakea payroll as Phil's primary caregiver. She is unavailable for any other position, now or in the foreseeable future. In the trust FP set up for her, he stated his firm desire that Miss Eleanor remain—his words are quite clear—Phil's companion and confidante as long as the boy, and eventually young man, feels he needs and wants her in that capacity. If and when he should decide she is not essential to him, Phil will discuss this with me and my son, and together we will determine what should happen. Until that time, the special rela-tionship between Eleanor Gaines and Farnsworth Phillips Fillmore IV is sacrosanct."

"What if Gaines decides she no longer wishes to be Phillips's companion and confidante?"

"I doubt that will happen, but if it does we will deal with it."

What more could Catherine say? She was shaken by the news that she was responsible for paying her personal maid's salary; this she had not known. She had never paid Gaines, but Gaines was apparently always considered part of the Oshatakea staff. Why hadn't Giselle said something about not being paid while they were in Boston? Could that be why the idiot girl had been in a perpetual French snit?

Charles Hunnewell did not mention Catherine's decision to keep Phil out of the academy. Did that mean he recognized her authority? Excellent! Her first encounter with the trustee had ended in a draw. Hunnewell might say Gaines would remain Miss Eleanor, but whichever name she went by, she would be living within a household ruled by Catherine even if she could not hire or fire anyone. Life could become increasingly complicated for the stubborn little English woman, who might, if she were sufficiently unhappy, return to Cliveden.

Before leaving Oshatakea, Hunnewell went to the third floor to report to Miss Eleanor on his meeting with Farney and Catherine, telling her she must not allow herself to be pressured into relinquishing Phil's care. "I have a suggestion. To remove yourselves from Catherine's immediate purview, you and Phil should take over FP's apartment above the Galleried Library. FP would approve."

Miss Eleanor thanked him, said she would think about it and discuss the idea with Phil but for the moment would like to remain where she was. "I think it important for Phil to not feel forced from rooms that have been his home since he was born. The boy's life has been disrupted enough, by his grandfather's death and his mother's return. He is also coping with the bitter disappointment about not being allowed to go down to the academy."

Charles smiled. "FP knew exactly what he was doing when he left Phil in your charge. Everything you say confirms the wisdom of his choice."

Miss Eleanor said no more. Her head was spinning. She had worked diligently to secure the loving sanctuary Phil's grandfather created for him. With FP gone, she was similar to a sole surviving parent, striving twice as hard to keep her child safe. Farney was doing what he could to take FP's place, and making headway, but for Phil, at least at present, his father was no substitute for Gramps. She was sure over time father and son would develop a closer relationship, though she doubted it would be the strong bond that was forged between FP and Phil during Phil's first years, or between Phil and herself when he was expelled bloody and bruised from his mother's womb into her hands. No one, especially his mother who never loved him, would be allowed to threaten him if Miss Eleanor could prevent it. She welcomed Hunnewell's support based on FP's trusts, but it was neither legalities nor a promise made to FP that fired her vigilance. It was her deep devotion to the child who might seem to have everything but in truth had much less than most children.

She knew her actions would add to the boy's distress if she were to openly challenge Catherine. Not that the challenge itself would upset him, but he would suffer from the violent vituperation that would follow. Such a challenge did not daunt Miss Eleanor who had learned survival tactics in back-stairs turf wars at Cliveden. Catherine Fillmore could be mean and conniving, but she was not in the same league with Nancy Astor. There were many ways Miss Eleanor could circumvent Catherine's commands if she thought them detrimental to Phil's welfare. Ever optimistic, Miss Eleanor hoped Catherine might quickly become bored pretending to be a mother involved in her son's daily activities, and withdraw, leaving Farney and Miss Eleanor to resume the parental roles they had played while she was away. Farney's instincts were sound. He and Miss Eleanor would know what was best for the boy. Though she thought Farney's idea to enroll Phil in the academy was exactly right, she did not interfere with Catherine's dictum that Phil was to be tutored at home.

Catherine's tutoring posture could be as temporary as her maternal interference.

But if he wasn't to be with other children at the academy, he must not lose Loren, his one peer in the nursery classroom. Ironically Loren's parents gave Miss Eleanor more trouble in continuing the nursery tutoring arrangement than did Catherine. Mr. Gage was strongly opposed to Loren doing anything different from other boys, and what other boys in the valley did was go to Fillmore Free Academy. After listening to pleas from Farney, supporting Miss Eleanor's contention that Loren's companionship was essential to Phil's well-being, Mr. Gage gave grudging and qualified approval, "but this year only." Which is what he said every year thereafter until the boys were ready for ninth grade.

Catherine, feeling extremely smug about Hunnewell's recognition of her authority, was blind to the pleasure Phil derived from Loren's presence. Had she known how important Loren was to her son, she would have quashed the companion arrangement as ongoing retribution for suffering she had endured bringing him into this world. Accepting Loren, Catherine told Miss Eleanor to contact Mrs. Nash, the boys' kindergarten teacher, to see if she would teach first grade. Catherine knew little about the woman except she didn't cause a fuss nor as far as Catherine knew talk to outsiders about the Portuguese Wing. Mrs. Nash was delighted to return to Oshatakea. "Phil and Gage are such eager learners," she said, "and an ideal pair. Each spurs the other one on. I'll soon be able to go beyond first-grade subjects because they are capable of advanced material." Based on Mrs. Nash's requests, Catherine approved orders for books and other educational requirements. Charles Hunnewell didn't question the invoices, and paid Mrs. Nash's salary without comment. Amazing, Catherine mused, that he did not use this opportunity to ask why Phillips was not going to the academy. His lack of curiosity disappointed her somewhat because she had prepared answers she hoped would flatten the attorney.

Satisfied that she had taken charge of Phillips with no real objections from Miss Eleanor or Charles Hunnewell, Catherine proceeded to test other loathsome trust rules. It would be fun to outwit the sly fox. With a lightness of heart she had not experienced since that dreadful day in the Galleried Library when Hunnewell revealed what FP had done, she called Sol Hurok's office. The impresario was pleased to hear from her. "I want to book a quintet for a Mozart weekend," she said. "I prefer to pay as little as possible for the best available group. If they haggle, remind them they will be getting first-class room and board as well as use of Oshatakea facilities. If they don't know what that means, tell them. If they continue to be difficult, impress upon them the honor I bestow when I invite artists to perform here." She heard Hurok's tight little laugh, but let it pass.

As she plotted, she realized she didn't want to ask Charles for an extra penny to cover increased food costs while the musicians were at Oshatakea. After all, how much would five scrawny string players eat in three or four days? She could afford whatever the difference was. And there'd be no houseguests. She didn't want extraneous people cluttering up the place. Her first thought was to restrict the quintet's audience to herself, Farney, the Kropotkins and Isabelle, but then she had the terrible thought that musicians might be offended if it appeared only a handful of people cared to hear them. This might affect their playing. If it did, she'd be the loser because she wanted to hear Mozart performed as it should be. "I have decided to open up the concerts, let anyone on the staff or in the valley who wants to come, come. We will do it by reservation as we did before, reserving seats in the order of requests," she told Farney. She brought Annie Dingle back on an hourly basis to handle paperwork and telephone calls she knew would be touchy because valley people always rushed to anything free at Oshatakea; there'd be more requests than could be accommodated. "Be sure to tell them we are not serving food," she instructed Annie.

When Farney heard this, he made a major commotion, telling her, as had FP, such parsimony went against two centuries of Oshatakea tradition. They fought for days, but Farney would not give ground. At last, when everything else had been settled and she was so impatient to hear the quintet play she didn't want to forgo that, she relented. "If you insist, we will have a simple buffet supper after each performance. I'll pass the bills on to Hunnewell, and if he complains you can pay for it out of your pocket."

Bones was excited to have more people in the house; family dinners weren't demanding enough for him. He went to work and came up with a menu he thought would please Catherine, but when he presented it she was not. "We don't need this. Give them cold ham, potato salad and cookies, that sort of thing." Bones had acquired temperament and attitude along with skills from the chefs with whom he had studied. He returned to his kitchen and threw a fit. When he cooled down he made a valiant attempt to fulfill Catherine's wishes but was unable to produce anything as nondescript as cold ham and potato salad. Defying her, he laid on a substantial buffet though not nearly as spectacular as his drop-dead displays of the past.

Charles Hunnewell surprised Catherine yet again by not objecting to the extra expenses that appeared with that month's statements, but he let her know they had not slipped past him with a remark that so irritated her she vowed henceforth she would pay every cent of whatever it cost to have music, dance or theater at Oshatakea. She could have done that for a time, but she had never written checks to pay for the weekends her fancy contrived. When after several serious shocks to her financial system she came to understand the thousands, sometimes tens of thousands of dollars required, her penurious Dudley breeding kicked in and she announced it was essential to "cut back." To hell with what the musicians, dancers or actors wanted for an audience; they were being paid, they better damn well give their finest performance regardless of how many sat there listening. Emboldened, she returned to her original notion of restricting audiences to the family, including Isabelle of course, and Miss Eleanor who would be there to keep Phillips awake and quiet. Phillips had to be present because Catherine wanted him exposed to the performing arts. Very different from exposing him to the children of farmers and tradesmen, but if the brat wiggled she'd have his head.

Suddenly everything was easier. Except for breakfast, the performing artists ate meals with the family, which gave Bones some needed incentive. Charles Hunnewell paid all bills including performers' fees and travel expenses, again letting Catherine know he was aware of what she was doing, this time with a positive comment. "We regard the cost of these weekends as part of Phil's education." Catherine could hardly believe it. Perhaps living at Oshatakea with Hunnewell replacing FP as paymaster wouldn't be as bad as she feared it would be. At least Hunnewell didn't ask for work sheets and need to approve menus. Residents of the valley and staff members who had availed themselves of the opportunity to attend performances weren't as sanguine, blaming Catherine's selfishness and arrogance for their exclusion. Deaf to complaints Catherine sent a memo to the household saying doors would be left ajar during a performance so those interested could hear the music if they stood in the corridor and remained silent. This did little to soften their hardening bias against her, though some were relieved that she would allow them to sit in back rows of the Baroque Theatre for dance and theatrical performances. However, the last line of the memo negated even this minor positive reaction. "Members of the staff are NOT invited to any post performance supper."

As Catherine learned to live with the new arrangements at Oshatakea, she became more expansive with performers' fees, buoyed up by Hunnewell's comment about the costs being part of Phillips's education. Artists Hurok had signed for the pittance she was willing to pay in the beginning did not live up to her standards. She missed first-desk players and knew the difference. If she was going to all the trouble entailed, even for a private performance, she wanted the best and original casts, not road-show second companies. With an open checkbook, Hurok and other agents were able to fulfill her fantasies. When still no objection was heard from Hunnewell, she set about "knocking the socks off," to use one of Bones's favorite expressions, those who constituted her select clientele. Isabelle and Adelaide were most appreciative of the major artists she brought in, sharing Catherine's knowledge and her enthusiasm, and Bones produced mind-boggling meals. After one particularly sublime dinner, the world's premier cellist leaned toward Catherine sitting next to him in the Gibbons Room and said, "Madame, had I known I would be served food such as this, I would have come to Oshatakea for nothing." If she were penny pinching, Catherine might have used his compliment in an effort to recover his staggering fee, but there was no need: "going top drawer all the way" was possible.

A major benefit of bringing professional artists to Oshatakea was, as in earlier years, the forming of friendships. Old friends returned and new friends were made during long walks, rides through the countryside in Farney's carriages, gay lunches or teas at the Kropotkins' dacha and cocktail parties at Isabelle's villa, and of course while eating around the table in the Gibbons Room. With these people Catherine dropped the aloofness that had been her signature characteristic. Delighted to be learning more each time artists came to the hill, she broadened her scope, inviting players of contemporary music and going beyond ballet to modern dance. Not that it mattered, beyond amusing her, but Farney was becoming deeply involved, and Phillips, thank God, was not nearly the distraction she thought he would be, though she paid no attention to what or whom he most appreciated. As long as he was quiet and remained out of her line of vision she didn't object to Phil joining other members of the family to greet or bid farewell to the performers. She had never bothered to greet boring houseguests, but these people were fascinating. Catherine wondered why she had not insisted on such exclusivity always. FP wouldn't let her. Thank God he was out of the way.

Having been excluded by Catherine, valley people turned their backs on the happenings at Oshatakea, paying little attention to the comings and goings of performers unless they were truly celebrated: Ethel Barrymore, the Lunts, Helen Traubel, Fritz Kreisler and others of that magnitude were greeted at the Fillmore Depot by autograph seekers, but few knew anything about modern dancers. Martha Graham, Jose Limon and Doris Humphrey could have been invisible when they stepped off trains for the total lack of interest in them.

Catherine's early reaction to Martha Graham was a combination of captivation and confusion. She admired the dancer's steel-hard determination and envied her unquestioned domination over the dancers in her company, but she could not accept as art dances Graham presented with such apparent anguish. Thrashing around inside a tubular gown was interesting to behold, but what was it? Catherine was not alone in her questioning. Isabelle grumbled about "all that groveling on the ground and tortured posturing. She wants us to think what she does is nigh on to impossible."

"Ballet dancers perform seemingly impossible feats and make them appear effortless," said Adelaide.

Louisa made the final pronouncement. "Markova is lighter than air and accepts accolades with humility. Graham looks like she can't get off the ground but thinks she's a goddess."

Catherine could question those she brought to Oshatakea, but when others did she leapt to their defense. "Graham says her dancing is just dancing."

"I read that piece too," Adelaide said, "where she says she wants to impart the sensation of living and energize us into a keener awareness of the mystery, humor and wonder of life. I'm not sure she's succeeding."

While not totally accepting, they were intrigued by Martha Graham. Her dances were a conundrum to be studied. This resulted in repeated invitations for the icon and her company to come to Oshatakea for extended periods, not just to perform but to make new dances as well. Along with these invitations, which provided an expense-free venue, came promises of complete privacy, and for contributions toward the production of future Graham projects.

Phil never nodded while watching any dance performance, ballet, folk or modern, whereas Miss Eleanor had to shake him if a chamber music piece went on too long. Perhaps it was their visual impact, but dancers so mesmerized the boy she had to pull him back into his seat as he leaned farther and farther forward until she feared he would fall on his face. Hyperstimulated, he didn't sleep afterward, making Miss Eleanor wonder if he should be allowed to attend evening dance programs. Had she tried to keep him away, she would have encountered fierce resistance. Phil, sensitive to her worry, tried to lessen it by pretending to be sleepy, and though he died to dance around his bedroom on those supercharged nights, he let her tuck him in and turn out the light. Then when he was alone, his imagination illuminated lifts and extensions, splits and slow rises until he danced in his dreams, one with those other glorious phantoms imparting the wonder of life.

Martha Graham chose to work and teach on the Baroque Theatre stage, which, she thought, offered the ultimate protection from prying eyes. However, Phil and Loren had, on childhood explorations, discovered a secret door that opened into a second-tier box. Here in their early years they played scary games of hide-and-seek. Somewhat later, in the glow of flashlights, the boys compared genitals. Later still, and alone this time, it was from the second-tier box that Phil watched the goddess Graham choreograph. He sat spellbound as she concentrated, then did a turn, a low bend or high reach, a short run, demonstrating movements for her dancers. Then looking into a dancer's eyes, she'd say, "Try it." Or ask, "Do you feel it? Do you understand?" From his hiding place Phil observed and heard and worried that if the dancer did not understand she or he might be horribly punished, so determined and intense was Miss Graham's demeanor.

Phil had been spying for weeks when, at dinner one evening, Graham cast her kohl-outlined gaze across the table into his eyes. Carmine-painted lips parted only a fraction over large teeth. "Young Mr. Fillmore wishes to dance."

"He does?" Farney asked.

Catherine would for intellectual exercise occasionally dispute Miss Graham who could argue until dawn over which came first, peach the fruit or peach the color, but all she said was, "Oh?"

"Isn't that true?" Graham asked Phil, her cobra stare pinning the boy to his chair.

Miss Eleanor gave Phil's knee a tweak under the table, meaning, answer the question. "Yes," said Phil.

"Oh," Catherine repeated, this time in a descending scale to scorn the ridiculous notion.

Miss Graham's mouth smiled and Phil saw a smudge of red on her white teeth. Her eyes held him. "You will learn nothing hiding in that box. Join me on the stage tomorrow morning at nine o'clock."

Letting out the breath he had been holding, Phil choked, "Yes ma'am."

A male dancer asked, "Are we starting class early tomorrow?"

"No. Nine o'clock is Phil and I, alone."

"I don't think," Catherine began, but stopped when Miss Graham asked to be excused.

At the door she paused to look back over her shoulder. "Nine o'clock."

"Nine o'clock," Phil repeated.

Chapter 25

LOSING LOREN AS A CLASSMATE AND DAILY COMPANION when the boys reached ninth grade was a serious blow to Phil. Loren was his pal and the only friend he had who was his age. The boys trusted each other and held nothing back but were highly competitive, especially after an incident when Mrs. Nash stuck a gold star on a crayoned picture Loren drew and a silver star on Phil's. Not yet aware that only at Oshatakea was he the main attraction, Phil made a scene. Why should he settle for silver when Loren got gold? After Mrs. Nash calmed the little boy she told him he would never get a gold star unless he deserved one, regardless of who he was or how much he carried on. "If Loren was not here, you still would have received a silver star for that drawing because you are capable of doing better work." Clever Mrs. Nash struck a nerve and started an Olympic race for the gold that ran from that morning through all the school years that followed. Loren's excitement and enthusiasm never ceased. He tackled each new subject with an explorer's eagerness, carrying Phil along with him on the tide of discovery. Phil wouldn't have given a fig about school if Loren hadn't been with him. When they reached the ninth grade, the first year of high school, Loren was forced by his father to go to the Fillmore Academy so he could play what the boys called "fucking football." Phil fell apart.

"It's stupid," he shouted at the breakfast table. "Loren and I have the same teachers. They lecture him at the academy, then drive up here and say the same things to me, or visa versa. Give me one good reason why I can't go down there with him." He was rebelling against his mother, but she ignored his pleas. He couldn't argue with Mr. Gage wanting Loren to play football; Loren was a natural athlete, a winning player on the junior varsity from his first game, which didn't surprise Phil, for everything Loren did was first rate, but Phil was hurt when Loren told him on the telephone he was having a blast. They spent practically every day together until they were thirteen, sharing all there was to growing up, then suddenly they were separated. Loren was doing just fine in a whole new world less than three miles from where Phil was miserable, a bug stuck in amber. The only "what's new?" that meant anything during nightly telephone conversations were Loren's descriptions of his day. Phil with nothing new to report resorted to kicking the wall. Loren said he was "wrecked" without Phil, but he didn't sound wrecked. Phil was sick with envy, and wildly jealous of friends Loren was making at the academy. In an attempt to spark a concerned response, Phil told Loren he wasn't bothering with homework, hadn't read a single assigned book, had stopped pretending to listen to his tutors tooting. "Tutors tooting" was an in-joke that used to crack them up. "I don't give a fiddler's fart about biology or algebra or the friggin' Lake Poets if you aren't here for me to breeze past."

Loren laughed, but Phil tried to hear something more than appreciation of his attempt at humor.

Miss Eleanor stopped having breakfast with Phil and Farney in the Portuguese Courtyard when Catherine returned from Boston and gave her so much grief about returning to being a maid, but Phil provided a full report to her when he went back upstairs to brush his teeth before going across the driveway to the converted monastery classroom. Several mornings during the first week of ninth grade, to express his distemper he threw a glass on the bathroom floor. Hearing the by now familiar shatter, Miss Eleanor rapped on the half-open door. "One of these days, you will cut yourself. Smashing things is something you inherited from your mother."

"I inherited nothing from my mother." Miss Eleanor's comment infuriated him.

"If you directed your energy to thinking things through instead of carrying on like a child of six, it might occur to you there is a slight chance your mother's position on this could ease, but only if you stop arguing with her. Shouting is bad enough, but saying her decision is stupid guarantees she won't give ground."

"But it is stupid."

"And so is your refusal to listen. Stop being pig headed Phil, some of us are trying to help you."

She and Farney were. Farney's naive way was to try for the umpteenth time to get his son more involved with horses, thinking Phil might then forget how miserable he was at being separated from Loren. Farney had been pushing horses toward Phil since he was born. His first gift when his son was only weeks old was a miniature horse hitched to a tiny basket cart. Phil slept soundly in the cart while Farney led the little horse around. He was not that passive when, at one year, he was lifted into another basket, this one attached to a saddle atop a Shetland pony. Phil's squalling scared the placid pony into becoming a bucking mustang. Strangely, Phil didn't make a whimper when they put him in the same basket saddle on a big black Newfoundland dog that lived in the stables. A string of steeds followed, each one meant to capture Phil's fancy. His anything-to-please father never stopped trying. If Phil had hinted he'd prefer riding an elephant, Farney nonplussed would have found an elephant. He could not believe his son, flesh of his flesh, blood of his blood, did not share his all-consuming passion. Stablemen teased him, saying Farney was part horse, usually the "back end." There probably wasn't an equine in the world

Farney couldn't have had a loving relationship with. What he really wanted was that kind of relationship with Phil.

"I'd like you to ride with us tomorrow morning," Farney said at dinner.

"I hate to hurt your feelings Dad, but I don't want to ride, tomorrow or any other morning. I think I'm allergic to horseback riding." The corners of Catherine's mouth lifted in an I-told-you-so smile.

"Tomorrow you may find riding a new and different experience." Farney's wink, an attempt to appear conspiratorial, made him look goofy.

"How different can it be?" Catherine asked. "Are you planning to mount from the other side?"

To please his father and make up for his mother, Phil was at the stables at seven o'clock the next morning. Pearl was giving her mare a final wipe down before putting on the pad and saddle. Phil said good morning to her, and went in the direction of Farney's voice. He was talking to somebody around the corner in one of the side aisles. As Phil approached, Farney looked up from cinching a bellyband. "Phil this is Sally Rowley, Jock Rowley's daughter. She's going to ride Jewel."

"How do you do?" Phil stepped forward, automatically put out his hand then quickly withdrew it.

Sally had lots of red hair. When she smiled she tried to hide a gap between her front teeth. "Hello."

"For you Master Phil," Farney's eyes gleamed, "I have a new horse."

"You always have a new horse for me." Phil meant to sound resigned, but realized he was being sarcastic.

The new horse was a handsome chestnut Morgan gelding. Farney said he was a sweet animal looking for a special person. Beau did have a sweet disposition and an easy movement. Phil was fairly comfortable riding him, but still he was not happy. This wasn't the horse's fault and it certainly wasn't Farney's. Phil could tell by his

father's halfhearted smile he knew he'd failed again. Back in the stable, feeling guilty because he had disappointed him, Phil wanted to
throw his arms around Farney's neck, but he never hugged his
father. Gramps was the only man Phil knew who liked to be hugged,
and Miss Eleanor the only woman. What he did instead was carefully cool Beau down so Farney would see he was taking good care
of his gift. Sally was doing the same for Jewel. After the horses were
wiped dry and let out to run, Sally said, "I'll see you tomorrow."

"You will?"

"Your father said I'd be doing him a big favor if I would come up
and ride with you every morning."

"I see." Phil saw. It wasn't just horses Farney was trying to involve
him with. "I'm not sure I'll be riding tomorrow, but you are welcome to if you want." After sleeping on it, Phil decided, what the
hell, he'd extend Dad the courtesy of not giving up after a single
try. He still felt guilty, so rode Beau alongside Sally on Jewel each
morning at seven o'clock for eight days. That was the most he
could do. He called it quits. Farney didn't plead or argue. Farney
argued with no one except Catherine when she was in a mood to
fight and wouldn't let him walk away. Father and son talked.

"I had no ulterior motive when I asked Sally to ride with us.
She's looking for experience. You need a pal Phil. I know you miss
Loren's company. I thought maybe an hour with Sally in the morn-
ing might help."

"Sally isn't Loren Dad. But you are right, I do need somebody."
Then he added quickly, so he wouldn't hurt Farney's feelings again
if he seemed to exclude him as a pal, "my own age. Sally is that,
and she is okay. She's kind of pretty once you get past the hair and
that gap in her teeth, but . . . "

"There's no need to explain. I understand," Farney said.

Miss Eleanor also understood, but they couldn't really understand. Loren was the only one Phil had told about his hours with
Martha Graham, how he was changed by every second of the sixty

minutes, becoming possessed as if a demon had entered his body and brain forcing him to do its bidding. Was this "dance" that had captured him? When Graham, so softly Phil had to strain to hear her, talked about "dance," dance became holier, more sacred than all the combined comparative religions whose histories Loren and Phil had studied. He was silent when she spoke, but inside he was repeating, amen, amen, as if in affirmation of prayer. When she said one could become a dancer, only, if to breathe, to see, to live, one could do nothing but dance. Yes, yes, Phil longed to shout. He thought every word she uttered must have been whispered in his ear eons before by a forgotten deity because he knew what she meant as she said it. The words were familiar and true. He was aware she said nothing to him she hadn't said to others, but that was what goddesses did. The first time he told Loren all this, he became so overcome with emotion he cried and was unashamed. That's the kind of friend Loren was; Phil could cry in front of him and not be embarrassed. Loren had listened with his mouth slightly ajar, which is what he did when he was enthralled.

Phil told Loren in excruciating detail what happened when Martha Graham asked him to remove his shoes and socks so he could follow her through a few "simple" exercises. "Do exactly as I do," she instructed. Phil tried, but could not. When she stood straight as a rod, Phil knew he was bent. When she planted her bare feet apart to give herself what she called a broad base, he moved his feet so far he thought from the catch in his groin he had torn something vital. When he made a correction, his feet were too close together; he had trouble maintaining balance. She inhaled deeply and slowly exhaled. He did the same. "Deeper." Phil did it again, inhaling as long and as deep as he could. "No, no, no, not in your head, use your diaphragm. Suck in then force out." She pressed and released, pressed and released. He became confused, breathed in when she was pressing out. Who would believe breathing could be so difficult? It took a few minutes of imperfect deep breathing at different speeds before they returned to positions.

She bent her knees ever so slightly and, with no warning, slapped the insides of her thighs with the palms of her hands. The clean sharp slaps startled Phil. When he did not immediately do as she had done, just stared at her, she barked, "Wake up!" He bent his knees and slapped the insides of his thighs. His slaps were muffled, sounded spongy. "Your muscles are mush. Come here, feel my thighs. Don't be afraid, boy." She grabbed his wrists and placed his open hands against the inside of her thighs. Through her loose skirt her thighs were sculptured steel. "Everything comes from here," she hissed. "Thighs and leg muscles, back and arm muscles — and head muscles." She rapped a knuckle on Phil's head. "You must develop proper muscles if you are to be a dancer."

As a partially cut through tree falls, her body above the waist went from upright to parallel with her legs, and her palms pressed flat against the floor. Phil watched but did not attempt to do what she had done. She resumed her former stance and fixed hard eyes on him. "I don't think I can," he said.

"I know you can't. Try."

He tried and couldn't. She didn't have to tell him to keep his legs straight; he knew from watching her he should do that. He thought he was bending from the waist but she told him his back was a croquet arch. Phil tried until his toes cramped. They then moved to a barre along the back wall to do stretching exercises, which made him want to groan even when he wasn't stretching. When she finally said, "Enough," Phil thought he'd pass out. "Tired?" she asked.

He was drenched with sweat and disheveled but she who had with no apparent effort done all the things Phil couldn't begin to do was casually cool, her makeup and coiffure undisturbed. "Yes," he puffed. The muscles in his legs jerked with spasms, his lower back felt as if he'd never be able to stand erect again.

"Expect pain."

Her dancers were drifting in, singly, in pairs and groups, arriving for class. "How'd it go?" one asked. Another tousled Phil's damp hair.

"Stay and watch if you wish," Miss Graham said. Phil was eager to watch, and desperate to lie down on his bed. "But do not make a sound."

Shoes and socks in hand, he hobbled off the stage, down to the first row, where he sat with a wince. Dancers warming up did pretty much the same exercises though not together, or in the same sequence. Graham disappeared into the wings with Louis Horst. Stiffness was gripping Phil's body, not the kind that comes when one first rides horseback after a long time not riding but a deeper less specific, all enveloping, creeping paralysis he feared might be terminal. But as badly as he was hurting, in the next few hours he was raised to a higher plane of elation than he had ever known. He realized he hadn't accomplished one tangible thing in his hour, hadn't been able to breathe the way she told him to breathe despite total concentration and immense effort, to say nothing of how limp he was trying to do those exercises, but something had happened to him, something beyond discomfort and disappointment, something that made him different from what and who he had been before. Watching Graham and her dancers, as locked in agony as he was, he did not want to sit watching from the safety of a seat in the audience; he wanted to know what these dancers knew even if it meant greater pain. He was willing to do anything she asked and do it over and over and over again, as they were doing. "And again," she said. He wanted to be as airborne yet as rooted in the earth, as agile, graceful and powerful, as magnificent as were her acolytes, perspiring, aspiring gods and goddesses in training. He didn't want to watch; he wanted to be one of them.

All this he shared with Loren. Only Loren would know how vital those painful hours of learning and trying and watching were.

Chapter 26

⁓

AFTER A HELLISH YEAR IT BECAME EVIDENT, EVEN TO Catherine who for all her interference paid little real attention to her son, that changes had to be made if Phil was to be prepared for Harvard. A compromise was reached. From the founding of the Fillmore Free Academy in 1826 by Christina Farnsworth Fillmore, a Fillmore had chaired the board of trustees. Farney, who now sat at the head of the table, encountered no overt opposition to his proposal, transporting students enrolled in advanced Latin, English Honors II and calculus up to Oshatakea for those three classes. These were courses scheduled for Phil if he could be brought up to standard by summer tutors, and Loren in the first term of his sophomore year. Farney persuaded Catherine to let Phil attend the academy for physics and chemistry, which Loren would also take. She approved because of the academy's labs, but drew the line at physical education. "He can get all the physical education he needs right here at home," she said.

Farney's experiment, described by him as simple in theory, became wildly complicated in practice. As soon as word leaked out that certain classes would be taught in the ancient monastery at Oshatakea, the rush to enroll in them was overwhelming. Only strict adherence to prerequisites kept class sizes manageable, but nothing kept the transportation aspect from becoming chaotic. Only five, including Loren, were in all three Oshatakea morning classes. The other thirteen students had to be moved up or down the hill for subjects that preceded or followed in the schedule. There was major curriculum realignment at the conclusion of a semester that came close to unhinging everybody involved. This incensed faculty members who already resented what was being done to accommodate a single student. There could have been resignations but for the attractiveness of the Fillmore Valley as a place to live and teach and academy salaries and benefits that were above the state average. Disgruntled teachers stayed on, confining their carping to supposedly private places such as the faculty room. Grumbles escaped but did not dampen the enthusiasm of those students who spent a portion of their school days on the Oshatakea estate.

Phil's after-lunch descent to the academy for physics and chemistry caused no problem for anyone but himself. More than just the new boy in school, he entered encumbered with myths, rumors and the indisputable fact that he was Catherine's son. Myths and rumors could be dealt with; he was after all part of the Fillmore/Oshatakea legend. But the maternal factor could not be altered and that put him at a distinct disadvantage, not just with fellow students but most adults who worked at the academy. They had suffered Catherine's disdain and were bitter because relations with the Fillmores before Catherine married into the family had been personal and friendly. Farney was loved; FP had been nearly worshiped and was still mourned. Affection for Adelaide and Louisa was genuine. Tit for tat, nobody liked Catherine, including those who gave her credit for at one time allowing them to attend her wonderful concerts. Seldom mentioned by name, valley women, out of respect to the rest of the Fillmores, referred to her as "that woman"; valley men called her "the bitch from Boston," or simply "the bitch." Phil, known to most of the community only by sight, was "the bitch's pup." Farney's plight as Catherine's husband engendered sympathy. No one seemed to be aware that Phil also had a plight as

Catherine's son, the prevailing attitude being he was a younger, male version of his selfish, tyrannical mother. Arriving for classes each afternoon in a chauffeur-driven Buick did little to disabuse onlookers of burning prejudice. Phil's lab stool disappeared with predictable frequency in the first months. "Let the bastard stand," the instructor said sotto voce before inquiring in a bemused tone, "Does anyone know where Mr. Fillmore's stool might be?" If Farney had learned of this teacher's behavior, the same follow-up question might have been asked of him, but Phil didn't tattle to his father; he blew off steam in Miss Eleanor's sitting room. That several of the students who were most evil to him at the academy were most obsequious during morning classes in the monastery made Phil want to piss on them, he told Miss Eleanor. Miss Eleanor raised her eyebrows but did not rebuke him.

The constant antagonistic atmosphere depressed him, distracted him from studies at which he felt compelled to succeed now that he and Loren were competing side by side. Forcing himself to ignore taunts siphoned off energy he should have expended on his work. He lied when Farney asked if he was happier now. Farney thrived during his own academy years when he was "one of the boys." He wanted Phil to have the same carefree experience. Phil justified lying with the truth that he preferred putting up with what he and Loren called bullshit to being tutored by himself. He did not seek shelter from the attacks, figuring the best way to beat not only the turds who taunted him but also the anything-to-be-popular teachers who went along with the crap was to study as if each day were a final exam. Results proved worth the effort. At the end of his sophomore year, he earned and was given, not graciously but nevertheless given, Fillmore Free Academy's award for highest achievement in science. He had an insane urge to do cartwheels down the hall, not because of the beribboned citation but because of the sour faces of his science teachers. Loren congratulated Phil on "getting the gold," and bet him he could not do it again. The feat was repeated at the end of his junior and senior years, three years in a row! Nobody in the history of the academy had won the science award three years in a row. Farney nearly exploded with pride. Miss Eleanor wept. Those in the valley who had nattered about favoritism the first year were reduced to complaining by the third, "It's unfair to be as rich as he is and damned smart too." Girls added, "And so handsome."

In contrast to muscular farm boys who did half a day's physical labor before they came to school and another half day of chores after school, Phil in his sophomore year resembled the ninety-pound weakling in the Charles Atlas ad, the one who has sand kicked in his face. Tall, thin and gangly, with a fair unblemished complexion and black wavy hair that was derided by his detractors, Phil stood out in a population of robust, ruddy-faced youths with unruly mops. His teeth were straight without benefit of braces; theirs would never be used in an Ipana ad. His manner was mild, theirs aggressive. Valley boys knew their present and future prosperity depended in large part on the Fillmores, but antipathy to the heir overcame acknowledgment of this fact. Brazen bravado rode a steed of assumed masculinity. As do young men everywhere when encountering one who differs in any respect, they sniped at Phil's sexuality.

These studs-in-waiting knew about sex. Procreation was part of their daily lives, not human but pigs, cows, sheep, chickens, horses. They not only watched but sometimes had to supervise the breeding process. Determined to act out fantasies fed by sexual activity surrounding them on their farms, they had limited opportunity for actual experience with girls. The valley was a close community where everybody knew pretty much what everybody else was doing. Hot or not, the boys had to be exceedingly cautious in satisfying lustful curiosity. It was dangerous to fool around with a girl who had brothers. Occasionally an equally curious female cousin visited, and there were a few brotherless girls who thought affection would follow if they did what boys wanted, but mostly the young men of Fillmore Valley did what young men historically do—they lied about their prowess with numerous conquests. A large part of their harassment of Phil was to bolster shaky egos and give substance to false reputations.

The first time Phil overheard, "Here comes the queer," followed by snickers, he knew the gibe and nasty laughter was aimed at him but didn't know what "queer" meant. When Loren explained, Phil shrugged. "Well, I'm not, so who cares what they say?"

Loren's loyalty was steadfast. Never did he hesitate or pull away, sticking to Phil's side, prepared to physically protect him if it came to that. Big, powerfully built and with a reputation for fearlessness earned on the football field, nobody challenged Loren. The intensity of his friendship with Phil, and the obvious need each one had for the other, however, led to speculation about Loren's sexuality as well as Phil's, not that anyone dared question it openly. The approach was devious, cloaked in locker-room camaraderie, such as: Did Loren know Kate Reilly was hot to trot with him, and "she won't put out for anybody, we've all tried." Incapable of subtlety they could not hide, even as they showered Loren with compliments, their growing suspicion that he might be "one of those" was obvious. "If you fuck the way you play football, man, you must be the answer to every girl's prayer. You must make 'em so happy they want to keep you all to themselves, because not one woman, and there must be a shitload out there begging for more, not one woman has ever peeped about bagging the boy wonder of Fillmore Academy. Why do you think that is Loren?" Loren grinned and shrugged his broad shoulders. He had other fish to fry.

That Phil would attend Harvard was taken for granted. Six generations of Fillmore men had attended Harvard University, and two of Catherine's Dudley ancestors were members of the first class to graduate from the Cambridge institution. Going to Harvard was Phil's undiscussed destiny. During the years when he and Loren were dazzling private tutors with their brilliance, it was suggested Loren should also think about Harvard. Upon hearing this, Farney not only endorsed the idea but on a visit to the Gage farm assured Loren's family Fillmore funds would support it. Then when Loren became as bright a star on the field as he was in the classroom, academy advisers told him he could get an athletic scholarship to any university he chose to attend. Such a scholarship was first put forward when Phil was languishing alone at Oshatakea. Charles Hunnewell's son George, who had taken over as Phil's managing trust officer, knew nothing about Loren's chances, but warned Phil's parents that their connections with Harvard, including a long history of major gifts from both families, might not be enough if Phil refused to learn. It had been George's warning that convinced Catherine to go along with Farney's compromise agenda of sending him part-time to the academy.

The dream of staying together in college held for Loren and Phil until the fall of their senior year. Loren was intoxicated by the prospect of a future based on a Harvard degree, and even more by his fantasy of what life could be for the two of them away from the valley and hassles heaped on Phil by locals. Phil was equally excited because he would be beyond his mother's reach, which made his major fantasies possible. He didn't really give a damn about Harvard; getting a degree was not part of his goal. Once he was on his own, he could seriously pursue his ambition to become a dancer. Martha Graham fed his obsession with guarded responses to floods of Phil's questions in letters that flew between Oshatakea and wherever she happened to be; guarded because she did not want to jeopardize Catherine's intermittent financial support, and she was not convinced by Phil's assurance that no one saw his letters to her or hers to him except his friend Loren Gage. Loren Gage meant nothing to her. Catherine worried both correspondents. If Catherine suspected the contents of the occasional Graham to Phil letter she spied in the morning mail, she would put a halt to their exchange, but Catherine never took seriously

Phil's murmerings pertaining to dance. She thought Graham was writing to her son from all over the globe as a kind gesture or perhaps to add exotic stamps to the collection he'd inherited from FP.

Graham told Phil in forceful and unmistakable language that there was no one in Boston capable of preparing him to eventually study with her, his stated goal, but after being worn down by his nonstop entreaties she gave him the name of a dance studio run by Shirley Biddlecomb. "She will be of little use to you, but won't do any major harm." He didn't dare attempt contact by mail with Shirley Biddlecomb, sure Catherine would intercept the dance instructor's reply. Impatiently he bided his time; when he was at last in Cambridge, his first act would be to find her studio.

This blissful picture of conjoined hopes with differing fantasies was shattered by the aftermath of the Presbyterian Church carriage-shed incident, which occurred on a Saturday night, September 19, in the boys' senior year.

"I'm taking a lot of guff because I'm still a virgin," Loren told Phil after a swim in Gramps's pool. They were lying naked on towels letting the warm fall sun dry them.

"Virgins are girls."

"Technically true, but you know what I mean. I've never slept with one, which Dick Mathey and Gary Cushing suspect."

"Why do you say that?"

"From the way they question me."

Phil laughed. "I sent a stable boy tail over teakettle when he asked me if I'd popped a cherry yet and I didn't know what he was talking about."

Loren rolled on his side facing Phil, his upper body raised, resting on an elbow. "Dick says he'll line up a girl, somebody he says is hot for me, if I want him to. I bet he could also get a girl for you. What do you say?"

Phil thought about it with his eyes closed. "I'm not sure I'd know what to do."

"You've watched stallions breeding mares for Pete's sake. It's the same thing."

"That can get pretty wild, with lots of screaming, the mare kicking, the stallion biting . . . "

"Not that part jerk. I mean when the stallion pushes his dick in her. Mares stop kicking when stallions start pumping. I guess it's the same thing with girls." Loren laid back and closed his eyes.

After a minute or two of silence, Phil went up on his elbow to look down at Loren. "I'd be willing to give it a try. Be a change from whacking off."

Dick Mathey and Gary Cushing made the arrangements, telling Loren that he and Phil didn't have a thing to worry about. Because Loren was "built like a bull, and a fucking Fillmore Furies hero," they were sure any girl would go along with their scheme to fix him up with an all-the-way blind date; probably even Kate Reilly, who as far as they knew honestly had never put out. However, their senses of humor being warped, the plotters did not go after Kate or any other valley beauty, but Liz Macomber, a plain girl whom no boy had so much as asked to go for a walk. Liz, hungry to be noticed, almost fainted when jaunty Dick Mathey sat down beside her on the bus, and then said in a low voice, "Loren Gage wants you to meet him Saturday night in the old carriage shed behind the Presbyterian church. You know what for Liz, so don't play hard to get. He'll never give you another chance." Liz didn't care about a second chance with Loren Gage, but she had her heart set on going to a good women's college, and was worried that never having been touched by a boy would make her as much an oddball there as she was in high school. Before Dick Mathey stood up to get off the bus, she said yes, she would meet Loren Saturday night. She spent every available minute between assent and assignation scrubbing her face with lotions guaranteed to remove all signs of acne and turn her "pebbly teenage skin to silky satin."

Despite their suspicions about him, for Dick Mathey and Gary

Cushing Loren was merely bait to haul in the bitch's pup. Phil the pretty prig would roll with Mamie Osgood, who had humped Dick and Gary and a thousand other guys at the academy, though she said she preferred men in their twenties from outside the valley. "You boys with hot nuts don't know what a woman wants," was her famous tag line when those who used her rolled off. "Compared to Fillmore the Fourth, Mamie will think we're love pirates," Dick Mathey snickered while setting up the deal, but he didn't say that to Mamie, telling her if she played her cards right she might one day move into Oshatakea. Nor did they tell her about Loren being initiated at the north end of the Presbyterian church sheds while she was laying the Fillmore heir at the south end because they knew she'd prefer fucking the football star to an improbable future in a big house on the hill. Gary Cushing told Mamie to talk as dirty as she knew how to overcome Phil's shyness. "Get him fired up, then go after him. Pretend he's raw meat and you're a leopard. We don't want you to just fuck him Mamie, we want you to scare the shit out of him." Mamie practiced a snarl. "You guys are turning me on. I didn't think you were up to it."

Phil lied about going to bed early with a sick headache. Excused from the table, he left the Gibbons Room, sneaked out of the house and ran through the woods to meet Loren, who was waiting for him at the front gate in his brother's beat-up blue Dodge. He nodded when Loren asked if he was nervous. "As shaky as the bumpers on this wreck." Attempting to calm himself and amuse Loren, he added, "I've been saving up for five days, three actually."

"Me too."

Dick and Gary were waiting for them in the dark behind the church where no gaslight's glow penetrated. Dick put his finger to his lips to indicate neither inductee into the halls of Eros was to make a sound. Gary took Loren's arm and whispered, "Follow me." Loren glanced over his shoulder to shrug "what the hell" at Phil who was looking even whiter than usual in the moonlight. Dick waited a minute, then grabbed Phil's arm and pulled him toward the carriage shed. When they got to the first bay, he shoved Phil inside and slammed the doors.

An odor of mildew permeated the blackness. Totally blind, praying his eyes would quickly adjust, Phil did not see that Gary, back from taking Loren to Liz, had joined Dick and three fellow conspirators leering over a partial partition between the bay he'd been shoved into and the one adjacent. Before adjustment to the dark came, naked Mamie reached up from kneeling on a blanket and began clawing the front of Phil's pants. "Come on Fourth, I wanna see if a Fillmore cock is bigger 'n better than an ordinary guy's." Phil's frantic attempts to free himself from her hands failed. He tried to push her away but could not. Her hands were everywhere; she was undoing his belt and yanking his pants and briefs down over his slender hips.

"Give me a minute. Please."

"You've got more'n a minute buster, you've got all night." Mamie stood up to rip the shirt off his shoulders, then pressed her soft bare breasts and hard nipples against his chest. She pulled his head down so she could stick her tongue in his ear, while riding her damp crotch up and down his leg. "Mamie's going to give you the fuck of your life, baby, the works—if she can find anything to work with." Using both hands, she grabbed his flaccid penis, stretched it, slapped it, massaged it. "Come on pretty boy, get hard. You can get a hard-on can't you?"

"Yes." Phil's voice was little more than a quaver. He fervently prayed for an erection.

"Maybe it'll help if I go down on you." She knelt.

Maybe it would have helped had Dick Mathey at precisely that moment not guffawed from his perch on the partial partition, "Jeez Mamie, I'm ready to shoot my wad looking at your big tits from up here and this queer fairy can't get a boner." The rest of the gallery howled. Mamie shrieked for them to shut their fucking faces.

What remained of Phil's penis retreated like a terrified turtle into its shell.

Loren's shouts were unheard above the boys' ongoing hilarity and Mamie's bellowed obscenities. Loren leapt off Liz, pulled up his pants and ran down to the bay, where Phil was trying to protect himself from Mamie's ongoing attack. He threw the doors open and saw Phil, his knees bent, shoulders hunched, arms crossed over his groin while Mamie bit and scratched and the gang of four yelped crude encouragement from above.

The following Monday morning, a battered and psychologically bruised Phil prayed again, this time for something, anything, it didn't matter what, to strike him dead before he had to walk to the old monastery building for class. Falling downstairs and striking his head would do, but he didn't fall. Choking on a fish bone from the kipper he put on his breakfast plate for that specific reason might be the answer, but he didn't choke because he didn't eat the kipper. He could not swallow. His father asked if he was feeling all right. He said he was. He contemplated a fruit knife, wondering if, jabbed between his ribs, it would be long enough to pierce his heart.

"Loren!" Farney's greeting broke Phil's trance. "What brings you here this early? Come sit down, have some breakfast."

"I borrowed my brother's Dodge," Loren said looking across the courtyard toward Phil.

"Where did you park?" Catherine didn't want farmers' cars cluttering Oshatakea drives.

"Back of the monastery." Loren had a small cut above his left eye.

"Don't sit down." Phil jumped up. "I'll get my books." They left the courtyard and went to the third floor where they locked themselves in Phil's bedroom.

Facing each other, Loren was the first to speak. "Are you okay?"

"No. What happened to your eye?"

"I was stupid. I let Dick Mathey get in a jab before I broke his nose."

"You broke Dick Mathey's nose?"

"Flattened it."

Phil clenched his fists. "Wow. What about Gary Cushing?"

"Remember his crooked front tooth? Gonzo."

Phil fell back onto his bed laughing. He was hysterical.

"They wouldn't give me the names of the other assholes who got away, but I'll find them eventually. Grab your books, we'll be late for class."

Phil stopped laughing and sat up. "I can't go to class, they'll crucify me."

"Yes you can go to class. C'mon, get your tail in gear."

"Loren, everybody knows."

"Of course they know. Does that mean you're never going to leave the house again? Like it or not Phil, you live in this valley, it's your home. You own most of it. You can't let a couple of dickheads take it away from you, and that's what they'll do if you let them."

"I know, I know, but . . . "

"It wasn't your fault, none of it was, nothing that happened—or didn't happen."

Loren grinned. "If some wiseacre makes a crack, tell him you only get it up for quality. Everybody knows Mamie Osgood is common trash."

They were walking across the lawn toward the classrooms when Phil put a hand on Loren's arm. "I've told you everything, but you haven't told me anything. Did you?"

"Get it up? Yeah, and in, for about thirty seconds, not long enough to understand what all the fuss is about."

Chapter 27

NOT MUCH MORE THAN THIRTY SECONDS WAS ALL IT took to alter the carefully designed scheme for Loren's future based on a Harvard degree. In a tearful encounter behind the bleachers overlooking the football field on which Loren had won trophies for the academy and laurels for himself, as Indian summer breezes riffled her wispy brown hair, Liz Macomber told him she was pregnant.

"You can't be."

"Can or can't, I am." Her bitterness was partially about her disappointment at the emptiness of those few clinical minutes in the carriage shed.

"What are you going to do?"

"We, Loren, what are *we* going to do! I was dumb, but I didn't do it all by myself."

"Right." He moved to the left to keep late afternoon sun from shining directly into his eyes. "I'm sorry about this Liz, about the whole episode, really sorry."

"Sorry doesn't do it."

"I know. Give me a chance to think."

"Don't take too long. I want this thing gone before it starts to show. I've got to get rid of it now." Her voice was rising.

Her wanting to be "rid" of this thing galvanized him. This thing was a baby, a baby he and she had conceived by mistake in that stinking carriage shed, but being a mistake was not the baby's fault; the baby shouldn't be killed because what he and Liz did was stupid. He understood her unhappiness, her panic, he too was in a panic, but he couldn't let her do what she wanted. Accepting full responsibility and honestly wanting to help Liz out of the terrible predicament she was in because of him, he needed time to think of a way out of this mess. When he told Phil, Phil joined him in pacing the floor but could do little else that was remotely helpful. Desperate Liz might do something before he could stop her, Loren revealed the whole story to his father in the cow barn during the evening milking. He expected wrath and recrimination, was prepared for whatever punishment his father might dole out, but Walter Gage's response was delayed and somber. "These things happen Loren. We'll talk to your mother, she's good in emergencies."

Sitting around the kitchen table, cups of coffee getting cold in front of them, the Gage family examined options until they came to a unanimous conclusion. Mrs. Gage would go to Liz and try to persuade her to carry the baby to full term, give birth and then let them, the Gages, take the child to raise. For the first time since Liz told him, Loren went to bed not feeling he was some kind of ogre. Relieved by what his parents were willing to do, he knew he would be able to sleep, something he hadn't done in the week of endless nights he'd lain awake burdened with guilt and worry. He was just dozing off when the bedroom door opened. "Are you too old to be tucked in?" his mother asked. He said he wasn't. She gave him a good night kiss. "No matter what Loren, your father and I love you."

"I know."

Liz rejected the Gages' offer. "I don't want anybody to take it and raise it. Can't you understand, I will not lose control of my body. I want me back as I should be." She grabbed Loren's hand and pressed it to her stomach. He couldn't feel anything. "It's getting bigger," she cried.

Farney overheard stable hands talking quietly in a corner and asked what the hot subject of tongue waggers might be. Their replies were embellished with lurid details of the Liz and Loren drama. Reluctantly they left out the juicy morsels of Mamie Osgood and Phil shrieking and screaming at the other end of the carriage shed. Farney was cross when he questioned Phil and discovered his son had known about all this from the beginning, and been kept informed of the Gages' offer to take the baby that was rejected by Liz and her family. "You should have told me, Phil. I might be able to help." He drove to the Macomber farm where Charley Macomber swore he'd shoot Loren Gage "if that filthy dog sets foot on my land. I won't go lookin' for him Farney, but be warned, he'll get kilt if he comes here sniffin' around my girl." Mrs. Macomber said she wanted to sell out, leave the valley and never come back. Farney's comment, intended to sooth, echoed Walter Gage's. "Margaret, these things happen. There is no disgrace. Everybody understands."

"This thing didn't happen to everybody, it happened to our family," Mrs. Macomber said.

Farney next went to the Gage farm where he sat down with Loren and Walter and Hattie in a kitchen redolent with the rich fragrances of brown bread and baking beans. Hattie told him the intent of their offer to take the child "is not just to solve a problem. We want this baby. Farney, it will be our first grandchild." Emotion crept into her voice. "If I didn't hold myself back, I'd be upstairs right this minute, painting and papering what will be the baby's room."

Walter picked up the strand. "Every day Liz doesn't say yes is painful. That girl is carrying a Gage, which may not mean a thing to anybody else, but means a lot to us."

"The Macombers are in pain too," Farney said. He commended the Gages for their positive position in a difficult situation, and left with, "I'll do what I can."

It was not easy for him because Mrs. Macomber was as adamant as Liz that this embarrassment should be dealt with promptly, put behind them as soon as possible.

"If I was sure she'd not die along with what's inside her, I'd mix up a batch of herbs an old Indian woman told me about and give Liz a double dose."

"Please don't do that." Farney listened and cajoled with no lessening of the Macombers' resolve. Disgusted with the gab, Charley Macomber went to the barn, leaving Liz to mournfully tick off all the things that were ruined for her, most important her hope to go to one of the good women's colleges. "I knew there wasn't much chance, but now," she wailed, "but now, even if I could go, no good college would have me."

Farney pursed his lips. She had given him a wedge, but he mustn't jump too fast. "I have an idea."

"What?"

"Stop crying and listen to me. Please Liz, listen carefully, you too Margaret." Liz sniffed. Mrs. Macomber's defeated eyes focused on Farney's. "If you will have the baby and release the infant to its father, I'll send you to a good women's college for four years." Liz and her mother stared dumbfounded at Farney. "I understand how difficult it is to be here in this condition. If you want to get away from the valley until after the baby is born, I'll find a place for you to go and pay for that as well."

Liz recovered first. Without looking at her mother, she spoke with no hint of sob or choke. "If I accept your offer, and I do, I have to graduate from the academy. If I go away I'd lose a year, which means I will stay where I am thank you. The money you would spend on a place for me to stay until I have the baby you can put into a savings account I can draw on when I finish college, before I get settled in a job."

Farney smiled. "You do understand my conditions Liz and accept the terms?"

"I do."

"All of them?"

"All of them."

"Excellent." He stood, his lower back hurting from sitting so long in one of the Macombers' straight kitchen chairs. "George Hunnewell will put our agreement in writing so there can be no misunderstanding. Thank you Liz, you'll not regret your decision." He wanted to be out of there before Mrs. Macomber, who had said nothing, could object or raise the ante.

Liz had grit. Regardless of how she felt, and she had a problem-plagued pregnancy, she didn't miss a day of school, without any support from anybody at the academy. A heavily pregnant, other-wise skinny teenager walking the halls was disruptive. Failing to admire her courage and determination, members of the faculty were appalled. They viewed Liz as a naive girl who got in trouble and was shamelessly flaunting her condition. "And the trustees let her get away with it." Conversely, Loren's standing as academy idol was enhanced by his part in the pregnancy.

Students were too busy giving Liz grief to lean on Phil, though his carriage-shed fiasco was common gossip. When Dick Mathey and Gary Cushing, both bearing scars, returned to school follow-ing several days' absence after the incident, boys who would oth-erwise have made Phil's life miserable confined their harassment to lewd grins and limp-wrist gestures. Not one of them wanted to tangle with Loren.

Phil and Loren received official notices of acceptance from Harvard and were advised their freshman residence would be Massachusetts Hall. Phil completed and sent off the next day the forms they were asked to fill out, regarding them as steps toward freedom. Loren was evasive when Phil asked if he had done the same. Pinned down, he shook his head. "I won't be going to Harvard. I have to take care of my son."

"I thought your parents were going to do that."

"He's my responsibility. I can't go off and leave him."

"You keep saying 'he.'"

"He?"

"You said, 'he is my responsibility,' and before that, 'I have to take care of my son.'"

"I can't say "baby" all the time, and I don't like calling him 'it.'" Loren cracked a smile. "Maybe if I say 'he' and 'my son' enough times, it will be a he."

Resisting pleas from his family, from Farney and Phil, from his academy teachers and the administration, Loren dropped out of school. "I'm going to start a small business to pay for the birth of my son and to support him," he replied to all who asked him, "Why?" Loren was a man on a mission, the star athlete and straight-A student rising before daylight to do barn chores, then driving an old Chevy he'd acquired to a building on the village square that had once been a grocery store, which, with money withdrawn from his now defunct savings account, he remodeled into Loren's Diner. Observant valley residents knew why he was doing it and decided to help. Shopkeepers, bank tellers, mechanics and truck drivers, who had heretofore eaten breakfast in their own kitchens, began coming to Loren's Diner for toast and eggs that were passable and coffee that was poisonous. Regulars referred to it as donkey piss, until Loren learned how to brew freshly ground beans, as he would learn how to make toast without burning it, how to flip and scramble eggs and fry crisp bacon. As his cooking skills developed and the business grew he expanded his hours to include lunch, and again residents supported his endeavor. They stopped carrying brown paper bags and lunch pails to work, running instead over to Loren's for a quick meal, meals that were substantially improved when Loren's mother took charge of the kitchen. For someone who knew nothing about cooking, Loren was from day one incredibly successful. Personal popularity based on athletic feats was expanded by his decision to care for and support his child. As a rule those who lived in the valley huffed about illegitimates, or babies that came cross lots (born before the parents had been married nine months), but they admired this teenager who turned down the bright beginning of a career to accept adult responsibility. Unfortunately, their admiration did not extend to Liz. What Loren did in the carriage shed was accepted as a blip in a young man's sexual development. Poor Liz was labeled loose and careless.

While Loren was developing his business, Phil made sure his friend would graduate from the academy whether or not he attended classes. Each afternoon, sitting on opposite sides of a table in a booth at the diner, Phil taught Loren what he had learned that day, gave him his notes to study, made him do homework assignments and write required reports, which Phil then turned in to their teachers. He primed Loren for tests and at the end of the semester crammed him for final exams Loren had to go to the academy to take. As might have been expected, Loren's grades and test scores could not have been higher had he attended school every day. By an overwhelming vote of the faculty he was granted his diploma. The single abstention was the baseball coach, who could not forgive him for abandoning the team in his senior year. Afraid it would appear as if they had totally buckled under, the faculty barred Loren from the commencement ceremony. If Loren couldn't attend, Phil would also skip it.

Celebrating by themselves on the secluded terrace alongside FP's apartment above the Galleried Library, they got staggering drunk on a humid June night slugging single-malt scotch whisky Phil remembered his grandfather kept in a cabinet in his study. In an alcoholic haze that made him mellow and more than a trifle sentimental, Loren admitted to Phil that not going to Harvard was a heartbreaking disappointment. "I wish, I really wish, sincerely wish, honestly, I wish I was, were, going with you. Not just for myself, but so you could dance with Shirley Biddle-di-comb while I was in class and then, at night, I'd teach you stuff the way you taught me so I could graduate. If you hadn't pushed your notes . . . "

"Passed on."

"Passed?"

"You said, 'pushed your notes.' I passed them on."

"Passed what?"

At that opportune moment Phil, without meaning to, let go a long loud fart. "Gas," he said. If they hadn't already been lying on the terrace's tile floor they would have fallen down laughing.

Returning to seriousness, Loren continued. "The two of us working together and playing together the way we always have, there in Cambridge, me at Harvard and you at Fiddlestick what's her name's, with my help you could fulfill your family tradition of a Harvard degree for every Fillmore whether he deserves it or not and your ambition to tippy toe, at the same time."

They drank to that.

"Let's work out something." Phil took a deep breath, attempting to speak without slurring his words. "I've got money, what I mean is, I can get money from George Hunnewell to support 'he.' There's plenty Loren, you don't need to work. This is just some holier-than-thou burr you've stuck under your saddle. I don't even know what a burr is. If anybody in this whole wide wicked world deserves a burr-free Harvard degree, it's Loren Gage."

They drank to that.

"A son needs more than money," Loren protested. "He needs a father."

"And I need you Loren. I won't make it without you."

Then, they both threw up.

Chapter 28

———

THE MORNING AFTER, PHIL AWOKE RACKED, STRUCK BY a plague so insidious death, swift he hoped, would be welcome release. All night, or what was left of it when he fell onto his bed, his good old bed had lost its bearing, rocking from head to foot and side to side simultaneously, rising and falling in defiance of gravity. He held on with both hands so he wouldn't be thrown off, waiting to die, wanting to die, knowing death would be pits of eternal flames. Rays of the rising sun seared his welded-shut eyelids. Thank God for the welding. If he could open his eyes he would have to face the hairy dragon sitting on his chest belching putrid fumes in his face.

"Miss Eleanor," he moaned. "Miss Eleanor," he yelled. The reverberating decibels widened cracks in his skull. Why had he given her that cottage she wanted at the foot of the hill? If he hadn't she'd be near, hear his cries for help and come running. "Miss Eleanor," he screamed.

"If your mother hears you and comes up here and sees you as you are . . . "

"My mother has never been in this room. Who the hell are you?"

"Your father. And you are what stable boys call shit-faced."

"Hi Dad. You said it, I feel like shit."

"Get up Phil. Get out of those stinking clothes and go stand in the shower until you sober up. Now!"

His father's sharp "now" cleft Phil, but he did what he'd been told. "Sweet Jesus, I should be given a medal for bravery." He shed his vomit-stenched clothes in a heap on the floor and tottered off to the shower where he stood for a hundred years. The shower helped, but not much. He emerged dripping in front of the full-length mirror, staring at a desecrated image. Pain-seared eyes were unable to see bruises, burns, gashes that must cover his head and body. When he was sure his sight had returned, he could not believe what he saw. Except for bloodshot eyes deep in dark blue pits there was no hint of the valley of the shadow he had trudged through. The telephone rang, making his nerve endings jump in a melee of short circuits. His impulse was to pull the damned thing out of the wall, but habit kicked in. He lifted the receiver.

"Phil?"

"Loren, please don't shout."

"Phil, I have a son, born at eight-forty-three this morning. He weighs eight pounds, seven ounces and he's nineteen inches long. His name is, wait until you hear this, his name is Daniel Valentine Gage. Our 'he' routine worked Phil!" Loren let out a victory yell that scrambled Phil's brain. When Phil tentatively brought the telephone back toward his ear, Loren was saying, "Get your butt down to the door, I'm on my way to pick you up, and I don't dare park the Chevy, your mother would kill me. We're headed for the hospital so you can see him. You won't believe me. You have to see him with your own eyes. He's the most beautiful baby ever born."

Phil was sitting on a granite step under the east portico, holding his head in his hands, when Loren's Chevy scrunched gravel around the corner of the house. "I'm numb, but I jangle all over. How can that be?" Phil asked as he got in. Why wasn't Loren suffering? Could becoming a father cure a hangover?

Phil peered through the window at a chubby-cheeked cherub with long dark eyelashes and whispered, "You're right Loren, he's beautiful." After an eternity of gazing, and making comments about Daniel Valentine being better looking than the rest of the crop sleeping in identical cloth containers, they went to see Liz, but the NO VISITORS sign on her door meant what it said. A nurse, who looked as if she might also be suffering from hangover, snapped at them when they asked if they could go in. "Can't you guys read?"

"Is she okay?"

"She's fine. She'll probably go home tomorrow."

At the Fillmore Florist Loren ordered a dozen red roses sent to Liz in the hospital, with a card on which he wrote, "Thank you for Daniel, Loren." Phil sent a separate bouquet. On his card he wrote, "Good job Liz, Phil," as if she'd won a race or passed a test. He thought she had.

Liz didn't go home. She and Mrs. Macomber went from the hospital to some faraway place. Margaret Macomber came back at the end of August, but Liz didn't return for decades. In his agreement, Farney promised Liz he'd pay for four years at a women's college meaning four college years, but Liz made it mean what it said. By not taking any breaks, she received her bachelor's degree in three years, then used the fourth year to start on a master's. George Hunnewell, amused that a farmer's daughter had outwitted the terms of a contract written by Hunnewell, Hunnewell and Hunnewell, coughed up funds for Liz to continue and complete her master's. But that was later.

Weeks dragged between the end of June when the boys had gotten drunk and the beginning of September when Phil would leave for Harvard. Loren's life now centered on Danny and the diner. He didn't have time for anybody or anything else. He and Phil talked on the telephone every night but didn't see as much of each other as they used to. For something to do, Phil helped Miss Eleanor plant gardens on all four sides of her cottage. Farney offered her a crew of Oshatakea gardeners, but she said she wanted to work the gardens herself. She accepted Phil as part of herself. Farney was so busy with his horses Phil saw him only at breakfast and dinner, and Catherine was even more preoccupied than usual, shutting herself in her suite much of the time. Her husband and son thought she was planning fall events.

Planting perennials, after Miss Eleanor had shown Phil how, required little conscious thought, which gave Phil time to think as he dug holes where she told him to, mixed well-rotted manure and compost into the soil with his bare hands, then plopped a plant in, watered it and moved on to repeat the process. He pondered his future alone at Harvard, and worried he'd make a flop of it if he was alone, the way he screwed up ninth grade when Loren wasn't there to keep him on track. Not that he cared a damn about Harvard except for not letting his Dad down. Harvard's purpose was to provide cover for what he really wanted to do, but if he didn't have enough self-discipline to make the cover work, he'd screw up everything else. On the other hand, if he spent all his time studying, there'd be no time to dance. Learning what he needed to know was not only possible but fun if Loren did it with him. Alone it was dismal and tedious. Maybe he should forget Harvard, go directly to New York to knock on Martha Graham's door and say, "Here I am, make me a dancer." Why did life have to be so difficult?

Dinners in the Gibbons Room were grim when it was just Catherine, Farney and Phil. Farney might say something about his horses. Catherine would not reply, as if she hadn't heard. Lost in woolgathering Phil seldom spoke. If he did, his father would respond but not his mother. Most nights, from soup to savory, except for Farney and Phil thanking Dale each time he served them, only the clock ticking broke the silence. Thus it came as a shock when, several times during that deadly summer, Catherine started chattering aimlessly. She wasn't a woman who chattered, had always been tight with words. Phil thought she listened to what everybody else said and didn't reply so she could remember remarks she'd use later to prove how stupid people were. Her mood on the chattering nights was incredibly light, almost gay, though it didn't allow for much real interchange. If Phil tried to say anything, she'd smile in his direction but not pause to give him time to speak.

Farney wondered if something had unhinged her. He'd never seen her behave this way. To escape what he couldn't comprehend, he'd excuse himself from the table and go to the stables. Phil thought she might be drunk, but she never finished the vodka and tonic that was her warm-weather predinner cocktail and most of the time didn't take a single sip from her glass of wine. Strangest of all, she seemed incredibly happy on those nights when she talked and talked and talked, even laughed at a joke only she knew. That's it, Phil decided, she's plotting something. She has put something over on us and can barely contain herself.

On a Wednesday night when Adelaide, Louisa and Isabelle had come for dinner, Phil saw Adelaide and Isabelle exchanging furtive looks as his mother leaned forward in her chair to emphasize a point and laugh as if what she had said was terribly funny. In an attempt to rescue her from the embarrassment of their silence, Phil made the mistake of laughing with Catherine. The mother he had always known returned with a vengeance. "You have no idea what you are laughing at Phillips." She spat out the words to reprimand him and make him appear stupid. To avoid similar attacks, regardless of how strained the situation became because no one knew whether it was better to join Catherine in her great good humor or merely acknowledge it with half smiles, everybody focused on eating and tried to avoid eye contact with her.

Bridge was a given following Wednesday dinners. Catherine, Adelaide, Louisa and Isabelle went from the Gibbons Room to a card table set up in one of FP's period rooms where coffee and liqueurs were served. Sometimes Farney and Phil played cribbage or backgammon; more often Farney retreated to the stables. When he did that, Phil read for a while, then said good night and went up to his room. He was still reading when his mother announced, "Bridge is a game for idiots."

"It is not," Louisa countered. "I love bridge."

"You would."

Phil glanced over at the foursome.

Not sensing trouble, Louisa didn't let her defense of bridge drop. "You think that Catherine because you can't be bothered to keep track of what has been played and what is held. You could be an excellent bridge player if you'd put your mind to it."

"I have put my mind to it Louisa. I shall never play bridge again." Catherine stood, smiled down on her seated guests, and grasping the edge of the bridge table with both hands flipped it over, scattering cards, coffee, liqueur, score pads, all that had rested on its surface.

Her partner Isabelle bore the brunt of the eruption. As volatile as her hostess and equipped with a colorful vocabulary she cried, "Jesus H. Christ Catherine, what do you think you are doing? Look at my dress. I'll never get these coffee stains out. Have you gone nuts?"

Phil watched from his chair next to the fireplace where a cool draught flowed across his feet and up the open flue as Catherine said, "Good night ladies. Dale will see you out," and strode from the room. He was positive he heard her humming.

The bridge game upset was nothing compared to the chaos created on a hot August evening when Catherine tossed a grenade onto the dinner table in the Gibbons Room. Only she, Farney and Phil were dining that night. "I have acquired a lovely house on Chestnut Street. Joe Wengren found it for me."

"In Boston?" Farney asked.

"Is there a Chestnut Street in Fillmore?"

"There is," Farney began. "It runs parallel to . . . "

"Don't be simple. I am speaking about Chestnut Street on Beacon Hill."

Farney sat back. "You sold your house on Mount Vernon, why would you buy another on Chestnut?"

She smirked. "The answer to that is obvious. Phillips has to live somewhere while he attends Harvard. The house on Chestnut Street will nicely accommodate us and the few servants we'll need."

"Catherine, Phil will live on campus, in Cambridge."

"Phillips will live where I say he will live."

"I'm going to live in Massachusetts Hall," Phil broke in.

"You will not live in a dormitory."

Farney spoke up again. "Catherine, I don't know what you think you are doing, but what you suggest is impossible. Phil will live in the yard at Harvard where he is supposed to live. If you want to have a house on Chestnut Street that is your privilege, but—"

Catherine's voice was harsh, her face a mask of case-hardened steel. "Until Phillips is of age, he will do what I tell him to do. I am his legal guardian." Farney tried to say he was also, but she ignored him. Her attention shifted to Phil. "You will like the house I think. Joe Wengren sent a portfolio of photographs. There is a handsome drawing room and a large dining room on the first floor, a library and guest suite on the second and two master suites on the third floor. The fourth floor will be yours to arrange as you wish. There are maids' rooms on the fifth, plus a cook's room next to the basement kitchen. I will be taking Bones with me," she smiled at Farney. "Obviously not as grand as Oshatakea, but we all know no house is. I can't wait to be gone from it."

Phil was eager to list the reasons he could not live with her in Boston, trying before he spoke to sort out those he could reveal and those he could not, when Farney said, "I didn't realize you are still unhappy here. Before Dad completed the Portuguese Wing, I knew you were, but after that you made quite a place for yourself at Oshatakea, and you came back when you could have stayed in Boston after he died. I thought—"

"You thought. You haven't had a genuine thought in your entire life."

Farney threw his napkin down and pushed back from the table. "Dad, please for once don't go off to the stables. We have to talk about this. I can't live with Mother in Boston."

"And I won't live in Cambridge," Catherine said as if the question was simply where they would live, Boston or Cambridge, not whether he would live in Massachusetts Hall where he belonged or in a house on Chestnut Street. She nodded to Dale, who pulled her chair back. Dropping her napkin onto her unfinished dessert, she smiled at a stunned and miserable Phil and an angry Farney. "End of discussion."

Chapter 29

—

"DON'T WORRY, YOU WILL LIVE IN MASSACHUSETTS Hall." Farney tried to calm Phil. "Your mother isn't your sole guardian. I have arranged with the master for you to be assigned the same rooms I had my freshman year. I hope that's okay. I don't want to interfere, but there are times when I think I've not done enough with you. For some reason, it's important to me that we share the experience of those corner rooms, not that your life in the yard will be anything like mine. I was there a long time ago."

Phil was sensitive to his father's attempts to bring them closer. "I don't mind. Except for trying to wed me to a horse, you've never interfered Dad, and on that score I let you down. I never tried hard enough. I don't care where I live, but thanks for wanting me to be in your old rooms so we could share that experience. I won't live with Mother, and if she persists I'll refuse to go to Harvard." Phil was thinking he'd go to New York instead.

"You will go to Harvard." Farney said, "And you will not be accompanied by your mother."

Farney knocked before entering Catherine's suite as a rule, but he didn't knock that night. Giselle was brushing Catherine's hair. She was seated in front of the dressing room mirror with her eyes closed. They snapped open. "You forgot to knock," she said to his reflection.

"I didn't forget. Excuse us Giselle. Mrs. Fillmore will ring when she needs you."

"You dismiss my maid? Am I about to be raped?"

"Catherine, mothers do not go to college with their sons."

"I am not going to college with him. I am providing a house for Phillips while he attends Harvard. It isn't unheard of. Sara Roosevelt did the same for Franklin. Phillips will live with me on Chestnut Street and be driven to his classes in Cambridge. It's that simple."

"Did your brother live at home on Mount Vernon Street when he went to Harvard?"

"My ass of a brother did not live at home from when he was sent to boarding school in the fifth grade. What he did or did not do has no bearing on what Phillips will do." She stood and changed the subject. "I bought this house furnished as Adah Whittemore left it when she died. There were a few good things, but most were awful and had to be replaced. Tons of rubbish was cleared out. All new plumbing has been installed and wiring, and every room has been painted and papered, so it is clean and ready for us."

Farney followed her into the sitting room. "You must have owned the property for some time to have accomplished so much."

"About a year." She opened the portfolio of photographs. "There is a lovely front door with double columns on each side and a fine rail. The brass is original. Tall windows to the left are in the drawing room, the bow above is in the library."

"If you have owned this house for almost a year, why didn't you mention what you had in mind earlier? Why wait until days before Phil is to leave? We could have discussed this calmly."

"We would not have discussed, we would have bickered. I made up my mind and I do not need permission. Phillips and I, Giselle and Bones, a maid and footman yet to be selected will travel to Boston on the Jefferson, September fifth. If George Hunnewell says anything about those staff salaries, tell him to stuff his money,

Phillips's really, I'm prepared to pay my own way." She returned to the album. "This is the backyard. It isn't large but the plantings are mature."

What Catherine referred to as bickering escalated into a shouting match. She threatened Farney with legal action if he tried to stop her, insisting she had the authority to say where Phillips would live, at least until his eighteenth birthday, and, she said, she would stretch that authority until he was twenty-one. If anyone objected, she was prepared to go to court. Farney said he would file a countersuit depriving her not only of the power to decide where Phil would live but also her right to see him.

While this fractious dialogue was taking place, Phil was trying to reach Loren on the telephone. Hattie Gage's exasperated whisper when she answered made it plain the timing of the call was inconvenient. "Phil, why do you call now? Danny was falling asleep and now because of the phone ringing he's wide awake again."

"I need to speak to Loren, it's an emergency."

"Loren went to bed at seven o'clock. He milks cows at three-thirty in the morning so he can open the diner at six. You'll have to talk to him tomorrow." She hung up.

"Shit, fuck!" Phil slammed down the receiver of his telephone. He had to talk to Loren tonight. There was nothing to do but go to the Gage farm and wake Loren the hell up. Why should Loren be sleeping peacefully when he was having a crisis to beat all crises? The Gage farm was a long way to walk; he could do it, but it would take too much time. He could saddle a horse, but his dad was probably out there shooting the breeze; he didn't need further conversation with his father that night, regardless of how much Farney wanted to help. The only way to get to Loren fast was to drive.

Phil had never driven, had no interest in cars or a driver's license, which every other boy in the valley obtained the day he reached legal age and considered his most important possession. He went to the garage and entered through a side door, flipping on the lights so he could see the oak panel on which sets of keys hung from hooks above labels identifying the car that went with each set. Packard convertible, that had been Gramps's favorite car. Oldsmobile station wagon, was his dad's runabout. Phil stopped reading and snatched a set of keys, took them to the car identified on the label and could not make the damned engine turn over. He got out, slammed the car door and went for another set. This car started, coughed and then lurched forward into a post where it stalled. Phil had not disengaged the clutch. His third attempt was the Buick coupe he'd been driven to school in the past three years. Though he had not paid attention, he thought he must have absorbed enough necessary details sitting next to the chauffeur Dick Fallon to start the Buick on his first try. He depressed both the clutch and the brake, turned the ignition key and the Buick neither lurched nor stalled, just sat there purring. It was maddening trying to figure out how to turn on the lights, but he was ready to wheel at last. Then he noticed he hadn't opened the garage doors. He turned off the ignition but not the headlights, got out, and when he pushed the doors open, standing in the headlights' beam, wearing striped pajamas, was Dick Fallon holding a shotgun pointed toward Phil's chest. Dick cradled the gun. "Jeez Phil, it's only you. I heard noises down here and thought cars were being stolen. If you want to go somewhere just say so, I'll drive you."

After Phil assured Dick that nobody would see him and if they did what difference would it make, Fallon crawled behind the wheel and they took off. When they were approaching the Gage farm, Phil told Dick to turn off the headlights so they could turn into the yard and, it was hoped, not wake up Loren's parents. Phil jumped out and felt around under a tree until he found a couple of sticks to toss up at Loren's window. The noise from the sticks striking against the house started a dog barking. The barking woke the baby. Danny's cries woke Mr. and Mrs. Gage. Lights went on in two bedrooms, but there wasn't a glimmer in Loren's. Phil grabbed a handful of gravel from the driveway and could hear it splattering against the glass of Loren's window. If he could hear it from where he was standing, why couldn't Loren hear it for Pete's sake? The gravel sent the barking dog into a frenzy. Heeding Dick's warning that they might be getting themselves into serious trouble, Phil got back in the car and was driven home in a ferocious funk.

The next morning he ran down the hill and was at Loren's Diner by 6:30, where he had to wait impatiently for a lull in the breakfast rush before Loren could be persuaded to go into a back room with him. They had to be alone when he detailed the latest outrage perpetrated by his mother. This could be terminally disastrous for his dance ambitions, he warned Loren. "To say nothing of making me the laughing stock of Harvard." He slumped down on a crate of vegetables. "I'll kill her. I swear to God I'll kill her."

"My mother was ready to kill you last night, waking Danny up twice. That was you throwing stones at the house, I assume."

"They weren't stones, they were pebbles and before that sticks. If you heard, why the hell didn't you come out?"

"How did you get there?"

"Dick Fallon drove me."

Loren shook his head in disgust. "Phil, when are you going to learn to drive? It's ridiculous for you to be dependent on somebody else to cart you around."

"Don't change the subject. This is serious. I need your help figuring out how to stop my monster mother. She says I have to do what she tells me to do until I'm eighteen and I won't be eighteen until November twenty-fifth. Do I?"

"Do you what?"

"Have to do what she tells me until I'm eighteen?"

"How do I know?" Loren was no more useful to Phil than Phil had been to him when the problem was pregnancy, but he did reciprocate with an equal amount of sympathy, worry and pacing.

Farney telephoned George Hunnewell and told him at length

about the deteriorating situation at Oshatakea, enlisting the attorney's help in convincing Catherine she should cease and desist. Phil had also called George, but their conversation was short and verged on hysterical from the Fillmore end. "There must be something legal you can do. I refuse to accept that she has the power to make me live with her until I am eighteen. Throw the book at her George, throw anything at her that will get her off my back. How could she buy this house in Boston without your approval? I thought you had to approve everything. Why did you approve it George? Whose side are you on?"

"I had nothing to do with that. She bought the house with her own money. Joe Wengren is my counterpart for the Dudley trusts, but even he has little say because your mother is way beyond an age requiring trustee consent. If she wants to spend every penny he can't stop her, nor can he keep her from disposing of property that is now completely hers, much as he tried when she sold the Mount Vernon Street house and everything in it. She has asked Joe to buy back some of the furniture from that house, by the way."

"None of that has any bearing on what I'm talking about. What I want George is to go to Harvard without my mother."

"I hear you Phil, but there isn't much I can do about it, except write her a strong letter, which I will."

"She won't read it. She says FDR's mother did the same thing when he went to Harvard."

"I guess she did, but she didn't expect him to live with her. She just wanted to be close so she could keep track of his whereabouts."

"That's the trouble."

"Aha," George laughed. "You have plans you don't want to share with your mother?"

Phil stopped short. "Not really, but who knows what I might want to do when I'm on my own for the first time?"

"That's only natural." George laughed again, a conspiratorial kind of laugh, thinking he knew what Phil might want to do.

Actually, he could never imagine Phil's real desire, and if he should stumble upon it, he'd dismiss the notion as being beyond possibility. George promised Phil he would do what he could, and contacted the Harvard freshman dean to seek his support. The dean sent a letter to Catherine giving her the many reasons why it was important for freshmen students to live together, to form a community and help one another adjust to what the college expected of them. For many years Catherine had thrown unopened letters from Harvard in the wastebasket, thinking each one was a solicitation for money. The dean's letter suffered the same fate.

Miss Eleanor pressed Phil to be patient. "Do not fight with her. That has never worked. Every time you fight with her she wins."

"Not every time," he interjected. "There were times you and I outsmarted her when she only thought she had won."

"How clever of you to have observed that. There are people for whom the appearance of winning is more important than actual victory. Your mother is one of those people. Regardless of the outcome of this current contretemps, all will right itself when you turn eighteen on November twenty-fifth. That isn't a long time to wait. My advice is, relax." A small frown clouded her face. "I don't think this is anything I could stop, but I should not have moved into my cottage until after your departure. I feel I deserted you."

"You did."

She cuffed him.

When it became obvious Catherine would listen to no one nor give an inch, Farney made the decision also to go to Boston, where he would serve as a buffer between mother and son. He'd stay until Phil could move out of the Chestnut Street house in November. Catherine's reaction to this was, as expected, nasty and negative, but Farney would not be deterred. The housemaster, contacted yet again, assured Farney he would hold Phil's rooms for him. Farney selected two horses to transport to Catherine's farm in Dover.

Getting from Chestnut Street out to Dover every morning would be a damn nuisance, but he wouldn't let Phil face this totally ridiculous situation alone. He'd miss riding with Pearl and bantering with his men in the stable; hell, he'd miss the entirety of his life in the valley, but it was a small sacrifice and he was willing to make it. Though why it was necessary baffled him. He had never understood Catherine's passion for controlling Phil when she returned from those months away following FP's death. As far as he could tell, she still had no real interest in their son, had never displayed the slightest affection, not that she was affectionate with anyone. She didn't care how Phil was doing as he grew up, never gave a thought to what he might want, never did anything to make him happy. Why then was she hanging on to him like grim death now?

"I would think you'd stay here with your housekeeper," Catherine said. "With me out of the picture, and Phillips away, you and the uncultured Pearl could have Oshatakea to yourselves. You'd be able to ride all day and play all night."

"Be careful Catherine, your obsession with Pearl will push you over the edge."

Chapter 30

THE NIGHT BEFORE THEY WERE TO LEAVE FOR BOSTON,
Adelaide, Louisa, Isabelle, Miss Eleanor and Loren came for dinner.
What should have been a festive going-away party wasn't. Only
Catherine was lively, and "festive" is not the descriptive word for her.
Triumphant is more like it. She was a victor gloating over those she
had defeated. Phil wanted to throw a knife at her; at the same time
he was embarrassed by her excessive behavior. As much as he hated
her at the moment, he hated more what others at the table must be
thinking. She was being meaner than dirt for the sake of being mean.

Farney was also putting on a performance. He was quiet, willing
to do anything to please, yet actually as unhappy as Phil. The few
times Catherine gave him a chance to speak he directed his attention to Loren, who was encountering Catherine for the first time
when her sails were billowing in gales of revenge, and the sight was
obviously taking its toll. Loren looked lost between Adelaide and
Louisa who were not unaware of Catherine's carrying on, but inured
to it. Across the table Isabelle was sniffing the air like a pit bull ready
to take on all comers should a brawl break out. If it didn't, Loren
thought she might start one. Her fender was askew, but she made no
effort to straighten it. From where he was sitting, Loren couldn't see
Adelaide's glances rife with warning at the diva. He peered sideways
at Louisa. Louisa could outtalk Catherine if she wanted too; maybe

she'd had prior instructions to keep quiet. Loren wished Miss Eleanor were his dinner partner even though her eyes were rapidly blinking in what he thought was anger. Miss Eleanor had shielded him from Catherine as firmly as she had Phil when they were kids.

Phil watched Loren picking at his food. Usually he devoured whatever was put in front of him and never said no to second helpings. In other circumstances Phil would have teased him, but there'd be no teasing this night. Against all odds he still hoped for a last minute reprieve. He had sent a telegram to Martha Graham pouring out his frustration and pleading with her to take him as a pupil in November. If she said yes, he would stay at Oshatakea until the morning of November twenty-fifth, locked in his room if necessary, then hop a train to New York, forgetting the Harvard ruse with apologies to his dad. If his mother moved alone to Chestnut Street that would be a bonus, but whether she did or didn't was of no consequence. He tipped his jacket sleeve back to check his watch. In less than fifteen hours, the Jefferson, a staff/baggage car and a stable car would be attached to the eastbound express and his mother, dad and he would be en route to Boston. When Graham hadn't replied to his telegram by noon, he called her office and was told she was on tour. They would read his telegram to her over the telephone when she called in, they said. He asked for a number where he could reach her, talk to her himself, to plead his case, but they wouldn't give him one. Please Goddess, come through for me.

Catherine hadn't stopped talking since they'd sat down at the table, going on and on about her new life on Chestnut Street. As the evening wore on she spoke slower and more distinctly. The savory was being served when she said, "Adelaide and Louisa you must pay us a visit—and you too of course Isabelle. Don't all come at the same time please, or do if you wouldn't mind staying at the Ritz. It's close by." Four days prior to this dinner, marking the end of summer on September first, she had switched from sipping a light vodka and tonic to gin martinis, straight up. Farney told Phil his mother had a low tolerance for alcohol. She doesn't need much to be affected, he had said. Martinis can be lethal. The first taste hit Catherine in the pit of her stomach as if she'd been rammed with a poker, and inflamed her cruel streak, melting the steel resolve that made her self-discipline so remarkable.

"The Chestnut Street house has two guest rooms, plus my husband's, which might as well be a guest room. He'll be in Dover with horses most of the time—when he isn't rushing back here to mount his favorite mare." Her attempt at an arch expression failed. Farney said nothing. Catherine addressed Adelaide and Louisa. "We must plan your visit around museum openings and concerts." Turning toward Isabelle, she said, "If you come, you will be as glad as I to be in real theaters instead of our make-do facilities here at Oshatakea." Her crooked smile was condescending.

Isabelle responded. "The Baroque Theatre is a gem loved by all who perform in it, and FP built an amphitheater that professionals raved about."

"Exactly," Farney said.

Catherine wasn't listening, she was talking. "Adelaide, I retain my mother's subscription for Friday afternoon symphony. We have two excellent seats. You may join me when you are in Boston. We'll find something else for Louisa to do." For a moment she looked as if she might close her eyes and not reopen them. Then she did. "Louisa you can go to Tuesday recitals at Fenway Court." She put a finger to her lips and her face lit up; she'd been struck by a sudden inspiration. "As Isabella Stewart Gardner's god-daughter, I have connections. Can you still sing Isabelle? If you can, wouldn't it be amusing if I could arrange for you to do a concert at Fenway Court?"

All eyes were on Isabelle. Phil wondered why she didn't smack his mother. Loren, realizing he was beneath Catherine's ken, was beginning to be fascinated by the Fillmore family at dinner. Nothing this extraordinary ever went on at the kitchen table in the Gage farmhouse.

Isabelle wasn't fast enough to get a blow in before Catherine continued. "If you are as bored with this backwater as I am, you'll come to Boston soon and often. No one told me when I married into this ridiculous clan I'd be deprived of the things that mean most to me. If they had I would have shot myself." Wine sloshed out of her glass when she raised it toward Farney. "Or shot my husband."

"I doubt that. Nobody deprived you of music Catherine. There has been more music at Oshatakea the past few years than most places ever hear. As for being stuck in a backwater, you hate travel. That's what you say. You've never spoken a good word about your luxurious yearlong, grand-tour honeymoon sans spouse." Isabelle yanked up her fender.

"Farney and I couldn't stand the sight of each other. He bored me for three months, then ran home to Oshatakea. We all know why, don't we? Once he was gone, I had a marvelous time. Gaines and I should have kept going around and around and around. Could we have broken an around-the-world record?"

"Catherine, you are sauced," Isabelle said.

Louisa broke in. "We had fun in Paris Catherine."

Catherine returned to the fray. "I have never understood the fawning attention paid to Isabelle Chapman by this family. It must be because of your isolation here in the wilderness. Adelaide enjoyed Paris more than we did Louisa. We went to buy clothes. Adelaide had something else in mind. Do tell us what happened the night you spent with that Hungarian. We want a full confession Adelaide."

Adelaide resisted the temptation to respond in anger or provide the information Catherine sought.

The old custom of women withdrawing after dinner, leaving men to their cigars and brandy, had never been observed at Oshatakea, so the company was surprised when Catherine stopped sniping and said, "Ladies we will go to the Chinese Room for coffee and liquors. Farney is dying to hug his horses and the boys want time to themselves, to talk about whatever it is boys talk about. Don't stay out late Phillips, we must be on the Jefferson by quarter to nine tomorrow morning." She was not engaging in an act of kindness, releasing Loren and Phil from purgatory; had she not been more than a little dazed she would have insisted they accompany the ladies to the Chinese Room thus prolonging their discomfort.

Relieved to be free, Loren and Phil walked outside, strolling across the lawn to get away from the house. They didn't say much until they were wandering in the boxwood maze. "Cheer up Phil, you'll have a good time at Harvard."

"I doubt it."

"I don't regret what I've done, but still, I wish I were going with you."

"Please come. It isn't too late. Dad can get you in, I know he can."

"It is too late, but that's okay."

They turned in tandem without conscious thought, hands in pockets, until they came to a spot that had always been tricky, though they had both figured out the maze when they were children. Loren turned right. "No, this way," Phil said, turning left.

"Are you sure? We haven't done this is a long time."

Phil's laugh was abrupt. "I come down here a lot. Doing the maze unties knots in my head. I know its secrets."

"Speaking of secrets," Loren began.

"Secrets? What secrets could we possibly have from each other? We've been together practically every day since before we could walk."

"True, but I have one," Loren said.

"I do too. My secret is I'm at least as scared as I am excited about what happens after tomorrow, excited about the dance thing, which may have to be put on hold, and scared about Harvard. Thank God nobody will know me there. They won't have expectations I can't meet."

In the moonlight Phil could see Loren shake his head. "They'll know you Phil. Fillmores are known beyond this valley, most certainly where you're going."

"I suppose. I wouldn't be afraid if you were with me. I'll write at least once a week, and if I have anything to report on the dance front, I'll call you at the diner. I don't want to write dance stuff in a letter somebody else might read."

"Telephoning might not be smart now that my mother is helping me. The telephone is in the kitchen, she'd overhear what we say."

"I thought about that. We'll use a code, the way we did when we were kids. If I make contact with Shirley Biddlecomb, I'll tell you I'm living on graham crackers—Martha Graham—get it?"

Loren groaned. "Not subtle. I don't think you're ready for Harvard."

Phil's laugh was real. "Right. We should go in. I won't sleep, but I want to get to bed early."

Loren put out his hand and touched Phil's arm. "I need to say something."

He couldn't have explained why, but Phil knew what Loren was going to say before he said it, not the words he'd use but what Loren thought would be news to him, the secret he thought he had kept. Nor could Phil remember when he first knew; it wasn't something that dawned on him one bright day, but knowledge that developed, not consciously on either part but in the way they were with each other. The acrid odor from the towering boxwoods surrounding them filled their nostrils. Phil thought of the dozens of times he and Loren had been lost in this maze, afraid they couldn't get out and nobody would find them.

"Do you remember," Loren began. He shifted his weight, jammed his hands deeper into his pockets and began again. "Do you remember when we used to fool around in your dad's shower?"

"Diddling each other's dicks you mean?"

"Yeah."

"Miss Eleanor caught us once."

"She didn't do much of anything except shake us and bawl us out." Loren paused. "We more than diddled if you recall, in the loft of my father's cow barn."

"I had forgotten that," Phil said. He had not forgotten. "We said we were experimenting, seeking new sensations, something like that."

A cloud scudded across the moon, and was gone. "Phil, it wasn't experimenting for me. I knew what I was doing. I wanted you to need me as much as I needed you. We did it more than a few times, but then you pushed me away. You said you'd had enough of that. I could never have enough of you."

"What more of me is there to have?"

"All of you, I want all of you, I want us to be one."

"We are one Loren. That's why I fell apart when your dad insisted you go down to the academy and my mother wouldn't let me go with you."

"That's not what I'm talking about. You felt alone then, left behind. I'm trying to tell you what I feel is love. Love. I'm in love with you Phil, and I have been forever." They stopped walking. "I need to explain that Dick Mathey and Gary Cushing had it wrong when they called you queer. You aren't, but I am."

"You can't be queer Loren, you knocked up Liz Macomber. You have a son. I've still never done it with a girl. Maybe I could have that night in the carriage shed if the stupid cunt had given me a chance and we hadn't had an audience. Once the goons began making fun of me it was all over."

Loren inhaled deeply. "You know why I have a son? Why I plowed Liz? I was so goddamn horny picturing what you were doing at the far end of the shed I got hotter than I'd ever been in my life. I jammed it into her without thinking I might be hurting her, and I came on the first thrust when I pushed it in. There was only one. When I heard the ruckus down where you were, I pulled out. I never even said slam, bam, thank you ma'am, I was in such a rush to rescue you. No wonder Liz was mad as a wet hen about getting pregnant. I hurt her Phil, and not just physically, because in my head it was you I was with. When I thought you were in trouble it was you I had to get to. I treated Liz like a scumbag. I didn't mean to but I did." He shook his head, as if he couldn't believe what he had done. "That's why she didn't want anything to do with what she called 'it.' And here's the clincher Phil. Are you ready for this? You're going to think I'm sick, but it's the God's honest truth. My obsession with keeping the baby, the 'he' that turned out to be Danny, was because in my screwed-up brain he was conceived by us—by you and me together. He belonged to us."

"I don't know what to say."

"You don't need to say anything. Don't worry, I'm past thinking most of that stuff now. Danny is mine, all mine. He's the gift from Liz she didn't want to give. I love him, not the same kind of love I feel for you, but he's still little enough so he likes to be held. I've never been able to hold you the way I want to. I'll always love you Phil. I had to tell you before you go away, so we're straight with each other." He laughed a nervous little laugh. "You knew I loved you. Miss Eleanor taught us to love and take care of each other. She couldn't have counted on me falling in love. There's a big difference between love and in love." He blew his nose. "From here on, no more secrets. You are going off by yourself to be a dancer. Me? Hell, I'm a terrible dancer, but you can't expect a bulldozer on the football field to be graceful on the dance floor. Write and call when you can." He paused again in a struggle to control himself. "I'm going to miss you like an arm."

Phil felt empty, desperately wishing he could love Loren the way Loren said he loved him. He wanted to but he couldn't. He said, "If I give you a hug, hold you for a minute, promise you won't pat my ass?"

Chapter 31

PHIL DID NOT SLEEP. THERE WAS TOO MUCH TO THINK about. Without a last-minute reprieve, they would shortly head for Boston. He felt feverish with anticipation and foreboding; he'd never been away from home, had slept in the same room every night of his life. Though it would not happen until November after he turned eighteen, living in a dormitory worried him, despite the battle with his mother to do just that. Massachusetts Hall sounded sufficiently magisterial to be secure, but the prospect of living in intimate contact with dozens of guys was frightening. If those in the valley who were somewhat dependent on his family made him an object of their scorn and the butt of all their jokes in school, what might a bunch of stranger housemates do? He was positive they'd think him a nerd, and nervous as he was, he would be, laughing like a jerk when he shouldn't, not laughing when he should because he didn't get what they were talking about. Loren clued Phil in when somebody said something he didn't understand, but Loren wouldn't be there. His father told him most of his classmates probably had been in boarding schools together; they'd arrive at Massachusetts Hall with their own codes, their own language and habits of behavior. He'd be the odd man out. As he brushed his teeth the morning of departure he realized he had never meant anything more sincerely than when he'd said last night he wished Loren were going with him. He was also worried about Loren. Loren was pretty emotional revealing what he thought was a secret. Phil would call him before they left.

"The only part of Oshatakea I shall miss is this lovely courtyard," Catherine said, spreading bitter orange marmalade on unbuttered toast. Phil thought it incredible she could be as smashed as she appeared to be at dinner and this morning at breakfast act as if she'd never had a drink. Farney came in wearing his riding togs. Catherine and Phil were in traveling clothes. "You should be changed and ready to go."

"I haven't ridden yet. I told Pearl I'd grab a bite first." He pulled a watch out of his pocket, looked at it and put it back. "There's plenty of time. I've been down at the siding loading horses. Horatio needed calming. We've given him a tranquilizer. He hates enclosed spaces. I've never been able to trailer him for hunts outside the valley. I should have known he'd raise hell being led onto a railroad car."

"Why take him if he's that difficult?"

"I need to work him. He'll be fine for the Dover Hunt."

"There are hundred of horses in Dover. Borrow one."

"Wouldn't be the same." He took a long drink of orange juice at the sideboard while examining the contents of silver-covered dishes. Drinking orange juice this way was strictly forbidden by Catherine, but Farney always did it.

"If you feel that strongly about your"—she paused to give added emphasis to her next word—"horses, why go to Boston? Phillips and I can manage without you. Unload Horatio and stay here where you belong."

Farney was filling his plate with cheddar grits, eggs and a couple of sausages. He paid no heed to Catherine's gibe. "I'm eager to go—not promising I'll stay long, but it's worth the effort to see my son settled in." He smiled across the table at Phil. "I doubt many in your class will come close to matching the Fillmore record for number of generations matriculated at Harvard. You might pick up spare change placing bets on that legacy."

Catherine said, "Place your money betting on my family Phillips. We were in Harvard's first class. See if anyone there now can match that. On the subject of family Farney, you keep saying 'my son,' referring to Phillips, as if you are absolutely certain he is your son. Has the thought never crossed your mind he might not be?" A bemused expression brightened her face. "You were in Europe more than you were at Oshatakea during the war when Phillips was conceived."

Farney stopped eating, his fork midway between his mouth and his plate. "What do you mean?"

Delighted she had without raising her voice managed to strike a blow with sufficient force to elicit an angry reaction, Catherine asked, "Why so agitated?"

"Are you saying Phil is not my son?"

"I was merely commenting on your smug self-assurance. One should never be blind to alternative possibilities."

Phil could not raise his hand from the table where it had flopped flounder limp when his mother seemed to say his dad was not his father. That's what he heard even as she was insisting she had merely commented on something else. "Dad is my father," he said, but they didn't hear him. If he wasn't, who was? Jesus! Phil opened his mouth to protest, to ask them to stop shouting, when he heard his mother ask, her voice dropping to its lowest, coldest register, "Do you think you are the only one to look elsewhere for, for what it is you look to Pearl for?"

"For God's sake Catherine, there is nothing between Pearl and me, never has been anything beyond friendship and you damn well know it. If you have something else to say, say it!"

Responding not to his request but to his statement she said, "Well if I do know it, then ponder this—I could be one up on you."

For a moment, Phil thought his father was going to lunge at her, but then Farney straightened himself from a half-crouching position, stood so abruptly he sent his chair flying across the tiles, left the table and crashed from the room, shattering panes of glass when he slammed the terrace door. Phil saw him half-running toward the stables.

"It seems I upset your father." Catherine popped the last bit of toast into her mouth, took a swallow of coffee and rose from the table. "Finish your breakfast Phillips. I want us to be settled aboard the Jefferson before the Boston train arrives."

"Mother, is Dad my father?"

"Of course. You look pale. I hope you aren't going to be car sick."

"What was all that about just now, what you were saying to him? I don't know what to believe."

"Phillips, do you think your grandfather would have given you everything if there had been any question about his son being your father?"

"Probably not."

"Definitely not. Unfortunately, you are a Fillmore, but you are also a Dudley. I resent your intimation I could have been unfaithful. What kind of son would think such a thing about his mother? Fallon will be at the east portico in one hour and"—she consulted her watch—"approximately thirteen minutes." John Johnston, the breakfast footman, came from behind the screen when Catherine rang the silver bell, a little woman in a full skirt. "Before you clear, pick up that chair and call maintenance. Tell them glass needs to be replaced in the terrace door."

Phil said good-bye to the few staff people he had not seen earlier, then went upstairs to call Loren and to make sure all the things he wanted had been taken to the Jefferson. Standing by his bedroom window, he saw his father riding Triumph hell-bent for leather across the grotto field toward a hedgerow. Phil could sense his dad's anger even at that distance, and knew his face was red, his mouth set in a tight straight line, as they had been when he stormed out of the courtyard. Triumph was not a horse to take over a hedge; Dad would certainly turn him away at the last minute, Phil thought. Then, Pearl astride Kestrel diverted his attention as she closed the gap between herself and Farney. At that second Phil realized his father was going to jump Triumph after all, but the horse faltered, refused, and tried again. His momentum lost, he could not clear the hedge. The stallion's right hind foot caught as he and Farney disappeared over the other side.

Phil heard Pearl screaming when she and Kestrel flew over in close pursuit, screams immediately joined by ear-piercing animal shrieks. He raced down the stairs, across the lawn and field to a break in the hedge where he came upon a tangle of bloody, broken horses. Triumph and Kestrel were now deathly silent, but there was pleading panic in their eyes and their bodies shuddered ripples of terror and agony. Kestrel was on top of Triumph, her left hind leg kicking out, her other three twisted beneath her. Bubbles of pulsing blood foamed from Triumph's nostrils and across his muzzle to puddle on the ground.

"Help!" Phil shouted. "Somebody please help me."

"Nothin' we can do until Jake gets here with men and guns." Farney's stable manager Gus walked toward Phil with outstretched arms trying to shield him from something Phil shouldn't see. But he did see.

Off to the right his father was lying at the base of a walnut tree. Pearl was beside him down on her knees, begging, "Farney please don't die." Phil knew, before he took a step closer, that his dad was already dead. Farney's head tilted at an impossible angle against his shoulder; his eyes were wide open and unblinking. Phil dropped down to join Pearl rubbing Farney's arms and patting his hands, both aware their attempts to comfort were futile. Phil wanted to call out as Pearl was doing, to say good-bye, to whisper "Dad," but he couldn't. The ritual continued until they were jolted by revolver shots. Pearl moaned and, raising herself so she could bend to look directly into lifeless eyes, said, "Farney, Kestrel is gone. Syrah's beautiful filly that we raised together." Thinking she might throw herself on his father's body, Phil gently pulled her back. She collapsed against him, her tears soaking the front of his shirt. His fell on her hair.

Dr. Montrose said Farney had died instantly and closed his eyes. Phil should have done that. He did help lift the body onto a stretcher, gagging when he saw gobs of cranial matter and pieces of skull embedded in the bark of the walnut tree. With other men he carried his father across the field, past paddocks and into the stable block. Pearl walked beside them, her fingers touching the blanket that covered the corpse. "If I hadn't ridden so close behind him. If I had not jumped."

Gus tried to ease her pain. "Farney was thrown into that tree when Triumph caught his hoof in the hedge. I saw it. That's what killed him Pearl. Had nothing to do with you. Farney was not there when Kestrel landed on his horse. What gets me is why did he jump? Triumph couldn't do it. Farney knew that. What was he thinking? He wasn't thinking about the horse or about jumping, that's for sure. He had something else on his mind. When Farney threw the saddle on Triumph he acted like a man possessed. Never saw him in such a lather. Something powerful was botherin' him."

Walking ahead of Gus, carrying his father's body, Phil knew what had been bothering him.

When Catherine was told Farney had been killed, she went berserk, bellowed and made terrible sounds, but spoke no words. She struck out with her fists and her feet, hitting or kicking anyone who tried to touch her. Phil heard none of this at the time because he refused to leave his dad until the undertaker insisted they could not do what they had to do with him standing there. Slowly climbing the stairs, each step requiring greater strength than he knew he had, he didn't stop when Giselle hissed from Catherine's sitting room door, "Dr. Montrose has given her a sedative." In his bedroom, Phil stood again at the window looking out, not seeing much through the distortion of tears, but he tried. He wanted to see clearly the place in the hedge where his dad had disappeared, where he last saw him alive. He wanted to erase the image of him lying with his head askew at the foot of that walnut tree, parts of his brain clinging to the bark. Would he, when he thought of him, always see his body lying on a table in the tack room? Could he ever forget his father's red-faced anger and clenched teeth when he'd left the courtyard? Why couldn't he go back a few minutes before that to remember how he had looked when he smiled across the breakfast table? That smile is what Phil wanted to remember. From what Gus said about his mood when he got to the stables, the smile he gave Phil was probably his last.

Thank God for Gus. He was the first one there, knew Farney was dead but sent for Dr. Montrose anyway, had somebody call Turner the undertaker, told Dick Fallon to get Miss Eleanor and bring her back to the house. How he knew Miss Eleanor was the one who should tell his mother was beyond Phil's comprehension. Miss Eleanor dropped her pruning shears and came at once. She found Catherine in her bedroom, doing the same kind of last-minute checking Phil had been doing in his room directly above. "You've come to say good-bye," Catherine said. "Or have you decided to apologize for turning your back on me? If you ask nicely and are contrite, I may forgive you. On the other hand, since you've taken so long to come to your senses, I may not."

"Please sit down."

"It's too late for sitting down Gaines. Phillips and I will leave for the station any minute. My husband, who can't tear himself away, may miss the train. I hope he does."

"Your husband is dead. Killed in a riding accident. I don't know details, but I am told he died instantly."

This, Miss Eleanor told Phil later, was when Catherine went

crazy. Before the bellowing there was a dreadful silence and then came—Miss Eleanor didn't know whether it was anger that defied language or pain raging beyond description—larger more powerful sounds than Miss Eleanor had ever heard, strangling sounds that seemed to rise from the depths of her being. When Miss Eleanor described the scene to Phil, his response was a phrase he'd picked up from Catherine. "I couldn't care less."

Others cared. The entire staff and everybody in the valley rallied around. Miss Eleanor called Isabelle and asked her to relay the sad news to Adelaide and Louisa. Putting their own grief aside, the women rushed up to Oshatakea to join Miss Eleanor in doing what they could to help Catherine and Phil. As a memento of her good intention, Adelaide carried for days afterward an ugly purple bruise on her right cheek where Catherine's fist connected. Fighting like a tiger to escape capture, she flailed at Adelaide and bit Miss Eleanor's hand. In the din, they were unaware that Dr. Montrose had arrived in the suite until he stepped forward with a hypodermic. Catherine stopped when she saw him. The doctor jabbed a needle into her arm. She rubbed the spot where the needle had entered, then backhanded Dr. Montrose with such force his glasses flew off and blood spurted from his nose.

"That does it," Miss Eleanor cried. She gave Catherine a mighty shove that sent her sprawling backward, partially onto the chaise longue, the rest of her on the floor. Shock and surprise combined with the onset of the injected sedative robbed her of an immediate reaction. Taking advantage of this opportunity, Dr. Montrose asked Miss Eleanor and Adelaide to help him get her into bed and suggested that for her own protection and the safety of others she be restrained.

George Hunnewell was at Oshatakea before anybody knew he was on the way. Phil was in his bedroom, hypnotically staring out the window when George and Miss Eleanor, the Kropotkins and Isabelle crowded into the old day nursery that had been converted into a living room. They trudged up to the third floor to comfort him when he refused to leave the window. If he and Loren could make an unborn child be a boy just by saying "he" all the time, maybe if he stared out that window, long enough his dad and Triumph would reverse direction and fly back over the hedge, alive and whole again. He didn't think he'd voiced that hope, but he may have, after Dr. Montrose had given him a sedative, not injected as was his mother's but a couple a pills.

He awoke late afternoon, confused. Why wasn't he on the Jefferson? He'd never ridden a train and was looking forward to that part of the trip. Had he missed it? Oh yes, he remembered. Through a haze he recollected George saying the family would gather at four o'clock in the Galleried Library to "formulate plans." It was four-twenty. He washed his face, brushed his teeth, changed his clothes and went to the library. The entire family, except Catherine, was there. Phil was glad George, who was talking when he walked in, had included Miss Eleanor and Isabelle. "Farney's service should replicate the service for FP." Hunnewell paused while everybody greeted Phil, and asked if he was all right. "We are discussing your father's funeral."

"Which isn't up to us to discuss," Isabelle noted. "Farney's wife and son should decide what they want. If our input is needed, they can ask for it."

"We are trying to ease their burden." Adelaide's rebuke was gentle. "Unquestionably Catherine and Phillips should make final decisions, but a number of things have always been done at funerals in our family. Those we can discuss."

They wrangled over who should and should not do what until George stopped them. "The head of the family is with us. If he approves, there is no reason we should not proceed with arrangements. I would like to finalize as much as possible this afternoon."

Phil did not notice immediately, but when George said the head of the family was present, the women turned to look at him. If his mother heard George Hunnewell refer to him as head of the family, she'd have the attorney's head on a platter. He raised his hand as if he were in class. "Nobody is better at planning events than Mother. She'll have a fit when she wakes up if somebody else has planned Dad's . . . " He couldn't say funeral. "Not only is she good at that sort of thing, she owes him the best party she's ever done."

"Exactly!" Isabelle crowed.

"Are we planning a party?" Louisa asked.

That ended the meeting, to George's chagrin, but things would get worse for him.

A week passed and Catherine didn't wake up. Dr. Montrose said she could not possibly still be under the sedation he had given her, but he was unable to elicit any conscious response. Without removing her to the hospital for sophisticated tests, he said his examination indicated she may have had a stroke.

Farney's body was not placed in a coffin atop a bier in the center of the Great Hall as was FP's. He stayed for eight days laid out on a table in the tack room, dressed in hunting pinks, his head resting on a saddle, a blanket of red roses covering him from mid-chest down. Shifts of stablemen stood guard around the clock. Valley people came in droves, long lines stretching along the service road, inching slowly forward, nobody pushing, each person given a moment with the friend who had everyone's affection as well as respect. Gus set up tables in the pine grove next to the stable yard that Bones kept plenished with sandwiches and hot coffee. To the side was a table with kegs of beer and Vernor's Ginger Ale. Too many to count commented on the appropriateness of holding Farney's wake in the stable with his horses looking on. Phil had not meant to change the way things were done when he suggested they wait for his mother to wake up before proceeding with funeral plans, but that's what he did with his request for no action at all and it was received as a head-of-the-family decision. From there on events marking Farney's demise developed spontaneously.

George gave the news to the *New York Times*, where it was picked up by an international news service. The *Times* said a date for the memorial service would be announced. People from outside the valley sent telegrams and letters of condolence, including Mrs. Roosevelt, whose husband had used Farney as a private courier during the war, but there was no deluge as there had been when FP died. Farney was a private person. Nor did Oshatakea fill with guests. Most of the house was under dust sheets. The staff didn't know whether to reopen rooms or continue to close them. Since FP's death household orders originated with Catherine and were passed down through Pearl, but Catherine was unconscious and Pearl was nowhere to be found, had not been seen since she and Phil were shooed out of the tack room by Turner's embalmers. Miss Eleanor sent footmen and maids to look for her in every room of the house. Gus led groundsmen and stable boys searching outside. Phil refused to believe he was the last person she'd spoken to. When they had walked to the house from the stable, entering through the servant's hall, she'd hugged him, told him how much his father loved him, then went to her apartment. Nobody saw Pearl after that.

George came to Oshatakea every day, busying himself with paperwork in Farney's office. He asked an assistant to temporarily assume management of the farms, and conferred with Gus about the stables and Günter about the grounds. Not forgetting where Phil was supposed to be, George said he had talked to the Harvard dean, who understood the situation, but warned, "Phil should not miss too much time because it will put him behind and that is especially difficult in the freshman year." Harvard is what Phil thought George wanted to talk about when he made his second climb up to the third floor, and was prepared to tell him that it didn't matter if he never got there, but that wasn't what concerned George.

"Phil, Mr. Bishop from Turner's advises me we should no longer delay placing your father's remains in the crypt. Unpleasant consequences may result if we do not proceed with the burial."

"You don't think we should wait for Mother?"

"I don't know what is happening with your mother, nor can Dr. Montrose predict when she will be awake and, more important, coherent. He tells me she is weakening. They are feeding her intravenously."

Phil knew she might not wake up anytime soon, but he hadn't thought beyond that. "What do you suggest?"

"A committal service with only the family present. When your mother recovers, she can plan a memorial."

"Whatever you say."

"Mr. Bishop thinks it should be done this afternoon."

"It's that bad?"

"Your father died eight days ago."

"I know when he died George. This afternoon will be fine. I want everybody from the stables there. He'd want them more than anybody else. Ask Miss Eleanor who should be asked from the rest of the staff, probably Dale Morris. Dad liked Dale. Hell, he liked everybody. I wish we could find Pearl."

"The crypt isn't large enough for too many."

"We'll do the talking part in the chapel where there's plenty of room, and then the family will go down to the crypt."

"I'll call Reverend Davis."

"Tell him to keep it short. Dad was not preacher oriented."

That is how it was, short, no eulogies or choirs singing hymns. After Mr. Davis said what he had to say, Gus, a couple of men from the stable, George, Loren and Phil carried Farney's coffin down the stone stairs and lowered it into its spot beneath the floor. It was rough for Phil, leaving his dad there. He stayed behind when the others went back upstairs, watching masons slide the heavy piece of slate in place and seal it. After they were done he stood alone looking down, wondering how this all could have happened, wondering what would happen next, trying to remember his father's smile.

Chapter 32

⸺

CATHERINE REMAINED IN A PECULIAR STATE OF SEMI-consciousness, not responding to anything that was said to her but ripping intravenous needles out if she was not rigidly restrained. The restraints drove her to animal-like behavior. Afraid she might seriously hurt herself, or others, during violent struggles, Dr. Montrose said his only recourse was sedation on a regular schedule that would keep her quiet while allowing periods of cognizance during which she could be fed a thin gruel and given liquids. She also fought this regimen until he said loudly, suspecting she could hear, that the next step would be a tube through her nose into her esophagus. She became somewhat less combative.

Miss Eleanor came each morning at eleven, a supposedly alert time, to talk to her and perform personal tasks she thought might comfort Catherine. Adelaide and Louisa alternated afternoon visits with Isabelle. Isabelle made it clear she thought Catherine was faking her semiconsciousness.

"If she were faking, Dr. Montrose would surely have brought her out of it by now," Adelaide said. The doctor admitted he could not with any assurance say exactly what was physically wrong with Catherine, but surmised she was suffering the aftereffects of acute psychological trauma. His solution was to keep her nourished, try to gentle her and hope that eventually her spirits and outlook "will, of their own volition, bounce back, at which time and with her help we can more effectively treat her." Adelaide knew Dr. Montrose had a growing reputation in the valley of using sedatives to treat questionable ills. A number of his patients were having problems with addiction. Worried this might happen to Catherine, but not wanting to offend him, Adelaide said, politely, "Please doctor, do not fill her with morphine."

Phil was having a harder time coping with the loss of his father than he could have expected. Before the accident, Farney had been there for him, though in a passive manner except for unceasing and unsuccessful efforts to transfer to his son some of his own passion for horses. When Phil thought he was going to Harvard, it never occurred to him that he might miss his dad. He was touched by Farney's attempts to solve the house dilemma and his willingness to move to Boston until Phil was eighteen, but those efforts and that sacrifice didn't foster an increased companionship between the two. Farney was his father. Phil loved him, but didn't know how much and didn't understand the depth of their relationship until he was gone. Now there was a great hole where Farney had been. Phil tried to fill it by spending time in the stable block with the men, but watching them work without Dad in their midst, listening to their rough conversations without hearing his father's voice and being surrounded by Farney's horses who seemed to nicker constantly for him made his loneliness worse. If his father couldn't be found in the stable there was no place for Phil to look.

Miss Eleanor was living in her cottage down at the foot of the hill. Loren was involved with the diner and with Danny. Catherine might as well be dead. Phil was alone as he never had been before. He was lost, miserable and without purpose. He had cherished privacy and yearned for independence, couldn't wait to be free of his mother's restrictions. Dad was gone and Mother could not tell him what to do, but he did not feel free.

His extended family went to considerable effort to support him. Miss Eleanor joined him for breakfast in the Portuguese Courtyard each morning, driven up from her cottage by Dick Fallon. The Kropotkins, Isabelle and Miss Eleanor came every night for dinner in the Gibbons Room, a practice, Adelaide informed Bones, they would continue until further notice. While these dinners were not gay, the conversation was livelier than it had been when just Farney, Phil and Catherine were at table. Phil appreciated what they were trying to do but did not conceal his disinclination to play host. Loren came through too, appearing on occasional late afternoons lugging Danny in a basket. He assumed Phil would derive as much pleasure watching Danny nap as he did. As with what the women were doing, Phil appreciated the gesture but was not diverted. The two friends were on different tracks, and had little to talk about.

As the lives of those who loved Phil were drawn back to their ordinary activities, concentrated attentiveness dwindled. The Kropotkins returned to daily rounds of good deeds they'd been doing for decades. Dispensing largesse along with comfort and expressions of concern was a career inherited from their mother. Now, in their mid-eighties, after a tiring day the sisters looked forward to a quiet dinner at the dacha with Boris and Magda looking after them. Isabelle, dressed to the nines, had people in for cocktails. On those nights when she didn't, she had dinner on a tray in front of the television, wearing a bathrobe and slippers. Miss Eleanor kept a large pot of soup simmering on the back of her stove, the rarely emptied pot kept going with additions of vegetable scraps, leftover meat and rice, fresh infusions of chicken stock, beef bouillon or tomato juice and occasional dollops of cream. She preferred a bowl of this soup, which could never be described, to a four-course dinner in the Gibbons Room. Eating supper in her kitchen with her shoes kicked off, stocking feet tucked on a padded stool, reading a book propped against the sugar bowl was heaven.

She was relieved, and so were the others, when Phil discouraged them from gathering as frequently as they had. Miss Eleanor would continue coming to Oshatakea for breakfast each morning, to keep Phil aware of what was going on outside Oshatakea. What little Phil needed to say to somebody else, he could say to her.

Phil didn't know what he needed. He did not want constant company, nor did he want to be alone. The only thing he was sure of was that he would not go to Harvard when his mother recovered. Harvard had been a means to an end. At the moment he had no idea what that end might be. He placed a call to the dean everybody else had called on his behalf and being totally honest said he could not come to Cambridge before Christmas at the earliest—"And I don't want to enter midyear." The dean said he understood. Responding to what he thought was disappointment in the dean's tone, Phil lied, "I'll be there next fall." Phil wished he had the courage to say he would be the first Fillmore in three hundred years not to attend Harvard. Consoling himself, he borrowed his father's phrase about Loren and Liz: these things happen.

When a check refunding advance tuition, room, board and fees was sent shortly after their conversation to the offices of Hunnewell, Hunnewell and Hunnewell, George exploded over the telephone. "Phil you cannot drop out."

"I'm not dropping out George, I was never in."

"Oh yes you were. Be reasonable—your mother is going to be fine, it just takes time. There are plenty of people to care for her. She has nurses and that doctor will see her every day. She doesn't need you. I'll call the dean, return the check and have you reinstated. If you don't want to travel to Cambridge by yourself, which is understandable, since it's your first trip, I'll go with you. Can you leave tomorrow?"

"George, I'm not going." Phil replaced the receiver in its cradle.

Several nights later, he was sitting alone at the dinner table in the Gibbons Room. "Dale, do you like lamb?"

"Very much."

"Good, get a plate and slice off a piece for yourself. Take some potatoes too."

Dale shook his head. "Thanks, but I can't. I'll have mine for supper tomorrow."

"Why wait? I'm serious, get yourself a plate. There are stacks in the pantry."

"I shouldn't."

"Yes you should. And pile on the potatoes and peas. Bones is an expert with roasted potatoes—if you like garlic and rosemary, and I do. Sit across from me, where Dad sat. He was very fond of you, and he'd be tickled to have you sitting in his chair."

"I couldn't sit at the table with you sir."

"Dale how long have we known each other?"

"Since you were born."

"Why do you call me sir? You never have before."

"I don't know what to call you—in the dining room."

"What does the dining room have to do with anything?"

"I'm on duty. This is where I work."

"For me, Dale, you work for me. If we were in the kitchen or outside, you'd call me Phil, and that's what I want you to call me wherever we are. That's an order." Phil tried to soften what might seem a stern statement with a smile.

"I take orders from Pearl when I'm on duty."

"Pearl isn't here is she? Pearl took orders from my mother, but Mother isn't here either, so I'm giving you a direct order. Dale Morris, fill a plate at that sideboard and sit down, I want somebody to eat with me."

Dale hesitated. "Okay, but you explain to Pearl because when she hears about this she's going to have a conniption."

"I'll explain to her you did it to keep me from starving." Fellow conspirators, during the next hour in the soft glow of candlelight they ate, drank good wine and enjoyed themselves. Dale told Phil about his two daughters, and how well they were doing at the academy. One was taking piano lessons and showed real promise. Putting discretion aside, as Phil had, Dale asked if Phil knew when he'd be able to get off to Harvard. Phil said he wasn't going.

"That's too bad. I'm really sorry, I know you looked forward to getting away."

"I did."

Dale didn't press further, but he was dying to ask if that meant the staff would remain as it was at Oshatakea. George Hunnewell had told them that when the family moved to Boston there would be changes, but nobody knew what that meant. Dale got up to clear after each course and to serve the next. After dessert, Phil made the footman sit while he cleared plates and brought a tray of cheeses and bottle of port from the sideboard. Dale jumped up to get a bowl of fruit Phil had forgotten. When dinner was over, Phil said he wanted Dale to join him for dinner every night. Dale agreed, if Phil really wanted him, if Phil made it an absolute order, and if, "a big if—you don't tell anybody. I don't want to get into trouble."

"It's a deal." Leaving Dale to put the Gibbons Room in order, Phil walked into the Long Gallery. He didn't drink coffee, so none would be waiting in the Galleried Library. It was too early to go up to his room. He could walk outside, but he didn't want to do that. He meandered toward the Belgian Room, opened the door and stepped back as if he'd been dealt a blow. Everything in the room was covered with white sheets. He went to the Gothic Room and found the same thing, and the Chinese, and the Dorset. Running from one period room to another, he found them all filled with ghosts, hulking bulky ghosts. Gramps was right; rooms do die if they aren't lived in. Opening the doors to the Welsh Room, he charged in and grabbed at the sheets. Some offered no resistance, others caught on arms of chairs, twisting them or knocking them over. Others caught on drawer brasses. He was creating havoc.

Back in the Gibbons Room Dale heard the commotion and hurried along the gallery to find Phil shouting, "Get these fucking ghosts out of here. No more ghosts, I never want to see another goddamn ghost in this house as long as I live."

The next morning, Phil was sitting in the Portuguese Courtyard, alone at breakfast because Miss Eleanor had a cold and stayed home so she wouldn't give it to him. Drained from lack of sleep, his mind a blank, not eating, not seeing what he was looking at, he didn't hear Bones clearing his throat by the pantry door, nor was he aware of the cook's presence until Bones was standing next to the table. "I hate to bother you, but I don't know what to do. I brought menus to your mother each morning. We'd planned them a week in advance, but she liked to review that day's on the day—she was very definite."

"I know."

"She taught me a lot. Your mother made me want to better myself. She, if you'll pardon me talking about her, took me when I was nothing and made me into something. I miss her."

Phil looked up. Bones was sincere in what he was saying. "My mother isn't seeing anybody now. She can't speak, or if she can she doesn't. Meeting with her wouldn't mean much."

"I'm not talking about seeing her."

"I don't care what I eat Bones—make it easy on yourself."

Bones stretched his fingers as if he were doing an exercise. "I try to prepare dishes that will appeal. Phil, you've got to eat to keep up your strength. I appreciate your trust, letting me do what I want, but I'm not here about myself or about meals. It's the household, the staff. Phil, we're at sixes and sevens. Nobody is in charge. The maids were very upset that they'd made you angry."

"The maids made me angry?"

"If they had known, and Pearl would have known and told them you didn't want the rooms on the Long Gallery closed—you know, covered with dust sheets—they'd have had them open, cleaned, ready for company, the way your mother and grandfather always had them. The last orders Pearl gave the morning we were supposed to leave, the morning she disappeared, were to close the house. Your mother never met with Pearl the way she met with me. She sent Pearl's orders in writing. I've seen her written order to 'close the house from top to bottom.' Pearl acted on that order. The maids did what they were told to do. It's that simple. I have the paper here." He reached into his jacket pocket and pulled out a piece of Catherine's household stationery. "Nobody told them to open those rooms again."

"I don't need to see the paper," Phil raised his hand. "Apologize to the maids for me. I fell apart last night. It had nothing to do with anything they did. It did, but it wasn't their fault. I hope I didn't break too much ripping the damn sheets off. Say I am sorry, and tell them to never cover the furniture again"

"I will. It's not my place to say it, but we all think you've been courageous during what's happened, losing your dad and now your mother so sick. You set an example Phil, as your father and your grandfather did. They'd be proud of you."

"Thank you Bones."

"I will make a suggestion if I may. Mrs. Gillons has been Pearl's assistant since Pearl succeeded Mrs. Blackburn as housekeeper. Mrs. Gillons knows the house, what needs to be done and she's a responsible person. If you'd name her housekeeper until Pearl comes back, there'd be somebody in charge again and things might get back to, well not the way they were certainly, but better'n the way they are now. You of course would tell Mrs. Gillons what to do, until your mother is better."

"Until Pearl comes back."

"Pearl won't be back," Bones said.

"How do you know?"

"She's dead. Don't ask me when, where or how, but I'm sure enough to say, I know she's dead."

"Tell Mrs. Gillons she is housekeeper—until Pearl returns. I'll call George Hunnewell to change her wages. I don't think I'm up to writing instructions, so just tell her I want the first-floor rooms and my grandfather's apartment above the Galleried Library kept exactly the way he had them, including fresh flowers every day. I don't care about rooms above the first floor."

"Except in the Portuguese Wing?"

Phil paused. "Yeah, I guess, the rooms on the upper floors of this wing should be open. That's where my mother and I live."

Chapter 33

OCCASIONALLY — NOT EVERY DAY BUT A COUPLE OF TIMES a week — Phil went into Catherine's dark and dank-as-a-cave room. Her nurse explained, "Your mother is not as restless if we keep the draperies closed and only the small lamp next to her bed lighted." That lamp with a 25-watt bulb filtered through a mauve silk shade did little to dispel the gloom. When Phil said a window should be opened to let in fresh air, the nurse said they were afraid she'd catch cold. They kept her in a reclining position on a pile of pillows propped against the headboard of her bed, so she would not choke on her own saliva, which she might do if she were lying flat, and, the nurse said, "because her eyes are partially open, we want to give her something more than the underside of a bed canopy to look at in case she can see."

Catherine's partially opened eyes stared from a jaundiced, emaciated face at Phil.

"You would feel better if you cried," he said from the foot of her bed. "I know Dudleys don't cry. 'Dry-eyed we bury our dead,' is the family motto. I'm a Dudley, Mother, and I've cried a lot these past weeks. I couldn't help myself. Sometimes I don't know I'm crying."

"We aren't sure she hears," the nurse, who had crept up, whispered.

"She hears. You hear me don't you Mother? I can tell you know what I'm saying." The nurse made busy sounds. She wanted Phil out of there. "Take a break nurse. I'll sit here and not take my eyes off her eyes until you get back. If she needs you I'll holler."

"I can't leave until my relief comes. She isn't due yet."

"Take a break nurse!" Surprised by Phil's bark, the nurse withdrew, swiveling the round pillows of her rear end. He sat in the comfortable chair where nurses held vigil and crossed his legs. "Did I tell you what Gus said Mother? I don't think I did, but if I repeat myself, forgive me. Gus said Dad died because something was bothering him, something big, so big he wasn't thinking what he was doing. Gus said, if he had been thinking what he was doing he'd not have tried to take Triumph over the hedge. Triumph wasn't a jumper. Did you know that Mother? Dad wasn't thinking about Triumph. He took that horse over the hedge because he was thinking about something else—and they both died."

Phil uncrossed his legs. "Were you looking out your window when they jumped? I was and I saw everything from the window directly above yours." He got up from the chair and opened the heavy draperies. When he pulled the cord, they made a hissing sound and bright sunshine flooded the room. "Ah, yes, you can see the hedge from here as clearly as I can from my window upstairs." Catherine closed her eyes, either against the light or to shut out what Phil was saying. "Were you watching Mother when he killed himself because he was not thinking about what he was doing? We know what he was thinking. You and I know what was on his mind. He was thinking about what you had said to him." Phil moved to the side of the bed. "Dad didn't commit suicide, fly into that tree on purpose. He was killed because his mind was elsewhere." Phil leaned over her. "You know where his mind was, don't you Mother?" She turned her head away.

Catherine's eyes were opening, squinting in the bright light but open enough for Phil to see dark pupils darting behind narrow slits. "Dad embraced the world. He actually tried sometimes. He'd throw his arms wide and say, 'Isn't that the most beautiful sight?' Or the finest, or the grandest. He looked like the last of the Mohicans when he did that and he sounded like Gramps when Gramps said a room was his favorite room, or a door or window his favorite thing in all Oshatakea. Every view of the valley or the sky was Dad's favorite view. He loved that big old walnut where he died. If you think about it, Gramps and Dad were happy people. All of us could be." Catherine was looking straight at him. "Have you ever been happy Mother?" She closed her eyes again.

"Dad was happiest on horseback, no doubt about it. Riding doesn't thrill me, but I loved watching Dad when he was astride a horse. On a horse he was nothing like the silent tortoise he could be in the house, seldom looking up from his plate at dinner, except to say something to Raymond or Dale. When you weren't around, Dad carried on conversations with them just the way Gramps did, but if you were there, he settled for, 'Thank you, yes please, just half a glass.' I don't remember ever hearing you thank a footman Mother." Her eyes at half-mast revealed nothing.

"That last morning in the courtyard, Dad wasn't silent as a tortoise. He came in smiling. Remember? He'd been loading horses. You said something about what he was wearing. He stood at the sideboard and drank a glass of orange juice. You never let me drink orange juice standing up. Then, he sat down and began packing in the grits. He told me how to pick up spare change at Harvard. He must have done that when he was a freshman. If he hadn't how would he know to tell me?" Phil returned to the window. "I was relieved by his upbeat mood because I knew he didn't want to go to Boston, but what made me ready to burst was when he said he was looking forward to getting me settled. It wasn't what he said, but the way he sounded when he said it and the way he smiled at me across the table." Phil gazed at the hedge beyond the lawn. "I never loved him more than that morning when he smiled at me."

Going back to the foot of the bed, he grasped a post. "You wiped the smile off my father's face when you told him I might not be his son." Catherine's eyes shut so tight her lids wrinkled and deep creases appeared on her brow. "Can you see, is it etched on your brain as you lie on those pillows with your eyes closed and your head rolling, how he looked when you said that? I'll tell you what I see Mother, what I'll see until I die, the pleased cat-that-caught-the-bird grin on your face when he erupted. You were ecstatic that you had given him something poisonous to ponder. When you watched from your window, if you did watch from that window, could you tell his teeth were clenched, his face still red? He was in pain. Your poison was taking effect. When he flew over that hedge into the walnut tree, he was thinking about what you had said. That's what killed him, Mother."

Catherine was making choking sounds, her head jerking spastically from side to side. Phil watched but did nothing when the nurse and Dr. Montrose rushed into the room.

Chapter 34

PHIL DRIFTED INTO OCTOBER, A SERE LEAF ON THE surface of a stagnant pond, initiating no action beyond one-sided confrontations with his mother that were kept to a minimum by nurses who had instructions from Dr. Montrose to never leave him alone with her. Continuing old habits, he was out of bed before seven, brushed his teeth and shaved. He hated shaving, but blue-black stubble that began poking through his white skin when he was fourteen had to be scraped off at least once a day. After a long shower, dressed neither as carefully nor as correctly as when he'd gone to breakfast with his parents, he descended to the Portuguese Courtyard where Miss Eleanor frequently awaited him. Now that Catherine was not there, he drank orange juice while surveying the contents of the covered silver dishes kept hot on the sideboard. If Miss Eleanor was not present, he might converse with John, the breakfast footman, or merely exchange greetings. Boston and New York newspapers lay on the glass-topped breakfast table, but Phil seldom read them beyond checking to see if they contained any news of Martha Graham.

After breakfast, he left the courtyard through the terrace door for his morning walk that, without premeditation or design, covered over the course of a week most of the grounds. Günter's crew perceived these walks as tours of inspection similar to those FP had made periodically and were inspired to keep everything in perfect order. Arborists policed the woods, removing downed and broken limps, cutting back anything that reached out toward the paths on which pine needles, bark or peat was maintained at depths comfortable for walking. Because this was as it had always been, Phil was unaware of the intensive labor and meticulous attention to detail undertaken to please him.

One morning toward the end of October, after walking along the cushioned woodland paths, he found himself standing at the main entrance to the estate where, dwarfed by Hester's iron gates, he halted momentarily and then ambled onto Ontyakah Road, turned left and kept walking past Isabelle's stucco villa, Miss Eleanor's white clapboard cottage and the redbrick firehouse, the first time he'd been off the hill since his father was killed. Across the village square he saw the carved LOREN'S DINER sign he had given Loren as a graduation gift.

When he entered, Phil was greeted like a wounded soldier come home from the wars. Loren squeezed him in a bear hug and made him sit on a stool at the counter. "What can I give you for lunch?"

"I didn't come for lunch. I'm just walking."

"You're here, it's almost lunch time, you'll eat."

"Yes Mrs. Goldberg," Phil said, harking back to the radio program they listened to when they were in high school, absorbing Mrs. Goldberg's syntax into their private lingo. "Bones will have lunch for me," he said looking up at the schoolhouse clock ticking on the wall. "I'd better get back."

"Screw Bones. I'll call and tell him you're here. Wait till you taste today's special." Loren's energy and enthusiasm enveloped Phil like refreshing rain. Before his dad died, his humor never failed to be elevated when Loren arrived bubbling and eager at Oshatakea, ready for anything. He hadn't felt hungry when he came in, but aromas from the kitchen were stimulating his appetite.

Loren set a heavy plate on the counter in front of him. After a few bites he asked, "What am I eating?"

"Baked potato."

"I know baked potato, what is this?"

"Meatloaf and the purple glop is Harvard beets."

"They make me regret I didn't get there, but it's the meatloaf that knocks me out. If I don't ask what's in it may I have more?"

The next morning Phil sent word to Bones he'd not be home for lunch. At 11:30, he loped through the woods and past the gates, heading for Loren's Diner. "I'll have meatloaf."

"Meatloaf was yesterday. Today's special is corned beef and cabbage."

Every day thereafter, except Sunday because the diner was closed Sundays, Phil trotted down to sit on a stool at the counter and stuff himself with the wonders of Loren's common cuisine. He ate everything, liking Loren's meatloaf with baked potato and Harvard beets the best, Mrs. Gage's chicken and dumplings next, followed closely by Friday's fish fry with cole slaw and french-fried potatoes. Thursday's liver and onions he liked least in spite of slices of excellent bacon Loren draped on top.

The lunches led to an argument with Loren over payment. Phil didn't carry money, never had. This Loren knew and told Phil he wasn't to worry. "After all your family did for me, the least I can do is feed you—if you stick to daily specials." Phil, not comprehending diner economics and daily specials, wouldn't accept that, insisting Loren charge him and send the bill to George Hunnewell the way everybody else did. Loren said that was too much trouble. Phil said he'd stop coming in. To stop the discussion, Loren gave in and thereafter sent batches of chits to the Hunnewell office.

George had not harassed Phil recently, but the telephone call to say Loren would be sending bills gave his trust officer an opportunity to apply pressure. "Of course, I'll pay for your lunches at the diner, no problem, but damn it Phil, I should be sending checks to you at college. Accept the fact your mother is in the hands of people who know what they are doing. You have no valid excuse not to do what your father and grandfather would expect. Get yourself to Harvard. An education is your major responsibility now Phil. Hanging around the house is nonproductive."

"Yes George," Phil hung up.

On cold days, if it was raining, Phil walked indoors instead of on the grounds, going through the first-floor rooms and his grandfather's apartment, noting everything with the same scrutiny that had galvanized Günter's men and had an identical effect on the household staff. No speck of dust was allowed to loiter, no tarnish darkened silver or brass. Windows were washed, floors waxed and polished, fresh flowers placed where FP had them. Inside or out, at 11:30 Phil set off for Loren's Diner. If it was pouring, he donned a yellow slicker, rain hat and L.L. Bean boots to jog across the lawn and through the woods, no matter how teeming the deluge. Dick Fallon, fretting that he had nothing to do except drive Miss Eleanor occasionally and oversee the two men who kept a garage full of unused cars tuned and shining, said he'd take Phil down to the village, but Phil declined, saying he needed the exercise. One early November day, a steady sleet pelted down, turning the grounds into an ice-coated fantasy and making the paths treacherous. Mrs. Gillons saw Phil leaving the house and called Dick Fallon. Dick started the Buick and driving as fast as he dared on the service road's slick surface was waiting above the main entrance on Ontyakah when Phil steamed out of the woods. "Get in here," the chauffeur shouted, "you'll break a leg and catch your death."

"No thanks."

"Stubborn like his mother," Fallon groused and returned to the garage.

Phil was usually back at Oshatakea about two o'clock, energized by Loren, good food and a two-mile sprint up the hill followed by close to another mile from the gates to the North Portico. He came into the house through that farthest-removed entrance because it gave him immediate access to the Baroque Theatre. Bounding on stage Phil lighted a rehearsal lamp, shed his clothes down to briefs and T-shirt, went to the barre barefoot to work up a sweat stretching and doing limbering exercises he had seen Graham dancers do. The length of time it took him to perceive even modest improvement was frustrating but not defeating. He wished he could have an observer's honest appraisal. Loren could be trusted not to talk, but Loren wouldn't know what to look for.

On November 25, the day before Thanksgiving, Phil became eighteen. He awoke aware of the signal date but did not muse on the irony of his situation until he was in the shower. Three months ago, his eighteenth birthday was anticipated as a day of deliverance, the day he would be able to leave his mother's house on Chestnut Street and move into Massachusetts Hall, from which he could escape to classes with Shirley Biddlecomb. Yet here he was on that important day more constrained than he had ever been, not because his mother was forbidding him but because he refused to leave her. He continued to turn a deaf ear to the importuning of George and the four women who had appointed themselves his caretakers. This was not to pay filial lip service; a sense of duty had nothing to do with his decision and there was certainly no normal mother-child bonding with Catherine that kept him at home. Miss Eleanor had cared for him, held, hugged and kissed him, sang to him, taught him, guarded him and, most important, loved him. Even when he was little he sensed that his mother hated him. She didn't want him near her, wouldn't touch him, recoiled if he reached out to her. Miss Eleanor scolded him and sometimes spanked him, but as she slapped his bottom he never doubted her love. Catherine's punishments were never physical, but they were cold, constant and cruel for reasons he didn't understand. Still, she was his mother.

He asked himself if he was using his father's death and his mother incapacity as excuses, covers for the fear he'd fail if he attempted to become a dancer. The answer was no. Success or failure had become inconsequential. During his weeks alone, he had learned that he just wanted to dance. Before an audience no longer mattered, nor did being a professional. He simply had to dance—for the joy of dancing. Martha Graham had said that to dance is to live. He felt this, but the words did not mean to him what they meant to her. Dancing alone made him feel alive. For what he wanted, he now knew, it was not necessary to rush off to Shirley Biddlecomb or to the goddess herself.

Punctuality was a trait he had inherited from both Fillmore and Dudley forebears. On November 25, he popped into Loren's Diner as the Presbyterian church bell tolled twelve—and he stopped short. Yellow, orange and brown crepe paper streamers spanned the room and framed a large painted poster at the far end that said in glittery gold script, "Happy Birthday Phil!" Miss Eleanor, Isabelle, Adelaide and Louisa sat at a round table under that poster, wearing crepe paper hats and blowing kazoos, as were grinning patrons at other tables, in booths and at the counter. They all laughed and clapped at Phil's befuddled expression, then sang a raucous "Happy Birthday." "This way, Mr. Fillmore." Loren doffed a brown bowler hat and bowed low, pointing toward the round table. The scene was silly and the goings-on somewhat childish as those the valley people referred to as "astocrats from the hill" provided more entertainment than they realized.

"It was Loren's idea," Adelaide said. "We wanted to do a party for you at the dacha."

"I wanted to do it at the villa," Isabelle interrupted.

"They all wanted to do it, but Loren persuaded us to do it here and we're having a grand time." Miss Eleanor's face was pink from puffing into her kazoo.

As other customers finished lunches and headed back to work, they came over to wish Phil a happy birthday, a few touching him on the shoulder. Several said they'd never forget the day he was born. More told him how much they missed his father. Nobody asked about Catherine.

It was pot roast and spaetzle day, but Loren made meat loaf and Harvard beets for Phil, who went beyond seconds to a third, albeit smaller, portion. Adelaide and Louisa raved over the pot roast, which they didn't think they'd ever had. When Loren explained his schedule of daily specials, the sisters said they would return next Wednesday. "Please reserve a table for us." Isabelle said she'd join them.

Two weeks before Christmas, the most disagreeable nurse on the team taking care of Catherine told Phil she was giving herself a present. "I'm quitting this booby hatch." She had much more to say, excluding what she had already told anyone who would listen: "The son is as cracked as his mother." Dr. Montrose commiserated with Phil but explained it would be difficult if not impossible to replace a nurse just before the holidays.

Giselle, who had done nothing but drink coffee and read slick magazines in the servant's hall since Catherine needed nurses rather than a maid, was pressed into service as a temporary substitute. She refused to give injections; needles frightened her, she said. This meant Dr. Montrose had to make two trips to Oshatakea during Giselle's eight-hour shift. However, she could not get out of spoon-feeding Catherine nutritionally enhanced gruel and keeping her clean. After three days of this Giselle went to Miss Eleanor to complain. "I wouldn't mind washing her face and combing her hair if she didn't grab at me all the time I'm doing it. If I try to do it while she's asleep I can't get the snarls out, you should see what those nurses have done to her lovely hair. They cut it so it looks horrible even when it is brushed. I could cry. But that's not the worst of it. They expect me to empty things."

"You mean bedpans?"

"Yes," Giselle whimpered, turning the corners of her mouth down in disgust. "If she used them I would have to empty them, but she doesn't, she dirties herself, so I have to change the bed and try to wash her. Merde, it's merde, merde, merde from one corner of the bed to the other. I am not a nurse, Miss Eleanor. I am a lady's maid. I do not clean up sheet."

"You will do what needs doing Miss Uppity Drawers or be sent packing," Miss Eleanor retorted.

Giselle went to Phil. "I fix hair, press gowns, wash silk under-things if they are not too soiled, draw bath water, hand Milady towels, help her dress and undress. I will not change the diapers Dr. Montrose has put on Madame. She does nothing to help herself and when I try to help her she scratches me. I can't stand it Pheel, I will leave at once."

Phil accepted her resignation and, rather than make further fuss less than a week before most people would be celebrating Christmas, decided to take Giselle's shift himself. Having inherited from his father a what-will-be-will-be approach to coping, he entered his mother's dark bedroom with no sense of martyrdom, but the first time he removed the top sheet covering the sight and stench that had incensed Giselle, he reeled backward and barely made it into his mother's bathroom before retching. He splashed cold water on his face and queasy but determined returned to her bedside, chanting, "It has to be done, it has to be done, it has to be done." But how to do it? What to do first? Standing a few feet away to gain perspective, he tried to devise a logical sequence. Remove the filthy nightgown from his comatose mother, then the dirty diaper, and then the foul bottom sheet? That wouldn't work; she'd be dirtied again from what was on the sheet. If he did the opposite, remove the sheet first, the rubber pad underneath would be soiled more than it was already. Pondering accomplished nothing. There's nothing to it but to do it, was another Farney saying. Holding his breath, he stepped forward, set to and, in the cleaning-up sessions that followed with stomach-churning frequency, tried every possible way and found none less odious than any other.

Whatever he tried, single-minded concentration was essential to completing the task. The punch line to a dirty joke he had heard in school came to mind: "I close my eyes and think, I am doing this for the emperor." He would never be able to wash excrement off his mother's body by carefully cleaning creases without gagging. When he wasn't repeating doing it for the emperor, he was bemused by the fate that had brought him and his mother to this point. Not long ago, she wouldn't let him touch her hand and now he was washing, drying and applying lotions to her most private parts.

The nurses that remained became increasingly unreliable, not showing up to relieve Phil, which meant he had to cover a second eight-hour stretch, or he would be told that the nurse whose shift preceded his had not arrived in his mother's suite, which also meant sixteen dismal hours at a stretch. When neither preceding nor succeeding nurses appeared, he caught on that they were playing a nasty joke, initiating him into the hell of a twenty-four-hour stint.

Dr. Montrose objected to Phil's assumption of his mother's care but had no alternative solution. However, he said he could not possibly keep running up to Oshatakea to give Catherine shots when registered nurses weren't there. Whether he wanted to or not, Phil must learn how to inject his mother. The doctor explained Catherine's basic regimen of medication to keep her somewhat sedated, with periods of sufficient consciousness so she could be fed the repulsive gruel, had changed. "Unfortunately, her dependence on morphine is mounting. She requires an increasing number of doses to keep her calm."

Surprised at the doctor's openness in discussing his use of the addictive narcotic, a practice Adelaide had warned Phil about, he asked, "Will she ever get well if all we do is keep her knocked out?"

Dr. Montrose's mousy mustache twitched. He looked at Phil through rimless oval glasses. "Regardless of what we do, your mother is not going to get well. She suffered irreversible hysteria when your father was killed. We aren't keeping her knocked out, as you so colorfully put it, we are attempting to keep her comfortable."

"Shouldn't we ask another doctor to examine her, maybe come up with a different treatment? George Hunnewell could bring somebody out from the city."

"Are you willing to risk having her committed to an asylum for the insane if that should be another doctor's recommendation?"

"The first nurse who quit said Mother is already in a booby hatch."

"I assure you son, the care she is getting in her own bedroom is far superior to anything she would experience in a mental hospital. Though she does not speak, she has lucid moments when she is aware of where she is and who is with her. Knowing your mother, can you imagine her reaction if she were to wake up in a straitjacket, tied to a narrow bed in a barren room with no curtains and bars on the window? Do you want to condemn her to that?"

Catherine showed no reaction when Phil pushed needles into her flesh; he winced.

An extreme cold front the weatherman called a Canadian clipper blew through the night of December 23, plummeting temperatures to eighteen degrees below zero. The morning of the twenty-fourth was bright, but the sun raised the thermometer to only seven below. At sunset it dropped again and winds blasted as if they came straight from the North Pole. Stefan's men tried but could not bring the chapel temperature higher than a frigid fifty-three degrees despite shoveling tons of pea coal into the furnaces. Unused since Farney's September burial, cold had so permeated the stone walls and floor of the chapel it would take more than banging steam pipes to warm pews and drive out bone-penetrating chill. Those who attended Christmas Eve services in the chapel knew from past experience it was wise to come muffled in furs and woolens even when the temperature outside was not below zero. Choristers behind the carved medieval screen customarily wore hats, mittens and heavy coats under their scarlet robes.

Christmas Eve at Oshatakea was for family, others considered family, houseguests and close local friends. The congregation would be sparse this year. There were no houseguests, and the Gages who usually attended wanted Danny to have Christmas Eve at home. This left Phil, the Kropotkins, Isabelle and Miss Eleanor to gather at five o'clock in the Galleried Library, huddled around the hearth for hot toddies. If one didn't stray farther than a few feet from blazing logs it was not too bad.

"I am deeply grateful for this hot drink." Adelaide held a steaming silver cup in her gloved hands, smiling at Phil from Farney's high-backed wing chair where she sat swathed in a hooded Russian sable cloak that fell to the floor in lush swags.

"If it weren't for this, I'd not make it through the service," Louisa chirped. "May I have another please?"

"If you have another, you will sleep through the service." Adelaide's bright laugh was taken up by the other women. Phil nodded at Dale to refill Louisa's cup.

"Thank God," Isabelle said, holding her cup up to be refilled, "you dispensed with homilies, though I shall miss hearing someone read the nativity story. Your grandfather was good at it, but Farney was better. Won't you please read just those few verses Phil?"

"No."

"Well, so much for that. I salute you for asking Jack Smead to provide a service of music. We are so lucky to have him at the academy. What he does with students is incredible. I never miss his beautifully staged productions of operettas and musical comedies. He has real flair. I'm sure his program tonight will be glorious." Isabelle wore a black mink cloche set at a rakish angle. Her voluminous purple silk satin cape was lined with relatives of the hat, but it would take more than a Canadian clipper to force her into gloves, which would deprive her of her rings. Several stacked fingers were already turning blue.

"We might take turns, each of us reading a verse or two from

King James. 'And it came to pass . . .'" Miss Eleanor looked dream-ily into the fire. " I nearly died the year your father had a bad cold and that young man took over and used a modern translation. I still shiver thinking about his deep voice proclaiming, 'Mary was preg-nant.' Do you remember Phil?"

"Pregnant, or with child, it's the same thing," Isabelle said.

"It isn't at all," Adelaide countered. "I agree with Miss Eleanor. These new versions of the Bible may convey the same information, but their language is harsh. Without poetry extraordinary events become mundane. Language used in Holy Scripture should not be the same as that used every day, not if we expect it to raise our thoughts to the Lord."

"I'm not convinced Mary was a virgin," Louisa said.

"Please dear, not on Christmas Eve," Adelaide shushed her younger sister, but she did not raise an eyebrow when Louisa asked for and received a third cup of grog.

Phil was the first to hear "A Mighty Fortress Is Our God" resound-ing from the chapel organ. Jack Smead played the forceful hymn to let them know Christmas Eve service was about to begin. Should he have invited Smead to join them for dinner? Gramps and his father would have. It was too late now. Everyone stood. Phil moved away from the fire to lead the tiny procession out of the library and along the Stone Corridor to the heavy chapel doors. Adelaide's sil-ver-tipped walking tick tapped to the beat of Martin Luther's hymn. She was pleased Mr. Smead had chosen the majestic Bach config-uration. Into the hoary chapel they marched, vapor puffs appearing each time they exhaled. Phil went to sit by himself in the front pew on the right side of the center aisle. Adelaide and Louisa sat behind him. Isabelle and Miss Eleanor took places in the third.

As the choir sang anthems, airs and carols their voices combined with that of the organ to reverberate in resonating waves from the vaulted arches. The minute congregation sat expressionless, staring transfixed at flames of clustered gold-sticked candles whose flickering light created an impression of movement among carved figures in the reredos. Toward the end of the service, the introduction to "In the Bleak Midwinter" sounded, and Phil, Adelaide, Louisa, Isabelle and Miss Eleanor sank to their knees on tapestry -covered fall stools. If a minister were present, this would be the signal for those so inclined to go forward to receive communion while others knelt in place, heads bowed in prayerful contemplation. Tonight, without benefit of clergy, the survivors remained motionless, on their knees, elbows on the back of the pew in front of them, hands cupped, ready to receive the mystical symbols of Christ's body and blood.

"In the bleak midwinter, frosty wind made moan, earth stood hard as iron, water like a stone; snow had fallen, snow on snow, snow on snow, in the bleak midwinter, long ago."

Adelaide's back was a straight line against which a carpenter's level could have been placed without the little bubble wavering in its glass vial. Only women raised when ladies of a certain class were defined by posture, carriage and manner would hold this position while the choir sang all verses, their soft voices spreading a blanket over the worshipers.

"Our God, heaven cannot hold him, nor earth sustain, heaven and earth shall flee away when He comes to reign: in the bleak midwinter a stable place sufficed the Lord God incarnate, Jesus Christ."

Adelaide was remembering sitting in this pew as a child, hearing the same words sung while glancing from beneath lowered lids toward parents she thought were the most precious in the world. She continued to believe they were. Eyes closed, inhaling the pungence of burning wax candles, she was sure she could also detect the delicate fragrance of her mother's perfume and the scent of her father's cologne. Filled with an ecstasy experienced only on Christmas Eve in this place during the singing of this particular carol, Adelaide thanked God for what she acknowledged had been a life of privilege, adding a plea for Him to keep her strong so she could care for her sister as long as Louisa lived. And please God, release Catherine and Phillips from the prison in which they find themselves this Holy Night.

"Angels and archangels may have gathered there, cherubim and seraphim thronged the air; but his mother only, in her maiden bliss, worshiped the beloved with a kiss."

Louisa's posture never matched Adelaide's. Short and plump, she had none of Adelaide's innate grace but had never yearned for parental approval. There was no need. From birth, luminous dark eyes and long lashes brought adoring smiles and spontaneous embraces from a mother who found it impossible to ever be truly displeased with this beautiful child and a father who saw in Louisa the reincarnation of his own iconic mother, but Louisa was not thinking about her parents as she knelt. Gazing toward the altar through misted eyes she saw amidst the slender tracery and burnished gold not the Savior, or saints and angels she knew were depicted there, but the figure of a young man who had been brutally taken from her. For too many years whenever she thought of him, she imagined the torn and bloody flesh his beautiful body had become when the train ran over him. It required more emotional and mental control than Louisa could muster to blot out that terrible image and replace it with the memory of their final loving moments in the grotto. Her cupped hands reached up, not in anticipation of receiving the blood and body of Christ but in supplication for a miracle that would let her once again touch the boy, the man, whose loss she still mourned. A moan escaped her.

"What can I give Him, poor as I am? If I were a shepherd, I would bring a lamb; if I were a wise man, I would do my part; yet what I can I give Him—I give my heart."

Miss Eleanor leaned forward to touch Louisa's coat. Louisa looked up and with Miss Eleanor's guidance eased herself back onto the red velvet pew cushion. Alert, Adelaide's lips formed a silent thank you to Miss Eleanor who seemed to always know how to comfort members of this family. Louisa patted Miss Eleanor's hand resting reassuringly on her shoulder.

Isabelle watched and wished Miss Eleanor would comfort her once in a while, but then, Isabelle mused, I never appear to need comforting; yet appearances can be deceiving. Phil seemed oblivious to what was happening behind him. Was he hearing the music, listening to the words, Isabelle wondered? Did they mean anything to him, move him? He is a conundrum. Why is he playing nurse here when he should be raising hell at Harvard? Filled with impatience, as she often was when trying to figure out what made Phil tick or not tick, she stifled an urge to rise up, stride to his side and grabbing him by the collar shake him until his teeth rattled. "It wouldn't do any good."

"Sssh," Miss Eleanor hissed.

"What?"

"You are muttering." Miss Eleanor put her finger to her lips.

"Sssh yourself."

"In the bleak midwinter, frosty wind made moan, earth stood hard as iron, water like a stone; snow had fallen, snow on snow, snow on snow, in the bleak midwinter, long ago."

When the hymn concluded, Jack Smead went directly into the recessional, and Phil led his flock to the Gibbons Room for a roast beef dinner followed by an exchange of modest gifts in the Galleried Library. After the women hugged him and wished him a merry Christmas at the South Portico, Phil changed his clothes and went to the mauve suite to relieve the nurse whose eight-hour shift ended at midnight.

Chapter 35

JOGGING DOWN THE HILL FOR LUNCHES OF COMFORT food and Loren's intoxicating high spirits stopped when Phil assumed responsibility for his mother's care from midnight until four in the afternoon. A night nurse from the village came on at four to give him an eight-hour break. As soon as she arrived, Phil went across the hall to his father's bathroom and stood for twenty minutes in the big green marble shower stall letting hot water pelt him from three sides and above. The shower did not do for his head what Loren's infectious enthusiasm did, but it reinvigorated his tired body so he could go to the Baroque Theatre for an hour of barre exercises. Though he was doing these exercise sessions after sixteen hours of caring for his mother, Phil thought he was making greater progress than when he had done them following lunch at Loren's. He decided dancing was more demanding than swimming after eating.

Following the practice session, he went to his third-floor rooms, took a quick second shower, shaved, dressed and hurried down to the Gibbons Room for a fast dinner with Dale Morris. He tried to be in bed by seven o'clock, because he had to be up again at 11:30 to get downstairs to his mother before the village nurse left at midnight. In the hours before his mother began stirring, Phil dozed on a chaise across the room from her bed or read one of the books he'd brought with him from the Galleried Library. Bones rang around seven A.M. to ask if he wanted anything special for breakfast, a question Phil found impossible to answer. He'd never had to decide what to eat until he looked over breakfast choices available on the long sideboard in the courtyard. Phil missed the sideboard selection, but Bones did his best, sending up to Catherine's sitting room as much variety as was possible on a heated room-service cart.

Though he'd been deprived of breakfast in the courtyard and a normal night's sleep, Phil managed to be fairly cheerful when Catherine was awake during his long attendance, including when he was bathing her and changing her nightgown and bedding, giving her injections and persuading her to accept the disgusting gruel he was feeding her. "I know it isn't to your taste Mother, but you'd choke if we gave you solid food. You know that don't you. I don't mean to keep repeating myself. There you go, a nice big spoonful. Look at it this way— No, no, please don't spit it out. As I was saying, look at it this way, you are a creature of habit, scrambled egg, bacon, toast with orange marmalade, yuck I'll never understand how you can eat that bitter marmalade three hundred and sixty-five days a year. Now you have this lovely gray-green, or is it blue, concoction for breakfast, lunch and dinner. How's that for habit? No, don't hold it in your mouth, swallow, there's nothing to chew. Why don't we pretend? You and I know it's not true but let's pretend what we have in this bowl is an egg scrambled soft the way you like it, crisp lean bacon, thin-sliced toast and bitter marmalade whipped together into a loose mousse. What do you suppose gives it this blue-green color?"

Catherine opened her mouth and the gruel dribbled out, down her chin and onto the clean nightgown that was such a struggle for him to put on her. Bibs had been dispensed with because they enraged her. Gruel settled into the folds of her neck. "Sorry if I upset you Mother, there'll be no more pretending."

If Phil's good mood lasted through Catherine's breakfast, he read aloud to her, starting with society news from the Boston papers. He frequently broke off reading to ask if she knew the people Allison Arnold wrote about in her column, or if, when she lived in Boston, she had attended the opening of the flower show. Once reports on the top drawer were out of the way, he read from books he thought might interest her or were related to her past experience. If she grew restless, which she usually did, he restarted one-sided conversations.

"Gramps has been much on my mind recently. I suppose it's because of the holidays. Holidays meant a lot to him, everything meant a lot to Gramps. But that isn't what I want to talk to you about. It occurs to me you and Gramps shared the goal of creating harmony. Don't laugh. I know you can't, but if you could you would. You'd tell me I don't know what I'm talking about. You'd say you would rather stir up trouble than bring people together. Discord over harmony every time. Right? The harmony I'm talking about is what Gramps accomplished putting this house together, taking disparate pieces from all over the world and melding them in such a way he created harmony. That's why Oshatakea is unique, they say, not that I know another house to compare it to. People tell me the same about you. You brought all kinds of artists together, planned programs, food, flowers, everything, so at the event all were of a piece. Isabelle says there has never been a hostess anywhere who came close to you. You understand the importance of relating music to mood, she says, and the dramatic principle of building toward a climax, and you did it every time. That's quite a compliment coming from Isabelle who doesn't like you any more than you like her.

"If you and Gramps were so similar in your goals, why didn't you get along? He admired and respected you, Adelaide told me that. Did you admire and respect him? Why couldn't the two of you create your own harmony? You used his Oshatakea as the setting for your successes and he used your—Miss Eleanor calls it genius—to show his house to the world. You were a great team Mother, you and Gramps. Too bad you were so antagonistic. Think about it while you lie there with nothing to do." He plumped her pillows. "Oh, oh. My nose tells me you need to be cleaned up again. No, none of that, keep your hands to yourself. Your nails should be clipped. I'll get to it. There's no need to roll your eyes, or kick the covers. Time for a shot. I'll give you one and then clean you up. You are easier to handle when you're unconscious." Phil sometimes thought he was losing his mind as he prattled at her.

A few days later, a little before four o'clock in the afternoon, the night nurse tiptoed into Catherine's bedroom. Catherine was asleep; Phil was nodding in the chair at the foot of her bed. He jumped when the nurse tapped him on the shoulder. She put a finger to her lips and jerked her head toward the sitting room. He followed.

"I'm glad to see you." He closed the bedroom door behind him. "I'll head out now and be back at midnight."

The nurse chewed her lower lip, looked down, then up again. "I'm quitting. I'm sorry, but I can't put in another hour of this duty. It's a hard thing to say, but what's being done to your mother is killing her. I became a nurse to help sick people recover. I refuse to be a party to what's going on here."

"You mean the morphine."

She nodded. "I do. It would be a kindness to give her an overdose, put her out of her misery. That will happen one day, there'll be a slipup, nothing intentional, but somebody will make a mistake and she'll be dead, a blessing, but I don't want to be here when it happens." She told Phil she was not just leaving Oshatakea, she was leaving the valley. "If I dared, I'd write a letter to the newspaper or another doctor somewhere, talk to the sheriff about this case, but I'm afraid to do that. Doctors are like crooks and police, they stick together, cover up for each other. I have two kids to support, I can't risk being blackballed. I'll keep my mouth shut until they are on their own, then, maybe, if she's still barely alive like she is now, and if I have a safe job far away, maybe then I'll do something."She offered to stay with Catherine for half an hour. "I hate to do this to you kid, I really do."

Phil thanked her, said he understood her position, was sorry to see her go—she could not know how sorry. "Don't worry about me, I'll be okay." He was numb.

"I worry about you." With a rueful smile, she added, "For her sake Phil, and yours, I pray she goes to sleep soon, and doesn't wake up."

Phil accepted her well-intended quick embrace, wished her luck and watched her go through the door into the hall, then he sank into a Bergere, which is where Miss Eleanor found him when she came into the sitting room. The worried nurse had stopped on her way down the hill and told her she was leaving. "I've come to help. The others will be here shortly," Miss Eleanor said.

Isabelle barged in, followed by Adelaide and Louisa. "Don't get any harebrained notion you can do this alone Phil, you can't," Isabelle boomed.

Adelaide's "Phillips you cannot go on like this" came out a half-beat behind Isabelle's words.

Phil broke his sodden silence to hush them. They complied for the few seconds it took him to open Catherine's bedroom door and make sure she had not been roused by the commotion. The door safely closed again, they resumed their gaggle of objection.

"I called George Hunnewell and told him to get his ass down here pronto, and bring a doctor with him who will know what the hell to do. He's being paid enough, it's time he took some responsibility." Isabelle crossed her arms over her bosom.

"Isabelle, you made a New Year's resolution to clean up your language," Adelaide chided.

"I've been making the same resolution since I was twelve."

"That was a long time ago," Louisa said.

Phil cut in. "Isabelle, call George back and tell him not to come, he'll just add to the confusion, and explicitly tell him to not send another doctor."

"Why for Christ's sake? Do you condone what this quack is doing to your mother?"

Phil took a deep breath and explained what Dr. Montrose had said.

"There's no such thing as 'irreversible hysteria,'" Isabelle scoffed, which brought a sharp rebuke from Adelaide as her eyes darted toward her Louisa.

Phil told them Dr. Montrose said another doctor would commit his mother to an insane asylum. "At least she'd get proper treatment there," Isabelle argued.

"I'm not so sure." Adelaide's quiet comment got their attention. "Terrible things have been known to happen to people in those places."

Grasping at Adelaide's hesitation, Phil said, "She couldn't stand being tied to a bed in a room without curtains and bars at the windows."

"You are wrong Phil," Miss Eleanor stopped him. "I am not advocating she be sent to a mental hospital, but there is nothing your mother can't stand if she puts her mind to it—not that she has control of her mind now."

"She couldn't face Farney's death," Isabelle sang out.

"And she wasn't on morphine then," Phil said.

The argument was interrupted when Louisa said she heard tapping on the door.

"Can it be Catherine?"

It could not. The tapping was on the sitting room door in the hall. Miss Eleanor opened it to reveal Bones, who was surprised and embarrassed when he saw a gathering. "I'm sorry, I came to talk to Phil. I didn't know he had company. Will you be staying for dinner? I'll have places set in the Gibbons Room."

"Thank you Bones, we are not staying," Adelaide said.

"I apologize, but I do need to speak to Phil, alone. It's important."

"I can't leave in case Mother should wake up," Phil replied. He looked at the huddled women. "Would you mind waiting in the hall? No, go across into Dad's study." His question and request met with dismay, but they went.

Bones's face was flushed. "This won't take long. I would not be here talking to you like I am, at this time, if I could help it, but an emergency has arisen, an opportunity actually, one that requires an immediate response."

When he didn't continue, Phil prompted, "Yes?"

"There's nothing for me to do now at Oshatakea. I prepare meals I think will appeal and you hardly touch them. I'll forget all I worked so hard to learn." He searched Phil's face seeking help. Phil had none to offer. "I talk to Chef LeBourne on a regular basis. He knows all about the situation here. Anyway, he called this morning, he needs a sous-chef." Without intending to, Bones puffed out his chest. "He's offered me the job! I could not believe in my wildest dream Chef LeBourne would ever want me to be his sous-chef. Do you know what that means Phil?"

In shock, Phil put out his hand. "Good show Bones. Keep in touch."

Bones was grateful to Phil for not making it difficult by begging him to stay, but he was hurt by his easy acceptance of a not yet proffered resignation with no expression of regret. "I hope you aren't mad at me. When your mother is better, if she moves to Boston, or if you decide to reopen Oshatakea, let me know. I'd love to come back."

"We'd love to have you Bones."

"Adrian Wells, my sous-chef, can do almost anything I did. He's done staff meals for a long time."

"I know. We'll be fine. You get yourself to Chef LeBourne, and good luck."

Reluctant to end a conversation that terminated his happy years at Oshatakea, Bones asked, "Will you explain to Mr. Hunnewell? I'll leave an address where he can send my final check."

Phil nodded. Hearing sounds in Catherine's bedroom, he excused himself. She was getting restless. He checked; she didn't need changing. In her bathroom he prepared the morphine, walked to the bed and pushed a needle into her arm. Pulling the covers up and tucking them around her shoulders, he saw she was watching him. Her eyes looked directly into his. He forced a smile to conceal his panic. "Mother, from here on, it's you and me — just the two of us. Do you think harmony is possible?"

Chapter 36

—

AROUND PHIL, MRS. GILLONS HAD ALWAYS BEEN QUIET, as assistant and then housekeeper doing her job effectively and without fuss. He learned she could be a virago when Bones and the last nurse left. Bones had told her about his offer from Chef LeBourne before he told Phil. Mrs. Gillons advised him to accept, said his absence would not cause a ripple in the household inasmuch as he cooked for the family and what family remained didn't eat anything that required a chef, but the nurse's departure ignited a spark in the seemingly stolid woman. Much to Dale's chagrin, she took Phil's dinner cart up to him. "I need to talk to you," she said when he opened Catherine's sitting room door expecting to see his favorite footman.

"Oh God, no," Phil groaned.

"Sit down and eat those chops while they're hot."

"I'm not hungry."

"Don't talk—eat!" She opened the door into Catherine's dressing room. "Just as I thought, there's plenty of room." She picked up the house telephone. "Stefan, you and the boys bring that rollaway to Mrs. Fillmore's suite, and tell Marcia to come along with linen and blankets." She lowered the telephone. "Do you need a special pillow or will any pillow do?"

"What are you doing?"

"I'm setting up a bed for you in your mother's dressing room, so's you'll have a place to sleep until this nurse mess is straightened out, which it will be shortly." She spoke into the telephone again, "Stefan, tell Marcia to bring a couple of pillows."

"I don't need a bed. I can sleep on the sofa."

"You will sleep on a bed, a cot, truth to tell, not first-class accommodations but better than a sofa. It'll only be for a few nights if I have to take over one of the nursing shifts myself. You're a bright boy Phil, but that doesn't mean you know what you are doing. You aren't invincible. You think because you're young you can do anything, well you can't. Now, while we're waiting for them to get your bed up here, I have to talk to you about the staff."

"Are they all quitting?"

Mrs. Gillons frowned. "Why would they quit? They're living on easy street. Won't they be surprised when I lay a bunch of them off—if you'll let me. I can't find enough work to keep everybody busy and idleness makes me frantic. Rooms above the first floor were buttoned down when we thought you were going to Harvard. People should have been let go then but they weren't. Now, all we have is the first floor, your grandfather's apartment and this wing to keep ready for the queen in case she should drop in. We don't need sixteen housemaids and five footmen when three maids and a couple of footmen, plus Stefan and Peter, can keep those rooms the way you want them. I've had two long conversations with George Hunnewell about this. Two because the first time I called to say what I had in mind, he was in his pontificating mode. My second try went better. That man listens if you talk fast and don't give him a chance to get a word in edgeways. The important thing is, he agrees with me, we should cut back. All I need now is for you to give me the nod and I'll do the rest." She tucked in her chin and thrust out her chest in defiance should Phil not go along with her.

"Do what?"

"Fire sixteen people. Pay attention to what I'm saying. Why aren't you eating?"

"Don't those people need their jobs? What will they do if we let them go?"

"Some are old enough to take early retirement, and the rest will find work somewhere that'll require more than sitting on their posteriors flirting with trouble. Don't give me grief Phil, I know what I'm doing."

Phil felt like he did when he was little and Miss Eleanor laid down rules. "I won't give you grief."

"Good. I doubt you'll be as easy with step two."

"There's more?"

"There is. When your mother stopped entertaining years ago the indoor staff was cut back quite a bit, we're down about half of what we were when the house was going full tilt. The girls that are left, and some of the boys too—they have fits when I call 'em girls and boys, which is why I do it—the girls and some of the boys are unhappy about sleeping in the servants' quarters up under the eaves. They hear noises. Most, not all, think the noises are a ghost. Half believe it's Pearl wandering around, dead or alive. If she is alive they're worried she's mad as a hatter, and that scares them more'n if she's a ghost."

"Do you think the noises are Pearl wandering around?"

"No. Why would she wander up there? Pearl never lived in the servants' quarters. From the time she came here she lived in the housekeeper's apartment on the ground floor, first with her aunt, Mrs. Blackburn, and then on her own when she became housekeeper."

"Maybe we should do another search. We haven't tried to find her since right after the accident."

"Do what you want, but don't change the subject—and eat! What I'm getting at is there are sixteen maids, five footmen and three kitchen staff, a total of twenty-four adults sleeping up there who say they're nervous. With the changes you just approved, there will be eight, and I can tell you they'll complain to high heaven about rattling along echoing halls lined with empty rooms. My suggestion, and George Hunnewell goes along with me on this too, is to close that floor, evict the lot and give them a housing plus partial board allowance, which most won't need because they'll go home to live with their families in the valley, but if we take away housing and the evening meal as part of their pay we have to compensate them some other way. They'll see the allowance as a raise, especially since they won't be on call twenty-four hours a day. The extra money we're talking about for allowances to those still on staff will be more than offset by letting a gang go and by what we'll save if we don't heat that floor."

"Are we worried about saving money?"

"Not that I know of, but a penny saved is a penny earned. Dick Fallon can pick up the few staff who'll be staying first thing each morning and deliver them home at night. It'll give him something to do. They'll have breakfast and noon dinner here and most will be on their way down the hill by late afternoon. Adrian, a kitchen assistant and a footman to serve you will stay until after you've had your dinner, and then they'll be taken home. The reason I'm passing it by you is because if we do this, and I think we should, it means you'll be alone in the house at night—you and your mother. Stefan will be out in his little house next to the old monastery, which isn't far away, and Peter is moving in with Dick over the garage."

"Where will you be?"

"Didn't I mention I bought a house on Partridge Road in the village? Molly Matthews and Lynn Jones are going to room with me."

"It seems you thought of everything before you came to me." What difference could it make? "I don't care. I want Dale Morris and John Johnston kept on. Beyond that, if George says it's okay, go ahead."

"Now hear me Phil, if you are nervous about being alone nights, with your ma sick, I can schedule a rotation so there'll always be a footman downstairs. He can polish brass, do that sort of thing to keep busy, and be available if you need him."

"That's not necessary. As you say, Stefan is just across the driveway, and if Pearl is wandering around the house, maybe she'll come if I ring a bell."

Mrs. Gillons glowered. "That's not funny."

"Sorry."

"You won't be alone long. George Hunnewell and I are going to get a full staff of nurses lined up within a couple of weeks. Now eat, you haven't touched your chops."

He didn't eat, and they didn't line up a staff of nurses. It was as if a curse had been laid on the house; no nurse in the valley nor in metropolitan areas where George advertised signed on. Nurses, who had been disagreeable when they were at Oshatakea, went out of their way to be nasty when they left, embellishing lurid tales of Catherine's witchiness and her doctor's unconscionable use of drugs. On the telephone, Loren told Phil ugly rumors were keeping valley nurses away. Phil thanked him for calling but asked him to please not do it again. "When the telephone rings Mother goes into convulsions. I'll call you."

Lying on the rollaway in his mother's dressing room, he pondered the rapidly deteriorating situation, and tried to find something positive in the circumstances. Perhaps the inability to hire nurses and his consequent around-the-clock attendance on his mother was meant to be. The last nurse to go, the one whose conscience troubled her, said she didn't want to give his mother those shots of morphine but she had no choice; as a nurse she had to follow the doctor's orders. I'm not a nurse, Phil thought, I haven't sworn to do what a physician tells me, but if what that nurse said is true, I am participating in the slow murder of my mother. He rolled off the cot and went to check on Catherine. If it weren't for a rasping, light snoring sound she could be taken for dead already.

It took nearly a month for him to screw up the courage to act. He knew nothing about addiction or withdrawal; worse, he didn't know what it was he didn't know. He knew his mother became irritable and demanding if he didn't give her a shot of morphine promptly every four hours. Increasingly, she couldn't go that long between injections, so he was prepared for her to fuss and carry on if he should skip a dose. Willing to do whatever was necessary to distract, soothe and comfort her until she forgot what she had not had, he was not prepared for the scalding experience of an out-of-control creature tearing at bedding and ripping her nightgown when he put his plan into action by withholding her four o'clock injection. Before his eyes she transformed within the space of an hour from an invalid into a maniac, pulling out clumps of hair and clawing her face and arms until blood flowed and the bed resembled a crime scene. Phil tried to calm her with a soothing touch and soft voice pleading with her to relax. When that had no effect, he felt compelled to use force in an attempt to hold her down, warning her in cries of desperation that she would hurt herself if she did not stop. In so doing, he acquired a black eye and deep scratches on his own arms and face. Since the day she had been struck dumb, the only sounds emanating from Catherine had been low-pitched moans and growls. Now there were shrieks, garbled imprecations and inconsolable pleas in an indecipherable language.

As the battle raged, though Phil needed help, he was glad no one else was in the house. With the windows closed there wasn't a chance Stefan could hear across the driveway. His determination to make this the night of his mother's purification was waning as her condition deteriorated and then grew steadily worse after he withheld a second injection, the one due at eight o'clock. Devising this operation, he had assumed she would settle down within a couple of hours, but after denying her a midnight dosage and as four A.M. approached, except for brief moments of panting stupor as if she were in the eye of a hurricane, the storm showed no signs of subsiding. He had to make a decision; would he stick to his original plan or surrender this first attempt, give her an injection, allow her to win the battle and withdraw until he was prepared to try again? Stubbornness kicked in, a trait inherited directly from the wreckage of the woman before him. He'd not relent. They had endured to this point; they would continue. There would be no respite for Catherine's wracked body and ruthlessly demanding nerve endings.

With all good intentions, but with no comprehension of her suffering, Phil opted for a new tack—he would remain firm but appeal to her reason. Holding a cold washcloth to his swollen eye, he approached cautiously. "Mother, you can raise hell as long as you want, but I will not give you one more needle filled with poison. You've had your last dose of morphine. That's it. Fini."

Her panting ceased. Bloodshot, black-ringed eyes glared at him. Desiccated breasts lay limp and flat on her bloody chest. Mistaking stillness for surrender, Phil stepped forward to begin the formidable task of restoring order and cleaning up. Catherine lunged. He jumped back. She clawed the air, wildly seeking something to clutch and slipped with a dead-weight thud down between the bed and the bureau. The mauve shaded lamp crashed to the floor, plunging the room into darkness. Fumbling and cursing, Phil at last found the wall switch for a chandelier hanging from the ceiling. The illumination was surreal. He tried to pick her up and pull her back into bed, but her cold sweat-coated naked body was wedged between two immovably heavy pieces of furniture, her head and shoulders near the floor, her left arm twisted grotesquely across her back. Only her right leg remained on the bed.

"Help," Phil shouted, struggling to grip her, afraid if he pulled too hard to get her out from between the bureau and the bed he would hurt her more. He didn't like the look of that twisted left arm. Climbing onto the bed, he bent over and attempted to put his hands around her slippery waist. The only way he could reach was to lie across her leg, and then he had no purchase. He had to have help. "Damn it, why didn't I insist somebody be in the house nights?" No one, not even Catherine, heard his cries for help. He rang Stefan on the house phone, woke him, told him to call Peter and get up to his mother's room at once. "As fast you can Stefan."

He tried again to move the bureau but couldn't budge it. "Don't worry Mother, we'll have you back in bed in a second." There was no response. He wished she'd moan, show some sign of life. In the light from the chandelier, which was harsh compared to the dim glow of the small bedside lamp, he realized how much she would hate being seen as she was, bloody, naked and soiled. He tugged a blanket from the bed to cover her, then, afraid she'd suffocate if the blanket shut off air, yanked it away. Stefan in pants pulled on over long underwear and Peter in a terry-cloth bathrobe were in the room within minutes. "Please don't look," Phil implored.

Stefan and Peter grunted but managed to move the bureau, letting Catherine's limp body slump onto the floor. Assuring Phil they weren't seeing a thing, Stefan and Peter then carefully lifted her onto the bed. Phil straightened the sheets, cursing himself for not thinking to remake the filthy bed before they laid his mother down. Stefan said it was unimportant, advising, "What you have to do is get the doctor here as soon as possible."

Incredibly, though Stefan and Peter had seen more of the despised Catherine Fillmore and her horrible condition than anybody else other than her son, no aspect of that night became part of the Catherine legend. Nor did Dr. Montrose reveal for the town to talk about Phil's attempt to rescue his mother from her deadly addiction. After doing what had to be done—she had a dislocated shoulder, a serious concussion, multiple bruises and other physical conditions usually associated with a barroom brawl—Montrose gave Phil a verbal thrashing for nearly killing his mother with actions that were well-intended but based on total ignorance. "Now, young man, you do what I tell you or we will remove her to a sanitarium without another word."

Phil was too frightened by what had happened to ask the doctor to tell him what he needed to know so he could one day try again to accomplish what he had set out to do.

If Miss Eleanor, the Kropotkins or feisty Isabelle had learned of that April night in Catherine's bedroom, George Hunnewell would have been called upon to intercede at once. He probably would have removed Catherine from Dr. Montrose's care and placed her in a metropolitan hospital. But none of them heard the story, thanks to Stefan and Peter, who kept their word not to reveal what they had seen. Phil had started to tell Miss Eleanor what he was going to do before he did it, but at the last minute he controlled his tongue. If she had known in advance, the pain and fear of an April night that echoed through months and years to follow would have been avoided. Catherine suffered indescribable mental as well as physical agonies, but it was Phil who would pay the dearest price.

What Phil said to Miss Eleanor instead so confused and scared her she sought help, help Phil would construe as betrayal. As the last of Phil's extended family to be accepted by him in his self-imposed exile, shutting Miss Eleanor out condemned him to solitary confinement with a living corpse in whose eyes he read nothing but hatred.

When the last nurse departed, Phil asked Isabelle and the Kropotkins to stop visiting his mother. "You agitate her so much, it takes me hours to calm her down." Not visiting Catherine meant not seeing Phil, because he wasn't leaving her suite. The result was cessation of all contact between them and him. He promised he'd keep in touch on the telephone, but he never called.

Miss Eleanor continued coming, but only into Catherine's living room, where she and Phil conversed in whispers so as to not disturb his mother lying unconscious in her bedroom. And she lunched there with Phil once or twice a week and occasionally cut his hair. She fretted that, consumed by Catherine's illness, he was becoming too preoccupied, and he didn't listen if she talked about anything other than what was happening within the confines of these rooms. She resisted chiding him for being sullen, but worried aloud that he wasn't eating enough. With her prodding he'd eat a few bites, then put his fork down. When he was alone, food was often returned to the kitchen untouched. Miss Eleanor was careful not to say anything about his appearance, hoping that if she accepted him as he was his self-confidence might be restored. She was wrong about diminished self-confidence. She hadn't understood he was becoming increasingly self-confident as he approached his mother's moment of truth. What she saw as brooding preoccupation was concentration on plotting Catherine's rescue. Unconsciously aping his mother, he proceeded precisely as she had when she'd planned events. If he told Miss Eleanor, it would be to use her as a sounding board, not to seek permission but to explain what was going around and around in his head so he might detect while listening to his own voice weaknesses or potential problems with his plan. Freeing his mother from her dependency on morphine could be the most important accomplishment of his life. It was essential for him to think through every strategy; he must not fail.

Miss Eleanor was leaving the suite after lunch on the day he would stop Catherine's injections of morphine, when, like a small boy wanting to show his teacher a picture he had painted, Phil called after her, "Miss Eleanor," and she stopped. Then he said, "I thought I'd tell you what I'm going to do, just so you'll know, but I've decided not to. It won't be easy, but there's no other way." He gave her a quick kiss on the cheek and closed the door.

Fear was not native to her nature, but Miss Eleanor was frightened. A terrible thought struck as Dick Fallon drove her back to her cottage. By late afternoon mounting uneasiness turned into full-flushed certainty. Praying George Hunnewell had not left his office, she rang him and poured out her fears, describing Phil's behavior as a descending spiral. "He has not spoken a completely coherent sentence in weeks until today when he was pushing me out the door and said, 'It won't be easy, but there's no other way.' I don't want to sound hysterical Mr. Hunnewell, but I am. What does he mean?"

"Do you think he's suicidal?"

George had spoken a word she'd held at bay; that word and another, even more frightening. "I don't know, but I'm sure something is going to happen to his mother, or him, or God help us both. Please come."

"He won't see me. He hangs up when I telephone and doesn't reply to my letters."

"You have to see him, he might listen to you."

George thought this highly unlikely, but his ego was stroked. "Understand Miss Eleanor, I manage his trusts. I am his legal and financial adviser, I am not his guardian. I have no authority over his actions or personal decisions. If he had not reached eighteen, I might be able to—"

Lawyers! Miss Eleanor interrupted. "This is not a time for legalities Mr. Hunnewell, lives are at stake. I hate to trick him, but if it's the only way I will. I am to lunch with him on Friday. I'll take you in with me."

"What time do you want me there?"

"Eleven-fifteen. Park under the South Portico. Since her illness Catherine hates daylight—they keep the draperies closed in her suite. I doubt Phil would see you if you came to the Portuguese Wing entrance, but better not take a chance. I'll meet you in the Galleried Library."

Friday morning a badly shaken Phil was desperate to recover his equilibrium. He bathed Catherine, trying to not hurt her as he gently pulled the washcloth over bruises and dabbed at open wounds. "I'm getting to be a professional," he said, easing her from one side of the bed to the other so he could make it afresh from the rubber pad through layers of sheets and light blankets to a mauve silk coverlet. "I hope the time will soon come when we won't need to do this. You will be able to sit in a chair while your bed is being changed. When you start feeling like yourself again, we'll call Giselle, ask her to come fix your hair. I'll send word to Bones to get back here so we can celebrate no more gray-green gruel with a fancy dinner in the Gibbons Room, all candles burning and a fire in the fireplace. When you get better. We all want you to get better. Should we have music at your coming-out dinner? What do you want? We need lush music to go with luscious food: Tchaikovsky, or perhaps Rachmaninoff. Do you think Pyotr Ilich was dreaming of delicious food when he composed?"

He smoothed the coverlet. Her gaze seemed to focus on his black eye. Please God, he said to himself, make her well again. "There you are, fresh and clean. Now, I'll give you your medicine." He picked up the prepared hypodermic syringe from a tray on the bureau, injected the morphine and rubbed an alcohol-dampened cotton ball where the needle had punctured her blue-white arm, then pulled her sleeve down around her wrist and tucked the covers loosely around her body. Propped against the pillows, Catherine watched him. "I'll get rid of this dirty laundry, then clean myself up before Miss Eleanor comes for lunch." At eleven-thirty he checked. His mother hadn't stirred except to close her eyes. Soundlessly he shut the bedroom door.

Miss Eleanor's knock was as usual two light raps with the knuckle of her right middle finger. Phil opened the door. "Phil, dear, George Hunnewell is with me."

"Hello Phil, I hope you don't mind."

Phil slammed the door and turned the bolt. He went rigid, not moving or speaking as Miss Eleanor knocked again and then again, her taps light but urgent.

"Phil, please."

"Phil, stop being childish and open this door." Miss Eleanor was pleading, George Hunnewell commanding.

Phil was paralyzed by Miss Eleanor's betrayal. How could she?

There was a full four-knuckle knock. It was Dale. "I've brought lunch."

"Take it back."

If Miss Eleanor had not attempted to slip George in to talk to him, Phil would have told her why he had abruptly stopped the injections of morphine. Miss Eleanor would not have known any more about narcotic addiction and the dangers involved in its treatment than he did, but she would have understood he had meant no harm to his mother. He wanted only to help her.

Chapter 37

MISS ELEANOR'S DECEPTION AND HIS MOTHER'S CONDITION after the attempt at a forced withdrawal drained Phil of all optimism. Dr. Montrose's tongue-lashing broke his spirit. A wounded animal, he bolted the doors to his mother's suite and would not admit maids to clean or footmen to deliver food. Spiders spun webs freely and dust accumulated. The door was unlocked only so he could push the laundry trolley out if no one was lurking in the hall. When Dale came with the food cart, he knocked to let Phil know it was there, then retreated because Phil would not open the sitting room door until he heard Dale descending the back stairs. Then he'd pull the cart in to retrieve Catherine's thermos of gruel and, if uninterested in investigating what Adrian had sent up for him, push the cart out again and relock the door. If he felt hungry, he uncovered dishes and nibbled. A warrior under siege, he removed from the cart those things he thought he might need later, stashing away in Catherine's dressing room fresh fruit, crackers, jam. He stopped stockpiling bananas when they rotted. Phil removed the offensive drawer in which they'd been stored, stacked it on top of the room-service cart and pushed the whole business out the door. Regardless of whether or not he ate, he always returned the cart to the hall because his mother would need another thermos of gruel for her next meal.

Dr. Montrose was the sole exception to his no-admittance policy. Phil had never cottoned to the little man who could have been a cigar salesman with his slicked-back hair parted in the middle, but when he understood what Montrose was doing, distaste became dislike, and after the attempted-withdrawal catastrophe and the doctor's virulent reaction, Phil regarded him as some kind of devil. The dime-store dandy checked in every morning following Phil's folly until Catherine's physical injuries were under control. He never alluded to any psychological damage. Then he came every other day, every three days and finally once a week, unless Phil called him for what he thought might be an emergency. As long as Catherine was kept drugged there were few real emergencies.

Prior to the lockdown, while maids were cleaning the suite, Phil had gone up to his own rooms for a shave, quick shower and change of clothing. Now, he could not risk that, as there'd be no one to hear his mother if she needed help. For more than two weeks he didn't shower and wore the same pants, shirt and socks around the clock, until the doctor, who normally barely acknowledged Phil's presence, stepped around him one morning as Phil was relocking the sitting room door and said, "You stink to high heaven."

Phil knew he must smell pretty bad, but he had not faced the problem of personal hygiene until Montrose made it an issue. He considered filling his mother's sunken bathtub but didn't think he could get out of the damn thing in a hurry if he had to, and what would he put on after he'd soaked and scrubbed—certainly not the rotten clothes he'd taken off. The green marble shower in his dad's bathroom was a possibility. Over there he'd also have access to his father's clothes. After much thinking about pros and cons, he decided to give it a try. As a rule, Catherine went into a deep sleep about twenty minutes after a shot, and stayed comatose for a couple of hours. He waited for an injection to take effect, then scooted across the balcony that was a private passage between his mother's and father's bedrooms, leaving doors open at both ends so he could hear her if she made a fuss. He was elated by his daring. After wandering through his dad's suite to make sure he was alone, he locked doors to the hall, then stripped and stepped into the shower. He would have liked to linger but forced himself to soap up, rinse off and get out. Toweled dry, he went into his dad's dressing room and began pulling out drawers. Farney's socks were too tight, and his shoes impossible. The only footwear Phil could squeeze into was a pair of rubber boots. He put on a flannel shirt and a pair of khaki pants that would have fallen down if he hadn't threaded a necktie through the loops, pulled it taut and tied it in a knot. Gathered like a broomstick skirt around his waist, the pants' cuffs were midway up his calves. Clean and refreshed, he returned barefoot to his mother.

As he came to feel secure in his expanded fortress and new routine, black depression lightened, not with brilliant bursts of sun but with receding shadows. He took comfort in telling himself he had tried the only way he thought he knew to rescue his mother; failing a sincere attempt was preferable to not trying at all. He now understood that she could have died, and almost did, according to Dr. Montrose, but she hadn't. That was a positive. She wasn't better, was actually getting more injections than before, but he'd done his best and would continue doing so until real nurses were found. Montrose said it was only a matter of time. It couldn't be too soon.

Nine months later, in February of what should have been his sophomore year at Harvard, Phil, rather than prowling student haunts in Cambridge and Boston, was moving about in a tightly restricted domain but growing bolder, no longer scooting across the balcony for a quick shower and hurrying back. Now, each morning, after completing the major task of cleaning his mother up and tucking her in, he gave her an injection and then went to stand surrounded on three sides by green marble for half to three-quarters of an hour, relaxing his mind and body, luxuriating in repeated latherings with aromatic hard soaps, rinsed off by pounding sprays, adjusted as a finale from steaming hot to numbing cold.

He fantasized he was walking in the rain, was immersed in the deep end of the swimming pool or standing under a waterfall. He remembered when he was a little boy taking showers in this glorious space with his father and, when he was older, playing grab ass here with Loren. Drying could be time consuming, but there was no rush, he had no place to go. He hadn't shaved since the day Miss Eleanor tried to sneak George Hunnewell in, nor had his hair been cut. He knew he should do something about a haircut; it took thick bath towels to soak up the water from his long beard and shoulder-length curls. A second canvas laundry trolley was now placed outside his father's door for towels and clothes. The putrid garments he'd discarded in the laundry hamper the first day he ventured over for a shower were never returned, not that he cared; his father's closets were full and he got a kick out of wearing what his dad had worn.

Dad's dressing room and wardrobe were wonderlands of discovery, journeys of exploration and nostalgic revelation. He'd given up completely on footwear except for the rubber boots, which he could put on in an emergency. Mostly he went barefoot. He tried on hundreds of shirts, pants, vests, jackets, combining them into outfits that became his daily attire. Neckties pulled tight solved the trousers problem. He made a game of donning things that didn't match, old green twills with a stiff-fronted dress shirt, into which he stuck his father's gold studs, or Dad's fancy salmon-colored linen slacks worn with a red and black checked shirt. On days he felt really good, he wore kilts. Every day became a costume party. He'd like a reaction from his mother, amusement or even disapproval, but her eyes revealed nothing of the sort. After every wearing and laundering, he carefully returned each article of clothing to where he'd found it. If Farney were to walk into his dressing room, he'd not notice any change—except that his neckties were taking a beating being used for belts.

While poking around in a closet one morning, he heard his

mother's all too familiar throaty exhale. Thinking she might have dragged herself across the balcony, he glanced over his shoulder. She wasn't there. He found her right where he'd tucked her in. With only the ticking of the tall case clock on the lower landing to break the stillness of the Portuguese Wing, he realized he need not be in the next room to hear Catherine if she should be in trouble. Taking this as a further reprieve, he broadened his routine, indulging himself with an evening shower, his second of the day, after Catherine went to sleep following the eight o'clock shot. This time, instead of putting on pants and a shirt, he took to wearing one of his dad's long dressing gowns. Most exciting, he felt free, after checking on his mother, to return to Farney's study to read. Books shelved there had to do with horse breeding, land management, forestry and agribusiness, subjects that held little appeal, but he had no other choice. Once again making a game of it, he climbed the library ladder and took down the farthest book to the left on the top shelf. *Doane's Facts and Figures for Farmers*. Just what I need, he groaned, but read the book he did and when he finished, several nights later, he replaced it and took down the next volume, *Forages: The Science of Grass Agriculture*. Continuing his post–second shower reading through months and years, he read all books in the study in the order of their shelving. When he finished the last book on the far right of the bottom shelf, he put it back, climbed the library ladder, reached up and took down *Doane's Facts and Figures for Farmers*.

Two years into his seclusion, on the first day of November, while uncovering breakfast dishes in the hot compartment of the room-service cart, he spied an envelope on which was written, "Open at once! Await instruction." He tossed the envelope back. When he investigated the cold compartment, there was an identical envelope propped against a pitcher. Somebody was playing a joke on him. He didn't like jokes. He'd been hungry when he pulled the cart into the sitting room; now, damn it, he didn't care to eat. As he spooned gruel into his mother's mouth, for which she now opened automatically as if she were a nestling, he seethed. Seething didn't satisfy curiosity, but curious or not he followed without the slightest deviation his established morning ritual, bathing Catherine, rubbing her body with moisturizing lotions, brushing her hair, putting her into clean diapers, nightgown and, this morning, a satin bed jacket, then remaking the bed so she'd be fresh from skin to coverlet. With Catherine's weight down to approximately eighty pounds, she was easy to pick up and put down elsewhere for sheet changing and for the frequent repositioning Montrose said was vital to keep her free of bedsores.

Phil no longer chatted while he fed or bathed and changed her. He had run out of small talk. As for trying to cheer her, she had never reacted to falsely optimistic predictions of how much better she would be if she did what she was told or to those that threatened doom if she refused to cooperate. As long as she had powerful injections of morphine she presented few problems. Phil had no notion of what was going on in the real world; newspapers were no longer scanned. He could have told her what he was reading at night in his father's study, but he knew she wouldn't be any more interested in that material than he was. Because he rarely spoke, Phil sometimes worried he might have lost the ability. Could I speak if I wanted to? he'd ask himself as he lay on the narrow cot in Catherine's dressing room. To test himself, he asked the question aloud. His voice was hoarse but otherwise unimpaired.

Without a monologue to focus his thoughts, Phil's mind roamed while he went about his chores. Something as silly as the lyrics and melody of a tune popular when he was in school might take root in his brain and could not be dislodged. Or a word, new to him, one he'd come across in his dad's books and looked up in the dictionary, would capture his imagination and he'd spend hours trying to fit that word into sentences. If something ridiculously inconsequential upset him, he obsessed. Try as he would that

November morning, he could not keep his roaming mind from returning, like a tongue to a cavity, to the damned envelopes with their cryptic message. What could "Await instruction" signify? Who was playing with him?

Willpower held as he placed his mother's gruel thermos back into the room-service cart's hot compartment, where he could see the envelope lying there like a coiled serpent ready to strike. He actually pushed the cart into the hall and locked the sitting room door, but then he reversed the lock with a sharp click, threw the door open and, without looking to see if anyone was in the vicinity, grabbed the cart, yanked it back inside, slammed the door and relocked it. He snatched up the envelope and shook as he ripped it open. On a piece of paper inside Adrian had written: "You have a twenty-first birthday coming up. Can I fix something special for you?"

Not that day, nor the day after, but several days later Phil replied on a piece of his mother's engraved notepaper: "Find out how Loren makes meat loaf."

Chapter 38

THEREAFTER, ON PHIL'S TWENTY-SECOND, TWENTY-third and twenty-fourth birthdays Loren's meat loaf was delivered to Catherine's sitting room in the hot compartment of the room-service cart. As time went on, the day, month and year had little meaning for him, so meat loaf was a pleasant surprise, accompanied by astonishment that another birthday had come around. Adrian always placed among the covered dishes a small card on which was written, Happy 22—or 23—or 24 Birthday. If he hadn't Phil would not remember how old he was. There were other cards on the cart from Miss Eleanor and from Loren, from the Kropotkins and from Isabelle, as well as members of the staff and George Hunnewell, but these were in sealed envelopes Phil did not open. In his first months caring for Catherine, he had stacked mail on his mother's desk, thinking he'd get to it later, but later never came. When the envelopes were piled so high they slid off the desk onto the floor, Phil no longer retrieved them from the cart, and instead he sent them back untouched. Adrian also marked holidays for his reclusive employer with turkey, oyster stuffing, pearl onions, mince pie, all the traditional dishes of Thanksgiving; goose with chestnuts, plum pudding and other goodies on Christmas day; roast beef with horse radish sauce and Yorkshire pudding on New Year's and so on, but these special dinners meant little to Phil after his first full year of seclusion. He had nothing to celebrate.

On the sixth Easter Sunday locked in with his mother, Phil retrieved the lunch cart and was surprised by what he found. Adrian had made a *pashka*, that extravagant Russian Easter concoction of pot cheese, egg yolks, sugar, heavy cream, butter, candied fruits, shredded almonds and fresh vanilla bean flavoring, a recipe Phil had memorized as a child when he'd watched Bones laboriously combining the rich ingredients. Fresh strawberries from Günter's hot house, crystallized violets and silvered candy shot decorated the tall white cake shaped like an upsidedown flowerpot nestled in a necklace of brightly colored Easter eggs. The elegant confection was breathtaking to behold; he had to show it to his mother. Picking up the *pashka*, Phil carried it aloft the way a bishop carries a crown to be set upon a monarch's brow. Catherine was awake, but for no good reason she clamped her eyes shut when he walked in. Pleading with her to look at what Adrian had made didn't persuade her to open them.

Exasperated by her stubbornness, Phil decided to make a ceremony of presenting the *pashka* to himself. Marching into the dressing room to the beat of drums and blare of trumpets he alone could hear, he set the *pashka* down to turn on the round frosted bulbs surrounding Catherine's makeup mirror and arrays of tiny bulbs in the mirror-lined three-sided alcove. Their brilliance hurt his eyes. Momentarily blinded, he proceeded with his pantomime, raising the *pashka* high above his head, this time as a casket of jewels is offered to a potentate, stepped into the mirrored alcove, bowed low and said, in a raspy voice suited to the role he was playing in a comic drama of his own devising, "For your delectation, the most magnificent *pashka* ever." He straightened and standing at attention slowly lowered the cake. As his vision adjusted to the glare he gawped, not at the mirrored reflection of a glorious white confection but at cascades of black hair mushrooming from the top of his head down over his shoulders and chest. There was no way to tell the difference between head hair and beard; they were one mass, enough to fill a bushel basket. Staring out at him from this ebon cloud were two frightened eyes that were frightening to behold. Were they his mother's peering from beyond fathomed depths? Or were they eyes bestriding the chiseled nose of a mad man? His gaze lowered to reflections of hands holding an Easter cake. The image in the mirror was neither Captain Kidd nor Rasputin; the abhorrent apparition was himself. His heart pounding, he turned and carefully placed the *pashka* on Catherine's dressing table, leaning there to more closely examine himself in the makeup mirror. Repelled and apprehensive, he combed long fingers through the beard and black curls, hair he washed and dried with thick towels twice a day. It should not have surprised and shaken him, but it did. He didn't look in a mirror after showering, and if he had his father's bathroom was not brightly lighted. He had assumed he was the person he'd always been. Existing as a robot, doing what had to be done, not anticipating change, accepting what is as the way it will always be, forcing himself to not care, unseeing, unaware, months had accumulated into years. Time and disciplined detachment had made him grotesque.

He could find no implements in either his mother's or his father's suites that were adequate to removing all that hair. He tried first his mother's scissors and gave up, realizing after a few snips he'd die of old age before he'd completed the task. Shears from his father's desk were made to cut paper not hair. He called the kitchen, thanked Adrian for the *pashka*, said it was a wonderful surprise. "I'll eat a piece shortly, and return the rest to the kitchen. Share it with the staff." Adrian was not prepared to hear Phil's raspy voice for the first time in two years but was pleased by his gratitude and touched that he wanted to share it with the staff. Then Phil asked for a sharp butcher knife and a dozen straight razors.

"Why do you need a butcher knife?"

"And razors, don't forget the razors, I'm going to shave and cut my hair."Within fifteen minutes Dale knocked and forced himself not to stare when Phil opened Catherine's sitting room door. "What took you so long?"

Dale held out a wide-bladed butcher knife and a pair of sturdy kitchen shears. "Here are these. We don't have straight razors." Dale found it hard to believe the handsome, well-groomed youth he had sat at table with in the Gibbons Room could be the old man of the mountain standing before him.

"Barbers must have them, and the drugstore."

"It's Easter Sunday, they won't be open."

"Call them at home, it's an emergency."

Dale did what Phil told him to do, but not until after he had described Phil's appearance in grim detail to Adrian, who listened incredulous. The only two staff members in the house at the time, they agreed it would be best to keep to themselves what Dale had seen, much as Stefan and Peter had promised Phil they would not tell anyone about Catherine's condition, a promise of which Adrian and Dale knew nothing. However, the minute the cook and the footman walked into their own homes that evening neither could resist telling his wife, swearing her to secrecy but not cautioning the children. Big-eared little pitchers went to school the next day, and by noon on Monday every child in the academy had heard, twisted, added to and retold a tale more suited to Halloween than to Easter. The rendition that set hard as cement and would not be changed included footlong hairs growing out of Phil's nose and eyebrows that covered bloodred eyes. Sam Weller, third-generation proprietor of Sam Weller's Pharmacy, confirmed the story because he had supplied the razors. "It took near two dozen of them to get through his beard. I billed more'n regular price, it being Easter Sunday, but I guess he can afford whatever I charged."

Loren hearing the story tried to call Phil, but Phil had disconnected the bells on telephones in the two suites. He could call out, but was oblivious to incoming calls.

From the time Dale delivered the kitchen knife and shears until he returned with razors, Phil hacked away in Catherine's bathroom. Kitchen shears he threw down when they seized up if he tried to cut a too-thick hank of hair in a single snip. The butcher knife was only marginally better. Dale's delivery of the straight razors, bone-handled beauties, each in its own chamois sleeve and polished wooden box, were answers to Phil's prayers. "Sam thought you'd need this," Dale said, handing Phil a leather razor strop. He was making real progress being careful not to slice off a piece of ear when Catherine began fussing; it was time for her four o'clock injection. "Just a goddamn minute," Phil shouted from the dressing room. Instantly reverting to acceptance of duty, he put the razor down on the sink, dissolved tiny tablets in a shallow saucer, sucked them through a sterilized needle into a syringe and pumped the solution into his mother's arm. If he looked at her when he placed her arm back under the covers, he would have seen frantic eyes scanning the creature tending her, one side of his face covered with ragged remnants of beard in varying lengths while the rest, including his neck, sprouted long black curls. A pale ear stuck out on the partially shorn side, lonely in its isolation, and the top of his head looked like he'd been attacked by an inept scalper.

To sustain himself during the long shearing process, Phil ate *pashka*, a forkful at a time, letting the vanilla-flavored buttery cheese, fruit and almond delicacy melt in his mouth, coating his tongue with velvet. The horror that had gripped him when he first beheld himself faded as memories of earlier Easter *pashkas* at Oshatakea came to the fore, followed by wide-ranging images from the time before his father's death, which changed everything. Freeing himself of the fright wig was almost as complicated as learning the maze. His smile drew on muscles so long unused they pulled but didn't disturb his recollection of Loren and himself as little boys unheedful of Miss Eleanor's warnings to stay out of the maze unless she was with them. Inevitably they became lost or separated, triggering screams that brought Günter's men running to the rescue and Miss Eleanor's stern reprimand based more on relief than on anger.

Under ordinary circumstances a thin slice of *pashka* would have sated, but the circumstances were not ordinary. He twisted and turned every possible way but still he could not see the back of his head. For a sixth of a second he considered calling Miss Eleanor to come and give him a real haircut, but that would have denied him the sole responsibility for his great unveiling. When he was twelve, he had pulled a cord that dropped the shroud from a statue of Gramps, paid for and erected by valley residents in the village square. Bands played that day and buildings were draped with bunting. There were no bands in the dressing room and no bunting, but Gramps's unveiling, while impressive, could not compare in significance to what was taking place in Catherine's bathroom. "And nobody has to listen to long boring speeches," Phil said, forking in another mouthful of *pashka* from the plate perched on the closed commode. He was drawing once more on his father's credo—what will be will be and what has to be done has to be done. He was also beginning to think that what he was doing was funny.

At the statue unveiling, barrels of beer were consumed and untold cases of wine drunk. Phil's mouth was gummy. He reached for the house phone. "Anybody there?"

Adrian answered. "You caught us as we were going out the door."

"Is it too late to ask for a bottle, make that two bottles, of white wine, a Graves, I think, with a bucket of ice and a glass?"

Was it the dawning of a new era, Dale wondered, when he knocked on the sitting room door and Phil shouted from the bathroom, "Come in, it's unlocked. Put the tray on the library table. Thanks Dale, Happy Easter."

Phil had a moment of panic when he went into the sitting room to get the wine and saw the room-service cart there as well. Jeeps! He'd forgotten to feed his mother. Thank God the thermos had kept her gruel warm. He gave her the eight o'clock shot an hour early and went back to the bathroom to continue his tonsorial transformation. He finished as Catherine's midnight medication was approaching. Holding both wine bottles bottoms up, he shook a few remaining drops into his glass, raised it to the mirror and grinned at the very different yet still exceedingly strange reflection of a pale young man with a butchered haircut and multiple pieces of toilet paper stuck to his cheeks, jaw, chin and neck to stop the bleeding where he had nicked himself. There was only soapy water to soften his stubble, but the finest lubricating shave cream would not have helped because his skin was covered with previously undisturbed minute pimples hidden by the beard. Every scrape of the razor sliced off pieces of skin. "Here's to Farnsworth Phillips Fillmore the Fourth"—his name came out as series of phonetic puffs—"who resembles the Cherry Valley massacre on the most remarkable Easter Sunday of his life, so far. Who knows what the future holds?" He drained the drops of wine. "Something tells me you are going to be sick as a dog Easter Monday." His belch was long and loud.

Chapter 39

PHIL VOWED HE WOULD NEVER AGAIN EAT AN ENTIRE *pashka*, even as he recognized the part Adrian's Russian Easter cake had played in his reawakening. He also vowed there would be no more hideous surprises as he emerged from the shower, dried himself on a large bath towel and examined his reflection in his father's three-way dressing room mirror. Trimming his own hair was an art difficult to master, especially in the back, but he did manage to even up jigsawed lengths as they grew out, and he shaved daily with a straight razor sharpened on the strop Sam Weller had sent, using his father's brush to make a satisfactory lather from bath soap. With practice he learned to accomplish this without turning his face into a plate of carpaccio. Checking out his physique, he perceived that the musculature he had taken for granted was soft, had lost its definition. Twisting so he could see his derriere, he tried buttock tightening; not much happened. "I have to get to the barre," he mumbled, knowing that was impossible. The footboard of his father's empire sleigh bed was close to barre height, and its concave curvature allowed space for his knees when he squatted. He began exercising at once, but it took weeks to produce results, and he was so badly out of condition he panted if he pressed himself too far, either at the foot of the bed or when he was doing floor exercises. He added jogging in place and jumping: feet together, arms at side; feet apart, arms overhead; feet together, and again and again.

His determination to restore physical fitness was a conscious effort; his mental and emotional return to the land of the living was more subtle. A marker was set on a June evening when he replaced the last book to the right on the bottom shelf of his father's study, climbed the library ladder, reached up to take down the first book farthest to the left on the top shelf, *Doane's Facts and Figures for Farmers,* and didn't. With nothing to read except books he'd read twice, he resorted to remembering books shelved in the Galleried Library. Would his mother be okay if he ran down to get one or two of those books? No, the Galleried Library was too far and, once there, he'd be seduced to browse. "Tomorrow, I'll ask Dale or Mrs. Gillons to bring books to me."

On impulse, he pulled the drapery cord at one of two east-facing windows in his father's bedroom. Having grown accustomed to covered windows, this was the first time he'd touched these draperies, which were closed by maids when Farney died. What he saw when they swooshed open shook him. The view from his father's window was the same as from his bedroom on the floor above and from his mother's room. Across a great expanse of lawn, looking toward fields and woods, he could see in the distance shimmering in the soft light at the end of day the hedgerow where Triumph tripped, but it wasn't memory of the accident that caught his breath, it was the green carpet of lawn, tweed-textured fields and the colors of leaves at the edge of the woods. This east view from the house was the least structured at Oshatakea, with no formal flower beds, no sculpture or fanciful folly. He had heard Gramps describe his ancestor Thomas Fillmore's emotional reaction when he looked down on the valley from the bluff where he would later build his cabin. Old Thomas never saw a manicured lawn such as the one Phil was looking at, nor knew nurtured fields, but that June night, looking not from a bluff but from his father's window, Thomas Fillmore's descendant experienced similar emotions. This space of lawns and fields and trees were Oshatakea as much as the house Gramps had built. It was Oshatakea's land his father loved. Standing at the window looking out Phil felt connected with his dad, his grandfather and even old Thomas. Sounds of Catherine choking interrupted his reverie. He closed the draperies and went to dissolve little white pills in distilled water.

The next morning he called Mrs. Gillons and asked her to come up when she had a minute. When she knocked on the sitting room door he invited her in and to sit down, then handed her a list of titles he'd written on a piece of notepaper. He explained what he wanted her to do and described in particular detail sections of the Galleried Library where she would find the books.

"I have a better suggestion," she said. "I'll stay here and you go down to the library. You know where to look, and you may see others you'd like to read."

"I can't do that."

"I'll call you on the house phone if your mother makes a peep. She'll never know I'm here and you're not."

"Thank you Mrs. Gillons, but I can't."

The housekeeper found the books was impressed by the accuracy of Phil's directions. Like his grandfather he knew every nook and cranny of this house. She failed to find just one of the books he requested. It was not where Phil said it would be, but he didn't complain, merely commented, "Somebody must have borrowed it. Did they leave a slip in the box?"

"I don't know about any box. Other than family, the only people who might know are Mr. Ames's men who clean and oil the bindings. I'll ask him."

"That's not necessary. The box I'm talking about is carved sandalwood. Gramps brought it from India. I'm sure you've seen it on the two-drawer stand at the foot of the brass staircase to the right of the fireplace. Anybody who borrows a book writes the date, title and their name on a slip of paper from a little pad that's next to the box and puts the slip in the sandalwood box. When they return the book, they remove the slip, write that date on it and drop the slip in the top drawer. It's a simple system Gramps devised so he'd know where his books were. He never used it himself." Phil's face lit up. "Aha, Gramps! Mrs. Gillons, go up to my grandfather's apartment and look around. I'll bet you'll find the book in his bedroom." She did.

Though Phil's days and nights became increasingly busy with his own activities, he didn't reduce by a millisecond the time spent caring for his mother. He was talking to her again, prattling really, about inconsequential things. There was no more fantasizing about the future. Nor did he reveal anything about his exercises in Farney's bedroom, undertaken only when Catherine was in a deep post-injection sleep. He also didn't mention the sublime pleasure he experienced observing changes in the landscape from his father's windows after he threw open all draperies in the suite across the balcony. He almost made a slip one day in the midst of a monologue when he heard himself expounding on the brilliance of autumn foliage. Realizing where he was going, and concerned his mother would guess he had uncovered windows, he changed course to quote Thoreau and Frost. In the thrall of his enthusiasm, he couldn't let it go with their poetry. "No words, not even theirs, come close to what it means to actually see our trees changing color." Oops.

With his reawakening came an awareness of the sorry condition of the rooms he lived in. He set about putting them right, brushing away cobwebs, dusting, polishing and vacuuming with supplies and equipment provided by Mrs. Gillons, who insisted he let maids in to do this work, but he said he enjoyed it, felt a sense of accomplishment when everything in his mother's suite gleamed in spite of the perpetual gloom, and sparkled in his father's sun-filled rooms. Pushing a vacuum cleaner around, or the quieter carpet sweeper in Catherine's bedroom, Phil turned menial motion into surreal choreography, dancing to music in his head. His greatest reward came when, just after the outside of the windows in his father's suite had been washed by Oshatakea maintenance men, he washed the inside surfaces with a magical spray sent up by Mrs. Gillons. The resulting crystal-clear view he embraced as his father had, opening his arms to the sky.

November 23 was cold. After Catherine's eight P.M. shot and his second shower of the day, Phil put on his father's heaviest wool robe and moving close to the fireplace in Farney's study sat down to read. Routinely he read until the midnight medication, and then returned to read more, putting out the light minutes before Catherine's four A.M. dose, after which he'd retire to his cot for a few hours' sleep. This was his schedule the night of the twenty-third. After the midnight injection he found a blanket to wrap around his legs, thinking as he settled into the easy chair, that his mother's arm felt cold when he'd tucked it back under her covers. Maybe he'd put an extra blanket on her bed. But then he became absorbed in *Out of Africa*, and was within half-a-dozen pages of finishing when he looked at the clock on Farney's desk. It was 4:20 A.M. His mother should be fussing, but she wasn't. He'd finish the book; it wouldn't take long. The clock chimed the half hour. He jumped up, turned off the light and, still wrapped in the blanket, crossed the balcony. Catherine's eyes were open, but she didn't notice him when he hurried past to prepare her shot. Returning, syringe in hand, he said, "Sorry I'm late. Blame Isak Dinesen, she had hold of me and wouldn't let go." He pulled the covers back to raise his mother's arm. It was colder than before and stiff. He placed his hand on her forehead. "Mother? Mother can you hear me?"

When Dr. Montrose answered his phone, Phil said in a calm voice, "I think my mother is dead." While waiting for the doctor to come, Phil tried to close her eyes, remembering his regret that he had not closed his father's, but Catherine's would not be closed.

Did she call out and he did not hear her? Could he have given her too much morphine at midnight? Or too little? He was positive he had done neither.

No greetings were exchanged, no questions asked. The doctor's examination was cursory and conducted without comment. Stepping back, he lifted the coverlet over Catherine's face. "Don't do that," Phil said. Montrose sucked his teeth, put his stethoscope into his black leather bag, snapped it shut and left the room. Phil followed him out into the hall. "I guess I won't be seeing you again."

"Probably not," Montrose said going down the stairs.

"I can't say I'm sorry." Phil was several steps behind him.

"Nor I." The doctor was approaching the porte cochere door.

"As surely as she killed my father, you killed my mother, and I helped you."

Montrose stopped. "Think what you will, but be careful what you say. People in the valley know you are deeply disturbed."

"Are you threatening to have me committed, the way you threatened my mother?"

"I am advising you to consider consequences before you speak." Montrose stepped out onto the granite steps.

"And you, doctor, you be careful what you do. I am not alone in knowing your methods." Phil stood under the portico as the little German car jerked when shifted and, crunching the graveled drive disappeared around Oshatakea's south front.

There was no snow, but the lawn was white with frost. Stars were fading. Inside, Phil walked the length of the Portuguese Wing's front hall and Step Gallery, flicking light switches. Colors in the Impressionist paintings were more vibrant than he remembered. At the top of the gallery, he grasped iron circle handles that responded to his tug with only a modest squeal as the ancient and heavy olivewood doors swung toward him. The Stone Corridor was a black tunnel until he turned on electrified lanterns hanging from the apex of ceiling groins. Bare feet made no sound as he crossed into the Galleried Library where he lit two standing lamps that formed yellow pools for him to wade through. He went to his grandfather's chair, the seat his mother had assumed the day old man Hunnewell revealed the contents of FP's trusts, and looked up at Gramps's portrait hanging above the mantel. Shivering, wishing he'd brought the blanket, he continued his journey, leaving the library through doors under the marble landing. The Great Hall was filled with a milky mist, a combination of waning moon and coming dawn. Peter the Great's clock high on the wall bonged the hour of six. Phil entered the Long Gallery, early glimmers of day penetrating the opaque glass ceiling high above. In the Gibbons Room pinkish light slanted through French doors. He did not enter all rooms off the gallery, but in the Chinoiserie he turned on pagoda lamps, in the Belgian he touched dark tapestries, in the crimson-cubed Dorset and the ivory and Delft blue Dutch he just stood and looked. Fresh flowers bloomed in niches and on tables. Mrs. Gillons had understood his desire to keep Oshatakea open.

Thinking he might freeze if he didn't keep moving, he pulled the cord of his robe tighter and hurried along the west loggia, switching on cove lights but looking neither to his right, through a thicket of tubbed citrus trees indoors to topiary outdoors, nor to his left into the libraries. He walked across the north lobby into the Baroque Theatre. No need to turn on lights here though it was stygian black; he knew where he was going and how to get there. Running down the right aisle and up onto the stage, he bumped into the standing rehearsal lamp, but no harm was done. Switched on, the huge bare bulb's glare was harsh.

Phil undid the cord and dropped his father's bathrobe onto the floor. He went to the barre along the back wall and grasped it with heart-pounding ecstasy. After glaciers, blizzards, avalanches and years in deep crevices he had reached the summit. It was at the top, where the air was rarefied, that Mrs. Gillons found him by following his trail of lights through the house. "Thank God! I was scared to death. What are you doing? Who is with your mother?"

Naked and perspiring, Phil stepped away from the barre. "I'm exercising. Mother is dead."

Mrs. Gillons brought her hand to her mouth. "Oh Phil, I am so sorry. Has the doctor been here?"

"Yes."

"Have you notified people? You should have called me."

"I haven't called anybody, and I should, shouldn't I?" Phil bent to retrieve his robe, pulled it across his shoulders and holding the front closed left the theater with Mrs. Gillons hard on his heels.

In the Great Hall now bright with sun they parted, Mrs. Gillons headed for the stairs leading to the kitchen. "Where do you want Adrian to send your breakfast?"

Phil, on his way to the Portuguese Wing, stopped. "Would it be possible for me to have breakfast in the courtyard?" He squinted at Peter's rock crystal clock. "Say in an hour and a half?"

Chapter 40

CATHERINE HAD SNEERED AT THE RITUALS AND CUSTOMS
of death. Death should be dealt with discreetly and with dispatch.
The body must disappear at once, and be seen by no one but
embalmers or cremators. A bereaved relative or friend who
expressed a wish to look one last time upon a loved one's face disgusted her. Civilized survivors did not permit death to interrupt
their lives; they carried on as if nothing had happened once
arrangements were made. That was "how it was done." With no
knowledge of or interest in the why of wakes or how they came to
be, she had labeled them barbaric. Funerals were to be avoided if
possible because they gave clergy an opportunity to proselytize.
Memorial services were acceptable only if the eulogy was brief and
not maudlin; the less said the better. Catherine had accompanied
Farney once to a funeral in the valley, for a dairy farmer who had
served on the academy board and been active in civic affairs. At the
church, she balked when Farney approached the open coffin.
Asked by the widow if she did not want to view dear Charlie,
Catherine's reply became part of her legend: "No thank you. I am
not a cannibal."

In deference to her strongly stated prejudice, Phil decided there
would be no service, not even a concert Adelaide proposed be held
in Catherine's memory. "We'll meet in the undercroft of the

chapel Monday morning at eleven o'clock. Anyone who wants to say something can." He invited Adelaide and Louisa, Isabelle, Miss Eleanor and Loren. George Hunnewell invited himself. Knowing the staff had little regard for his mother, Phil did not invite them. If Bones were here, he would have been included, as would Annie if she hadn't died of emphysema.

On Phil's twenty-sixth birthday, two days after Catherine expired in her sleep, seven mourners plus Günter and Tommy, who opened the crypt and would close it, buried her next to Farney. Phil and Loren helped lower the polished mahogany coffin, unadorned except for a small wreath of waxed magnolia leaves placed there by Phil. As the heavy slate was pushed back over the granite tomb, thudding in place to become once again part of the floor, Isabelle exhaled a deep sigh. Those who heard her thought she was dusting off the last of Catherine, but Isabelle was huffing about the numbers of people who had fought to be asked to Catherine's parties, and now that she was gone, neither note nor posy came from them. What about those whose careers she launched, boosted, supported—where are they? Damn it they owe this woman. Here we pitiful few stand dumb. The bitch made our lives miserable much of the time; she never thought about what anybody else might want, was always bugged about something, but she did a lot of good in the music world.

Louisa was glad the long chapter of Catherine at Oshatakea was ended, and thankful no minister had preached about her being safe in the arms of Jesus. If mean-spirited people go to hell, and if hell is fire and brimstone, Catherine will never be cold again. Why don't they tell the truth at funerals? This man beat his wife and didn't take care of his livestock; for those and other crimes he is roasting on a spit. They'd get more converts if they were honest. Preachers use funerals to hook people when they're most vulnerable, sitting there thinking about their own deaths. They stand up and mouth lies, ignoring what everybody in the church knows about the dead person. If the person was religious, he should be praised for loving God, but if he wasn't, if he was an atheist, I don't want to hear some priest say he's happy over on the other shore. That makes me want to shout, I don't think so.

Adelaide was close to weeping. Catherine had exceptional ability and so many talents. There was nothing she could not do extremely well if she put her mind to it—and if she wanted to. If she didn't, no one could force her. Pour soul, I've never known another as unhappy; she had been poisoned by bitterness. Even so she brought a brilliance to Oshatakea that equaled Grandfather's creation. He knew better than anyone how hard she worked, and recognized what she did, respected her, but she closed her heart to him. Not just to him; she didn't give any of us a chance to love her.

Miss Eleanor was remembering Catherine the first time she had seen her, a mature bride burdened by boredom, who made no attempt to conceal her rancor or contempt. That changed as they explored Venice and Florence and Rome. Miss Eleanor thought that while they'd traveled around the world, the cold hard Catherine was gone for good, but returning across the Pacific, she got worse the closer they came to Oshatakea. By the time they stepped off the train at Fillmore Depot, she might as well have been encased in steel. Dear decent Farney never stopped trying to please her, and she made him suffer. When he went, it was Phil's turn. How he has endured these terrible years I don't know.

Which is what Loren was also wondering. He was seeing his well-loved friend for the first time since Danny was an infant, and now Danny at seven was helping in the diner's kitchen. Loren was both relieved and shaken by Phil appearance. His pallor was to be expected—he'd been cooped up inside—but he looked healthy and seemed to be in good physical shape. His hair wasn't as crazy as rumors reported, but why was he dressed that way? Phil had good clothes; when they were teenagers he was a sharp dresser. Why was he wearing a pair of his father's pants that didn't come close to fitting, held up by a necktie knotted around his waist? And a pink hunting jacket for Pete's sake? Couldn't he find socks and shoes? His mother must be spinning in her box if she knows he is at her funeral barefoot in rubber boots. Loren had not planned to go to lunch at the dacha after the committal, but he changed his mind when he saw Phil's getup. Maybe he could push him into a corner at the Kropotkins' for a private talk about his clothes.

George Hunnewell hoped no one noticed when he shot his cuffs to check his Lucien Picard watch. Joe Wengren had some time ago sent him a paper having to do with Catherine's estate in preparation for this day and he wanted to discuss it before lunch, so he could leave immediately thereafter for an investment conference.

Phil was not thinking. His mind was blank, had been for much of the last two days after his initial, impossible to believe release when he walked through the house without fear he'd not hear his mother if she needed him. He had actually exercised at the barre in the Baroque Theatre and stood at the sideboard in the courtyard drinking orange juice while he uncovered dishes containing a stupefying assortment of good things. Now, he was past feeling loss or the finality he had when he went back upstairs to his mother's body and experienced a sensation of falling from a great height. Sitting with her until Turner's men came, he could not accept she was gone. After they put her in the coffin, he returned and sat with her again. Alone, he tried to accept that he was free to do as he wished. He could go wherever he wanted to go, could resume his life. But acceptance didn't come. He was disoriented and unbalanced, could make simple decisions but nothing more. He went up to his own rooms, a stranger who didn't belong there. That first night he spent beside the closed coffin. Only he and Dr. Montrose would recognize the corpse inside. Catherine's hair, what was left of it, was white and she had shriveled to a fraction of what she had been. The next night, Phil resorted to long showers, taking one after another trying to revive himself, trying to comprehend this crucial moment in his life.

They were waiting for him to move out of the crypt when Isabelle's voice, soft and warm, intimate, not projecting as if she were performing, sang "The Lord's my shepherd, I'll not want. He makes me down to lie in pastures green; He leadeth me the quiet waters by. My soul he doth restore again; and me to wake doth make. Yea, though I walk in death's dark vale, yet will I fear no ill. For thou are with me and thy rod and staff comfort me still. My table thou has furnished in presence of my foes. My head thou dost with oil anoint, and my cup overflows. Goodness and mercy all my life shall surely follow me, and in God's house forevermore, my dwelling place shall be."

Slightly embarrassed by echoing silence when she finished, Isabelle resumed her posture of irreverence. "Somebody had to do something. Catherine was a pain in the ass, but she loved music. What I sang is from a seventeenth century Scottish psalter. Jessie Irvine wrote the melody. Not Catherine's dish at all. She would hate it."

They climbed the stairs to the chapel. Muted conversations commenced as they made their way along the Stone Corridor. In the Great Hall George approach Phil. "I must see you and Miss Eleanor for a few minutes."

"Now?"

"Yes, could we duck into the library? The others can go on, I'll drive the three of us down to the dacha."

Seated at the end of the long refectory table with St. George on his white charger and sword drawn to slay the green dragon towering behind him, George Hunnewell removed an envelope from his suit coat pocket and from the envelope a single sheet of folded paper. "Phil, I have something your mother wrote just before your birth, which she refers to as her will."

"Oh dear," Miss Eleanor said, fingers touching her cheek. "I should not be here for this." She started to rise.

"On the contrary, Miss Eleanor, you must be here." George waited for her to be seated and then continued. "It is a brief document. Catherine wrote it herself, as is evident." He held the paper up first toward Phil and then Miss Eleanor so they could see her handwriting. "She was anticipating your difficult delivery Phil, an unfortunately accurate premonition." Clearing his throat struck his small audience as stagy. " 'I Catherine Dudley Fillmore, being of sufficiently sound mind to know I will not live through the ordeal facing me, declare these few lines to be my last will and testament, nullifying an earlier document signed by me October 15, 1928. My husband, Farnsworth Phillips Fillmore III, has no need for anything I possess, nor will . . . ' " George looked up from the paper. "She left a blank space after the words, 'nor will.' " Again he cleared his throat. "Joe Wengren and I believe the blank space means she did not know what to call the unborn child. She continues, 'If there is a law that says I must leave my husband some portion of my estate, I leave him one dollar to discharge that stupid obligation. Everything else it is within my power and authority to bequeath, I leave to my only friend, Eleanor Gaines. Written by me November 22, 1945, and signed before Alfred Bones and Annie Dingle as witnesses.' " George glanced up. "Catherine's signature is unmistakable."

A muffled cry of distress seeped from Miss Eleanor. "I can't, oh no, I cannot, I absolutely cannot accept. She didn't know what she was doing when she wrote that. She was not herself; she was out of her mind with fear." Miss Eleanor's watery blue eyes pled with Phil to believe her.

George's smile was a smirk. "Miss Eleanor, you will be happy to hear Joe Wengren and I agree completely with what you have just said."

Phil did not hear Miss Eleanor's assessment of his mother's mental state when she wrote her will, nor George's delighted agreement. His blood was pulsing erratically. He was having trouble seeing. To stem increasing dizziness, he forced a fake grin and a hearty, "Fantastic." If he didn't move, he knew he'd fall to the floor. Leaping up, he ran behind George and around the table to pull Miss Eleanor into his arms and a crazy clog, laughing a hollow laugh and repeating, "Fantastic."

"Stop Phil, stop, please stop," she cried.

Phil ceased cavorting, and like a balloon losing its helium eased her back into her chair. George's expression had changed from smug to sour. "From your ridiculous demonstration Phil I take it you accept this document and will not want me to file a challenge on your behalf."

"Right George. Challenge it? I applaud it. This sheet of paper clears the air." He grabbed it from George's hand to read for himself what his mother had written. There the words were in her own hand. He knelt beside the stricken Miss Eleanor. "She wanted you to have everything and she knew what she was doing." He held the will for Miss Eleanor to inspect. "See? That's what she wrote."

"But I don't want anything," Miss Eleanor protested. "Oh, a handkerchief or a pin as a memento, but leaving me everything is wrong. When she wrote this I may have been her only friend, but then you were born into my arms Phil and she would have nothing to do with you. I had to take care of you, your grandfather and I. Your mother thought I betrayed her. She tried to send me back to England and would have if your grandfather hadn't stepped in. She never forgave me." Miss Eleanor's muffled sobs made it difficult for her to go on, but she did. "She forgot she ever wrote this silly will or she would have torn it up."

George slapped the table. "Right on the mark again Miss Eleanor! She also forgot she sent the paper to Joe Wengren. If she thought at all over the years about what would become of her property, she assumed the will signed the day before she married, naming her future husband beneficiary, was in effect. Joe and I think it still is, and so will the probate court. This worthless piece of hysteria, and that's all it is, will be denied. Phil, you are your father's sole heir, and therefore her's."

"Forget it George." Phil stood.

George was stunned by his tone, as cold and implacable as Catherine's. "You do understand, your mother could not alter the beneficiaries in her family trusts. Income from those trusts will now come to you. Joe Wengren and I believe her intention, if she had any real intention at the time she wrote this paper, was for Eleanor Gaines"—he nodded approvingly toward Miss Eleanor—"to have a piece of her jewelry, a pin perhaps, certainly not family pieces that Miss Eleanor understands should rightfully be yours. And she may have wanted Miss Eleanor to have her clothes, odds and ends of furniture, which was all she thought she had to leave, not knowing the house on Mount Vernon Street, the farm in Dover and the North Shore estate became hers outright and unentailed upon the death of her mother. She could do whatever she wished with them, and did eventually sell Mount Vernon Street, then bought the house on Chestnut Street. What I am saying Phil is your mother had the power, though she did not realize it on November 22, 1945, when in her delirium she wrote this note, to bequeath exceedingly valuable real estate. We are not talking now about the trinkets she had in mind." He pointed to Catherine's note.

"So what George?" Phil scoffed. "Miss Eleanor, you own four houses! You can do spring in your cottage here when your garden is at its best, summer on the North Shore, autumn on the farm in Dover and winter on Chestnut Street."

George could no longer tolerate Phil's nonsense. He rose like an Old Testament prophet, intending to intimidate the obstreperous heir. "Sit down. Stop your prancing and listen, we are discussing important financial matters."

Phil's grin vanished. "George, Adelaide is waiting lunch for us. We don't want to be rude. Come along Miss Eleanor." He helped her from her chair as she looked from Phil to George and back again, not knowing what to do. Phil led her toward the Stone Corridor door, where he explained, "I've had a thought. Adelaide can wait."

George, enraged by Phil's behavior and disregard of his attorney's advice, controlled himself sufficiently to demand, "Where are you going?"

"Upstairs to rifle mother's cache of jewels. I don't know the combination to the safe, but I'm sure Miss Eleanor does. We're going to pick out a piece for her to wear to the dacha."

"Oh no," Miss Eleanor pulled back.

"Oh yes," Phil said guiding her through the door. "You must take something that will outdazzle Isabelle's fender. Go on George, Dick Fallon can drive us down."

At lunch, Phil laughed as if all present were competing in a contest for best storyteller and he was cheerleader. Wary of his peculiar behavior, conversations were muted and halting because nobody wanted to speak if whatever was said would be followed by a donkey bray. When Boris moved to replenish wine in the glass Phil had emptied, Adelaide shook her head, but before Boris could pull the bottle back, Phil took hold of his sleeve and hissed, "Just a drop." Boris half-filled the glass that Phil then raised toward his unhappy hostess.

George glowered. He had arrived at the dacha before Phil and Miss Eleanor but did not mention the dustup in the Galleried Library, so when the two late guests joined the others in the conservatory for an aperitif, Louisa asked where they had been. "Miss Eleanor couldn't wait to get her hands on the loot," Phil cracked, pulling Miss Eleanor's hand away from her shoulder where a sapphire and diamond brooch was pinned to her blue silk dress. Watching for her reaction Phil thought Isabelle's eyes would pop out of their sockets and roll down her rouged cheeks. No one was amused by his attempt at humor, Miss Eleanor least of all. "Please, no more gratuitous remarks, you have caused quite enough havoc for one day." These were the only words spoken during the next hour that didn't send him into fits of fake laughter.

Though curious about the brooch and appalled by Phil's display, the Kropotkins and Isabelle could not ask questions in front of George Hunnewell. They would not learn of Catherine's will until the men were gone and Miss Eleanor was forced to reveal all, begging them to tell her how to handle the burden placed on her by that handwritten document.

At lunch, Phil didn't mind George glowering but was upset that Loren was staring at him. When Adelaide rose to take her guests to the drawing room for coffee, Loren said he could not stay. "I'm sorry, I have to get back to the diner." If Loren wasn't going to be there, Phil would make a bigger fool of himself than he had already. Without offering an excuse, he followed Loren out of the dacha, asking, "Will you drop me off?"

George was right behind him. "I'll drive you up to the house."

"No thanks," Phil said, providing one more reason for George to want to seriously maim his sole client. He expressed his anger by slamming the door of his gray Mercedes and roaring off through the birch grove without a wave or a nod good bye. "I don't really want a ride," Phil said, standing next to Loren's Chevrolet. "I just had to get out of there."

"Jump in, we'll talk."

"I want to walk through the woods."

Loren hesitated as if he had something important to say, then thought better of it. "Let me know when you're ready." He put his hand out.

Phil grabbed it and held on. He thought he was going to cry. Why cry now? He hadn't cried since his dad died. He dropped Loren's hand as if it were on fire.

"Tomorrow is meat loaf day at the diner," Loren said.

"I'll try to make it down."

"Do more than try Phil, be there."

Remnants of that morning's snow flurries lay frozen on the ground, crunching like Rice Krispies under Phil's feet. A harsh wind moved the trees and undergrowth, piercing his father's pink hunting jacket, nipping his bare ankles deep in rubber boots and making sounds that brought to mind Marian Anderson singing the song that gave him nightmares as a child. It was about an earl king chasing somebody through the woods. He had been so frightened, he could remember and hear the words: "Mein vater, mein vater, und horset du nicht. Was Erlenkonig mir leise verspricht?" Swaying branches overhead were black against the lowering sky. He wished he had accepted Loren's offer of a ride. By the time he closed the south front door, he was congealed, his face stiff, his hands blue, legs covered with goose bumps. Chills rippled around his shivering torso.

The house was empty. Mrs. Gillons had sent everybody home. He stood in the middle of the Great Hall. Why had he left the dacha so abruptly? He could be in front of a fire stuffing himself with Adelaide's Belgian chocolates. After lunch, in the drawing room, is probably when they were going to mention his birthday. He'd told Adrian not to do anything about it because he thought Adelaide would. The hell with birthdays. He wasn't with others in front of a fire; he was freezing alone in a vast empty space without a clue as to what to do next. He had to leave when he did because if he'd stayed another minute he'd have started screaming. He left with Loren, not because Loren was his buddy but because Loren was being quiet and Phil needed quiet. After years of living with nothing louder than his mother's labored breathing, he was assaulted in Adelaide's dining room by voices, silver clattering on china, rings clicking against crystal. He behaved as he did because he was being driven mad.

The only sound in the Great Hall was the heavy ticking of Peter's rock crystal clock. Phil turned to look, speculating on what Heinie Fiske went through once a week to wind it. Heinie, Oshatakea's clock winder, had to drag a ladder from somewhere, climb halfway up the wall, wind the clock and climb back down again, a daunting task for a man his age, and then put the ladder away, plodding on to wind clocks in other rooms. Phil doubted he had the patience to be a clock winder. What a boring job. Heinie didn't even fix clocks if they didn't keep time; a specialist in maintenance did that.

Drafts blowing from corridors and galleries across the Great Hall weren't helping Phil's freezing feet. If he stood much longer he'd turn into an ice sculpture. He walked under the marble landing toward the library, stopping at the power grid in a closet beneath the stairs to pull a master switch and was psychologically warmed by the display of sconces glittering on walls up to the dome. His mother hated those sconces, said they made the Great Hall look like the Paris Opera, which Dad said was precisely the effect Gramps wanted. Phil liked them.

It was impossible to turn on enough lamps to eliminate shadows in the Galleried Library. Shadows didn't bother him, but in his present mood dark corners did. Dull late November dusk filtering through the St. George window gave the white stallion an appearance of floating in a gem-filled sea as the emerald dragon spewed flames from below. His gut felt as if the dragon were inside him. It wasn't the altercation with George Hunnewell gnawing at him; it was his mother's will. He had forgiven her cruelty, tried to forget all the mean miserable things she had done to him and his father, but with a handwritten note she reached out from before he was born and slammed him one more time. He was glad she had left everything to Miss Eleanor. Miss Eleanor deserved it after putting up with her all those years. He didn't want, didn't need anything, not even something to help him remember her—"But Jesus Christ, I am not a blank space." She had written that her husband didn't need anything, "nor will" and then a blank space. "The blank space is me. I'm a blank space. To you I was nothing." He walked under the dragon window. Couldn't she have written my child? Slapping the table, he shouted, "God damn it to hell—if that's where you are you blistering bitch—I am not a blank space." He unclenched his fists and swiped at his eyes. "Your husband didn't need anything, nor will blank space. This nothing needed you. You were my mother Catherine Dudley Fillmore."

He rubbed his hands together to warm them. She wrote that paper before he was born; he shouldn't be so upset. She'd told him often enough he almost killed her. "You hated me for being ass-backward, what did you call it? A breech presentation, that was it." He could understand how she felt at the time, but later, when she was well again, couldn't she have written a new will? He wouldn't care if she had written, I don't want my ass-backward son Farnsworth Phillips Fillmore IV to have a thing that was mine because of all the suffering he caused me. If she'd written that, he would have laughed when George read the will. At least she would have acknowledged his existence.

George said she didn't remember the handwritten will; George is an idiot. Catherine was an elephant when it came to remembering, relishing every slight, real or imagined, every mistake anybody made, and everything she ever said. "I told you so" was her favorite comment on bad news. "I hope whoever is in charge of remembering in hell is the one throwing logs on the fire."

"No I don't," he sobbed.

Being consumed with rage was a Catherine Dudley trait. She had left him something after all. He threw his head back, looking toward the ceiling that had all but disappeared in the dark, and whispered, "You lose Mother. I, your blank space, do not accept your legacy. I will not be bitter, and starting right this minute I am going to forget you. I swear to God I am going to forget you ever lived."

He had to find a bed.

MRS. GILLONS PRESUMED PHIL WOULD EVENTUALLY USE his father's suite, having spent so much time in it. She offered to remove Farney's clothes and replace them with Phil's, thus putting an end to his eccentric attire, but Phil stopped her. He said he had no intention of living in the Portuguese Wing. Despite having lived there his entire life, the main part of Oshatakea, Gramps's house, was his real home. He stepped off the birdcage elevator into the Moorish foyer of FP's apartment and was enveloped in the combined aromas of bay rum, sandalwood, lemon-scented furniture polish and other scents too exotic to identify. It was returning to a happier time. Considering how long Gramps had been gone, he wondered if the aromas were real or tricks of memory, but then he heard water trickling into a shallow mosaic basin in a little round pool in the oriel. That remembered sound was real. No question.

So pleased was he by how much better he felt as he clicked on lamps, he gave way to the grandiose notion that his immediate mission would be to reilluminate not just the Great Hall but every room on all floors, turning Oshatakea into a beacon shining across the valley, the way it was when the house was filled with people and music. That's how he would let everyone know life had returned to this, his house. "There will be no more darkness," he told his reflection in a mottled mirror hanging between archways of carved plaster. Gramps's apartment contained choice Iberian architectural artifacts, the only Spanish rooms completed at Oshatakea. An elaborate stone fireplace and mantel anchored one end of the living room, opposite glass doors with iron-filigreed screens at the far end that opened onto the long terrace atop the Stone Corridor roof. Bookcases and chestnut paneling surrounded smaller fireplaces in the study and bedroom. Here, in his private quarters, FP forswore strict adherence to period and style, furnishing the rooms with a hodgepodge of objects because he wanted these particular pieces near at hand. Japanese screens, Grecian urns, Persian rugs, Chinese blue and white porcelain, Hindu deities, Russian icons, Yoruba masks, cloisonné, pre-Columbian ollas crowded the apartment. Hanging on the walls were paintings by Copley, Homer, Eakins and Peale as well as framed sketches and studies FP didn't think fit in downstairs.

In his bedroom an early eighteenth-century American chest on chest that had belonged to Thomas Fillmore shared space with a massive hooded bamboo carrying chair from Ceylon and, on a raised platform, a monumental lacquered six-post Chinese ceremonial bed with pomegranates and lotuses in its fretwork. Books were everywhere, on shelves and tables, the floor, stacked along the edges of ebony steps used to climb into the high bed. In its disarray, the apartment looked as if the person who lived in it had stepped out but would return shortly. Undisturbed, but cleaned and aired, though uninhabited for two decades the rooms were not musty but fresh.

Phil lighted the bedroom fireplace, picked up a book Gramps had left on a nearby table, crawled between posts into the great bed and pulled a fur robe over himself.

Chapter 41

—

THERE WAS MUCH HEAD SHAKING BY MEMBERS OF THE staff and the four women who made up Phil's family. No one could understand why he slept in his grandfather's bed and went way over to the Portuguese Wing to shower when there was a perfectly good shower off FP's bedroom. And why was he continuing to wear Farney's clothes now that his own were accessible? His daily schedule didn't make sense either. He was up long before staff arrived at Oshatakea. Doing what? He ate breakfast in the Portuguese Courtyard. Why? If he was living in his grandfather's apartment, wouldn't it be easier to have breakfast in FP's breakfast room? He lunched at Loren's Diner, then spent afternoons doing not much of anything, as far as the worriers could tell. His dinner routine was most ridiculous. You couldn't really call it dinner. Adrian told them he dined sitting on a stool at a butcher-block worktable in the kitchen. Truth to tell, which Adrian didn't know, Phil seldom sat; he stood at the refrigerator's open door and picked. If Adrian left a cold roast, Phil moved it to the butcher block for slicing, then stood between the worktable and the refrigerator reaching in both directions. He preferred cold chicken or turkey, pheasant, grouse, partridge, any fowl because he could pull the carcasses apart without resorting to cutlery, and he was partial to raw vegetables. When queried about his dining habits, he said, "I eat a big lunch. I'm not hungry at dinner time." The real reason was his wanting to be free to eat at night when the spirit moved him. He kept to a tight schedule for breakfast, seven o'clock sharp after an hour of exercises at the barre back stage, followed by a shave and quick shower, and he walked into the diner for lunch on the stroke of twelve. Why should he be punctilious for his third meal of the day? When he was hungry he descended to the kitchens and ate, sometimes as early as six or seven; more often not until midnight. Sometimes he didn't go down at all.

Except for his standup third meal, his daily routine was quite regular. Between breakfast and lunch he walked the grounds adapting Gramps's philosophy about rooms dying if they aren't lived in to the outside of Oshatakea. Several times a week, he stopped at the stables to check on Farney's horses and talk with the men who cared for them. As before, when it was too wet to be outside, he walked corridors instead of paths. All of this reassured him that he was taking care of Oshatakea, as Gramps would want him to. He seldom ventured into Hester's drawing rooms, which he found as funereal as FP had, or into the Portuguese Wing except for the courtyard, where he had breakfast, and his father's suite, where he showered and dressed. Occasionally he went to the upper reaches of the house, on the staff floor and into the attics. Up there he had an eerie feeling he had disturbed someone, sensed he had come into a room still warm from a recently departed presence.

No matter where he was on his walks, with the instinct of a homing pigeon he turned at a properly timed moment and headed downhill toward the village, his exactitude a phenomenon that brought people to windows, visitors to the town who were fascinated by tales of the exotic millionaire. Phil barely acknowledged greetings on his way to lunch. Those who wanted a word with him had better luck when he started back up the hill at half past one. Though never irascible or churlish, he was not at ease except when he was in the diner. He tried to forget but, like Catherine, had an elephant's memory. Many who called out to him as friendly or fawning adults had harassed him as teenagers. Following Catherine's death his carriage-shed phobia was complicated by knowing that many believed he had killed his mother. He believed that himself. He hadn't smothered her as some said, but he caved in to the doctor's regimen of morphine. Fear played no part in his elusiveness; he was wary, as a wounded deer is wary.

Loren was again his solid rock. Phil's hour and a half at the diner every day but Sunday provided pleasure as well as sustenance, and he loved being with Danny. Loren's precocious son knew he wanted to be a chef from the time he was a toddler running around the kitchen. He began cooking when he had to stand on a box to reach the stovetop. At age nine, with an earned reputation for the lightness of his omelets, Danny begged his father to let him stay out of school and cook full time. "Graduate first," Loren said. "I'd like you to go to college, but if you'd rather cook when that time comes, you can."

Phil took Danny's side. "What good did graduating do you or me? Let the kid cook. He's a natural." Loren told Phil to back off, and he did for a few years, but when Danny graduated from the academy at age sixteen, Phil persuaded Loren the boy should go to Paris. "He wants to study at Le Cordon Bleu. You promised him he could cook if he finished school." George Hunnewell made arrangements and paid Danny's expenses following Phil's instructions, including an allowance sufficient to cover the cost of meals in fine restaurants. Both Loren and Danny protested, but Phil brushed them off. "Supporting Danny's culinary education may be my only claim to fame."

While Danny was being taught haute cuisine from master chefs and gourmet dining in Paris, Phil was assiduously pursuing dance. He wanted to float and fly as ballet dancers did, and stretch and retract, contract and release, reach out and pull back as he'd seen modern dancers do. He wanted to leap, fall to earth and recover. Everything he did was based on his memory of the few hours Martha Graham had spent with him and the many hours he'd watched her and other dance companies rehearse and perform. He had prepared himself by slavishly developing what he heard dancers call their "instrument." His trunk was firm, toned but resilient; his arms and legs supple and sinewy. To the best of his knowledge, he had perfected barre and floor exercises. Now it was time for him to make a dance. How to begin?

Phil spent afternoons listening to records played on the big, old Capehart in the Galleried Library. Those that had any possibility of suiting his purpose he set to one side. Rejections were returned to the shelves. In addition to the quantity Gramps had accumulated before he died, plus his mother's collection brought over from the Portuguese Wing, there were stacks of unopened packages from Sam Goody containing hundreds more. These were from Catherine's never canceled standing order with the New York music store for new recordings in specified categories. Phil had a wonderful time opening and sorting through this uncharted cache, but after a while he worried he'd never catch up as more arrived. He asked Fisher Ames for an assistant librarian to sort, catalogue and shelve new acquisitions during the mornings before Phil went to the library to listen.

When the staff left late afternoon and he had Oshatakea to himself, he began experimenting, at first simply moving about the library, improvising to the music, responding to rhythm and beat, keeping time, incorporating steps and figures he knew, waltz, gallop, polka. Comfortable with that, he forced himself not just to listen but to hear harmonies, shifts in tempo and key, to become conscious of mood. Then—and this took months—he went from doing whatever he felt like doing at any given moment to trying to establish patterns, repeating exactly what he had done before when he danced to those particular phrases of music, and then repeating them again and again until they were set in his head. Transitions came next, and they were difficult. Letting yourself go, freewheeling, turning, running, jumping as the spirit moves you, is exhilarating and easy, but it isn't dancing. Part of the thrill watching Graham's dancers rehearse was their striving to belie the impression that they were following a set design, each motion activated not by memory but by music heard for the first time. As actual performance time approached the movements were so much theirs, it was not the music inspiring them; rather, they inspired the music. Phil could only begin to imagine what they must feel when they succeeded in convincing an audience of this. He wanted that feeling, but without an audience. The thought of being watched made him sick to his stomach. He had once been expected to perform before an audience, albeit unseen and unknown until they jeered. That experience scarred his psyche. He would never dance for anyone and risk their derision. He didn't need cheers or applause. All he wanted was the bliss of dancing. Dreading jeers and laughter, he danced only when he was alone in the house.

Phil began his creative attempts in the Galleried Library, repeating specific movements to music played on the Capehart. As his efforts expanded he needed more space. He turned up the volume and moved out into the Great Hall, but this wasn't a satisfactory solution. Because of his repetition of passages and motions, he needed close access to the record player. Almost more important, he had to be surrounded by the music and not hear it from afar. Moving the Capehart into the Great Hall wasn't impossible, but everyone would want to know why. Phil pondered installing a sound system in the Baroque Theatre, but he couldn't think of a good reason to give George, who would have to pay for it. Lying awake in Gramps's bed, Phil hit on a solution. At a quarter to five in the morning he called Hunnewell at home. George was annoyed but listened.

"George, do you know about Gramps's belief that rooms die if they aren't lived in?" Phil asked. "Well I believe that too, and I have a lot of rooms to live in. I don't mind, but I want music wherever I am, and the only place I can play records is in the Galleried Library. What I need is an up-to-date sound system installed in the Great Hall with speakers there and in the Long Gallery, so I can hear wherever I am. A storage room under the landing could be used for the equipment."

Phil nearly fell out of Gramps's bed when George replied, "I'll send a sound engineer down. Tell him what you want."

"Goddamn, thank you George."

"Phil, the next time you want something, please do not call me so early in the morning."

Phil was emboldened to go further. "As long as I have you on the telephone, the lighting in the Great Hall needs adjustment. I'm neither as tight as my mother nor as extravagant as my grandfather. I'd like more options than turning on every light or walking around in the dark. Send an electrical engineer down to look into that." George said he would.

Before all this was accomplished, late one night while Phil was still playing a record on the Capehart, leaving the library doors open and dancing in the hall, he heard a single clap from far above when he finished a piece. "Who's there?" he shouted, his heart pounding from fright and rage. Scanning the balconies and landing he detected no sign, nor was there another sound.

No one was supposed to be in the house after six. He didn't tell Mrs. Gillons he was dancing, just said he was in the Great Hall when he heard a noise from above. If anyone had stayed in the house, or came back after they'd left for the day, he wanted that person fired. Mrs. Gillons interrogated the entire staff and reported back to him that no one had been in the house after six. If he'd been spied on, Phil knew his dancing would become instant gossip throughout the valley, making him yet again the object of ridicule. He holed up in his apartment, not speaking to anyone. Loren telephoned to see if he was all right when he didn't appear for lunch, but Phil would not take his call. Nor would he talk to

Miss Eleanor when Mrs. Gillons asked her to speak with him. No one could understand why a noise from above was so disturbing to him. If he wasn't afraid to stay in the house all by himself at night, why should something that might very well be his imagination or maybe a mouse drive him to ground this way?

It was Mrs. Gillons's comment when she stalked unbidden into his bedroom that the showers in the house were in working order and he'd better use one soon that broke the spell. For all his anger and worry, Phil didn't want to revert to what he'd once been when locked in with his mother. "Are you telling me I smell?"

"I am. Take a shower and put on clean clothes. I'd suggest you leave your father's in his closet and wear your own, but I don't want you to think me rude." Phil tried to not laugh. No-nonsense Mrs. Gillons had saved him before and she was doing it again.

There were no more claps in the Great Hall, though Phil sensed a presence. If it was Pearl watching from above, she didn't bother him. He would keep her secret, if she kept his.

PART THREE: *Sylvia*

Chapter 42

LOREN SHOWED PHIL A METROPOLITAN NEWSPAPER whose headline screamed NAKED MILLIONAIRE CAPTURES DANGEROUS KILLER. The story began, "Reliable sources report Farnsworth P. Fillmore IV was awakened in the middle of the night by James Whittemore, an escapee from the state prison's criminally insane unit who had been incarcerated for murdering his parents. The unclad heir to the Fillmore fortune chased Whittemore through his mansion, and in the great hall wrestled the intruder to the floor, holding him captive until the police arrived."

"His name is James Whittemore," Phil said.

"Is that what happened?"

"Not quite."

"The paper says he went into a rage and stabbed his parents to death when they would not come to the aid of his older brother who was suffering an epileptic seizure. The next-door neighbor found the mother and father in pools of blood. This guy was on the floor holding his dead brother in his arms. Gruesome."

"I want to help him."

"Help him? He's a murderer Phil, he could have killed you."

"He's a kid, younger than Danny, and he needs help."

George told Phil, "Forget Whittemore. Be grateful you are alive."

But Phil couldn't forget. "We're going to do something for that man George. He doesn't have anybody. If you won't look into it, I will."

JERROLD CLEWES AND COMPANY BOOKED FOURTEEN OF the sixteen rooms at the Fillmore Inn. Five appraisers had to rent rooms in private homes, reigniting George Hunnewell's extreme annoyance with Phil. All had breakfast at the Inn before being picked up by Oshatakea cars, making the aging Dick Fallon happy to be doing something at last. Because both George and Clewes were anxious about the warehouse contents following Phil's admission that he'd let people remove things, all except two of the appraisers began their evaluation of what Phil considered his personal possessions and George called inventory in the long buildings beside the river. It would be several months before George was informed that Phil's open-door policy had not resulted in major losses. Mostly chairs, tables, beds and bureaus were taken, and many of those came back, all transactions duly noted on cards kept for each item. Clewes was amused by the irony that loaned pieces were primarily American in origin, furniture used by earlier generations of Fillmores and consigned to warehouses when FP had filled Oshatakea with his acquisitions from Europe and Asia. How could the savvy old man have predicted the soaring market for American antiques? He was also astounded by the quality of what he found throughout the warehouses and the generally excellent condition; thousands of items, from entire disassembled rooms to moon gates, columns, capitals, doors, tapestries, sculptures, and paintings, covering numerous periods and styles. There was a glut of decorative arts from around the globe. Each piece was numbered, catalogued and stored in marked bins. FP had taken care not to cram his excess treasure in too tight spaces, treating each with the concern and expertise of a professional curator. FP's fabled storehouses exceeded Clewes expectations.

The two appraisers who did not go to the warehouses each morning, Sam Wilson and his assistant Harriet Cooke, were driven to Oshatakea to appraise the libraries. In physical appearance and personality, it would be difficult to conjure a more unlikely pair. Sam, of African descent, was tall, distinguished in manner and attitude, a man of thoughtful demeanor in his late thirties with prematurely graying hair who wore three-piece suits. An easy smile saved him from being forbidding. Harriet was short, stocky and effervescent, a woman literally busting out all over. Too-tight skirts in primary colors rode high on Rubenesque thighs and matching jackets could not be buttoned over ballooning breasts. Blind without contact lenses, she carried in her purse spare sets in different shades to color-coordinate with her suits. Sam said little. Harriet talked incessantly. His chuckles let her know she was not being ignored. She dictated information into a small tape recorder for later transcription. Sam made notes on a legal pad.

Jerrold Clewes' complete corps of appraisers had been presented to Phil on their arrival at a Sunday afternoon reception and tour of Oshatakea organized by George Hunnewell. The whole thing put Phil in such a grump he made a point of not remembering names or registering areas of expertise. Becoming familiar with these interlopers would only increase the misery brought on by their presence. Sam and Harriet started in the Galleried Library the morning after the reception and were working there when he came to listen to records after lunch. He would not be put out of his own space, and they could not be persuaded to go elsewhere. Gregarious Harriet regarded the eccentric owner of Oshatakea as a challenge. Without missing a beat, she redirected her steady flow of remarks toward Phil, who just stood there. He hadn't engaged in repartee for so long he was unable to reply. That state of being struck dumb would have made him leave the room if he hadn't been fascinated by Sam. Phil had never known anyone quite like this man. It wasn't the rich color of his skin, but his quiet manner and the formality of his attire—suit, shirt, necktie and polished cordovans. Yet Sam was relaxed, couldn't have been more laid back if he were wearing fatigues. When Phil told him Oshatakea wasn't a bank, that he didn't need to wear a suit to work, Sam said he'd gotten into the habit of a jacket and tie at Exeter, and wasn't comfortable in sport clothes on the job.

"No comments on my clothes please," Harriet quipped. "I don't give a damn what anybody thinks about what I wear." Her green eyes panned Phil from the top of his head down to his floppy sandals. "Am I alone in that?"

Phil grinned, but was embarrassed. He hadn't thought about Harriet's clothes; he was just trying to tell Sam not to dress up as if he were in an office every day. Harriet rescued him with a cackle.

"Why don't we settle on, to each his own?" Sam said.

This kind of silly session gradually included Phil in the kinship that existed between Sam and Harriet. He grew fond of them both and didn't mind at all having them in the house. Even so, he could not listen to his records while they were working. He could go off and do something else, but Sam's remarks about the books he was appraising intrigued him. Behind Sam's flashy smile and easy laugh was a formidable breadth of knowledge. "I wish you had known my grandfather," Phil said. "He handled a book the same way you do."

"I'm sorry I didn't. By these books, I can tell he was an unusual person."

"He was."

Phil's morning schedule remained fixed. He exercised on the stage of the Baroque Theatre early, walked the grounds and headed for the Peasant Palate at the proper time. As Phil trotted down the hill, Oshatakea cars were bringing Clewes's people up Ontyakah Road for lunch. Phil had assumed they would eat with the household, but Adrian, excited to have more sophisticated palates to feed, said that wouldn't work because the two groups would be eating different meals. Noon meant meat-and-potatoes midday dinner to Oshatakea staff when appraisers from New York would want lunch. The appraisers ate from a buffet in the Double Cube Room.

Sam and Harriet finished the Galleried Library and moved to the French Library off the West Loggia about the same time Clewes and the other appraisers completed the warehouses and came up to start on Oshatakea. An unexpectedly happy period ended for Phil when the house became a disconcerting bustle of noise and confusion. Appraisers overran the place with Dictaphones, Xerox machines, X-ray and infrared equipment and rolling racks of FP's original inventory records, going about their business accompanied by relentless commentary that included disagreements about attribution, authenticity and current value, punctuated by Clewes's cries and exclamations, "Oh God, would you look at this, the mate to it is in the Victoria and Albert." Or, "I have never seen a finer example of this." Oshatakea was a hive of frenetic bees. Phil thought he would lose his mind when he sought refuge in his apartment and found them busy up there as well. He tried filling idle hours with Taurus, grooming him until the stallion's normally calm disposition cracked. "Why is he so crazy today?" Phil asked as Taurus pawed and whinnied.

"An old mare's in heat and he wants at her. It's not normal for a stallion with a full set of balls to behave like a gelding."

Phil stopped brushing and looked at the stable man, whose comment Phil took as a jab at him. The stable man wasn't talking about Taurus; he was implying Phil wasn't normal because he had a full set of balls and didn't use them. Phil wanted to yell: for all you know you jackass, I could be fucking every woman in the valley. He didn't because if he were fucking anybody, the stable man and everybody else for miles around would know who, where and how often.

Clewes and Company departed Friday afternoons to fly to New

York City for weekends with their families, returning on Sunday. Since the occupation began, Phil lived for Fridays, saturating himself while they were away with music played at maximum volume. He wasn't sure he'd make it until the invaders were gone for good. The sole exception was Sam. He'd be sorry to see Sam go. Fisher Ames had told George Hunnewell, that he would retire when the book appraisal was complete. If he meant what he said, Phil wondered if Sam might consider succeeding him as Oshatakea librarian?

When he shared these thoughts with Loren, describing Sam's stellar qualifications in detail, Loren said, "You sound like a schoolboy with a crush."

"I haven't got a crush. Sam is a wake-up call. He's better than any teacher you and I ever had. My brain goes into overdrive when he's talking and I hear myself saying things I didn't know I knew."

"If he's so great, how come he's playing with old books, why isn't he teaching in a college somewhere?"

"Books are his life Loren, you should see him with them. You'd like him. I'll bring him down for lunch."

"Has he told you about his girlfriend?"

"He's married."

"Was. And what has being married got to do with anything? You think these guys don't play around when they're away from home?"

"Who?"

"Who?"

"Who is his girlfriend?"

"Britt Benson."

"Billy Benson's widow? She never looked at anybody but Billy, and he was killed in Vietnam."

"You're right, she never did—until your friend Sam came along. They say she finds him exotic. I think 'erotic' is the word."

"Britt is a good person."

"Did I say she isn't?"

It hadn't occurred to Phil that Sam might have a life in Fillmore outside the libraries at Oshatakea. "Would you join me for lunch at the diner?" he asked Sam. "I walk or jog down and back. You can't do that in dress shoes. Wear sneakers, if you have sneakers."

"I have sneakers, and I jog every night before dinner."

"Not in those clothes I hope."

Sam's smile was broad. "Phil, one of these days I'm going to surprise you."

Sam and Loren clicked, which relieved Phil because he thought Loren acted jealous when he talked about Sam. Danny came out from the kitchen to be introduced and thought he'd died and gone to heaven when Sam started talking to him in French. Except for occasional conversations with Giselle or Lucile, Danny had no chance to use the patois he'd learned in the streets of Paris.

"You and your wife must be proud of him," Sam said when Danny went back to cooking. Without going into the whole story, Loren explained he was not married and Danny's mother hadn't seen him since he was born, but yes, he was proud of him. "Forgive me, I should know better than to presume. I'm divorced and have a twelve-year-old son, Sammy. Like Danny, he has talent, not as a chef or linguist, but he sings like a wicked angel, dances and paints. Mostly he is out of control. If he doesn't cool his jets he's headed for big trouble." Sam laughed while he recounted his son's assets and liabilities.

"Where is he?"

"In New York with his mother. Her name is Sylvia. She and I are good friends. We just married too young. I was a graduate student and she was studying dance at Sarah Lawrence. She's a fine dancer, that's where Sammy gets his talent. She's also a wonderful mother." Sam laughed his easy laugh. "I'm doing this Oshatakea appraisal because Sylvia pushed me. This is where her Seneca ancestors lived. She has been out here a couple of times and thinks the Fillmore Valley is paradise."

"Oh?" Loren and Phil asked in unison.

"She's descended from the man in the statue with Thomas Fillmore up at Oshatakea."

"Gahah?" Phil asked, incredulous.

"That's right."

"Why haven't you told me this?" Phil wanted more information about Sam's wife and Gahah, but Loren was too fast for him.

"Do you spend much time with your son?"

"Sylvia and I have joint custody. He spends a week with me, then a week with her. Both of us live close to his school so he can walk from either place. Now that I'm out here during the week, I have him on weekends when I go home, but that's not enough, I miss him."

Jerrold Clewes made no effort to conceal his envy that Phil had chosen Sam Wilson to befriend. He would have liked to brag that he and Phil Fillmore were buddies, and he was eager to lunch at the Peasant Palate. A wandering reviewer had written, "If the Peasant Palate were in France, Michelin would give it a minimum of two stars." Adrian's buffets were excellent, Clewes had no complaints, but he doubted they'd merit Michelin stars.

On a Monday following Sam's weekend in New York, as he and Phil were jogging down the hill to lunch, Phil said, "You are very quiet. Is something wrong?"

"Sylvia has an opportunity to tour Russia with the Alvin Ailey dance company. She's dying to go, but if she accepts she'll be away almost three months, which wouldn't be a problem if I were in the city to take care of Sammy. I want her to go but I also want to finish this job. I'll never have another crack at a collection of this caliber."

"Bring Sammy here."

"I've thought of that, but I'm not sure I can talk him into it. He's involved in a mess of activities at school and the streets of New York are his native habitat. If I can persuade him, which is a big if, do you think the Fillmore Academy would admit him for a single semester? He could share my room at the Inn."

"I'm chairman of the board of trustees, not that I do anything. George Hunnewell sits in for me, but be assured, getting Sammy into the academy is a cinch."

Sammy reluctantly agreed to the move after Sylvia described the Fillmore Valley and told him what she knew of Oshatakea. "If you go, you can research our Seneca ancestors."

Chapter 43

"WE'RE STARTING OUT FRESH, RIGHT? I MEAN, YOU don't know me and we're not related, so tell me what you want me to call you and I'll tell you what I want you to call me. Legally, I'm Samuel Marcus Wilson III. My grandfather Samuel is a judge. My father, Sam, you know. They stuck me with Sammy, I hate Sammy; it's nowhere. The only thing worse would be Sambo, so I came up with JJ. Before you ask what JJ stands for, I'll tell you. JJ are initials for Jasper Jamison. Nobody would want to be called that either, but I like the sound of JJ. Call me JJ."

"I haven't listened to a lecture that long since my grandfather died."

"What's a lecture?"

"An enlightening explanation. You told me why you want to be called JJ, now I understand. Call me Phil." They shook hands.

"Dad says you are legally Farnsworth Fillmore Phillips IV. That's a drag. I thought being a third was bad. I'm not going to stick numbers onto what I name my kids. Samuel Marcus stops with me."

"I agree."

"How many kids do you have?"

"I'm not married."

"You don't have to be married to make babies."

"I know."

"I'm an only child."

"So am I."

"It's supposed to be the pits, being an only, but I can't complain." The honey-colored boy with the bright eyes and a mouth that, according to his father, never stopped running, changed the subject. "I asked Dad how many rooms in this house. He said he didn't know."

"Neither do I."

"How can you live in a house and not know how many rooms it has?"

"I guess I never thought about it."

"Can I count them?"

"I don't know, can you?"

"You don't think I can count that high?"

"'Can' implies capability."

JJ's lip curled into an okay-you-got-me-grin. "May I, will you give me permission to count the rooms in your house?"

"You may."

"Thanks Teach. I'll make charts. Should I count bathrooms?"

"Why not?"

"Closets?"

"That's up to you, it's your project."

Their conversation was interrupted by Sam. "I told you to not bother Mr. Fillmore. Get out of here, he has more important things to do than listen to you."

"Phil," JJ said with strong emphasis on the name to let his father know he and Phil had moved past the mister stage, "and I are talking about how I'll count rooms in the house."

Sam shook his head and emulating his son's emphasis said, "Mister Fillmore doesn't want you running all over the place."

"Why not?"

"I said he could."

"No Teach, you said, I might—'yes you may.' Ha, caught you."

Sam closed his eyes. "Will you please stop?"

"I don't mind Sam, it might put to rest once and for all the eternal question. He'll be doing me a favor."

"Don't spoil him. If you let him do everything he asks, he'll ask for more. I warn you, this kid is a genius at stretching boundaries."

"Thanks Dad. Do you have any graph paper?"

"I'll donate a lined yellow pad to the cause."

"Can I, may I, go anywhere Phil?"

Phil covered his mouth to hide a smile. He was not helping Sam's attempt at discipline. "Why not?"

Several weeks later Isabelle called to say she was coming up. "I can't believe the stories I hear about the actions of those people who've taken over Oshatakea. I want to see for myself." Accompanied by Mrs. Gillons she trod through the house, stumbling over wires to electrical equipment and colliding with rolling racks of documents. She was astounded by the constant wave of items being picked up, checked over, compared to photographs, passed from hand to hand and put down again, to the accompaniment of stated opinions. "I'd kick the lot of them out the door before they smash something," she told Phil when she returned to the Galleried Library and accepted Mrs. Gillons's offer of a biscuit to go with a glass of Dubonnet.

"They haven't so far. Clewes tells them they must be careful."

"Careful schmareful, they're a goddamned bloody nuisance. George Hunnewell should stuff his appraisal and send Clewes and Company packing—all except that divine bookman. I wish he'd noticed me before he began romancing Britt Benson."

"You are too much Isabelle."

"You keep saying that, and you haven't a clue what you're talking about. Jack Smead is thrilled by the way to have the bookman's son at the academy, what's his name, JJ? Jack says the boy has a voice that should be heard. He's going to mount a production of *The Mikado* to showcase JJ singing the lead." Isabelle trilled "A Wandering Minstrel I." Stopping for a Dubonnet reinforcement, she went on, "He has to hold tryouts, but he's doing this particular Gilbert and Sullivan specifically for JJ, so there's no question who will get the part."

"That's great news. JJ hasn't mentioned it."

"He doesn't know yet—nor do you—so be surprised when you hear."

"Did Jack say how JJ is getting along with the other kids?"

"He's the class clown, which means of course he'll want to play Koko instead of Nanki-poo. His big-city slang expressions shock some of the teachers, and that makes him even more popular with the students." Isabelle barked a laugh. "The most delicious tidbit about him is that the baseball coach, you remember, the one who was so rough on Loren all those years ago, tried to recruit him for the junior varsity team. JJ thanked him politely for asking, but said he could not play baseball because if he injured his knees he might not be able to become a dancer."

"And nobody laughed at him?"

"Au contraire ma cher, they cheered."

Phil was out with Taurus when JJ came shouting across the field. The stallion instead of bolting watched JJ's approach with bland curiosity.

"Guess what? Guess what?" JJ cried.

"What?"

Really running off at the mouth in a nonstop rattle of words, JJ told Phil they were going to put on Gilbert and Sullivan's *The Mikado* at school and Mr. Smead wanted him to try out for a part. "Do you have a record of *The Mikado* I can listen to? Mr. Smead played some music and told us what it is about, but I'd be better prepared if I heard the whole thing."

The day of the tryouts Sam was too preoccupied to eat much lunch at the Peasant Palate, worried his son's heart would be broken if he didn't get the part he wanted, the role Mr. Smead told him he was better qualified for than the hokey Koko. Phil knew the preordained outcome but was thinking about community reaction if the new boy at the academy, and a temporary student to boot, was chosen over a valley resident. He remembered people's viciousness when he won academic honors, but then nobody was giving JJ grief because Dick Fallon picked him up every afternoon, and they had ragged Phil unmercifully about being chauffeured.

"I got it, I got it," JJ yelled rushing into the library office where his father was pretending to go over notes and Phil was waiting to be surprised by the news. "They picked me to play Nanki-poo!" Sam hugged him and then he ran into Phil's arms. "Gil Dodson, he's a friend of mine, wanted the part in the worst way and he's good, really good. When he and I checked the cast list on the bulletin board outside the music room, Gil got mad. He said the lead should be played by a valley native. I said, I am a valley native, my family was here before yours. That really ticked him off. He was ready to fight. I told him my mother is descended from Gahah. He said Gahah was a Seneca Indian and asked me, 'Is your mother an Indian?' I told him my mother is lots of things, she's Seneca, Jamaican, English, and drop-dead beautiful."

Sam's eyes shone. "Did you say that?"

"I did, and to prove it, I showed him the picture I carry in my wallet."

"May I see it?" Phil asked. JJ pulled a battered wallet out of his back pocket and opened it to show a tiny black-and-white photograph of a young woman with wide-set eyes, high forehead and the hint of a smile. "You're right JJ, she is beautiful."

"Hasn't Dad shown you the picture he carries. That one is in color. How does your girlfriend feel about Mom's photograph in your wallet Dad?" Sam gave his son a soft cuff. "Just kidding. I like Britt, she's a good cook. But back to what happened. I told Gil I couldn't remember all the begots, but I think my grandmother was Gahah's something-something-granddaughter. And then, I said to him, what does it matter, we're all polygot."

"There is no such word."

"Yes there is, it means a mixture."

"You are thinking of 'polyglot,' which has to do with fluency in several languages."

"Picky, picky Dad, it's the same thing."

"You shouldn't throw words around if you don't know what they mean."

"Gil didn't know either. I had to explain it to him."

"That must have endeared you to him."

"I don't think he's mad anymore if that's what you're saying."

From the start, JJ's room-counting project was sporadic. He drew lines on the yellow pad for columns to record numbers of rooms floor by floor, but then became involved in learning how to ride and take care of a horse with Phil as his instructor. Adelaide and Louisa further distracted him with an invitation to assist in preparing for an early spring picnic in the birch grove. The Kropotkins were enchanted by this enthusiastic, curious boy who listened when something was explained to him, as was Miss Eleanor, whose acceptance of his offer to help with the spring cleanup in her garden amazed them all. Miss Eleanor was so protective of her precious plants she wouldn't let just anybody touch them. JJ had never gardened and was thrilled to add that to his list of new experiences. When Jack Smead began afterschool rehearsals of *The Mikado*, Phil assumed that was the end of JJ's room count and exploration of the house, but JJ surprised him.

"I thought you said you are the only person who lives here," JJ said.

"I did and I am."

"I don't think so. When I was counting rooms in the attics I opened a door and found a room filled with trunks. At the end of that room was a low half door that was locked, I think with a hook on the inside because when I tried to pull it open it rattled. Then I heard other sounds in there. I said who I was and asked who they were, but nobody answered. I made noises like I was leaving and crawled behind some trunks. Nothing happened for so long I almost fell asleep, but then the half door opened. I couldn't see very well, but what looked like an old woman came out. She must have seen me because she turned around and scuttled back in and locked the half door behind her."

There are things one thinks one knows, but doesn't want confirmed, as there are questions best left unanswered. Phil was sorry JJ had seen someone in the attic. "JJ, can I—and I mean can, not may—can I trust you not to tell anybody if I share with you something that then only you and I will know?" JJ crossed his heart, and was mesmerized as Phil related the tale of Pearl's disappearance the day his father was killed, and how staff members thought they heard her occasionally on the upper floors.

"Have you ever seen her?" JJ asked.

"Not really, but I sense when I'm in the Great Hall at night that she may be watching me from above." He didn't tell JJ he thought Pearl had clapped once when he'd danced, and whose cry made him look into the face of the man who had escaped from the prison hospital.

"What does she eat?"

"She goes down to the kitchens late at night when no one is around and picks from the refrigerator."

"What will happen when Jerry Clewes starts poking around in that trunk room?"

"Nothing is being appraised on the mezzanine, the staff floor or in the attics. There's nothing but old clothes in the trunks."

"Are you sure nobody else knows about Pearl?" JJ asked.

"I hope no one else knows. We should leave her alone. That's why I ask you to not tell anyone."

"It's a family secret."

Phil looked into JJ's bright eyes. "That's exactly what it is."

"Cool. I'll keep it. Thanks for telling me."

Chapter 44

SAM HAD TO GO TO NEW YORK CITY TO DELIVER A PAPER at Columbia University. He'd be away overnight and when he returned would bring Sylvia to see JJ in *The Mikado*. Just back from her Russian tour, she would stay with Isabelle at the villa. "Sammy feels very grown-up to be left on his own at the inn," Sam told Phil. "He will go to Britt's for dinner."

"Britt and JJ seem to like each other."

"They do." Sam hesitated. "I haven't said anything because it's impossible, but Britt and I would like to marry."

"Why impossible?"

"Britt doesn't want to leave the valley, and I can't leave New York. In a few years maybe, after Sammy is in college, but not now."

Phil hadn't planned on bringing up the subject of succeeding Fisher Ames until the appraisal was finished, but Sam's comment on Britt and New York provided an opening. He explained that the old librarian was retiring, and when he left his elderly assistants would probably leave too. "I hope you will consider taking over his job. You could hire your own staff. Mr. Ames and I have talked about it, and he thinks you are the ideal person."

"You want me to be librarian at Oshatakea?"

"I do."

Sam's shoulders dropped and his chest caved as if the stuffing had been knocked out of him. Distinguished-gentleman demeanor gave way to overwhelmed youth. "I, Phil, I, what can I say? I'd rather work in the library at Oshatakea than do anything else. I don't think you have an inkling of what you have here. If the research facilities were updated, these libraries would be invaluable for all kinds of scholarship. And you ask me if I want the job? Am I dreaming?"

Sam's response made Phil want to shout hurrah, but he said, "I don't know what George pays Mr. Ames. If it's not enough, we'll come up with whatever you need."

"Not so fast. I haven't said yes. God knows I want to, but there are complications." He laughed again, a loud joyous laugh. "First it's Britt tempting me and now you. How can I say no? Yet I can't say yes. I need time Phil, will you give me that, to see what I can work out?"

Phil had been trying for some time to make a dance to Rossini's *La gazza ladra*, "The Thieving Magpie," whose rhythms and insistent drive offered sublime opportunities for movement. The piece had light phrases, dramatic passages and glorious crashing crescendos. He had plotted almost nine minutes, but had not completely memorized everything. The night Sam was away, he danced halfway through the piece to his satisfaction, then screwed up. He stopped and went to reposition the arm on the record when he heard— applause? "Shit!" He snapped off the stereo. "Okay, who is it now?"

"Hey, Phil, you are all right. Your recovery in that fifth bar, *ta ta ta ta ta dum*, could be cleaner and in a couple of spots you need definition, it's muddy now, but for an old geezer, you're pretty good. Don't get a swelled head, you are late hitting turns."

"JJ get down here, now!"

JJ tore around the third tier and down the stairs. "Don't be mad, man. I'm really impressed. You get into it heart and soul. My dance teacher would die if he could get guys in our class to apply themselves the way you do."

Was this kid running off at the mouth or did he mean it? "JJ, what are you doing here?" JJ would know what he was talking about if he critiqued Phil's dancing. "Are you pulling my leg?"

"I'm serious, you're good. You'll never to make it to City Center, but for an old poop foolin' around, you light up the sky. Start the music again, I have a couple suggestions."

"Old geezer? Old poop? How old do you think I am?"

"Older than my father, and he's old." JJ's smile was innocent and radiant with approval.

"You haven't answered me. What are you doing here? You should be in bed at the Inn."

"This might be my only chance to see Pearl. You said she watches from above when you are in the Great Hall at night." He twisted his mouth and dipped his head, peering out from beneath lowered brows. "What you didn't tell me is you dance up a storm, and that's why she's watching."

"You are avoiding my question."

"Sorry. When I left Britt's—she had a super dinner—I didn't go back to the Inn, I hotfooted it up here and hid behind the hangings so Pearl couldn't see me if she came creeping along. I wasn't going to do anything. I wouldn't speak or try to touch her. I just wanted to see what she looks like up close. I'm sitting there waiting when I hear this music." JJ was dramatizing the scene. "I peek over the banister to see where it's coming from and you are flying around the walls like Paul Taylor with pepper in his pants."

"Paul Taylor is an outstanding dancer, I wish I did look like him, with or without pepper."

"I didn't mean that the way it sounded."

Phil didn't know what the hell to do. There are only so many things this blabbermouth kid could be expected to keep to himself. Everybody in the valley will know tomorrow what he has seen tonight. "You are going to be a mess in the morning, we have to get you back to the Inn. There are two choices. I can wake up Dick Fallon and he'll drive you down, or we can ride Taurus."

"If people see us riding Taurus in the moonlight, they'll think Ichabod Crane has come to town."

"Must you always be a wiseacre?"

"Why can't I sleep here?" Phil tried to talk him out of it; he should have saved his breath. Nobody could outtalk JJ. As JJ climbed into Gramps's Chinese bed, he launched an entirely new line of chatter. "Nobody is going to believe me when I tell them about this."

"Do me a favor, don't tell them. Now go to sleep." Phil took a short shower in Gramps's too small shower stall, banging his elbows on the tile walls, but he wouldn't leave JJ to go over to the multi-nozzled green-marble monstrosity. He lay down on the bamboo carrying chair and wrapped himself in a comforter, listening to JJ's steady breathing. It was Phil's first experience sharing a room with a healthy, vital person; his earlier anger at being interrupted—worse, being discovered—ebbed. With it went his dismay that JJ had watched him try to dance. He thought the kid's crack about doing pretty well for an old poop was quite funny. Musing about once again being held up to ridicule, he was surprised that he wasn't as worried about that as he had been in the past. Perhaps, when JJ stated he wouldn't play baseball because he might hurt his knees and not be able to dance and nobody had scorned him, Phil's overriding concerns were somehow pacified. He understood he wasn't the crowd pleaser JJ was, but he was no coward. If the mobs roared and laughed and pointed fingers, he wouldn't collapse. Hell, he could handle whatever they threw at him. Lifting his head to look across at JJ asleep, he concluded that being alone in the house so he could indulge a secret passion was ridiculous—and not nearly as satisfying as sharing his house and his secrets with a bright, sassy twelve-year old.

When Phil rolled off the carrying chair at five o'clock, JJ asked, "Where are you going?"

"To do barre and floor exercises."

"May I join you?"

"If you promise not to laugh or pronounce judgments."

JJ ran circles around Phil, not literally but in the way he went through the routines, not talking until they were finished. "Maybe Mom will join us when she gets here. At her age, she can't afford to miss a day of exercise."

"Is she old too?"

"Not as old as Dad and definitely not as old as you."

Breakfast in the courtyard was raucous. JJ had something to say about every dish on the sideboard, piling a helping of each on his plate. "This is better than a cafeteria."

"You are welcome to all you want and can go back," Phil said, "but, to quote my grandfather, you have to clean up your plate every time."

"My grandmother says the same thing."

Dick Fallon came in response to Phil's call to take JJ to school. Before he left, JJ asked Phil to please not tell his father what he'd done. "You and I know why I did it, but he wouldn't, and if you tell him you'll have to explain about Pearl and Pearl is a family secret."

"I won't tell him."

"Thanks Phil. And I won't tell anybody I saw you in the middle of the night sashaying around the Great Hall. These farm kids wouldn't know who Paul Taylor is."

"Yes they would, their parents saw him perform here, but don't worry about it JJ." Good Lord, will the surprises never cease? He was giving JJ permission to say whatever he wanted about watching him dance.

Phil's morning walk took him to the white birch grove where the ground was crocus-carpeted in blue, white and yellow with clumps of early jonquils supporting heavy heads of swelling buds about to burst into bloom. Because he kept to the paths so as not to trample the flowers, Adelaide and Louisa spied him from the second-floor windows of their dacha and sent Boris out to bring him in. Putting a finger to his lips, Boris warned Phil to be quiet. "They have something to show you."

Adelaide was waiting at the top of the stairs in a peignoir, her brushed hair falling down her back. Phil didn't think he'd ever seen her with her hair undone. "Phillips, what an opportune time for you to drop by. Louisa is so excited she can hardly bear it." She led him through Louisa's bedroom into a sunny bathroom, where Louisa was sitting next to the window on the cover of a commode constructed to look like a caned easy chair. Louisa put her finger to her lips as Boris had and gestured Phil forward.

"Look in the astrakhan tree, a bluebird. That's the mister. Missus has inspected the hole where a branch broke off, and must be satisfied because now she's coming back with a twig, though he doesn't have the hole quite cleaned out."

"Louisa has been sitting here since early morning," Adelaide whispered.

"To watch bluebirds Addie! These are the first bluebirds we've had since that terrible winter killed the orchards, and they are building a nest!" Louisa took Phil's hand. "It's a sign Phil. Bluebirds returning to the valley will bring happy days to Oshatakea once again. I love bluebirds, don't you?"

"I do," Phil said.

"And they like us as much as we like them. I've been sitting here for hours watching. They see me but I don't worry them one bit. I may sit here until their eggs hatch and the clutch flies off."

Sam and Sylvia would arrive in Fillmore midafternoon. Isabelle had invited them and JJ, Miss Eleanor, the Kropotkins, Loren, Jack Smead and Phil to what she called a simple supper. It would be early because Smead and JJ had to go to dress rehearsal for *The Mikado*. "Phil, don't you dare come to my supper in a ridiculous getup," Isabelle said. "Wear kilts, if you can't find something more suitable. You're damn sexy in kilts. I don't understand why you haven't bought new clothes, or had those you bought for Harvard retailored."

"The clothes for Harvard are almost as old as the clothes I wear that give everybody fits."

"At least they'd be your clothes, not your father's or your grand-father's. I'm surprised you haven't raided the attics to see what you can put on your back from earlier generations."

Phil's smile did not reveal the fact that he had raided the attics and found a number of items he wore with some regularity, but to mollify Isabelle he donned kilts for her party, making sure every-thing was cleaned and pressed so she'd have no excuse to make snide remarks, other than her usual lame jokes about what he did or didn't have on under the plaid. He would have been on time if Jerrold Clewes hadn't stopped him as he was leaving to say the appraisal was taking longer than anticipated, making Phil cross because he hated being late. Clewes used any stupid excuse to start a conversation.

They were in Isabelle's music room when Phil came up the stairs from the lower-level entrance. A setting sun poured in through her window of souvenirs, objects such as amber, pieces of jewelry and lace, bull's-eyes embedded in glass to create an architectural memento of Isabelle's singing career. Sylvia was standing with her back to that window. All Phil could make out was the silhouette of a tall slender person standing as dancers frequently do when they are on stage. She had a long neck and a strong chin held at a forward angle. As he came closer, he saw she was wearing a white silk pantsuit. That was a first for Fillmore. Long black hair was pulled back into a small chignon. Large inquisitive eyes with long lashes and laugh wrinkles at the corners softened an otherwise severe expression. She wasn't as pretty as Phil thought she would be from JJ's wallet pho-tograph. That one must have been taken some time ago. He wasn't disappointed. She was striking and magnificent as a leopard is mag-nificent and exuded the same threat of danger. When she smiled, her mouth opened and he saw white teeth and a pink tongue.

Before he could introduce himself, Louisa rushed up. "Phil, Sylvia's Seneca name is Bluebird!"

Chapter 45

HE WAS SMITTEN. THE SUN BEHIND SYLVIA WAS SETTING, but for Phil it was rising, flooding the valley with a new day's radiance. The brightness blinded him to all but this woman whose smile was a question. He was as much a stranger to her as she was to him. When she spoke to amend Louisa's statement, her voice was like none he'd ever heard, low in pitch and throaty. "My grandmother called me Bluebird, but I was never actually given that name in a Seneca ceremony."

Phil's voice had disappeared. He sat dumb as a stick throughout Isabelle's supper, contributing nothing to the lively conversation and making only cursory responses when asked direct questions. Sylvia sat next to him, which tied him in knots. He wished she were across the table where he could look directly at her. Turning his head to watch her from the side, he held the position so long he got a crick in his neck. Her silk pant leg grazed his bare knee, electrifying the hairs on his own legs.

"My grandmother brought me to Oshatakea when I was four. I don't remember much other than the statue of Gahah and the Great Hall. That may have been all I was shown. Sam tells me the house is extraordinary. May I see some of it?"

"Yes," Phil croaked. Goddamn, he was long past voice-changing age. He cleared his throat and tried again. "I'd be happy to show you around. The cast party for *The Mikado* is in the Banquet Hall tomorrow night, so you will see that then, but if you are free in the morning I'll give you a tour."

"Accept his offer Sylvia before he changes his mind," Isabelle cried. "He's let nobody in for years, not until George Hunnewell forced these idiot appraisers on him. Forgive me Sam, present company excepted."

"Persuade him to let us give him a birthday party," Louisa said.

"That's expecting too much," Isabelle retorted.

Phil and Sylvia set nine-thirty as the time for her to visit Oshatakea. He would send Dick Fallon to pick her up. Isabelle offered to drive, but Phil declined. He was afraid Isabelle might linger and he didn't want her hanging around. After a fitful night, he was up at dawn, skipped exercising at the barre and went instead to his old rooms on the third floor of the Portuguese Wing, where he pulled clothes out of closets, trying to find something to put on that wouldn't look strange to Sylvia. He'd also need a suit, or jacket and slacks, to wear to that evening's performance of *The Mikado*. Before Sylvia came he hadn't given a thought to the attention he'd draw away from the kids on stage if he walked into the academy auditorium in one of his usual outfits. For the house tour he settled on a pair of khaki shorts and a blue oxford button-down shirt. What could be more ordinary? When he tried on a blue blazer and a pair of gray flannel slacks made for him to take to Harvard, they fit. So much for Isabelle's retailoring crack. His thighs were thicker than they had been when he was seventeen, but other than that the snug slacks were fine.

He struggled to appear relaxed as he and Sylvia walked through the house, but his mind was distracted with observations having to do with her. Her quick laugh was like Sam's; did they have those same laughs before they'd married, or did their laughs develop while they were husband and wife? Sylvia listened attentively, the way JJ did, but Phil held back so as not to overburden her with information. He didn't think she cared about all the details he'd learned from Gramps's lectures. Boring her would be the worst thing he could do, but he wanted her to know what Oshatakea meant to him. How to do that if he didn't express his enthusiasm? He had no idea being a tour guide could be this complicated.

They were in the Baroque Theatre when Sylvia first mentioned Catherine. "Which is the box where your mother sat while terrified dancers performed for her?"

Phil indicated a small curtained box to the right of the stage. "Terrified dancers?"

"Not just dancers, musicians too. Catherine Dudley Fillmore was powerful and an important figure to those people at the start of their careers. To be invited here was a great honor, but they were scared to death they might not please her. Agents listened to what she said. Her reactions and comments could launch or kill."

"I don't understand." He wasn't trying to.

"She demanded cream and could pay for it, which meant celebrated, first-rank artists came when they were asked, but she also gave unknowns a chance. If she liked them, she could help in many ways, not just financially. If she didn't, she shipped them back with such a blast everybody knew they'd flopped at Oshatakea."

"She did a lot for Martha Graham, but I had no idea her opinion mattered." Sylvia's smile, her lips, her teeth and pink tongue made him want to stop talking about his mother. What would she do if he touched her?

"There is still great regret that she didn't follow through on her plan to establish a performing arts colony at Oshatakea. She talked about it with a lot of people, as a place where serious creative work could be done away from commercial pressures. Then she apparently lost interest."

He was fantasizing about her mouth. "Explain it to me."

"Providing a place for works in progress to be tried before an audience, to give artists—primarily choreographers and composers, which were her greatest interests—the benefit of audience reaction, while at the same time the audience learns how a dance or a piece of music is made." Sylvia smiled again. He had to kiss her. "This lovely little theater, the outdoor amphitheater, the orangery—there are so many spaces for groups to work and plenty of rooms to house artists. It's a perfect facility, and would have been an invaluable gift to performing arts if she had followed through."

"'Invaluable,' is a word Sam uses. He thinks Oshatakea's libraries can be an invaluable resource for scholars."

"If Sam says it, he means it. He's thrilled to be offered the job of librarian."

"Is he going to take it?"

"I told him to accept, but he won't if he thinks it will hurt JJ. Sam is a very special father."

"That's what he said about you—that you are a very special mother."

The performance of *The Mikado* was a cheering, standing-ovation success. The cast sang encore after encore, stopping only when other students came down the aisle carrying bouquets for the cast and for Jack Smead. Grandparents, aunts, uncles, parents and siblings of cast members, plus every person who had the slightest connection with the production and their girl- or boyfriends, came to the party at Oshatakea where they consumed mountains of sandwiches and cookies, drank hundreds of gallons of punch and danced until two in the morning. Jack Smead's magic at creating illusion turned the replica of Henry Tudor's Banquet Hall into a disco with Mylar, flashing lights and a sound system that shook the rafters.

Phil tried to say no, shook his head vigorously, but Sylvia made him dance with her. What the kids were doing he didn't consider dancing, but once Sylvia had him on the floor in the midst of the ear-shattering, throbbing melee, he had a fantastic time. Starting out copying what she was doing, he grew bolder, throwing his arms, kicking his legs, strutting and whirling with total abandon. JJ ricocheting past gave him a high-five. Phil shouted at JJ, asking if he was still dancing like Paul Taylor with pepper in his pants, but his words were lost in the din. When Sylvia made it clear she had had enough, it was his turn not to accept no; he wouldn't let her off the dance floor, keeping her jumping until the party ended with a nuclear number that made ears ring for days afterward. As the crowd dispersed, Phil was swamped by people thanking him for a fabulous party. Kids threw their arms around him, some covering him with kisses. Older guests expressed their gratitude and happiness at being at Oshatakea again. "I thought I'd seen the last of the good times up here," Katishaw's grandfather yelled to make sure Phil heard him. "Let this be a new beginning."

Another party was scheduled, this one a private dinner the next night in the Gibbons Room, with JJ as guest of honor. Phil told Adrian to pull out all the stops. The guest list included the old family group of Kropotkins, Isabelle, Miss Eleanor and Loren, plus Danny and Danny's girlfriend, Margery Macmillan, and Jack Smead, plus the new family at Oshatakea, Sam, Britt, JJ and JJ's date, Jo Fox, who sang "Yum Yum," and Sylvia. He had known Sylvia would be there but didn't think of it as a problem until Sam told him how serious he and Britt were. Now, Phil wasn't sure. He hoped Sylvia wouldn't be upset. Unschooled in diplomacy, he came right out and asked while they were touring the house if she would rather not have Britt at JJ's dinner. Sylvia said she wouldn't mind at all. Sam had taken her to meet his lady friend, and she liked her very much.

Phil struggled with how to seat people around the table, moving the place cards in constantly shifting patterns. Finally, deciding it was time to make a statement, he put himself at the head of the table in Gramps's place, where his father had refused to sit. This would be the first time Phil occupied that chair. Opposite, at his mother's former place, he put Sylvia's card.

Mrs. Gillons, who was helping him, raised her eyebrows. "Shouldn't Adelaide sit there?"

"No."

She didn't give up. "People will talk."

"Good."

And they did, starting with Loren, who cornered Phil in the Chinese Room when they were having coffee. "Have you slept with her?" Phil shook his head. "Are you going to?" Phil shrugged. "Do you want to?" Phil nodded.

Isabelle thrust her fender against Phil's chest. "My my you do work fast when you see what you want. Have you proposed?"

"Isabelle, I've known her less than a week."

"She's returning to New York tomorrow. Take my advice, Handsome, and follow her. If you attack here she may break and run. Woo her on her home territory."

"I've never been out of this valley, how the hell am I going to find my way around New York? I'll get Loren to go with me."

Isabelle had the discretion to stifle a hoot. "It isn't New York you'll be finding your way around. Grow up for Christ's sake. This you have to do on your own. Hole up in a good hotel and stay there. Get her to come to you and then seduce her. You do know what I'm talking about don't you?"

Adelaide kissed him on the cheek, whispering, "I hope the seating arrangement means something wonderful is about to happen. She's perfect for you Phillips. Grandfather would approve."

Sam's comment was concise. "You have my blessing, friend."

George Hunnewell offered no blessing when Phil awoke him yet again in the wee small hours of the morning. "I need a ticket for the eleven-thirty New York flight and find me a place to stay. Thanks George." The ticket was no problem, nor was the place to stay. Phil's trust owned enough shares in the corporation that controlled the Carlyle, so when George asked to have the presidential suite readied for Farnsworth Phillips Fillmore IV, they hove to.

Sylvia knew Phil was lying when he told her he was on the flight with her because he had business in New York, and he knew she knew, but then nothing he'd done during the past three days bore any resemblance to reality. The plane lifted off the runway, and Phil felt as if he were going to throw up. It would be worth being sick if flying to New York and staying in some hotel meant he could seduce Sylvia. He wanted to seduce her. More, he wanted to marry her and take her back to Oshatakea. The plane shuddered and dropped when it hit turbulence. Phil asked himself why he was flying. Why couldn't he have just said, when they had a minute alone last night, Sylvia please marry me?

He was ever so grateful to be on the ground again, but what came next? Sylvia hailed a cab and offered to drop him off at his hotel. "Would you?" He hung on as best he could when the taxi careened around corners at the speed of sound and then swooped up to the curb in front of the Carlyle to stop so unexpectedly Phil's face almost smashed against the plastic barrier. "Would you have dinner with me tonight?"

"You don't look well. We should have dinner tomorrow night."

"I may not be alive tomorrow night."

Sylvia said she'd come to the Carlyle to pick him up so he wouldn't have to fight uptown traffic getting to her apartment. When he didn't make a move toward a wallet, she added, "I'll pay the cab fare, don't worry about it." He wasn't worried; he didn't carry money. No one had told him he should not go to New York City without a penny in his pocket. To hell with that. He grabbed Sylvia by the shoulders and pressed his lips to hers with such force their teeth clicked. She was startled, but didn't resist.

"Luggage?" the doorman asked, holding the cab door open.

"No luggage." Phil was in shock from the taste of Sylvia's lips and the touch of her teeth. He had tried to get to her pink tongue. However, he wasn't so far gone he didn't sense disapproval when he walked into the hotel past the doorman with his hand out.

"George, I need money and new clothes," he shouted into the telephone.

Phil couldn't have rested if he'd wanted to, or kept anything on his stomach. This business of seduction could destroy a man. He spent what was left of the day in his suite with a salesman and tailor from Sach's Fifth Avenue looking at suits and jackets, slacks and shorts, shirts, ties, coats and hats. The tailor tucked and fitted, marked with chalk and carefully labeled things Phil selected. He couldn't have been more congenial until Phil said he'd need one of the outfits by six. Congeniality collapsed. "What do you think I am?"

Thus, Phil was in the same Harvard-bound blue blazer and snug-fitting gray flannels he had worn on the plane when Sylvia knocked on his door. "I did shower," he said, so she'd not think he was exactly as she'd left him, "and I'm wearing all new, what the salesman called linen."

She flashed a knowing smile. "I'm glad."

"I have no experience at this, at least no experience that will help me at the moment. May I just kiss you?"

"You don't need to ask."

He kissed her and she let him. She opened her mouth and he tasted her tongue. "I love you Sylvia."

"I know."

"Do you love me?"

"Phil, we just met."

"Four days ago, today is the fourth day. Can't you tell whether you do or you don't?"

They talked and kissed, kissed and drank champagne, and concurred that dinner in the suite would be nice. When the room-service waiter presented menus, Phil said, "Surprise us." And then they talked less and kissed more and were in the bed when the waiter came back with dinner. "Leave it by the door," Phil yelled.

"Will you marry me?"

"Don't rush."

"I'm not rushing, I'm trying to catch up. I've never been in love, never seduced anybody—did I seduce you? Did or didn't, you are the first person I have made love to. Now that I'm in motion I don't want to stop. Let's not waste time Sylvia, I didn't think I'd ever find you."

They didn't feel the slightest chill as they sat naked on striped satin chairs and ate a cold dinner. "Are you at all inclined to pursue your mother's project of establishing a performing arts colony at Oshatakea?" she asked.

"I've been thinking of nothing else since you mentioned it," he said.

Phil opened the door only a crack so the waiter could hand him another bottle of champagne in a cooler.

"I too have a project," he said.

"Oh?"

"Locked away in a mental hospital is a boy who killed his parents. I'd like to free him if I can, give him a home."

"There's plenty of room at Oshatakea," she said.

Sunlight streamed into the room through the narrow space where the draperies at one window had not been completely closed. Because she said it with her face pressed against his neck, Phil wasn't sure he heard and asked her to repeat it.

"I will marry you Phil."

EPILOGUE

TELEGRAM TO LOREN GAGE:

You told me there was a difference between love and being in love. I thought I knew what you meant, but I didn't. Now I do and I tell you first because you offered yours and I took it without knowing the value of your gift. Knowing deepens our bond. —Love, Phil

TELEGRAM TO MISS ELEANOR GAINES:

Last night Sylvia asked, "Do you think Miss Eleanor will approve?" I hope you do. What I have experienced this week is the one thing you did not prepare me for, yet in a way you did when you told me if I tried to please others I would please myself. —Love, Phil

TELEGRAM TO SAM WILSON:

Accept librarianship at Oshatakea and marry Britt Benson. JJ can continue dazzling the academy, living one week with you and Britt and the next with his mother and me. The former Mrs. Samuel M. Wilson Jr. is about to become Mrs. Farnsworth Phillips Fillmore IV. —Love, Phil

TELEGRAM TO ISABELLE CHAPMAN:

Dearly beloved, gather yourself together for a wedding June 19 in the chapel. Sylvia and I want you and Jack Smead to plan the music. As a surprise for his mother, please include a solo by JJ. Thanks for pushing me onto that plane. If you are passing out grades, I get an A-plus in seduction. — Love Phil

TELEGRAM TO ADELAIDE AND LOUISA KROPOTKIN:

A fortieth birthday bash with all Oshatakea guest rooms filled and everybody in the valley invited is on. Start making lists. Sylvia wants to plan the entertainment. — Love, Phil

TELEGRAM TO GEORGE HUNNEWELL:

Because you know all about Gramps's trusts, I want you to be my adviser and financial manager when I assume control of the estate on November 25.

Thanks, Phil

P.S. I marry a Bluebird on June 19 and will need a strong ally as she reinvents Oshatakea. You thought Mother had an iron will? She was a piker compared to Sylvia.

AUTHOR'S NOTE AND ACKNOWLEDGMENTS

—

THE CLOUD DWELLER BEGAN WHEN I WAS HAVING LUNCH at the Gaslight Café in the lovely village of Wyoming, New York, and observed well-dressed women, obviously from out of town, taking great care to avoid a disheveled man sitting at a short counter as they were being shown to tables in the next room. It amused me to play the game of "what if?" What if this raggedy individual was the owner of Hillside, a legendary mansion they had driven many miles to see? Would they avoid him if they knew or approach him? With its colorful past, Wyoming provided fertile ground for my imagination and fond memories of people I knew there gave me several characters.

Parts of western New York State resembled rural England during a long period in its history, with great estates that were the homes of once powerful families. Power dwindled, but the families stayed on and became cultural forces in the area. Far from Boston and New York City, they established their own orchestras, opera companies, theater groups and art colonies. Lydia Avery Coonley Ward built an amphitheater at Hillside and brought professional performers to Wyoming. Harriet Saltonstall Gratwick and Bill Gratwick followed her example at their estate in Linwood. Though Catherine is neither Mrs. Ward nor Harriet Gratwick, her passion for music is a tribute to them.

There are parts of Bill Gratwick in Phil, his gentle nature, decency and determination, but Phil is not Bill. Bill Gratwick was unique, a man who forged ahead full speed on any project that caught his fancy, whether it be sculpting, developing new breeds of sheep and horses for the Olympics, writing an opera, singing, acting or creating a strain of yellow tree peonies with stems strong enough to hold their blossoms upright. If he ever had doubts he kept them to himself. As a man I admired enormously, I could only smile when someone in the village said, "With all his degrees, he never amounted to anything." Bill's quixotic spirit was with me throughout the writing of *The Cloud Dweller*.

I want to acknowledge members of the Westwinds Writers' Workshop—Judy Coon, Katya Coon, Bill Henderson, Bojan Jennings, Ayaz Mahmud, Mary McCrae, Jay Mitchell, Thelma O'Brien and Priscilla Weld—whose critiques and suggestions were invaluable. I am also grateful for the patience of organizations that remained supportive when I was unable to work with them as I had in the past: Authors on Stage at Wellesley College, the Chilton Club and the Women's Educational and Industrial Union in Boston. Josh Cutler, editor of the *Duxbury Clipper* and *Point South*, must also be thanked for putting up with the irregularity of my column, "Books & Bob Hale."

Adnan ElAmine is an extraordinary physician who kept me going, wouldn't let me give up and was able to put me back on track when health issues arose. I thank him for that and for his friendship.

The Cloud Dweller took me a long time to write. Always urging me on was a loyal fan and old friend named Eleanor Dacey. Mrs. Dacey never saw me without saying, "If you don't hurry, I'll be dead before the book is finished, and I want to read it." Unfortunately, I wasn't fast enough. I gave her parts of what I thought was the final draft. Her perceptive criticism convinced me it wasn't.

Many years ago, my almost-sister Jean Hale Burr and I spent hours drawing detailed plans for houses similar to Oshatakea. Creating one with words has given me as much pleasure as she and I derived with pencils and graph paper.

It is my extreme good fortune to have Don Congdon as my agent. Don has kept the faith from the beginning and done so much for so little—to date. I wish success for *The Cloud Dweller* to partially repay him for his unstinting efforts on my behalf. He is also a very sharp and useful critic.

My longtime editor and mentor Jim Mairs pushes more politely and persistently than anyone else I know. Not only did he never give up when I grew weary, he has twice said to me the sweetest words any writer can hear, "I want to publish your book." Neither *The Elm at the Edge of the Earth* nor *The Cloud Dweller* would have been written without him.

Most important of all is my wife, Lyddy, who prides herself on having no patience, but she has patiently put up with the long, long time this book has taken to complete, and not complained too much about my absence from domestic duties. Most amazing she never got angry when she walked into my study and I shouted, "Not now, not now!" Lyddy makes everything possible.